VEILED COURT

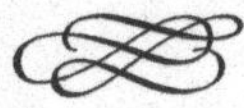

C.N. CRAWFORD

For Elizabeth Briggs, a wonderful writer and friend whose words continue to live on through her books.

CONTENT WARNING

Readers should also be aware that this book contains sexual scenes and magic-induced lust, swearing, suicide by hanging, violence, and execution by burning.

Some characters have a trauma history, including childhood starvation and hallucinations and memories of family deaths.

SUMMARY

Join the Trials. Fake a Romance. Kill the King.

Ex-assassin Syn Malleore hates kings. The last one poisoned her sister, leaving her to slowly die. Now that the monarchy has fallen, Syn can finally leave London and return to the Fey realm to search for a magic cure.

But the Fey nobility are already plotting to restore the monarchy. In a hidden court, aristocrats fight to the death in brutal trials to claim the throne.

Syn won't let another tyrant rise. Disguised as a baroness, she infiltrates the trials as a spy. Her first goal: steal a sacred relic to save her sister. Her second: destroy the monarchy.

But the greatest danger is Rion du Lac, a lethally seductive warlord. When he discovers she's an imposter, he forces her to pose as his lover to win the crowd's favor.

If he exposes her secrets, she'll burn for treason. And if she fails, a new tyrant will rise.

CHAPTER 1

or just a second, I let myself indulge in a vision of throwing a rock at my boyfriend's head right before he reaches orgasm.

I'm standing in a dark London alley in a damp T-shirt and soggy trainers, staring up at the Tudor windows of his flat, where he entertains a woman I've never met. There, against the leaded glass, he's shagging a blonde. The cheeks of her bare arse press against the panes—pale, like two little mounds of uncooked dough.

Cold rain slides down the windows, echoing as it drips from the stone eaves. I loved that bedroom until a few minutes ago—the way it nestles in an arch between two gray stone buildings, sweeping above the alley like the Bridge of Sighs.

Up there, it's warm and safe, all golden light and steamed windows. Down here, in the chilled damp of the passageway, a mouse scuttles past my foot and through a puddle.

The wind starts to pick up, whipping the April rain at my back.

How many times, exactly, was Owain lying to me when he said he was busy?

Sharp loneliness stabs me in the ribs.

In the window, Owain's hand tangles in the woman's blonde locks, yanking her head back. It's precisely the same way he grabs my hair when he's about to come.

The crack in my chest splits wider, an icy, hollow fissure.

What is he *doing?* Half our friends are dead. We need to flee the city, or we'll be dead, too. Tonight is our *one* bloody chance.

And he's throwing it away for this mortal woman?

I'm still staring at Owain. He hasn't seen me; his eyes are closed in ecstasy.

Thought it would be over by now. Do they *know* people can see them? Maybe that's the point. We never have sex in the window. Just in bed, after a few glasses of wine.

My cold sadness simmers into anger, and I grit my teeth. I storm up to his front door—blue-painted wood set in old stone under the archway. Slimy water drips onto me, sliding down my hair.

I press the buzzer. No answer. Of course not. Obviously, he's busy, but I suppose I'm not feeling very considerate at the moment.

I keep pressing it. Again and again, unrelenting, refusing to let them come. The doorbell sound grates through my skull like a baby's cry, but I don't stop until footsteps thunder down the stairs and I hear him yelling, "Fuck *off*!"

I wince, even though he doesn't know it's me. I'm not supposed to be here.

At last, the door flies open.

Owain is wearing nothing but a towel, and when he sees me, his face goes as white as the terry cloth around his hips. His throat bobs. "Syn...I thought we were meeting at the church in an hour."

I glare at him. I can't even figure out where to start.

His dark hair hangs to his shoulders, and his pointed Fey ears peek through the strands. Of course she wanted him. To a human like her, he's not only pretty but also immensely strong—and these days, a Fey lover is something forbidden. An intoxicating combination.

"That window has been there since Elizabeth I," I say, a razor's edge cutting in my voice.

He narrows his eyes—bronze, a color I loved deeply until tonight.

"Syn." His voice cracks a little. "Why are you talking about windows?"

"Because that girl's pasty mortal arse was mashed against it." I keep my voice cool, controlled. Icy. "You don't press your arse on something that survived the 1665 plague *and* the Great Fire of London, do you?"

He frowns, looking confused. Frankly, so am I. No idea where I'm going with this.

It really doesn't help that I haven't eaten since a breakfast of Extra Value bread this morning.

"Those windows were here for the dissolution of the bloody monasteries." Somehow, I feel like this is a cutting rebuke. "For the beheading of Charles I."

"Okay." His voice is quiet, shaky. "I didn't mean for you to see that."

The heartbreaking ache keeps intruding on my rage, which I hate. It's making my eyes mist as I stand here beneath the damp stone arch, and I really don't want to cry in front of him.

The girl must have heard me yelling about the dissolution of the monasteries because she comes whipping around the corner, wearing Owain's Cardiff City Football Club T-shirt. It hangs down to her knees. She's small, like me, but very human—and very young. Twenty, maybe, to my thirty-five. Absurdly, we're both wearing Owain's T-shirts right now, and mine has a cartoon picture of an old computer.

Unlike me, she's holding a champagne flute. She must have bought the champagne, because gods know Owain can't afford it. Apart from the nice flat, he has nothing here in London.

"What's going on, Owain?" she chirps. "Who are you

talking to?"

My fingers curl into fists. "Did Owain tell you he was leaving London tonight with his girlfriend?"

She wrinkles her nose. "Yes, I know? I'm his girlfriend? We're leaving tonight?"

Everything is a question.

Owain's eyelids are shut now like he's hoping this whole situation will somehow be gone when he opens them—like a toddler trying to hide from the world by putting a blanket over his head.

At last, he opens them again. "I told Vicky I'm leaving. She's going to come with me to the Fey realm. I'm sorry, Syn. After the war, you and I just...we stopped having fun, and I..." He trails off, looking agonized. "Well, I met Vicky. I planned to take her with me to the Fey realm. I was going to tell you..."

The rage bleeds out of me until all that's left is the dull, Sunday-grey throb of loneliness.

"You're bringing *a mortal*?" So much for our plan to start a new life together.

He looks back at Vicky. "She won't be in danger there now. The king is dead. Mortals are allowed."

"I don't understand. Who are you, Vicky?" Now *my* voice cracks, though I want it to sound ice cold.

Her facial expression seems to be frozen in a permanent grimace. "I'm a life coach for single women?"

Another question.

"Life coach?" My shout echoes off the stone above me, uncontrolled.

"I offer coaching for high-achieving women about how to find their soulmates..." She trails off, and her grimace fades into a blank expression.

I stare at her, still stunned. "People pay you for that bollocks?"

"Yes," she says sharply. "If you hadn't noticed, everything is fucking terrible these days. People want an escape. They want fantasy. They want *romance*."

"You're a romance expert, are you? And you're shagging a man who is cheating on his girlfriend?"

I glance at Owain again, and I can't decide if I want to tell him to be careful or not. Instead, I just blurt, "Well, you'd better pack your things. The portal isn't open all night. And look out for the Iron Legion so you don't get murdered by *mortals* on the way out. They hate our kind these days, you know?"

It doesn't seem cutting enough, so I add, *"Twat."*

I pivot on my heels and walk down the rain-slick alley, where streetlights gleam off the puddles.

I'm trying very hard not to cry, but the loneliness is eating at me.

I turn a corner, heading for the old medieval church in Smithfield. With my head down against the drizzle, I hurry through the modernist flats known as the Barbican. This used to be one of my favorite parts of London, where ancient Roman walls still stand. A water feature burbles across the landscape.

When I first arrived in London, I wanted to live here. Not that I could afford it. But once, I imagined myself giving history walking tours, rambling on about medieval walls and lost Roman roads. I dreamt I'd one day be able to afford a flat near the fountains and overgrown greenery. Sometimes, I imagined Owain and me living here—a sweet little domestic life of home-cooked dinners and tea.

But I stopped dreaming of those things when the war began. Now I dream of dragons scorching the skies, hunting us to death. And I dream of a beautiful Fey knight with golden tattoos, slaughtering everyone around him as he stands knee-deep in gore.

Even my favorite neighborhood doesn't feel the same anymore. The Barbican walls show the wreckage of the war. I glance at the silver Fey script still curling along the bricks, a faint glow that brightens under starlight. The Fey army made these markings last year, designating these flats as barracks—a pretty little reminder of the violence they left behind. And above that script, the walls are scorched from dragon fire.

As I walk, I can't relax for a moment. The war isn't totally over—not really.

I glance over my shoulder as I hurry along. Tonight, the quiet has a dangerous edge, and there is a sharpness to the air.

I'm not welcome in London anymore, and my time is running out.

I take off on my own into the city's dark alleys.

CHAPTER 2

'm running down a street lined with dark brick buildings, heading for my meeting spot with my sister—the thousand-year-old church known as St. Bartholomew-the-Great. With the portal key in my pocket and the ancient power of the church's stones, we'll be able to open a gate into the Fey realm.

But until we go through that portal, I can't let my guard down.

My hands tremble, the old tremor I've had since I was teenager. And along with it, a brutal headache blooms in my temples.

Of *course* I'm on edge. First, there is the heartache: the life coach, the knife-twisting betrayal, the fist gripping blonde hair—

Then, there's the danger. In London, they're hunting people like me.

Officially, the war between Fey and humans ended a few months ago. The mortals won, and the tyrannical Fey king was killed. And I hated the king more than anything. I never supported his invasion.

Still, it doesn't really matter what my politics are. When mortals look at me, all they see is a killer, and they're trying to rid their country of every last one of us.

With a shaking hand, I slip my sunglasses on to hide my purple metallic eyes. I sniff the air, then relax a little. I don't smell any iron—yet. It's just me and the scorched stone walls, the gaping holes in buildings.

Since the war ended, human paramilitaries have been roaming London's streets at night, looking for Fey to torture and kill. The revenge gangs call themselves the Iron Legion. They murder Fey with iron weapons—our weakness.

Fey corpses have been turning up all over the city— mutilated, hanging from walls with iron hooks. Some with blood-smeared signs that read *MONSTER*.

Walking faster, I cross into the old square known as Smithfield. Up ahead, the stones have been steeped in centuries of blood. Right here, kings and queens burned and mutilated a thousand so-called *traitors*.

Human or Fey, tyrants all wield power in the same way.

Nearby is a memorial sign and bouquets of dried flowers. It's the spot where an executioner disemboweled William Wallace.

I don't say these kinds of things aloud when I can help it. I have all the worst possible thoughts churning in my head at all times, but I don't go on about them to people because I am fucking fun, *Owain*, and I know how to make small talk. So even if I'm thinking it, I can, in fact, stop myself from saying, *Henry the Eighth boiled his cook to death in a great vat of blistering oil right where I'm standing.*

As I'm imagining what it would be like to be boiled alive, a voice pulls me from my thoughts: "Syn."

I turn to see my sister, Vero, with her best friend, Balin. His face flushed, Balin is lugging all the enormous duffel bags and rucksacks. He's also supporting Vero's weight as she leans on him.

My sister looks like she's barely hanging on to life.

Her big, lavender eyes are almost the only sign of vitality, and her cheeks and lips are pale as apple blossoms. Though the ends of her curls still hold their cherry red color, the rest of her hair is growing in white.

Years ago, the Fey king poisoned the river where my family lived. He was trying to kill anyone with mixed blood—the demi-Fey. Us.

People called his poison the River-Ague. Even if the poison doesn't kill you at once, the after-fever never goes away. Fifteen years later, the last of the surviving victims are dying.

My gaze lingers over her cheekbones, the way they stand out too sharply in her pale features. Faint blue veins trace their way up her chest and throat. The higher those marks climb, the sicker she gets. Now, they're nearly at her jawline. By the time they reach her eyes, she'll be dead.

My heart squeezes at the sight of her, and I want to scoop her up and take her somewhere safe, somewhere with magic that can cure her.

As she steps closer, I can hear how hard she's breathing, and my stomach tightens.

"We could have been the Iron Legion," she rasps. "And you're standing here thinking about…let me guess. History? Kings? Something morbid?"

I lift my chin, pretending she didn't just see right through me. "If you were the Iron Legion, I'd have smelled you before you ever got close. I have a nose for ferrous oxide. Now, my friends, let's stop chatting and get out of London before the Iron Legion actually turns up."

I loop my arm through hers so I can support her weight instead of Balin. I know she can't move quickly, and our slow pace has my pulse racing out of control.

With the paramilitaries roaming around, we're in danger every minute we're out here. Every day we spend in London is another day I could come home to find Vero carved open by the Iron Legion—or simply gone. If the disease doesn't kill her first, the hunters will.

Staying in London is a death sentence right now.

As we get to the church's old gatehouse, I feel relief for the first time in months.

Beneath a Tudor arch, Balin pushes the wooden door

open. We step into the mossy churchyard of grass and crooked gravestones.

On the far side of the cemetery path stands the thousand-year-old church where Balin works as a sextant. It's perfect for us tonight because we need the ancient stones' power to open the portal.

Vero coughs. "Have I ever told you two how much I love you for taking care of me so well?"

Balin's bright golden eyes gleam in the darkness. "You don't need to thank me, but I do like to be loved."

He uses a key to unlock the church doors. When he pulls open the heavy oak, we step into the church. We walk further up the aisle, where pale gray stone soars high above us and moonlight spills onto the checkered floor through stained-glass windows.

"Wait, where's Owain?" Vero asks, as she leans against my shoulder.

"He's coming through later, and so am I. Separately, though. I've got one more errand before I leave. The portal will stay open for a full hour, so we both have time." It finally dawns on me that our plans have totally changed now, and we need a new place to stay. "But, um…we won't be staying in Owain's aunt's mansion. And we won't be seeing much of Owain anymore."

"Why?" Vero asks. "What happened?"

I sigh, walking deeper into the church. "He has a new girlfriend. A mortal named Vicky who teaches rich women to find their soulmates, and apparently, she's found hers in Owain. They're going to be using *my* plan and my borrowed portal key to start their new life. They'll be staying in his aunt's mansion, and I don't imagine we're invited anymore. But there are plenty of empty cottages in the Fey realm, you know, from…"

I trail off because I was trying to come up with a cheerful thought, but the cottages are empty because of a tyrant king's brutal massacres.

I clear my throat. "Anyway, we'll find a cottage and fix it up. It will be all ours, and we don't need Owain."

"But Syn." Vero is staring at me, open-mouthed. "What a tosser. You know what? I never liked him. Do you remember that time he couldn't grasp the concept that two-thirds was bigger than one-sixth? Fucking idiot."

Balin quirks a smile. "You know what? I'd rather find our own cottage than live with someone's rich aunt."

"Exactly," I say, brightening. "We'll find a cozy little place, and we will find a magic cure for you, Vero. And when we do, we'll throw lovely parties among the primroses and bluebells and butterflies. And you won't be sick anymore."

She smiles at me. "Do you think we can find the grail? That would cure me."

"I think we can. It will be my only mission."

I release a long breath, finally feeling safe as I take in the gothic arches of the church. This place has been a sanctuary for centuries.

"Our last few minutes in the human realm!" Balin's voice echoes off the arches.

I put a finger to my lips. It's not exactly the sort of thing you want to shout if the Iron Legion is lurking around outside.

"You're sure you can't come with us now?" Vero asks. "What's this last errand?"

"I'll follow through soon." I pull the portal key out of my pocket. It's a silver hoop, like a bracelet, and it hums with magic. "I've got to get this key down to the Tower of London before I join you. We're only borrowing it, and I'm supposed to get it back to Tristan immediately. He needs it for some kind of secret spy mission. But you should go through now."

"Why can't Tristan meet you here?" Vero asks.

"He's on a spy stakeout, I guess?" I say. "I don't know. Everything he does for Avalon Tower is top secret. You two should wait for me on the other side, okay? I want to make sure you get through safely, and then I'll catch up after I give the portal key back to Tristan."

"And where will it take us, exactly?" Balin asks.

"Somewhere in the north of the Fey realm, by the sea. There's not much around there, I think. We'll need to make our way south. Tristan promises it will be safe as long as you don't go near the dragon's keep, and if you happen to see a large castle, don't go near it, either. He won't even tell me what that is."

Vero touches my arm. "You're sure you can still run fast enough to get back to the portal in time?"

"Of course I can. I can cover three miles in an hour. I'm thirty-five—I'm not dying."

I immediately regret the choice of phrase, and guilt twists behind my ribs.

She doesn't seem to notice.

"Okay," she says. "We'll be waiting just on the other side."

"Right. Here goes." I close my eyes. Holding the portal key, I chant a few words in Fey, my voice echoing off the arches.

Magic crackles over my skin, raising goose bumps on my arms. When I open my eyes again, I see a whirling vortex that seems to tear through the gray stone and shadowed alcoves of the church.

On the other side of the portal, my old homeland stretches out under the night sky. There, a weeping willow sways gently in the breeze, silvered in the starlight. In the distance, the sea laps the shore, glittering with silver flecks. My chest aches for its strange beauty, and my heart speeds up with longing.

My home lies just out of reach—the castles and forests and fields kissed with a magic that I crave. It was the last place I was truly happy, and I want it so badly, I can taste it.

With the tyrant king dead, we can go back to the halcyon days before the fall.

But it's not my time yet.

I shove the portal key safely into my pocket. With misting eyes, I watch Vero and Balin go through the portal. They step into tall grasses, then sit down beneath the shadowed branches of the willow tree.

For the first time in months—no, over a year—I feel happy. Vero will be safe in the Fey realm—Brocéliande, to use its real name. Later tonight, they'll be sitting by a warm hearth in a little forest cottage. My eyes sting, and I blink quickly to stop the tears.

But I don't have time to relish the happy thoughts.

I turn and hurry out the door. On the stone path through the churchyard, I break into a run past the graves, pushing through the gatehouse door into Smithfield again.

I'm hoping to make it to the Tower of London in fifteen minutes or less.

I grip the portal key, running toward the main road on my way to meet Tristan. Really, I haven't seen him enough since we moved here from the Fey realm. Once, we were best friends. Inseparable. But in the past fifteen years, he's been busy nonstop with Avalon Tower, his magical spy agency. And he can never talk about what he does, so we've started to drift a little. On top of that, it's not like I ever have anything interesting to tell him. While he's been off on missions assassinating evil Fey aristocrats (or whatever he does), I've been filling out paperwork and replacing pens and fetching ham sandwiches for colleagues.

Now, we talk to each other from across a chasm of different lifestyles. I miss our former closeness, though, almost as much as I miss the golden days of our early childhood.

I cross into a short, narrow alley. As I approach the high street, I scan my surroundings, surveying the narrow lane—and I skid to a halt.

Alarm bells ring in the hollows of my mind.

Iron.

The unmistakable toxic stench nearly overpowers me.

Fuck.

I slip back into the shadows. As I catch my breath, four black-clad members of the Iron Legion enter the alley. Their dark shirts are buttoned tight, with iron dagger pins gleaming on their lapels. Fear shoots through my veins until I realize they're not looking at me.

Their eyes are fixed on a skinny Fey woman to the right. She's dressed in a magical cloak, stitched with glowing silver thread.

The four men move closer, surrounding her.

She turns, and a golden glow radiates from her skull like a halo. More magic. What is she doing? The magic beaming from her head is a literal beacon for the paramilitaries.

She folds her arms, glaring back at them with an irrational confidence.

Is she stupid?

Then the tallest member of the gang pulls out an iron dagger, and my pulse races.

"You," he growls at the Fey woman, "put your hands where I can see them."

As the men with him draw their weapons, the pungent scent of iron curls toward me, stinging my eyes. My throat tightens.

They're going to kill her right in front of me, aren't they?

CHAPTER 3

One of them taps a knife against his thigh. "And what sort of magic is this?"

"Excuse me," the woman says evenly. "Why are you blocking my path? I hope you realize I'm a baroness of Listenoise."

Ah. That explains why she's this shockingly clueless. If I remember correctly, Listenoise is the Waste Land—a desolate, ravaged kingdom cut off from the rest of the world. I had no idea anyone could leave it, to be honest.

Standing stock-still, I weigh my options.

I could turn back and slip away, sneaking out the other side of the alley. This isn't my fight, and I have limited time. I've got to get this key to Tristan and make it back to the church before the portal closes. After all, I'm not the one wandering around London flaunting Fey magic—

Then again, she really doesn't know better.

If I still had the magic I possessed as a teenager, I could kill them all within seconds. Unfortunately, my magic is broken.

And yet—I'm Fey, and they're human. Even *without* magic, I'm faster and stronger than they are. The baroness must be, too. Two Fey can probably take down four mortals, even if we're unarmed and magicless.

"Fey bitch," one of the men spits. "Do you know what we do to creatures like you?"

Now her face has gone white as she seems to understand the danger she's in. "What's the meaning of this? You want to kill me simply because I'm Fey?"

She *really* missed a few key things when she was preparing for her trip into London.

The tall one points his iron dagger at her. "You killed enough of us, didn't you?"

He lunges forward and grabs her by the hair. Viciously, he throws her to the pavement.

She slams down hard, grunting. She's not much of a fighter.

Fuck.

"Why are you doing this?" she cries from the ground.

"The Fey army murdered my wife. An eye for an eye—"

The baroness pushes herself up, glaring at him. "But your wife's not dead. She ran away because you beat her."

The leader kicks her hard in the stomach. "Shut up."

A tether snaps within me, and I find myself marching out of the alley.

"Hi! Everyone all right?" I force my voice to sound cheerful, unassuming.

Just a curious little lady here.

As I cross toward the men, I blink innocently. But underneath, unease coils through me. I'm not exactly prepared for a fight these days.

One of them barks something at me about my sunglasses, but I'm busy assessing them. Three larger, armed with iron. One's smaller, with a steak knife and soft hands. Not much taller than me, and his knife is steel. He's the weak link.

I dart forward, knocking the blade out of his hand. In the next instant, I slam my forehead into his nose.

Pivoting, I face a man with an iron-plated sword just as he raises it above his head. I grab his forearm and kick him in the chest, and he falls back into his friend.

It's all sloppy and awkward, but it's enough to break the baroness free.

I grab the wrist of the Fey woman and pull her up. "Fucking *run*!"

We run faster than I have in years.

Behind us, they shout and give chase. Passersby stare but don't intervene, clearly happy not to be involved.

We hurtle down Cheapside, far faster than a human can run.

As we sprint, my gaze lands on the number fifteen bus,

its door still open. *Perfect.* I grab the baroness's hand, and we leap onto it just before the door shuts. Catching my breath, I reach into my pocket and pay the fare for both of us.

Slowly, it starts to roll east toward the Tower.

"Pull your cloak up and follow me," I whisper to her.

Keeping my head down, I push through to the back of the bus. It smells of sweat and beer. A woman is shouting that she got "fucked outside St. Paul's Cathedral last night" and it was "the most romantic thing I've ever done." She's dressed like Marie Antoinette for some reason, which is great because literally no one is looking at us.

Besides the baroness and me, the only sober person here is a thief pickpocketing a drunk American woman.

We cram into the back where the doors will open, and my Fey companion stands with her hood pulled up over her ears, covering her strange halo.

"I appreciate your assistance," she whispers. "I didn't know the humans were hunting Fey in this kingdom. It all seems rather barbaric."

Her posh accent is immediately apparent, clipped and aristocratic. That puts me on edge. I haven't had the best experiences with nobility.

Still, she seems harmless.

"They've been at it for months now," I whisper. "Organized this whole Iron Legion of paramilitaries. It's not safe here for us. We need to be discreet."

She narrows silver eyes at me. She's pretty with a small

mouth, a narrow nose, and elegant features. "Do they not want peace?"

They want revenge.

"You're a telepath, right?" I whisper. "That's how you know that man beat his wife."

She nods. "Yes, but look what good my magic did me. Not much use in knowing someone plans to kill you if you can't wield a sword. I wasn't trained as I should have been. There wasn't a chance for it in Listenoise."

I glance out the window and see that we're nearly to Aldgate High Street and the Tower of London.

Where are you headed? I ask her in my mind.

"The Tower of London. Do you know it?"

I nod. *I do. This is our stop. I'll walk you there.*

When the door opens, I jump off, and the baroness follows me onto the street.

Side by side, heads down, we walk south.

I peer over my shoulder a few times, checking for signs of the Iron Legion, but I don't see anyone. On weekend nights in the City, there aren't many people around.

What are you doing at the Tower? I think.

"I am not permitted to say," she says curtly.

I have a solid guess that she's meeting Tristan. This is his secret spy stakeout situation.

Her hood moves slightly as the woman shoots me a sharp look.

I try to make my mind go quiet, but that's impossible for me. My mind is never quiet.

I now regret offering to walk with her, since being around a telepath means she can hear every word in my mind, which is *deeply* intrusive, and also brings out my absolute worst thoughts.

There was a time when I practiced concealing my thoughts from telepaths, but I haven't done it in ages. It takes a few minutes of calm to muster up a mind shield, something King Auberon taught me long ago.

She turns to me with a half-smile and a wink. "Don't worry, stranger. We will have a new monarch soon enough."

Cold fury slides through my veins. "What do you mean?"

Her smile falls fast.

I glare at her, knowing she can hear every furious idea whirling through my mind.

I hate kings. Did you know that one summer, King Auberon burned over three hundred people to death? Their crime was refusing to worship him as a god. Some took hours to die. I can still hear their screams. And that bastard might actually be still alive, because no one saw his body—

I try to stop the next thought. I'm *really* not supposed to fantasize about killing a king, especially around a monarchist, which she obviously is. Auberon still has supporters. But that man ruined my fucking life. He broke my magic, destroyed my family, and poisoned my sister.

The next thing I imagine is smashing Auberon's blond

head into a rock, cracking open his skull, and watching his bloodied crown roll into the dirt.

The baroness stops walking and whirls sharply.

A wave of naked hostility radiates from her.

Of course, I've given her the impression that I possess the bloodlust of a Victorian serial killer.

"What is *wrong* with you?" she hisses. "Traitor."

"I've asked myself the same thing many times. But what's wrong with *you*? Stop listening to my thoughts. Walk ahead or behind me if you can't stop yourself. Your telepathy is very intrusive."

"You cannot injure a king," she snarls at me in Fey.

"And we're better off without a king," I whisper back in kind. "But you need to be quiet. We could be killed for speaking our language."

As I take a step, she grabs my arm in a vise-like grip. "You're the one who will ruin everything."

I narrow my eyes. "Your dear King Auberon cheated and lied his way to the throne. And even if he was the true king, descended from Bran himself, I'd kill him all the same. He's a monster. Why don't you stop listening to my thoughts, since you are so easily offended? Get out of my head."

I wrench my arm out of her grasp, marching on. But the woman grabs my bicep again—harder now—and spins me to face her.

"You could destroy the world!" she shouts, clinging to my arm. "Never has a Fey committed such a great wrong."

"Are you daft?"

"I know *exactly* what you are. Because of you, the land will lie in ruin, the powerful will sicken, and sorrow will reign in our kingdom. Cursed is the hour you were born," she hisses, her eyes flashing. "You must die."

My stomach plummets at the venom in her words.

Her brown hair is wild, her silver eyes frantic like a panicked animal's. She reaches for my throat, hands clamping around my neck, and slams me against a brick wall with unexpected strength.

She's trying to kill me.

Where was this power when she was facing down the mortals?

Gritting her teeth, her fingers tighten, pressing, choking. I can't breathe. She's crushing my windpipe, compressing my airway.

My thoughts go dim. The world slows. For a moment, I'm at peace.

I'm in the cottage again where I grew up, and sunlight streams in, catching on dust motes. I turn, running my fingers over the little flowers my father carved into the wood above my bed. Mother is outside, pulling weeds from her garden, and I can hear her singing to herself as she works...

Until—faintly— I hear a distant song.

A melody drowned underwater...

A raven's wing brushes against my cheek like a kiss...

Faintly, my old magic thrums through my veins in a slow symphony.

I jab up at the baroness's forearm with my fist and hear the snap of bone. Then I grab her by the hair and slam her head into the wall.

The sharp crack of her skull against the brick makes my heart lurch.

Even a Fey can't survive a crushed skull.

Her body crumples to the pavement, crimson pooling onto the gray.

I stare at her, stunned, horror sliding through my bones.

My breathing sounds wrong—everything is wrong. I've just killed the person I was trying to help. How did this night fall apart so fast?

And what, *exactly*, should I do with the Fey corpse at my feet?

CHAPTER 4

$\mathcal{A}$s I stare down at her body, her words reverberate in my thoughts like a ringing bell.

Cursed is the hour you were born...

I listen for the sound of footfalls, fighting a rising sense of panic at the dead baroness bleeding all over the pavement. Now it won't be only the Iron Legion after me —I'll also be running from the London police, and the Fey government on top of that.

Fuck.

In the distance, police sirens wail, and my stomach twists.

My blood pounds hard in my ears, a steady drumbeat. This night was supposed to be a sweet homecoming, and it's all gone so terribly wrong.

Breathing hard, I scan the street to see if anyone is around. Mercifully, it's empty.

I crouch and hook my hands under the dead woman's shoulders, then drag her through the shadows to an abandoned railway line. Her body leaves a crimson trail on the pavement. The scent of blood envelops me, sweet and metallic at the same time.

Dread coils through my chest.

Her limbs flop limply, and her jaw hangs open. Quick as I can, I pull her behind a rubbish tip.

Guilt twines around my ribs.

I'm just dumping her here like rotten trash.

Distantly, the sound of sirens grows louder. A sharp tendril of fear twists around my heart.

I can see my cozy, safe future in Brocéliande dissolving before my eyes.

When I step out into the light of a streetlamp, I see the blood on my wrists and hands, and my heart plummets.

I hurry back into the alley and wipe the blood on the woman's soft cloak. I'm sure I'm leaving fingerprints all over everything, but I don't know what else to do.

I take a few steps toward the street, then freeze at the sound of heavy boots on the pavement beneath the bridge.

I slink back into the shadows, watching as a group of drunk mortals totters down the road. Not the Iron Legion, thank the gods, and they're too wasted to notice me.

What the bloody hell was she talking about? I'm going to *destroy the world?*

Even for an Auberon-loving monarchist, that was an overreaction.

Once the drunk mortals have moved on, I walk quickly toward the Tower. My body is shaking, my heart pattering like a hunted rabbit's.

I tuck my chin down as I walk at a steady pace. I'm not running, not trying to draw attention. But if anyone looked at my face closely enough, they would see me losing it.

I jam my hands into my pockets and touch the smooth metal of the magical key.

I'm supposed to meet Tristan by Traitors' Gate at the Tower of London, right next to the river. It's the exact spot where those who offended monarchs saw the sky outside the Tower for the last time, Anne Boleyn and Lady Jane Grey included. They floated in from the Thames, beneath a stone gate and into the Tower prisons, before executioners cut off their heads.

I suppose that's an appropriate location for me, a person who fantasizes about crushing kings' skulls.

As the baroness just pointed out, I am very much a traitor.

As I hurry down toward the river, my mind flashes with images I'd love to bleach from my thoughts for good: Vicky's pale bum pancaked against the Tudor glass. The baroness's furious face and her blood on the pavement. The fragments of her skull. Her body limp behind the rubbish, mouth agape.

Nausea turns my stomach.

My senses are hyper-alert now, and I glance at the Tower of London before me, trying to stay calm.

I'm almost at Traitors' Gate.

I've always loved this place, but tonight—perhaps because of what I've done—it looks like a grandiose jail more than anything. It's not a single tower, but rather a vast stone fortress built around a central keep, with twenty-two towers in total, bound by massive stone walls that loom over the river. For centuries, this place was both a palace and a dungeon, a site of feasts and executions alike.

Up ahead is the gatehouse—two fat, squat little towers of white stone, joined by an arch above the door. Slowly, the portcullis rises, its groans echoing over the stone courtyard.

That's...odd. Why would the gate open at this hour?

I narrow my eyes, my gaze sharpening on a pair of Fey stalking gracefully toward the gatehouse. The man and woman stand out like north stars against the night sky. They're a foot taller than most mortals, with the same halo glow that the baroness had. And as I get closer, I can see the utter luxury threaded through their clothes. They wear the finest of cloaks trimmed with fur. This pair seem like they swept in from the Fey realm wrapped in gold and velvet. The woman's throat and wrists glitter with jewels, and a jeweled earring hangs from the man's ear.

Spinning sharply, the woman looks back at me. She's

beautiful, with shimmering cheekbones, pale skin, and eyes like amethysts. She wears a delicate, glittering tiara over her golden hair. Amber light radiates from her head. She looks as though she were dipped in gold.

My heartbeat picks up.

Whatever is going on here, I'm sure it's why Tristan is stationed at the Tower.

The woman has stopped, blocking my path—which is deeply unfortunate, because the last thing I want to do is talk to another rich Fey.

As I move around her on the cobbles, the Fey woman steps directly into my path, looming over me. She drags her gaze down my body with the repulsed expression you might give to a chunk of rotten meat.

I peer down at myself. I'm dressed in dark jeans and a worn black T-shirt Owain must have bought secondhand. It reads *Have you tried turning it off and on again?* with a faded cartoon computer underneath. It's a relic from a world that doesn't exist anymore. It must be over fifteen years old, dating from before the Fey arrived and our magic turned digital technology into ash.

I've never used a computer. I doubt these two glittering Fey aristocrats even know what one is.

My hands start trembling again, and I clutch them together to still them. Pain from my headache flashes through my skull.

"Are you *really* joining us?" the woman asks. Even her

accent drips wealth—pure old money. "Dressed like *that*? Is this a *joke*?"

I want to punch this woman in the throat and move on to Tristan, but I've had enough violence for one night.

I flash a fake smile. "Join you? Absolutely not."

Her gaze flicks down my body again, and her lip curls slightly. "I thought only the elite were included. And you're so *small*. I heard a rumor someone from the Waste Land was coming. I'm guessing that's you? Baroness of the Kingdom of Bones? You look worse than I thought, frankly. A little runt. I didn't believe the rumor until now. Frightful, really. They're letting anyone in."

That's when her companion turns, and my breath leaves my lungs. I've dreamt of this man for years.

He meets my gaze, and my heart skips a beat. The beautiful killer from my nightmares.

The gilded warrior—an elegant, gold-painted façade with coiled brutality underneath. Pale light streaks over his sharp cheekbones in strange tattoos, eerie golden lines that trace his features. The amber light emanating from him seems to drip over me.

A chill dances down my spine as realization takes root in my thoughts. How is it that I've dreamt of his beautiful face so many times? In my nightmares, he leaves piles of bodies and severed limbs in his wake. And in my fevered dreams…

Best not to think about those now.

I breathe slowly, staring at him. His pale, silver-blue

eyes pierce me, and his silver hair drapes over a fur-lined cloak. He looks half like a warlord and half like a libertine, with that jeweled earring and strings of necklaces. His jaw is sharp and masculine, but his mouth is soft, almost dangerously sensual.

I can sense the tightly coiled brutality that lies beneath the gilded surface.

But my real question is what the fuck is this knight doing here in the middle of London, dressed like he's going to the Fey Court?

He takes a step closer, his gaze pinned on me, and lifts my chin with a finger. A wicked, amused glint sparks in his eyes. Magic rolls off him in waves, stroking my skin like it's hungry for me. He drops his hand.

He laughs softly—a low and seductive sound that makes my breath catch. "Is this what the gods are sending us to decide the fate of the Fey?"

His aristocratic voice is surprisingly sensual, and it sends a strange shudder racing down my spine.

"To decide *what*?" I hiss.

"Honestly, we don't need the opinions of every provincial, filthy backwater baroness," the woman cuts in, her tone brittle. "The council of Fey should be small and *elite*. Refined. But she'll be easy to break, I imagine. Nothing functions in the Waste Land, and I'd wager that includes her mind."

She flashes me a dazzling smile and slips her arm through her companion's.

A dozen sharp retorts rise to my tongue about aristocrats being parasites, but I swallow them down. I've made enough enemies tonight.

"Well, 'bye." With that farewell, I march around them on the cobbled path toward the riverside.

The woman calls out, "Running from the council, I see, little wastrel. The wisest thing you could choose. You'd do better to take your chances with the Cloaked Ones than with us."

CHAPTER 5

$\mathcal{I}$ march on. Whatever was going on back there had nothing to do with me. All that matters is that I get the key to Tristan right now, with enough time to rush back to Smithfield, back to the bloody portal before it closes. Then I'll join Vero and put as much distance as possible between me and that poor woman's corpse.

With my blood pounding in my ears, I follow the cobblestone path that curves around to the left. The Tower Bridge spans the Thames in the distance.

I desperately want to see Tristan. He and I grew up together. Instead of a regular school, we studied in the Undercroft, Auberon's underground spy academy. Literally underground—beneath the king's castle. We've both killed more people than I can count. If anyone can handle the unwelcome news of my chaotic and violent night, it's him.

I spot him standing beneath a birch tree, looking out over the river. Moonlight gleams off his dark, wavy hair.

If he weren't in such sinfully perfect shape, he might pass for a tourist drifting through London at night. But anyone paying attention would see the way his shirt strains over shoulders carved by hours of swordsmanship. They'd notice the ink along his arms too, the dark leaves coiling over hard muscle, rendered with a craftsmanship that could only be Fey. And then there are his eyes, metallic green shot through with gold.

He always makes my heart skip a little beat when he looks at me too long. It's no wonder he's left a trail of brokenhearted women behind him. I've had a crush on him for as long as I can remember.

Technically, we were always *just friends*, but seeing him makes my cheeks flush. You can't blame me. The man looks like masculine perfection, and I spent my teenage years sleeping next to him.

Even now, after the night I've had, my pulse races when his eyes slide to mine, and all thoughts of Owain dissolve.

Tristan, however, doesn't look happy to see me. His jaw tenses, and he leans back against the railing, folding his arms like the very sight of me is exhausting.

When I'm close to him, he grabs my elbow and pulls me near, whispering, "*Who* did you kill, Syn Malleore?"

I frown. "What sort of greeting is that? How do you know I killed someone?"

He peers down at me. "Because I'm highly skilled in espionage, and you bear the distinct mark of a murderer."

"What mark?" I lean over the river's edge, looking at my reflection.

My heart jolts.

There, glimmering off the water's surface, are golden rays radiating from my head—a halo. "Oh, gods. What is this?"

"Unless you're an aristocrat, there's only one way to get that golden glow, and it's slaughtering the noble who possessed it."

My stomach tightens. "What the fuck?"

He crosses his arms. "First, tell me who you killed."

I turn back to him, heaving a deep, shaky breath. "The baroness from the Waste Land. I was trying to help her get away from the Iron Legion, and on the way here, she attacked me. She was a telepath, and she overheard me fantasizing about killing Auberon. Apparently, she was a fan of his, because she started shouting at me that no one should hurt a king, and that someone like me could destroy the world, and *cursed be the hour I was born*. Then she tried to choke me. She was completely unhinged. I had to fight back."

Tristan goes very still, staring at me, and my pulse quickens. I can tell he's exercising a large amount of restraint before speaking, which makes me wonder exactly how much trouble I'm in.

"Okay..." he says slowly.

"What?" I grab his forearm. "What are you not telling me?"

"You killed Alis of Listenoise. The niece of King Pelles of the Waste Land. This is bad, Syn. The monarchists will kill you if they find out. Did anyone see you?"

I shake my head. "No one saw me kill her. But I passed two more Fey with the same halo. They seemed certain *I* was from the Waste Land. They mistook me for the baroness. I think they were trying to reconcile the aristocratic halo with my shitty clothes."

Tristan's gaze bores into me. "*Fuck.*"

"What, exactly, is going on, Tristan? I know I'm not part of Avalon Tower's spy guild, but you *need* to fill me in right now. Why are all these rich Fey with halos showing up around the Tower?"

A muscle ticks in his jaw, and I can almost see the gears turning in his head, as though he's weighing how much to tell me. But I know him, and given the right circumstances, he has a hard time resisting a bad idea.

"Come on, Tristan. I know you're dying to tell me. I'm in danger, aren't I? I doubt that hiding information from me is going to keep me safer."

"Fine. You remember the Veiled Court?"

My heart leaps at the fortress's name, nostalgia twining with regret. I've never seen it, but I've heard all about it—a court that moved around the kingdom from year to year, hidden by magical mists. They say that once, it stood on the lost island of Avalon—and before that, in London. Some of Auberon's most powerful advisors lived in the Veiled Court. A *very* few of his most elite spies were granted the privilege of becoming Knights of the Veiled Court—even one or two lowborn rabble from the Undercroft.

When I was a teenager, I imagined myself there all the time. Curled up on a hard dirt floor, I pictured Tristan and me drinking from crystal goblets on a balcony above a garden. I envisioned fine gowns, soft pillows, crystal glasses of mead.

The golden possibility of the Veiled Court might have been the only thing keeping me going back then.

"Of course I remember," I say. "Do you have any idea how many times I've thought about it while stepping over a puddle of someone else's vomit outside my flat? I think about it every time I see someone in my neighborhood injecting heroin into his knob, which is more than you'd expect. I think about it whenever I have to buy value-brand margarine because butter is too expensive. Yes, you could say it's been on my mind once or twice."

Tristan cocks his head with a quizzical expression. "Right, well, King Auberon may not be dead, but he's gone, and so are his advisors. Many of them are now imprisoned in the dungeons by the commoners; others have been executed. But someone from the Veiled Court has been sending these invitations to aristocrats around the Fey world. Only they can get into the Veiled Court. Ravens brought invitations to every forgotten, hidden Fey island across the globe, summoning their high lords and countesses. You know the lost Isle of Shalott? Not lost anymore. The ravens found it, and they invited members of their noble houses."

"They want a new king, don't they? I *hate* the nobility."

"You and me both, Syn. I hate every bone in their bodies." He sighs. "Unless it's my own."

Of course—he really does have a history of shagging aristocratic women.

When it comes to work, he's strategic and completely logical, but the rest of his life is anarchy. Once, after a fight with a lover, he disappeared into the forest for two weeks. He returned to the Undercroft naked, bruised, and covered in dirt.

Auberon kept him locked in a dark hole for weeks after that, starving him.

Tristan absolutely cannot resist the lure of adventure, which is why he's been imprisoned more than once, even by his own spy organization in Camelot.

Sometimes, I wonder if he craves being locked up. After all, it's how we spent much of our youth. It's familiar.

"Tristan, what else do you know?" I whisper.

"People are getting into the Veiled Court with these invitations. The raven brings the invitation, explaining where to go. When the invitation is opened, the golden halo appears. It's a portal key, and it vanishes once a person crosses the threshold into the Veiled Court. But the halo will reappear if someone leaves the Veiled Court without being formally dismissed. If you never show up at all, you're stuck with it. All of this is only for the nobility."

"Then why do I have a halo? I come from a long line of peasants and gravediggers."

"Because if someone with the halo is killed, the magic seeks a new bearer. It's completely illegal to kill them, of course, but the Veiled Court's magic is older than laws."

"So, what is your role in this?" I ask cautiously.

"That's the third way in. I planned to infiltrate as a humble servant."

My eyebrows flick up. "I know you've played many roles in your life, but I'm not convinced *humble* is one you can reasonably pull off."

"It wasn't exactly easy to arrange, you know. I was supposed to act as Alis's manservant. The Waste Land's borders are completely closed. It's fog and swamps and decay if you try to get through. Messages can only arrive by raven, and even then, half of them die. We had to use magic enchantments in our letters to convince the baroness that I was one of her uncle's own valets, lost outside the Waste Land boundaries for decades. We were supposed to reunite right here. But then you killed her."

I touch his arm. "Who is sending out the invitations, exactly?"

He holds my gaze for a long time before he answers. "Someone called Niniane is in the Veiled Court. She's an ancient priestess, and she's an obsessive monarchist. We believe she's calling people in for a council of nobles to choose the next king."

"So, they're just ignoring the republic's new courts," I say. *"The first thing we do, let's kill all the lawyers."*

"Shakespeare again?"

I don't answer because I'm too busy thinking, *Fuck kings.*

Tristan and I have both seen what one can do. A Fey king shatters the bodies of anyone who objects to him and hangs their broken carcasses on gibbets. He goes after their families. He grinds his enemies into dust, and he'd never dream of letting the courts stop him. He'd destroy them all first.

Because everyone knows that a king's wrath is death.

Auberon once sent us to round up traitors from the villages and bring them to him for a mock trial. No real lawyers. No real judges. I did as commanded. That was the third worst thing I've ever done.

And when we brought him the "traitors," the peasants' sentences were preordained. If a king says a commoner is guilty, he's guilty. And if you criticize him for his harsh methods—well, that alone is treason or sedition. Then you're guilty, too.

"We can't have another king," I whisper. "We just got

rid of the old one. Why would anyone want to go back to that?"

It's a rhetorical question, but I think I know why. It's the bloody ceremony of it all, isn't it? When you step into Westminster Abbey and see where a monarch is crowned—when sunlight slants through the colored windowpanes onto the soaring arches—people feel awe. It looks godlike. When an anointed king sits on a throne glittering with jewels, he looks divine.

But who built those arches, the crown and scepter, that stained glass? Not the gods-damned king. *Artists* create the magic. Artists are divine; they channel the numinous voice of the gods.

All the bloody king did was show up and plant his arse on a throne.

"Many of the Fey in Brocéliande were happier with the monarchy," Tristan says. "They're not satisfied with being ruled by commoners, and it doesn't help that the republic keeps imprisoning every aristocrat and cutting off their heads. The commoners have no idea what they're doing. So, there's a growing royalist faction that's gaining power every day. It's chaos. The republic is off to a rocky start."

"Of course it's off to a rough start," I shoot back. "Half the leaders were running pubs or farms before taking power. They haven't had time to learn how to govern, but they will if people are patient. Choosing another king isn't the answer. Our monarchs live for thousands of years. If the next king is a monster, we'll be stuck with him forever. And even if he starts out fine, the throne will corrupt him."

Too much power rots the soul. The kings believe they are chosen by the gods, which means they can do no wrong. That belief is corrosive to morality.

I bite my lip. "Lydia the tavern wench and her mates running a kingdom—they can be replaced if everyone hates them. They've got to stay in line. No gods anointed them. They've got to be thoughtful to stay in power. *The kingdom needs tavern wenches.*"

My voice has grown too loud, and Tristan lifts a finger to his lips. I hear footfalls coming closer, people out for a nighttime stroll.

Tristan glances over my shoulder, then grabs me by the waist to pull me in closer against his muscled chest. A pulse of heat flares through me, and my heart skips a beat. Of course, I know this is only a spy ploy to make us look like lovers by the river, but I'm distracted by his clean, delicious scent all the same.

Tristan is the only person I knew before everything fell apart. When I see him, I remember lying on my back in tall grasses and honeyed light and running through the forest. I remember a childhood of looking for mushrooms and conkers, fighting with sticks. To look at Tristan is to see a lost sylvan idyll made of woodland cottages, and being near him opens a sharp hunger in my chest for a time of innocence.

"We have to stop the next king," I whisper.

"Yes, I know. That's why I wanted in to the Veiled Court," he leans down to whisper, a lock of dark hair falling in front of his eyes. "Avalon Tower needs to know what decision they will make. We need to know *when* it will happen. Problem is, the baroness is dead, and I no longer have a way in."

I breathe in the smell of him, like fresh rain on stone, and it reminds me of being young. Despite the horror of tonight, I feel safe pressed against his hard chest, and his body warms mine.

"I don't think you should give up just yet," I whisper.

Tristan holds my gaze, a line forming between his eyebrows. I can read him like a book, and his expression makes my throat tight.

"What else are you not telling me?" I say.

Slowly, he releases me. "That halo will remain as long as you are outside the Veiled Court. As you walk around with it, you'll find yourself followed by cloaked spirits who come in threes. They'll crawl from the shadows like phantoms. They're the *cugol*—the Cloaked Ones."

You'd do better to take your chances with the Cloaked Ones than with us.

"I think I've heard of them," I say. "What, exactly, do they do?"

"They'll find you no matter where you go. The halo is a beacon, and if they capture you, they will burn you. They serve the nobles, and you murdered one of their own."

CHAPTER 6

My throat is bone dry, and I turn to stare out at the Thames glittering under the night sky. I rest my arms on the rail next to Tristan, and a soft breeze kisses my skin. This morning, when I woke up, I imagined myself waltzing through the portal, arm in arm with my pretty boyfriend.

Unlike my family, Owain's was rich before the king exiled them. If things had gone to plan, we'd be traipsing into his aunt's mansion and sipping flutes of fine mead on a balcony overlooking the riverside while servants offered us fresh fruit. We'd be choosing from three stories of rooms to sleep in.

I'd fantasized about finding the cure for Vero, then throwing a party to celebrate— dancing with Owain in the ballroom, celebrating a glamorous new life of freedom and health and fancy parties under the stars.

Owain is probably on a marble balcony right now.

Just not with me.

A little blonde mortal is drinking my mead, looking out over the river in my place, delighting in the pleasures of a plan that I orchestrated.

Meanwhile, I'm going to be hounded by Cloaked Ones until I burn to death.

I take a shaky breath. "Do you know what I want right now, Tristan? A cigarette."

Without a word, Tristan pulls a pouch of tobacco out of his back pocket, one of his many bad habits.

I quit smoking years ago, but if I ever needed a cigarette, now's the time.

He starts rolling me a cigarette, adding in the filter and everything. When it's all neatly finished, he hands it to me, along with a lighter.

I light it, filling my lungs with smoke, and I exhale over the Thames. I wait to feel a buzz, a sense of relief—anything. But it doesn't taste as good as I remember. In fact, it just feels kind of like I'm sucking in poison and ash, and now I want to clean off my tongue. I take a few more puffs, trying to remember what I once liked about this.

Then I hand it back to Tristan like it's a spliff. "Yeah, it's not doing it for me. This is gross."

"I'm quitting, you know."

I thrum my fingertips on the guardrail. A little seed of an idea is starting to bloom in my mind. "The Veiled Court was built by the first Fey king, Bran, right?"

"Yes."

Roots of hope start to germinate. "King Bran, who created the grail."

"Right."

"People say the grail is kept in the Veiled Court, and it's the one thing that can heal any illness."

"Supposedly," he says. "Fuck knows if it's true."

My pulse races with excitement. "It *is* true. Tristan, I have an idea. You said the Waste Land is totally cut off, surrounded by fog and rot. So, does anyone actually know what Alis looks like?"

"No."

My eyebrows raise. "No one at all?"

He shakes his head. "The whole kingdom of Listenoise is bones and rocks as far as anyone knows. Until Alis got her golden invitation, no one could leave, either. The only reason she escaped was because of the halo."

A grin is starting to spread on my face.

I tilt my head up, meeting his gaze. Maybe this isn't the worst possible series of events. Maybe fate is offering me a solution to my most heartbreaking problem.

"Tristan, what if I took her place for this council meeting? If I show up as Alis, no one will know she's missing. I'll stay safe from the Cloaked Ones. You get to be a humble servant and complete your mission. No one will look for the baroness's body because she will be exactly where she's meant to be. In the Veiled Court."

He narrows his eyes at me. "No."

"Why?"

"Because what if they notice you're not full-blooded Fey? And you don't have an aristocratic accent. I also have no idea what they actually have planned in there. If it's dangerous, you won't be able to fight back because your magic is broken."

Once, I had a type of magic called the Song. I'd hear the Morrigan's music—the song of the war goddess. I'd feel the brush of her phantom raven feathers against my skin.

Then I'd kill everyone within seconds.

But I haven't heard the Song in fifteen years.

"I'm three-quarters Fey," I say. "I've even got iron scars like a full Fey. And you were perfectly willing to send Alis in without knowing what she was getting into. She's worse at fighting than I am. Obviously."

He nods. "But I didn't give a fuck if she lived or died."

My breath is rapid, shallow. "I don't see myself as having many options if Cloaked Ones will be trying to burn me to death anywhere I go."

"You're kind of fucked either way, Syn," he mutters.

"Story of our lives, isn't it? But it's not just me. I need the grail. You know I'd do anything for Vero."

"We don't even know if the grail is there." He turns toward the Tower and the Traitors' Gate, the dark stone archway where the river laps at the old stones.

"After all these years, you and I will finally get to see the Veiled Court. Aren't you curious? Don't you want the adventure of it all? Don't you want to find out if the grail is real? Or if they're going to choose a new king?" I lick my lips. "Think of all the pretty bejeweled noblewomen you can shag while their husbands sleep."

When Tristan turns back to me, his eyes are gleaming with excitement, and I know I have him. "You know I can't resist anything you just said."

I lean in closer. "Then let's go."

"You'll be in danger every moment you're there. A traitor among enemies. If they discover what you've done, they will torture you to death. You absolutely cannot let your cover slip, or your accent, even for a moment. You know what they'd do to a peasant who kills an aristocrat and infiltrates their secret court? They'll have you pulled apart by horses or slowly roasted by a dragon. If they find out who you are, they'll make you regret the day you were born."

The excitement leaches from my body, and a thin sliver of fear wends its way through my chest.

My eyes sting, but I don't want Tristan to see me looking emotional. I don't want him to think that living among humans dulled my sharp edges. We both know that being soft gets you killed.

This is about as hysterical as either of us ever gets. We trained together. We endured lashings together. We certainly killed a lot of people together.

More than once, the king demanded that we beat each

other, pitting us against one another in his twisted mind games.

But Auberon never broke our bond. Tristan was the guy who bandaged all my bloodied knuckles, treated my iron-laced wounds over and over, and held me as I fell asleep. Tristan pulled me from Auberon's grip when my magic broke, just before the king killed me for being useless. We fled the kingdom together.

But we never *cried* in front of each other. Crying happened silently, in the dark.

Or in Tristan's case, sometimes naked, running through the woods.

I clench my jaw and blink until my vision clears again. Overhead, a raven sweeps closer to me through the darkness. Dark eyes gleaming, the bird circles me.

Ravens—the Morrigan's creatures—always seek me out. Even now, with my magic broken, they still recognize me as a sort of kin.

"What else is going on?" he asks quietly.

"Owain has a new girlfriend, so my whole plan with him is ruined, anyway." I try to sound breezy, but my voice cracks. Right now, I can imagine Vicky walking through that portal with her bottle of champagne, eyes wide at the beauty of the Fey realm.

"He fucking *what?*" An edge slides through Tristan's voice, which I appreciate.

"Owain and his new lover are going to Brocéliande together."

"That absolute fucking twat. Syn." His hand brushes softly down my bicep. "You were always too good for him. You were never going to stay with a loser like him forever, and he knew it. He's just trying to get out of it with his ego intact. Let me guess—he left you for a young, simpering mortal girl who hangs on his every word?"

"Remarkably accurate." I almost smile, though I'm not sure how much better I feel about the concept that I was dumped by an absolute loser. "I caught them shagging in his window."

"The old Tudor window?" Tristan sounds outraged on my behalf. "You love that window."

I sigh. "Exactly. No respect for history. Anyway, he's taking *her* into Brocéliande, to his aunt's mansion, because humans are allowed there again—which, of course, is good. I fully support mortal rights. But..."

"But you'd rather this particular mortal was not welcome," he says.

"You always knew he was a loser?" I ask.

"I was waiting for you to realize. Fairly sure he was, too. He had that really nice flat, and you lived in that cramped shithole, and he never once asked you to move in with him."

It's true. I've been living in a literal closet. Vero and I have been cramming six people into a two-bedroom flat share. More often than not, I'm woken at three in the morning by a drug deal gone wrong right behind the building. Nearby is a field everyone calls Disappearance

Gardens after a woman was abducted there ten years ago. Behind my flat, thieves abandon stolen cars under a bridge and set them on fire. Sometimes refrigerators, too. It looked like a war zone even before the war. That patch of trash-strewn grass is called Homicide Park.

"Owain's new lover said she specializes in romance. Quite clearly, that is not my strong suit." My throat tightens. Do I even have a strong suit anymore? "Okay, you know what? I don't want to talk about her. Let's go back to the agonizing executions topic. Or tell me where the Veiled Court is, exactly. Is it the fortress you told us not to go near?"

"That's the one, in the north of Brocéliande, up by the dragon's keep. It's very hard to see, though, and you can only find it if you know where to look." He points to the gatehouse of the Tower. "If you're going in, you'll get there through a portal just over there, through the gatehouse. But Syn? You cannot *ever* let down your guard. I don't even want to think of what they would do to you."

CHAPTER 7

$\mathcal{A}$ shiver dances down my spine. "You won't come with me through the gatehouse?"

He shakes his head. "Only the halo gets you in there. The lowly peasants like me are supposed to go through separately with our portal keys. The one you were bringing me."

He holds out his palm, and I dig into my pocket to hand it to him.

"Then what?" I ask.

"You go straight in while the servants are vetted, I believe, and I very much hope there is no torture involved, unless it's the fun kind."

"Will you have time to tell Avalon Tower about the change of plans?"

"I'll send a message, yes."

I clear my throat. "Tristan, there's another thing. The

baroness's body isn't hidden very well. I dragged her behind the rubbish tip under the abandoned tube station on Minories. There's blood everywhere."

"You know, part of me is enjoying the fact that you're the one fucking up for once."

"I fuck up all the time, but thank you for pretending otherwise."

"I'll take care of the body. But I need to get you dressed in something more appropriate first. You look too human and far too poor for the Veiled Court."

"Okay, first of all, *thanks*." I look down at the cartoon computer T-shirt I'm wearing. "But those two Fey already saw me dressed like this. They assumed this was the best anyone could do in the Waste Land. Remember? I think it will look more suspicious if I waltz in wearing a new frock."

He scrubs a hand over his jaw. "Right. You'll have to go in as you are, then, I suppose, looking like you're wearing the ratty clothes you slept in."

I glare at him. "Nobody sleeps in jeans."

Though, as soon as the words are out of my mouth, I remember that I actually had slept in these jeans last night because my room was cold, and I don't have pajamas.

"Okay," he says. "I'll join you as soon as I can. Just make sure you can convince them that you're posh. Let me hear your accent."

I lift my chin. "You *must* fill me a bath, then scrub my back, but do it gently, you know, with that rose soap," I say in the clipped accent that I remember from Auberon. "Use your hands, not the rough cloth, and get all the crevices and folds."

His eyebrows rise, and he blinks. "Where did that particular idea come from? Is this a request?"

"The accent was good, though, right?"

"Very. I felt like Auberon himself was asking me to bathe him, and I'm horrified to say it slightly turned me on."

I touch his arm. "When you go through the portal, Vero will still be waiting there for me by a willow tree. Let her know I'm fine, but not to wait for me. Just tell her… tell her that I have a spy job to do with you. She'll understand she can't get more details. And maybe you can find her a horse? She can hardly walk."

"I'll take care of it."

"Try to help her find some food. She'll be hungry by now, and I was going to help her get dinner once we got through, but I won't be there. Make sure she knows how to get to the Melian Forest."

He nods. "You know she's an adult, right?"

"Barely. She's only eighteen."

And I still think of her as the little girl I brought over from Brocéliande, the one who woke up screaming at night because someone murdered her parents. I still think of her as the eight-year-old who slept next to me for months, snoring on my shoulder. To me, she's still a child who needs to be fully covered in stuffed animals to sleep, who uses her shirt sleeves as a tissue and gets excited by the wonders of chocolate milk and ice cream.

"Syn, I want you to know—" His gaze lifts over my head, and he goes quiet. I turn to see a faint flicker of movement in the shadows.

A dark shape shifts there, and a cowl sweeps over a pale face. The Cloaked Ones.

Ice sweeps down my spine.

Tristan whispers in my ear, "Time to go, Syn. Do not let your accent slip for a moment."

My pulse hammers.

Time to become someone else.

As Tristan stalks off into the night, I turn back to the Tower. Acutely aware that I'm being watched, I strike a haughty pose and stride along the cobbled road.

My vision blurs again as my throat tightens. Bordering on hysteria once more.

Gods above. Get it together, Syn.

Whatever this meeting holds, surely I've been through worse. Right? And this is all for the grail.

And yet, my nerves flutter as I slink up to the gatehouse, its pale stone walls looming over a cobbled path. As I draw closer, the halo around my head tingles and grows brighter, reflecting on the stones at my feet. I take another tentative step, and the portcullis rises with a groan that echoes over the stone.

Normally, I feel completely comfortable at the Tower of London. I visit whenever I can. I suppose it reminds me of home and the castle whose shadow I once lived under. But tonight, it feels different—otherworldly. Shadows coil around me, slick and cold, twining over my limbs like serpents. Already, a strange and ancient magic is at work.

Distantly, the sound of a clanging bell resounds off the stone, sending a chill up my spine. The Tower is beautiful, but it's also a place of death.

When I pass beneath the gatehouse arches, darkness envelops me. The gray stone dims, and I breathe in the scent of soil, damp stones, and moldering bones.

Around me, the Tower of London dissolves, sliding back into a castle old enough to remember the gods. I step into utter, primordial darkness.

Magic tingles over my skin, raising goose bumps.

So, this is how I leave London forever.

Tristan and I arrived in this city long before the war broke out. We were refugees, fleeing King Auberon's purges of demi-Fey. Anyone with mortal blood automatically became a "traitor" to the king.

Anyone who annoyed him could also be a traitor. I was both.

And for fifteen years, we were safe here. Nobody cared that I was mostly Fey, part mortal.

That all changed a year and a half ago when the war began.

Driven by a famine, the Fey army slammed into the UK and turned this country into a living nightmare. Dragon fire seared the skies. Fey swords cut down anyone in their way. Auberon's soldiers raided the cities, stole food from every corner of the kingdom, and left the British starving. Mortals here finally saw what Fey violence looked like and how ruthless we could be.

I reach out, touching slick, rounded walls on either side. I bring my foot down slowly, not sure what I'm stepping into, and encounter smooth, worn stone. It's uneven beneath my feet, compressed by legions of shoes over thousands of years.

Steadying myself on the cold stone walls, I slowly mount the perilous, slick steps. As I climb higher, thin rays of light start to pierce the gloom, and I reach a window in the curving stairwell—a jagged, gaping aperture, like a dragon ripped a chunk out of it. The view is dizzying, a few stories high with nothing to stop me from falling if I stumble in the narrow stairwell.

And I remember now: Brocéliande isn't like the mortal world. Its beauty will leave you breathless, but there are no modern comforts and protections here to keep you safe, no safety nets or caution cones.

I gaze out at the starlit, rolling fields spread across the Fey realm. Beyond them, the sea glitters, reflecting the light of the two strange moons, silver and red, the latter dappling the water with crimson sparks.

I breathe in the briny air of the ocean, sweetened with the scent of sea thrift and lavender. My chest twinges at the familiar smell. I thought I'd forgotten it, but it all comes back to me. The scent of my golden childhood.

I resume my climb, taking care not to slip, past narrow windows that let in the silver-red moonlight.

The higher I ascend, the more the stairwell seems to be shaped and polished by magic—smoother now, with straight stones of pale gold. Now, the walls are carved with ornate shapes: twisting vines and serpents, ravens and antlers, each carving shimmering with magic. On I climb, and I can almost forget Owain and the poem he once wrote me, one casting himself as an alder tree and me as the rain he needed to live. I can almost forget that Vicky will be lying next to him in silken sheets tonight.

At last, I reach a landing with a towering ceiling and an enormous oak door. A triple spiral shape is carved into the wood. Below it are letters in the ancient Fey language:

Whosoever pulleth this sword from this stone and anvil is rightwise king born of all Fey.

My skin prickles with the words, my heart fluttering.

I push through the doors of the Veiled Court at last and cross into a glittering, dangerous kingdom, a beautiful world filled with those who would tear my heart out if they knew the truth.

CHAPTER 8

I step into a great hall. Moonlight streams through soaring windows thirty feet high. In the center, a fountain burbles, and flower petals drift across its surface. Very pretty—even if the basin is carved with skulls. I scan the hall for any signs of a grail, but I suppose it's too much to hope I'll just walk right into it.

A breeze stirs the flowered vines that climb the honey-gold stone. Far above, lanterns float beneath a vaulted ceiling. They sway in the breeze, casting light and shadow. Around the hall, mirrors gleam and ripple like water. Rich food is set out on the tables—glazed fruits, goat cheese, venison and boar roasted with thyme, honeycomb, dates, and candied flower petals. Why do they get to eat like this when the rest of us have so little, simply because of an imagined birthright?

Still, my breath catches at the overwhelming splendor of this place. It's more beautiful than I ever imagined.

Hundreds of aristocratic Fey stand around, draped in gorgeous fabrics and sipping mead. Some linger by the fountain, talking quietly and eating fruit. Others lounge on pillows. Some of the women wear long gowns; others are clad in short skirts and tall boots or in sheer chain mail and lace. Dripping with jewels, they glitter and shine like a dragon's hoard. The crowd, overall, is sexy as hell—and just as dangerous. Each one of these gorgeous Fey would rip me to shreds if they knew that I'm a peasant.

I take another step into the hall. As the halo around me tingles, a herald calls out, "Baroness Alis of Listenoise."

I'd hoped to fade into the shadows. So much for that.

I go still as all eyes slide to me—the Waste Land raga-muffin in an old cartoon T-shirt. I lift my chin, attempting to strike the pose of a baroness. Fortunately, the attention of the Fey nobility only lasts a moment before they lose interest.

Plucking a glass of mead off the table, I survey the room, keeping close to the wall. The golden-haired lady I met outside the Tower leans casually against a column, her tiara set perfectly on her hair. With her lifted chin, she holds herself like she was born to rule.

Beside her, the man from my nightmares idly swirls a glass of mead between his fingers. His face is a study in contrasts: sun-warmed skin and gold tattoos and eyes cold as winter light. Black brows slash above his eyes, and a lock of his pale silver hair hangs rakishly down his cheekbones. He wears a fur-lined cloak that hangs open, showing off supple leather trousers, and a soft, Fey-wool shirt that stretches over his chest in dusky forest green. A few long chains hang around his neck, down to his waist, one adorned with the tip of an antler.

It's uncanny how familiar he looks from my worst dreams, and I can't stop staring at him. For so long, I've dreamt of his power and cruelty and unearthly beauty.

I have no idea why. The strangeness of it sets my teeth on edge.

Slowly, he lifts his glass to his lips, and the rose-kissed moonlight catches in his drink and sparkles on his gold rings.

When his icy gaze slides to me, my pulse races. I look away.

Clearly, some of them are already drunk because a tall man with long black hair is staggering around, sloshing a bright red cocktail. He lurches toward a lady standing by herself, breathtaking and glamorous, with wavy hair tumbling over one shoulder, perfect eyebrows, and golden-brown skin. She is wearing a figure-hugging white dress.

Well, it's white until the drunken man spills his entire crimson drink on her. "Oops!" He breaks into laughter.

The golden lady titters. "Oh, dear, what a mess."

The woman formerly in white stares down at her

ruined dress, and I pull a napkin from one of the tables and hand it to her. "Here."

She takes it from me, and I can see that her eyes are gleaming. "Thank you. You don't know how long I've been waiting to dress up and go to a party." She looks up at me, blinking. "But I suppose there are worse things in the world than stained silk, yes? Fuck it."

"There certainly are."

She tosses the cloth aside, and her gaze sweeps down my outfit. "You look like you went shopping in London on the way. How fun!"

I wonder for a moment if it's an insult, but she sounds genuinely curious.

I shrug and mentally rehearse the way Auberon spoke —quietly, with little expression. "I *had* to try out some of their exotic attire, you know? Bit of fun. I've always been curious about mortals, and of course, I couldn't leave the Waste Land to see any of them until the halo appeared. What luck."

Her eyes are coppery and gold, like metallic flames. "You know, I've always wanted to visit the human world, too. London, especially. But I was stuck here in Brocéliande, away from court for so long that none of them want anything to do with me." A shadow passes over her features, and her smile fades. "I've spent far too much time in my room, never getting to go anywhere. All I had were the books, the walls, and the somber quiet of my own thoughts."

"How dreadful."

She sighs heavily, her expression clearing. "Right. Yes. Nice to meet you. I'm Countess Elizabeth de Benoic."

"I'm Baroness Alis de Listenoise. So lovely to make your acquaintance, Elizabeth. Beautiful name."

"There was a mortal queen by that name who never married. Smart woman to reject men so thoroughly, don't you think? They called her the Faerie Queen." She leans in closer, and her voice drops to a conspiratorial whisper. "Will you tell me what you saw in London? Were you able to try a *sausage roll*? Or the wing of a chicken, fried in batter? Did you sample *jellied eels*? I absolutely must visit someday."

I clear my throat, remembering how the Fey think. "I'm afraid I didn't have long in the city, but I did pass a truck selling *ribs*. I don't know what creature they belonged to originally. I imagine they devour the bones of their enemies."

She nods, her expression serious, eyes gleaming. "Yes. Yes, likely. What about a cocktail bar? I read about them in a book. The writer went to a cocktail bar, drank gin with a healing tonic, and wrote his book. Imagine that. Just scribbling notes so the whole world could hear your thoughts, instead of keeping them all to yourself in a quiet coffin of a room."

"It sounds divine. Not much time for writing where I'm from."

Elizabeth nods. "No, not in the Waste Land. I imagine

you have to spend your days clawing food from the barren earth to live. But now we're here, yes? In this majestic place, with all the food and mead that we want, along with the people we don't want." She runs a hand through her hair. "I'm out of practice at being at court, you know. I've been trying to catch up with the gossip, though I mostly have to get it through eavesdropping, since no one particularly wants to speak to me. But what, *exactly*, do you think we're doing here?"

I drain my mead and smile at Elizabeth. "I honestly have no idea. Something with the leadership of Brocéliande, I imagine? I was so eager to get out of the Waste Land, I didn't stop to wonder too much about the details."

She pulls my empty glass from my hand and sets it on the table. "Well, me, too. I was absolutely delighted to be chosen for this—whatever this is. I've been so desperate for conversation. I believe the last party I went to was a strawberry festival in Brocéliande a hundred and fifty years ago."

"That's a long time."

She turns suddenly, snatching two crystal flutes of mead off a tray. "I'm going to drink as much as possible and probably end up in that fountain by the end of the night."

"Sounds like a great start to this...meeting."

She shoves a glass into my hand. "I hope we're not

supposed to be on our best behavior. I don't think I have best behavior anymore."

Charm is not one of my skill sets, either.

Though, as I established earlier, I no longer have a skill set beyond finding the cheapest biscuits in the supermarket.

I sip the mead, savoring it and letting it roll over my tongue. Faintly sweet and golden, it's like the last weeks of summer in a glass. I can't afford the good stuff in London. I usually drink discount white wine from the supermarket that tastes like vinegar and cardboard.

I lean closer to Elizabeth, hoping to pry information out of her. "You said you've been catching up on the court gossip? Can you fill me in?"

"Who shall I start with?"

I take another sip of mead, and my gaze slides to the man from my dreams. Another strange shiver runs down my spine at the sight of him. "Who is the man with the golden tattoos?"

Her expression brightens. "What a wonderful place to start. The High Lord of Tintagol—Rion du Lac. They call him the Ruthless Knight. He's the murderous High Lord who tortures people to death at his parties. My husband used to tell our children stories about him to scare them into bed. *Go to sleep now, or the Ruthless Knight will stick your head on a pike.* Do you know the real story?"

My heart races. Of course I've heard of the Ruthless Knight—a monster of a creature. This might explain how

I've dreamt of him. We've all heard the description. And in my nightmares, he kills everyone around him.

Elizabeth leans in closer to whisper. "Two hundred years ago, he arrived on the island of Tintagol, armed for battle. He's a warlord from the wild forest. He gathered an army of fighters, people with grievances against the High Lord. They slaughtered half the inhabitants, then *murdered* the monarch. Starved him to death in an oubliette. They say the Ruthless Knight really loves drawing out pain, making people scream. And he does the same for pleasure, too. They say he has a harem of women, and they're always begging for him to fuck them, and then he won't let them come when they want to."

I blink at her, startled. I have forgotten what it's like to be in Fey society, where people say things like that within moments of meeting someone. I swallow hard and say, "I see."

"The man who spilled his drink on me—the drunk one with black hair? Mabon. He's from Tintagol, too. He lived here in Brocéliande once, but he fled after poisoning his wife. The woman next to him is Igraine, a Countess of Tintagol. She's not very friendly."

I nod. "I met her briefly. She's as charming as a maggot."

But only one other man here looks as strong as Rion. He's enormous, with uneven, close-shorn hair. Iron scars mark his arms, like he was tortured.

On his wrist are tattooed words: *I pledge myself to the gods.*

"Do you know who he is?" I ask Elizabeth.

She cocks her head. "I overheard someone say he was sentenced to death years ago on the island of Ys. I'm not sure why. All I know is that he languished in prison for years, forgotten by the world. Lucky for him, the summons of the Veiled Court must be obeyed. His halo freed him, like it did us."

As if hearing us gossiping, he glances at us, his dark eyes glittering with curiosity.

"He looks powerful."

She lets out a long sigh. "Gods, it feels good to gossip again. I needed this." Then, more fiercely, she repeats, "I *needed* this."

I think of the pasty arse cheeks and the Tudor window again, and I raise my glass. "You know? I needed a change too, Elizabeth."

"And what's your story, Alis?"

I twirl the stem of my glass. "Nothing very interesting, I'm afraid. I'm from Listenoise—it's a Waste Land, of course—so I live in a hovel. There's not much food or money. I haven't eaten since the stale bread for breakfast."

The absolute truth. Really, I don't have to change much to describe the Waste Land.

Her eyes widen. "No wonder you're so tiny. Not enough nutrients."

"That's exactly it."

She turns, darting after a servant carrying a tray. In the next moment, she's handing me a korriberry tart. "Here. It's divine. Build up your strength, darling, for whatever lies ahead."

My mouth waters. "I'm so gods-damned hungry."

Sweet fruit, creamy custard. I've never had a Fey fruit tart before. In the Undercroft, we survived on stale bread, water, and dried meat.

"Tell me more about the Waste Land," Elizabeth says, her eyes bright.

"Terrible place. Right before I came here, I found my lover shagging another woman. She looked about twenty years old."

Elizabeth's jaw drops. "That is grotesque. Did you slaughter them both?"

"I let them live." I drain the last of my mead. "For *now*."

The conversation in the hall becomes a hush as a woman strides into the room dressed in a pale blue gown, a gauzy veil draped over her ink-black hair. Her body shines with pale light, and her arms are tattooed with the cycles of the moon. In the center of her forehead is a triple spiral symbol.

From the entryway, a herald calls out her arrival. "Lady Niniane, High Priestess of the Veiled Court."

She's tall, elegant, and glides through the hall carrying a silver goblet. Her dark gaze sweeps over the room.

The herald calls, "And Lord Cador, Squire of the Veil."

A male trails into the room. His hair is a dark, wine red, almost burgundy, and he wears a blue cloak.

Niniane holds out her arms to the side. "Welcome to the Veiled Court. Here, you will learn who you truly are. In this ancient castle, you will forge an unbreakable bond with your ruling ancestors. In the Veiled Court, we shall find our next monarch. From one hundred and eighty-one, we shall choose the next ruler."

A cold chill shudders down my spine at the thought of another king.

Niniane reaches out a hand, and her squire, Cador, quickly hands her a goblet. Their fingers brush, and she gives him a flirtatious smile.

Then, she holds up her goblet. "As we seek the strongest in our kingdom, we have summoned you here because we have no monarch to lead us. A kingdom without a crown will wither and rot."

Niniane seizes the wand from her attendant and raises it toward the rippling mirrors. "Few now remember the ancient days of the Fey—before the fall of Avalon, before Auberon raised the great forests of Brocéliande. Before mortal madness spread across our world. But once, there was a time when the Fey ruled the islands and wild groves of Britain. In the Golden Age, we shone bright with primal magic, and mortals worshipped us as gods. King Bran—first to unite the Fey—earned his crown through trials. Queen Morgan won hers through right of combat. And so you stand here today in the Veiled Court to prove yourselves worthy through courage, combat, and chivalric manners. When we are finished, one of you will wear the crown of the High Fey monarch in Castle Perrilos."

A murmur ripples through the crowd, and every Fey here is alert. And now, eyeing each other as rivals for the crown.

They can have it. All I want is the grail.

Niniane takes another graceful step closer. "Of course, the ancient prince Mordred has a claim to the throne. But he's exiled from Brocéliande, trapped in the ruins of Avalon and thus unable to rule. So, we must choose another."

I glance at Rion du Lac, who leans against the wall, swirling his drink languidly. He'd probably carve his way through the rabble and climb a mountain of dead men's skulls to get to the high Fey throne.

Niniane smiles. "There are three ways you can leave this castle. In a coffin, with a crown, or dismissed with the approval of the noble houses. When we dismiss you, your halo will be removed. But if you try to escape without our permission, my darlings, that golden beacon will reappear around your head. You will be hunted to death by our *cugol.*" She lifts her chalice, smiling. "Now, raise your goblets to repeat the oath. Swear here in the ancient Tower of Aether that you will never betray the Veiled Court, and that you will never lie to the Council of Nobles, on pain of death by dragon fire."

My blood has gone cold, but I keep my expression serene, raise my glass, and lie through my teeth.

When the hall falls silent once more, Niniane's sharp gaze lands on me, and my nerves flutter.

And in this moment, I'm certain this was all a mistake—that she'll know I don't belong here, that I'm a peasant who grew up underground, that my grandfather was a literal gravedigger, slinging dirt on the corpses of the executed.

She stalks closer to me, her gaze brushing down my body. My spine stiffens. From shadows behind her, the Cloaked Ones emerge, their faces shrouded by dark cowls. Dark magic pours through the room like ink.

"And who do we have here?" the priestess asks in a voice cold as snow.

CHAPTER 9

*P*anic means death. It robs a mind of rational thought, the one thing more than any other that can keep a person alive. It's more important than strength, more important than magic.

So, I breathe in slowly and keep my mind clear. Tristan told me a spy gets into character, then improvises.

I curtsy slightly, the way an aristocrat would, and flash my most charming smile. I summon the memory of Auberon's accent. "I am Baroness Alis de Listenoise. How delightful to be in the refined embrace of Brocéliande's high society—quite the change from my bleak island kingdom."

Silence reigns in the hall.

A chill ripples over my skin as I wait for her reply, and my heart thunders in its cage.

After what seems an eternity, she arches an eyebrow. "And this is what you decided to wear?"

Bloody hell. This isn't going over well.

The silence seems to grow thorns as I scramble to think of something else to say. "I stopped in a mortal city to shop on the way in. Perhaps my selection missed the mark. We are truly isolated on Listenoise, far from the fashionable designers or current trends."

Amusement curls her lips. "Well, we will find out soon enough who belongs here and who does not. And until that point, perhaps we can find you attire more befitting of the Veiled Court. People like us are supposed live in beauty, blessed with silks and satins and jewels. Luxury is the birthright of nobility."

"Of course." I raise my glass to her.

Inwardly, I'm wondering what the hell she means about *finding out soon enough.*

Niniane raises her glass in a toast and flashes me a sharp smile. Then she turns back to the hall. "Now, many of you will die here."

This is probably the least relaxing party I've ever been to.

"You have been chosen by the gods to attend the Veiled Court, but we take over from here. We must choose a monarch, so you will compete in trials to prove your worth. The Council of Nobles will watch you and award points for strength and regal bearing. The heads of each of these fifty-two noble houses will decide who gains points in each trial. In the end, there will be only one monarch, but the points they award can grant you lands and new titles." Another sharp smile. "If you survive."

Gods, I just want to hear about the bloody grail.

Surveying us closely, Niniane walks around the room. "The first trial will be combat. You need only fight one round. All who survive join the next trial, but many of you will shed your lives in the trials. The gods demand blood, after all. When another contender defeats you, you may surrender. The noble houses then decide if you live or die."

The hall falls to a hush, the mood shifting into something dark and sharp. *Trial by combat.*

"But fear not," Niniane goes on. "You have two weeks to enjoy the pleasures of this ancient palace before the fights begin. For some of you, two weeks is all you have left in this world. So, drink now, dance in our halls, and savor the treasures of the Veiled Court. Enjoy the bright days before they vanish into darkness. The purpose of a Fey's life is pleasure, after all. Better to live briefly in a garden of lush blooms than to linger endlessly through the withered winter of decay, entombed by time."

Those words stir something in me—a memory of my parents' garden, blooming with lilies my mother planted.

Niniane snaps her fingers. "Lord Cador, darling! Please take Baroness Alis to the wardrobe in the Lyria Tower. And Countess Elizabeth, too, needs a new gown.

Jasper will see to it that they're dressed in a style befitting their titles."

Lord Cador stalks closer to us. Beneath his cloak, I catch a glimpse of the twisting, vine-like tattoos that climb his arms, and he beckons me to follow him. "Please come with me." He glances at Elizabeth, his sweeping gaze taking in the stain on her gown. "You as well, Countess."

Elizabeth still looks rattled from the combat trials announcement, like maybe she regrets leaving those four walls of her room. Still, she manages a faint smile.

We follow Cador down winding stairs. As we walk, my gaze trails over the ornate gargoyles huddling above the windows.

The question now is: will I survive here long enough to find the grail?

At one point, I could have won the entire tournament, bagged myself a crown—then handed power over to the commoners again. But those days are over.

Quite simply, when it comes to a combat trial against properly trained Fey warriors like some of the large men in there, I'm fucked. And yet, there's no way out until this is finished.

Cador turns back to me, his silver eyes sparkling in the moonlight. "We're in the oldest part of the fortress right now. Aether Tower stands in the center. King Bran built the Veiled Court thousands of years ago."

My heart leaps at his name. "King Bran?"

"This was his home. He was the first king to unite the

Fey, long before the Romans invaded Britain. But of course, the Veiled Court moved around. It once stood in Wales, then London, Avalon, and now it shifts around Brocéliande, moving from one place to another."

My eyebrows rise. "Is it true that his grail is kept here?"

Cador's eyes sparkle as he smiles at me. "In a manner of speaking. Not *exactly* here, but it's connected to our castle. All I can tell you is that the grail truly is a wonder, imbued with primal magic from our Golden Age."

My body sings with hope. I *have* to make it far enough in these trials to figure out where it is. "What do you mean, not exactly *here*?"

He shrugs. "You may find clues about its meaning engraved across these very towers, if you know how to look. But most are not for you to find. Here, secrets are hidden behind locked doors. And you must not unlock them, ladies. That would be treason."

Elizabeth's eyes have a vibrant, fiery hue. "The grail was made with primal magic from the Golden Age, wasn't it? When we used to be powerful. It's all faded now, since the Fall of Avalon. Only the ancient objects hold that magic."

"Perhaps our next queen will bring back the true power of the Fey." Cador flashes a faint smile. "That's what we hope—for another Golden Age, when the mortals will worship us as gods."

"Lord Cador," I begin, "Niniane said some contenders

will be dismissed by the noble houses. How does that happen, exactly?"

He smiles benignly. "After each trial, some contestants who performed poorly will be sent home. That's it, really."

We cross through an oak door and emerge onto a battlement hundreds of feet above the grassy earth. My jaw drops at the world around me—more stunning than anything I could conjure up during my wildest fantasies in the Undercroft.

I turn back to look at the bone-white castle in the fortress's heart.

Here, everything is grander and more beautiful than anything I've imagined. Bridges radiate from the central tower like spokes on a wheel, connecting it to the interior wall and more towers. The walkways sweep over gardens, courtyards, and towering standing stones, just like Stonehenge.

But the most prominent feature of the place is the four towers that rise from the walls. One of them burns like a torch at the top, the stone glowing as if kissed by the first rays of dawn.

"Is it supposed to be on fire, Lord Cador?" Elizabeth asks.

Cador points to it. "Yes. That's Belenior, the sun and flame tower. You see the four major towers around Aether? They represent the four elements: air, fire, water, and earth. After tonight, you will all be assigned to one of these towers, depending on who you are. Belenior is for those who take leadership roles and like attention. It's a place for parties and loud music, and everyone talking over each other. Not my cup of tea."

"And the rest?" Elizabeth asks.

He smiles. "I've heard the Tower of London echoes the grandeur of this court, only in a stunted, mortal construction. Their royal history is a weak, rotten copy of our own, you know. A faint echo. Nothing like this."

I see it now, with the two fortified walls and rings of towers around a central castle. Aether Tower's stark walls gleam, brighter and taller than the White Tower of London, reflecting the light of the moons.

Cador points to our left, where a tower stands with glass rooms and balconies. Mist twines its walls, but beneath the fog, there's a shimmer of purple and coral, like a twilight sky. My heart squeezes at the otherworldly beauty of it glowing against the ocean.

"The Gloaming Tower," he says. "Air and sky. A bridge between worlds, between the living and the dead, where spirits roam. Those who live there are dreamy, intellectual, emotionally reserved. One foot in this world, one in the world of the spirits and the gods. I like them, usually."

We walk farther, toward another tower also along the coastline. Several of the floors have terraces with open pools that catch the moonlight. Star-flecked waves lap at the tower's base. Pale mist coils around the stone, and a silver basin gleams where the turret would be.

"And that," says Cador, "is the Lyria Tower. Water.

They're seductive, hedonist, pleasure seekers. Sinfully sensual. They're connected to their emotions, which is nice, but they will absolutely ruin your life, and you will never get over it, so I don't recommend taking a lover from Lyria."

"Men are an absolute nuisance," Elizabeth says. "I'd never bother again with that rubbish."

Cador then points to another tower, a vast column of green with stones enveloped in flowering vines. "And that's where I live, Druantia Tower. The earth and forest. We're the people who actually take care of things while others are throwing parties or daydreaming or seducing people. We're also very good at surviving in the woods, and we're resourceful. We're really the most reliable people around, even if we don't get all the glory."

"It's so beautiful," Elizabeth adds.

Between some of the towers and walls curves a wooden rail, and I have no idea what it's for until a wooden cart comes rattling along, carrying two passengers. They fly past, hair trailing behind them. It's like a primitive roller coaster that zips between stone buildings, painted blue and decorated with stars and moons.

On the far side of the walls, the sea sparkles with silver-red moonlight. I breathe in the sweet scent of honeysuckle and thyme. There's a vast amphitheater in the courtyard, where I imagine the trials will take place.

I peer over the nearest wall. Hundreds of feet below us is a courtyard with a walled menagerie. A fence encloses rare creatures: griffins, cockatrices, a phoenix, white bears, wolves...

Next to it is a stone court where a red-scaled dragon slumbers on a raised dais. Twenty feet below the dragon, a metal pole juts from the ground. Chains hang from it, charred black.

My heart thuds as I stare at the black scorch marks darkening the stone, and dread slides up my throat.

At the peak of mortal technology—before Fey magic started destroying it—the humans kept their populations in line through constant surveillance. Cameras everywhere, perpetual observation, digital tracking systems. But the Fey? Even to this day, our methods of control are simpler and far more brutal: a metal pole, a dragon to burn you. Sometimes, a rack to pull your body apart. Severed limbs, rolling heads. Blood and broken bones and burned skin.

It's really very effective, and just the sight of that burnt stake has me breaking out in a cold sweat.

Elizabeth tugs on my arm. "Don't look at that, darling. It sounds like we've already got enough to worry about here. Bloody trials by combat?" she hisses. "Did you have *any* idea?"

CHAPTER 10

I frown. "Isn't it how they chose the king in the old days?"

"I don't know anything about history," Elizabeth mutters. "I don't really want to live in the past."

"Come along!" Cador calls out.

We follow him across the bridge toward the Lyria Tower.

I try to push the mental image of that charred stone out of my mind, focusing instead on the tower in front of us. Water streams from large windows, and a light, misty spray kisses my skin.

We cross through an open archway, where a pool gleams in the center of a round chamber. Gowns hang from the walls all around, beautiful silken dresses in jewel and metallic colors.

By the window is a silhouetted figure, a man watching

the water trickle down outside. He's sipping a cherry red cocktail like the one spilled on Elizabeth's dress.

Staggering a little, the man turns and stiffens. Rings glitter on his fingers, and he stares straight at me. "What in the gods' names is this abomination? Did you bring me a peasant?"

His words are slurred. He's obviously drunk.

Cador gestures at us. "Jasper, I've brought you Baroness Alis of Listenoise and Countess Elizabeth de Benoic."

"What the fuck is she wearing?" He drains the last of the cocktail, then throws the empty glass out the open window. "Listenoise. The *Waste Land*. Is that *really* what we're doing here? It's all gone to shit, hasn't it? I once dressed icons of glamour and power. But they're gone now, aren't they? Prince Talan lives in the ruins of Avalon. The king is dead. And now they're just letting in ragamuffins and sluts from the Waste Land. Might as well dig up the two princely corpses from Aether Tower and dress *them*. They'd look more regal than this."

"She's a baroness," says Elizabeth sharply. "What is your title?"

"Ooooh, a *baroness*," he says in a high voice that rings with mockery. "Hardly a fucking prince, though, is it?"

"The Waste Land is very fucking interesting, actually," Elizabeth snaps. "It's as exclusive as it gets. No one can get in or out. We all live in luxury, don't we? Luxury is boring. Alis is something different."

Jasper goes very still, then cocks his head. He taps his fingers together. "True, yes. Very exclusive. And unique. You make a very good point, Elizabeth. It *is* interesting. Prince Talan always kept people guessing. He'd be intrigued…" He drops his voice to a scandalized whisper. "What is the Waste Land like? I've always wondered. I'd heard everyone there was dead."

"I'm not dead."

"They have nothing to eat there except stale bread," Elizabeth adds, "and their lovers are grotesquely unfaithful."

For just a second, Jasper quirks a smile. Frankly, he looks like he's hungry to binge on schadenfreude. "Nothing but old bread and cheating lovers?"

I nod solemnly. "There's no mead, either. There's white wine, but it tastes like vinegar."

Jasper's lip curls. "That's *vile*. What's your palace like?"

"I live in a hovel," I reply. "Not a palace. It's a literal closet, with clothes that hang above my head."

Jasper's interest is clearly piqued, and he stalks closer, eyes locked on me. His voice drops to a whisper. "Of course. And what's outside your hovel?"

The stolen cars come to mind, along with stray pieces of newspaper blowing through the street and the discarded chicken bones people leave on the pavement after a drunken midnight snack. It's been rough for centuries. I remember reading that long ago, a factory owner on my street was beaten to death in a marsh for mechanizing the looms.

I lift my chin. "Rubbish catches in the breeze, tumbling across the landscape like clouds of thistledown. The poor steal chariots and set them on fire. Gnawed bones are scattered on the street, and sometimes, angry mobs bludgeon the wealthy to death in swamps."

"Fascinating," Jasper says, eyes gleaming and voice raspy. "It's worse than I thought. Very exclusive, yes."

It stings that they accept my tales so easily when they should be saying, "But surely you look *far* too glamorous to be from that hellhole!"

"What are the Fey like in the Waste Land?" Jasper asks, taking a step closer.

I think of my neighborhood at three a.m. "Aggressive. Destitute. There's noise everywhere. Many stagger around vomiting. Others wander with dead eyes. There are some good ones, of course, but plenty who will rob you blind. Often in the middle of the night, I'm woken by screaming."

"Amazing." He points at me. "I like a challenge. *You* are a challenge. Something rare. And now, Alis, you're going to have something you never had before." His voice drops to a sensual purr. "*Luxury.*"

And he's not wrong about that. Before the Undercroft, my early childhood home was a little cottage in the woods, with rushes covering the ground and a bed stuffed with straw. A loving place, but spare. I didn't spend long there. I grew up in the king's barracks—underground, sleeping on the dirt floor in a small, crowded cell, hidden from the world. The warmth of Tristan's nearby body was my only luxury.

I suppose that little closet was the nicest place I lived, really. Our flat was clean, and we had running water, a modern mattress, *and* a pillow.

Jasper spares Elizabeth a bored glance. "Take whatever dress you want. I'm going to make something custom for the ragamuffin."

He grabs me by the shoulders and turns me to face a mirror set into the walls. "A woman from the fetid horrors of the Waste Land..." he whispers behind me. "Let me think of how to transform you."

I catch my reflection and grimace, guilt twisting my heart. I am my mother remade: prominent cheekbones, full lips, and dark lashes above lavender eyes. But the whole picture is worse than I'd expected. My shoulders hunch. My T-shirt hangs, half in and half out. Eyeliner smudges the skin beneath my eyes, streaked by the rain, and my hair is a frizzy mess, like it's trying to fly from my skull to escape the indignity of it all.

In short, I look like shit.

On the plus side, I really look like I'm from a place called the Waste Land.

"What shall we do with you?" Jasper mutters to himself. Then he barks in my ear, "Ranae!"

He snaps his fingers, and a Fey woman rushes into the

room. Ranae, I assume. She has ink-black hair cut in a bob and wears a gown of delicate silver.

Jasper has already found another cocktail from somewhere, and he takes a sip. "Ranae, we have a challenge here tonight," he says. "A vagrant of sorts. A vagabond. A wastrel." He shouts the last word, suddenly furious.

Ranae stares at me. "Is she *supposed* to be here? Shouldn't we report her or something? Because she might be carrying lice or another sort of critter."

"She's a baroness," Jasper says, whispering for some reason, then mouthing, as if naming a shameful venereal disease, "From the *Waste Land*."

Ranae's eyes widen, and her lip curls. "Oh, dear."

Jasper points at me, squinting one eye. "Go on, then," he slurs. "Take off your filthy rags, Baroness."

I'd forgotten this aspect of Fey culture—the part where they're totally fine with being naked around each other. It's not how things are done in London, but I try to get into my Fey mindset again. I pull off my shirt, my jeans—everything but my underwear. That stays.

Jasper clasps his hands together in a prayer pose, closing his eyes and breathing deeply. "Let me think. Inspiration from the kingdom of bones...a garden blooming from the ashes, a morning sky. Dazzling bowers of flame beneath a night sky. Light in the darkness. I want *dawn breaking*. A new beginning. Yes, sun rising over the festering bones, over the stale bread and the unfaithful lovers and burning machines. Ranae!" He shouts her name, although we are all standing close together.

"*What?*" she snaps.

"I want beautiful, but minimalist!" he continues. "Minimalist, yes? Show off her figure, will you, in an hourglass shape. Light and dark, yes? This is *revival.* This is a *renaissance* for a life of bones and filth and utter grotesque depravity."

Stings again, that I have described my real life, and this is how they summarize it.

Ranae chants a spell, and a smooth, silky fabric wraps around my body. Slowly, the silk dress stitches itself together over my form—simple, yet elegant, black chiffon pulled tightly over the colors of a fiery dawn. The overall effect is one of embers burning within ash.

A new woman wearing a pout comes in, her white hair draped over a violet gown. Arms crossed, she looks at me and says, "Another one trying for the crown."

Jasper swirls his drink. "Will you fix"—his voice drops to a whisper again, his eyes wide and urgent—"her *hair?* And whatever is on her *face.* I need her hair to shine and gleam like Lord Cador's. He uses linseed oil, I believe, so his hair doesn't look *like that.*"

I'm quickly starting to understand that he whispers whenever he finds something utterly repugnant.

"And Millie?" he barks. "Nothing too ornate. Under the grime, she's quite beautiful, so let her face be the finest jewel. Add shimmer and a blush to the lips as if she's just been thoroughly kissed. Like the way I kiss, Millie. *You know.*"

"It's *Tillie*," the white-haired woman spits.

Ranae adjusts my dress as Jasper barks orders and Tillie cleans my face with a cloth. When my old makeup is scrubbed off, she sets to work on my hair, first smoothing it out with oils, then running a wide-toothed comb through the curls.

You know? I could really get used to this life, maybe learn to live with the threat of death by dragon fire and the drunken insults. Like Niniane said, you might as well enjoy the last bright sparks before you die.

Finally, when the two women are finished, I'm staring at a totally new person.

The dress is perfection. It hugs my waist, sweeps over my breasts, and trails to the floor. The dark fabric blends into flaming hues of violet and peach near the hem, and my blue-black hair drapes in waves over my shoulders.

Cador sidles up to me. The moonlight streams in past the falling water, silvering his pale skin. "Gorgeous. Look at you. Reborn."

Elizabeth is now dressed in a gown made from cloth of gold, and she looks like a goddess. She smiles at me. "Utter perfection. Both of us. I mean, I liked our first outfits, but now we've got fancier gowns. Now, let's grab a bottle of mead so we can try to forget about the combat trials, shall we?"

Cador clears his throat. "You can get more mead, but then you'll need to head right down to the dragon ceremony."

My eyebrows flick up. "The what?"

"You're going to get your sigils," says Cador. "Your heraldic emblems. It's fate, Niniane says. In the menagerie, one of the animals will be called by your family's noble bloodline, and you will wear that symbol in the trials. These creatures are bonded to the noble houses, of course."

Shit. I don't have a single noble relative in my bloodline. There will be no unicorn waiting to bless my blue blood.

I force a smile onto my face before he notices. "That's so fun. But what happens if no animals choose us?"

Cador's expression darkens, and he leans in closer to whisper, "Well, let's hope that doesn't happen, because that's when Goch gets involved."

My confusion must be apparent, because he adds, "The red dragon."

Elizabeth stares at him. "Bloody hell. Really? I thought this would be more of a banquet and conversation situation. Cocktails and hors d'oeuvres, you know? I didn't realize we were going to face swords and dragons and warriors trying to kill us."

"But you two will be fine," says Cador with a gracious smile. "I know it. You'll help us revive the Golden Age of the Fey."

My throat goes dry, and heat inflames my skin like I'm already burning. "Elizabeth? More mead is an excellent idea."

CHAPTER 11

$\mathcal{A}$s I cross into the courtyard, my thoughts are a maelstrom. I can tell all eyes are on me now, watching the Waste Land baroness.

Torches burn in sconces on the wall, casting dancing shadows over a spiral pattern of pale stones in the stone courtyard. I move deeper into the square and settle into place near the menagerie. Part of me wonders if I should try to escape right now.

But the other, louder part of me will not leave here without the grail.

Inside the enclosure, a white lion pads in silence. A unicorn tosses its head, nostrils flaring, iridescent eyes narrowing. Behind them, the animals shift through the shadows—a black hound with flame-like eyes, a white boar with golden tusks and hooves, and a ghostly, radiant stag standing tall above them all.

Rion is standing to my right, and his powerful magic skims over my skin. In the darkness, golden light radiates from his tattoos.

But he's not the real threat right now.

My gaze darts to the dragon looming over the courtyard, and unease twists through my chest. The creature is enormous, easily the size of a two-story house, even coiled in sleep.

Around the courtyard walls, the magic mirrors ripple. The Council of Nobles is ready and primed to watch the unworthy burn tonight.

In everyday life, I'm perfectly worthy. I do my roommates' dishes. I take care of Vero. I help people when they've dropped things in the street. I give food to the homeless man named Billy who lives under the bridge by my flat. But in the world of Fey royalists? I'm a traitorous peasant, and they'd burn me to death in seconds if they knew the truth.

Elizabeth sidles up next to me and hands me the bottle of mead.

"Thanks." I take a long sip, hoping to dull my nerves. My gaze flicks up, scanning the shadows and parapets for signs of Tristan.

I'd really love a second opinion at this point. Should I run for the shadows and find a way out?

From the menagerie, a phoenix rises in a blaze of fire, wings scattering sparks before it bursts apart, raining cinders and ash across the night. Sulfurous smoke curls into my nostrils.

When I look back at the dragon, I see that he has opened a single golden eye—and it's locked on me.

If only *I* could return from the flames like a phoenix.

I hand the mead back to Elizabeth.

I glance at Rion. He sips lazily from his glass of mead, his rings catching the lantern light. And why would he worry? He's of noble blood, and he'd make the perfect king. A Fey king takes what he wants—a crown, a throne, a woman up against a wall.

Rion glances down at me, his steely-silver gaze sweeping the length of my body. His lips curve in a wry smile. "Do you really think you can survive here?"

From the other side, the drunken Duke Mabon leans forward, his black hair hanging down over a velvety cloak. His eyes are unfocused. "When she first came in, I swear to the gods, she smelled of *mortals*. Revolting."

Rion's half smile fades, his pale eyes raking over my face like he's uncovering my innermost thoughts. "I think you're keeping secrets—but no one lies to me for long." His voice cools, sharpening. "There *is* something painfully human about you. So delicate." He tilts his head and looks thoughtful. "I think I could break you as easily as I breathe."

The wind toys with my black hair. "But you can't break what's already broken. We're here to fight for the crown, and I've got something that none of you do, Rion du Lac."

Silver light sharpens in his gaze. "And what's that?"

"Nothing left to lose." I smile up at him. "That's what the Waste Land is, you know? *Nothing.* So, who do you imagine will be the most ruthless one here? A high lord grown soft on mead and banquets? Or the creature who crawled from the kingdom of bones like the dead rising from the grave to breathe again?"

I'm not leaving here without the grail. This is a world where power is granted by bloodlines and brutality, where they'd happily let someone like Vero die. To them, peasants are vermin and pests.

I want to heal Vero more than anything—but I also want to take something precious from them.

A dark, slow smile curls the corners of Rion's mouth, and his cruel eyes pin me. "The most ruthless one here, are you? This should be very interesting."

Then his expression grows bored, like I'm an old trinket that no longer amuses him. He turns away, murmuring something to Igraine.

As a cool breeze slips over us, High Priestess Niniane sweeps into the stone courtyard, holding her palms to the sky. "My glorious Fey nobles. The gods have called you all here today because we must choose a new monarch—a High King or Queen to rule over *all* the Fey kingdoms from Brocéliande. We must take back our great city Corbinelle from the peasant rabble and reclaim Castle Perillos. The commoners roam its hallowed halls like packs of wild pigs."

She turns to face the mirrors on the walls behind Goch and draws her wand. Cold magic slides across my skin as she speaks quietly. Her words carry in the air, though I only catch fragments. It's ancient Fey, a language almost no one speaks anymore. I understand parts of it: something about the Horned God, a wild hunt to choose a king, a binding to the land.

As her voice fades, the rippling water in the mirrors grows still, and their surfaces gleam with a faint silver sheen.

They're watching us now, the Council of Nobles. Fortunately, none of them would recognize me from the Undercroft. Spies are meant to be invisible.

Tristan says Avalon Tower prefers diplomacy and the delicate art of improvisation. Auberon's spy craft was nothing like Avalon Tower's. The king taught us the brutal arts: kidnapping, torture, and assassination. We killed anyone who saw our faces, so none of these aristocrats ever saw mine.

Those of us in the Undercroft came from nothing: from Corbinelle's slums, from ramshackle huts buried deep in the forest. Tristan's mother was a prostitute. My father was a hunter who barely kept food on the table. That was how Auberon motivated us—through promises of titles, land, and riches we could obtain only through making him happy. He rarely made good on those promises.

The animals, unlike the nobles, make me nervous. They might smell the poverty on me.

As if hearing my thoughts, the dragon raises its head, staring straight at me. Fear skitters up my spine. Fuck. Can dragons be telepathic?

Elizabeth hands the bottle back to me. "We'll be assigned to towers tonight. We'll find out who we really are, they say."

High Priestess Niniane turns back to us. Her expression is delighted, almost girlish. "As Lord Cador calls your name, please come to the center. You will be blessed by one of the beasts to wear his form as your sigil."

"Lady Lunette," Cador calls out, "come and discover your true heraldic sigil."

A woman with mahogany skin in a pearlescent gown strides into the center of the circle, wearing a flower crown of white lilies. She moves with elegant grace, stopping by the metal stake and standing still on the scorched stone. From a parapet, ravens swoop down, gracefully arcing above her.

Overhead, the ravens caw and call out, "She knows life and death. The beginning and the end. A heart broken. Music silenced."

From the menagerie, an ivory butterfly flutters out, landing on Lunette's shoulder. She beams.

"The Gloaming Tower," the ravens squawk.

Lunette grins as she steps back into the crowd.

From the edge of the courtyard, Cador's voice booms, "Countess Elizabeth de Benoic, step into the center and claim your heraldic sigil."

Slowly, Elizabeth walks into the center of the spiral. I hold my breath, watching as the ravens swoop above her in a circle. I realize too late that she's still gripping the bottle of mead—which is probably not ideal for this particular occasion. By now, we've both drunk so much of it that clear thinking is out of reach.

The dragon lifts its head, peering down at her with burning eyes. Above her head, the ravens chatter about isolation, about carving poetry into the stone walls. They speak of a murdered count, smothered by a pillow in his sleep, never to speak again. Then they fall silent.

An elegant white owl swoops out of the menagerie, then rests on Elizabeth's shoulder.

"Gloaming Tower," the ravens cry.

Elizabeth's smile looks a little uncertain.

As the birds fly from her, she hurries back to me, eyes wide. "I made it!" She thrusts the bottle of mead into my hand.

"Rion du Lac! Your sigil summons you," Cador shouts.

He stalks into the center, still holding his glass of mead. His silver hair hangs long over his black, fur-lined cloak, and his leather trousers hang low on his hips. As he stands by the stake, he takes a sip.

If he's worried about Goch, he doesn't show it.

The ravens arc above him, their cries loud enough to wake the gods. "Myrddin Wyllt…a king who keeps death at his court…a crown of bones…a true king screams from the oak. Balor, the one-eyed, rises from a forest forged with blood…madness runs in his veins…"

The ravens' chatter isn't doing much to improve my impression of him. Goch growls, low and deep, and the sound rumbles through my gut. Rion languidly swirls the mead in his glass.

At last, the gate to the menagerie swings open with a groan. The phantom stag trots out and stands proudly by Rion, and the creature glows like the stars in the night sky. The stag's antlers are a pale blue. His body drips with water, and his eyes are the color of a pristine lake.

"Lyria Tower," the ravens cry.

Cador calls, "Sir Dagonet," and the formerly imprisoned warrior stalks before the stake. Already, I'm making the calculation that I should avoid him in combat trials. His thickly corded muscles are covered in iron scars, and he's obviously no stranger to violence.

When a little dragon lands on his shoulder, he nods once, then returns to his spot.

One by one, each noble passes the test unscathed. Igraine is graced by a water serpent. Even the drunk finds himself paired with a salamander.

When little blonde Lady Blythe is called up, she walks gingerly into the spiral of stones. She's pink-cheeked and youthful, and a flower crown sits slightly crooked on her golden hair.

She smiles at us, but I can see her hands shaking. "I'm ready to discover my sigil!"

The ravens circle above her, screaming into the night.

"Weak…faithless…capricious…confusion in battle…unready…cannot protect us…"

Her smile falters, and Goch raises his head, rearing back. His great maw opens, and the dragon's teeth gleam.

My legs feel weak. "Blythe, run!" I say through gritted teeth.

As Goch stands to his full height, my blood roars.

Blythe turns bone white, and she's trembling harder now. But it's too late. She takes one step, two—

Goch unleashes a blast of fire, searing the air. Heat singes my skin. I close my eyes and stumble back, the air too hot to bear. I'm coughing, trying to find cool air to suck into my lungs. Smoke billows around us. Blythe didn't even have time to scream. When I open my eyes, I see a living torch burning down to bone. The smell of scorched flesh fills the courtyard, and cinders spark in the darkness.

The blaze roars, then dwindles until nothing is left of the pretty golden-haired Fey but a dark pile of ash.

Coughs break the silence as the wind carries pieces of ash into the sky, whipping it around us.

"What a shame," Niniane says with a sigh. "But it can't be helped. Not worthy."

I grab the mead from Elizabeth and take a long sip, my hand shaking.

And as I press the bottle to my lips, Cador calls out, "Baroness Alis de Listenoise."

The world tilts beneath my feet as the dragon's eye finds me again.

Am I about to die?

CHAPTER 12

My skull pounds like ocean waves as I cross into the center of the circle. I scan the parapets, searching for signs of Tristan. Where the fuck is he? Smoke still curls around me, bringing tears to my eyes. I doubt there's anything he could do to help, but at least he could bring word of my brave demise to Vero.

Slowly, I walk over the smoldering ashes, the last remains of Lady Blythe. Cinders glow beneath my feet, bright red embers in a pile of hot ash.

I find my place before the stake and feel its heat radiating over my back. The soles of my shoes feel like they're burning. Coughing, I take a few steps away from the stake, trying to find relief from the heat. I settle in a slightly cooler spot on the stones, but the smoke still wraps around me. Sweat trickles down my temples, and I try not to think about breathing in Blythe's charred remains.

Gods. I wish I'd taken the mead with me. I wonder if prayer will help me at this point.

I don't think the Morrigan hears me anymore. I heard her for a moment when the baroness was trying to kill me, but that was it. Just a whisper of a memory. She revoked her magic when she discovered I was irredeemable, stole it because of the terrible things I did.

Maybe getting the grail to Vero is the only way I can redeem myself.

I glance at Goch, and his golden eyes narrow on me. *Everyone has a weakness,* Auberon used to say. *All you need to do is find it and break them.* If I had the Song, that's what I'd go for. Even a dragon would flail with a torch jammed through an eye socket.

But it's just me here, magicless and ordinary.

Stop feeling sorry for yourself. Auberon's deep voice echoes in my mind. *What's your next play?*

Even without my power, I can still take action. Rational thought is more important than magic. That's always been the case.

Panic is death.

If the dragon rears his head, I can't hesitate like Blythe did. There's only one option if Goch decides to strike: sprint into the shadows and hide. I'll need to find a way out of here, live in the forests or something, always staying one step ahead of the Cloaked Ones. I may not be an elite fighter these days, but I am a survivor.

I scan the area, searching for a way out, and spy a route leading down a narrow cobbled path past the menagerie that disappears into darkness. There's a rolling cart nearby, something I can use to escape until I can find a way out of this place.

The ravens circle over my head, and my blood runs cold. Should I have run and hidden from the start? No, not even now do I think I should have run.

Vero will die without a relic like the grail, and this might be her only chance.

Overhead, the ravens start to speak.

"Murderer. Murderer."

Their cries rise, harsh and relentless, and I let the condemnation wash over me. They're not *wrong*.

The truth is, whatever Rion did, I've probably done worse. *I'm* not the sort of person who should ever sit on a throne. No one should, but particularly me.

"Not what she seems…not the one…"

Every inch of me is coiled tightly now, ready to run.

"Kissed by the Morrigan…"

A shiver runs over my skin.

"Dormant power…kill us all…"

Again, they're not *wrong*.

"An incarnadine queen ordained to stain the seas with slaughter…can she forgive…can she forgive…"

My heart slams hard. The menagerie gate isn't opening. It's just me and the ravens.

"Can she forgive..."

Goch lifts his head, narrowing his eyes. Cold sweat trickles down my temples, and I steal a glance at that dark, cobbled path. My gaze flicks back to Goch, who stares at me with a keen interest. My blood roars in my ears.

And just as I'm about to run for it, the ravens arc lower, flying in a ring around my body. They encircle me, almost like they're protecting me, surrounding me in a hollow crown of darkness and feathers.

The Morrigan's coronet. I feel as if she's giving me a whisper of redemption.

After all, ravens are her creatures.

"Killer!" the ravens cry around me. But they don't seem upset about it—in fact, they might be impressed.

Perhaps I'm still standing for my ruthlessness. That's what the buried magic of the Veiled Court seeks, isn't it? That's why I'm here in the first place—because I smashed someone's head against a wall and robbed her of the ticket in. The magic is older than civilization.

Blythe was weak. Merciful. I'm not.

A raven perched on my shoulder squawks, "The Gloaming Tower!"

I close my eyes, exhaling a slow, shaky breath. I've made it. The ravens know exactly who I am, and they *like* it.

When I open my eyes again, I see High Priestess Niniane's eyes boring into me. "How strange. How strange indeed."

* * *

BY THE TIME we leave the ceremony, I feel absolutely drained. Only Blythe died tonight, but the whole event was an extended exercise in terror.

Lord Cador leads Elizabeth and me to the Gloaming Tower. "Gorgeous night, isn't it?" he says.

I can still smell the smoke. "Quite lovely," I murmur.

Every moment, I'm scanning my surroundings for the hidden signs of the grail he promised.

Cador leads us beneath a stone arch, and the Gloaming Tower comes into view, looming above us. Wisps of lavender-tinged mist twine around it, and beneath the clouds, the tower shimmers like a starry twilight. Gorgeous.

You know, I feel like I belong here, even if I'm a peasant and a liar.

Overhead, lightning cracks the sky, and I jump a little at the boom of thunder. I'm still on edge. I feel the temperature dropping, like we're about to get hit with rain.

As we reach the base of the Gloaming Tower, I peer into a small garden encircled by stone walls. Apple trees grow among roses, peonies, and gillyflowers.

Cador spins back to us as we walk. "You're both lucky! Your tower has views of the sky and the sea beyond the walls, but you're also near the Rhiannon Garden. It's enchanted by the love goddess."

"Hmm, I'll avoid that," says Elizabeth. "One second, you're falling in love, and the next second, he's trapped you in a room."

Cador reaches over the fence and plucks a blushing rose. "But in the old days, they believed a monarch must find a consort. A fated mate. It was called the sovereignty bond, and if it's true, it was part of the Golden Age. If the king's family is fertile, so is the land. And if the goddess blesses you with fated love…well, it's a sign that perhaps you were meant to rule."

With a faint smile, he hands me a rose. I twirl it in my fingers and realize my hands are still trembling.

Overhead, someone zooms by on the rolling cart, and my gaze flicks up. I don't want to fall in love here, and I certainly don't want to burn to death.

But I *really* want to ride in that thing.

Ahead of us, Cador pulls open the blue-painted, star-flecked door to the Gloaming Tower, then presses his back against it, holding it open. He reaches into his pockets, pulling out a pair of keys. "This is where I leave you, but I'm giving each of you a key to your new rooms. Alis, your room is called Raven by the Mere."

Lightning flashes again, closer this time.

Cador hands me a large, silver skeleton key with a parchment tag attached. It's painted with an image of a raven swooping over a lake.

He turns to Elizabeth and hands her a similar key, with

a round-eyed owl. "Howlet's Nook. Just climb the stairs until you find your rooms."

"Thank you." Elizabeth stares up at the mist-twined castle. "Is this tower haunted, by any chance?"

Cador shrugs, stepping away from us. "It's a three-thousand-year-old castle. Every room is haunted. Sleep well."

I start the hike up the narrow stairs, and Elizabeth climbs behind me. "Do you have magic?" she asks. "Anything that could be useful in the trials by combat?"

"No, I'm afraid not. Only my wits, assuming I still have them about me. But there's no way around it at this point, is there?"

"No, and my magic won't do me much good in that trial," she says glumly. "I only *just* got out in the world. And I still want to go to England to try the bread slices with meat in it."

"Sandwiches?"

"Yes." Her eyes are wide with delight. "Those."

I clear my throat. "Why were you so cooped up, Elizabeth?"

"My husband thought I was unwell. Too spirited, he said. His mistress was quieter. More submissive, you know? Anyway, he's dead now. Ha!"

Elizabeth has clearly moved on.

I climb behind her on the stairs, still struck by the feeling that this place is far grander than I could have imagined. Open windows are set into the walls, each one with a balcony that curves around the walls outside. Clouds start to float past, stained coral and lavender, darkening to purple. Lanterns light up the stairwell, casting a warm glow in the gloom. Tonight, the air smells like it's about to rain.

At each landing, we find two rooms with painted doors and round heraldic sigils. We pass framed pictures of a pegasus, a magpie with tarot cards, a bat hanging from a yew bough, and a nightingale wearing a crown. Without numbers, I have no idea how long I'll need to keep climbing. All we can do is match our key to the picture on the doors.

My legs ache, and my eyelids grow heavy. I'm a faded, weak version of myself right now, like lukewarm tea not brewed long enough. I might need sleep before I hunt for the grail clues.

"I *like* the theme of this tower," Elizabeth says wistfully. "I like the idea of skies. Skies are freedom."

At last, we reach our rooms—across from each other, hers a few steps higher. Sharply peaked blue doors are set into the stone walls, each marked with a painted sign. Mine shows a raven in a Jacobean ruff standing by a pond. Between our rooms, there's a round door painted with a golden image of the rolling cart, which must be the entrance to the strange little roller coaster. I'm glad it's so close to me.

Elizabeth gives me a dreamy smile. "Sleep well, little raven."

"Good night."

I push open my door—and stop short. It's everything I dreamed about, and I only wish Vero could be here with me.

CHAPTER 13

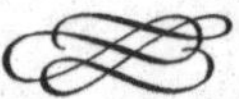

The chamber is breathtaking, the size of a grand dining room, with an entire wall of glass overlooking the outer walls and the sea beyond. Glass doors lead to a large balcony of white moonstone. The view here is mostly sky and the lilac-tinged clouds drifting past. Dark blue bookshelves span another wall, with a cushioned reading nook in the center. A moonstone table set with wine stands near the books.

By the door, ropes hang from the walls, each one joined to a bell in the servants' quarters. Beside every rope, a small brass plate bears a symbol: a key for my head servant (Tristan, I'm assuming), a pie for the kitchens, a dress for the laundresses, and a broom for any cleaning tasks.

Most of the room is deep purple and blue, and the ceiling is dappled with glowing stars that shift slowly like a moving solar system. Lanterns float above me, drifting through the air. A fire burns in a small fireplace.

Above the mantel hangs a portrait of another raven wearing a Jacobean ruff.

I open a door to find a private washroom with a copper tub. One wall is glass, and the air smells of starflowers.

When I turn back into the bedroom, a flutter of movement catches my eye. A raven peers at me from the bookshelves, a *living* bird wearing a lace ruff around his throat, looking utterly dignified. The raven launches into flight and glides through the open window.

I open the wardrobe doors to find that it's already full of clothes in my size, somehow, like the room has been waiting for me. There are gowns, chain mail, trousers, a dagger, training clothes, a silk bathrobe—even brooches and hairpins adorned with raven symbols.

My *Have you tried turning it off and on again?* T-shirt lies folded neatly at the bottom of the wardrobe.

But the thing that grabs my attention is the bed. It looks soft and inviting, with silver blankets and pillows, and I want to sink into it. A faint silvery mist roils around its base like a cloud. Quickly, I change my clothes, slipping into a silky white nightgown.

I start to blow the candles out, one by one, and the lanterns overhead dim, as if hearing my thoughts. Outside, clouds churn, and a light rain falls against the glass. A perfect sound for sleeping.

I'm too tired to do anything but crawl beneath the covers. I pull them over me, and my body sags into the comforting embrace of the bed.

This is the kind of place I dreamt about when I lived in my own little Waste Land—first the Undercroft, then the closet in London. Death lingers around every corner in the Veiled Court, and I don't know where the grail is yet, but I still feel a thrill that I finally made it in here after all these years.

I fall asleep to the sound of rain hammering against the glass, and a raven sweeping by my window.

* * *

I'M AT HOME—MY childhood home, tending to the garden near the sycamore tree. It used to be neat little rows of cowslips, violets, and rue. Now, it's overgrown. Abandoned. Tall grasses grow up high around the pale peach roses. I don't remember Mama planting those, but I never paid enough attention to what she planted.

I wonder if she thought of me when she chose them, because I loved roses. I only have vague memories of her tending to the gardens outside our tiny cottage. Now, everything seems old, forgotten. It's so quiet here without Mama's singing, and the silence gnaws a hollow in my chest.

The wooden fence around the chicken coop sags and crumbles. The rope on the swing is frayed, useless. Papa made that for me when I was six, carefully measuring it to make sure it was safe.

Did I thank him?

A sharp ache unfurls in my chest. It's darker here than I remember. Quieter. Desolate. I kneel among the roses under a dusky sky, trying to set things right. Frantically, I tug at the weeds, determined to fix Mama's garden for her. No one has been tending it since...

Anyway, she isn't here anymore. I haven't lived here since I was a child. Mama and Papa died long ago, and how did that happen? And no one took care of the garden, or the swing, or the fence. No one sits among the flowers.

And how did they die?

I don't want to remember. It's a secret that lives like a sleeping monster between my ribs, waiting to open its eyes again.

Gritting my teeth, I rip out nettles, dandelions, and bindweeds that grow wild, trying to reverse time itself. Trying to set things right. Maybe I can bring it all back to the way it was before the Fall. To the time of innocence.

But as I pull the weeds, blades grow from the earth where the flowers once bloomed. They carve into my skin, drawing blood.

* * *

I WAKE to the sound of my door opening and bolt upright. My throat is tight. I'm not sure if I'm relieved to be awake or if I want to go back to that cottage so I can fix the overgrown garden and stomp the blades into the earth. I want to go into the cottage.

Tristan stands in the doorway, holding a leather suitcase and a large duffel bag. "I knocked, but you didn't answer." He pauses, his eyebrows raising. "Are you all right? You look upset."

He drops the bags on the white table inside the room.

I blink, trying to regain control of myself. "Just a dream." I pull the sheets up. "How was Vero?"

He steps inside and closes the door quietly behind him. "She's absolutely fine."

Irritation simmers. "No, she isn't. Did you actually see her?"

"Yes." He holds my gaze for a long time. "Well, fine. She's sick, but you know that. She was coughing up blood, but she's holding on. I gave them money to take a boat to Balin's cottage, so they don't need to walk. And because I knew you were going to worry about it, I made sure they had food before they set off for the Melian Forest."

I close my eyes, exhaling a shaky breath. This whole night, I've been carrying the tension of worry about Vero —and that's at least one thing I can clear from my mind. "Thank you, Tristan."

"Don't worry about it." Already, he's opening the bottle of wine. "They gave me my own little room in the servants' quarters, but I wanted to find you first. You need to fill me in on what I missed."

"We went to a dragon ceremony, and the dragon didn't

burn me, so apparently, I'm worthy. And it turns out that people are going to fight in a series of trials to win the crown. Those of us with halos can only leave here if we're dismissed by the noble houses for performing poorly in the trials. So, long story short, I won't be able to leave until after I've fought in a trial by combat."

He stalks closer to me, holding two glasses of wine. "You're going to fight in a trial by combat? Are you mad?"

He hands me a glass, and I take a sip. Strawberry wine, sweet and tangy.

"There's no way around it. We will compete against each other, and the Council of Nobles judges us through mirrors. Fifteen rounds of eight contestants each, fighting to the death. Anyone caught lying will be burned. Anyone who performs poorly will be dismissed." I lift the glass again. "Also, yes, you were correct that if we leave without permission, we'll be hunted to death by the *cugol*, so I really have a wonderful array of death options to choose from. But if things go perfectly, I'll find the grail, fight terribly in the trials but survive, and go home."

His expression darkens. "You haven't fought in over a decade. You have no magic, and you're not trained anymore. It should be me fighting."

"Well, it's not. We have two full weeks to look for the grail. And when I'm not looking, I'll be training. Two weeks is plenty of time."

"First of all, no, it isn't, and you know that. Second, did anyone suspect anything?"

"Someone said I smelled of mortals, and they all thought my outfit was wildly inappropriate. But a dragon ceremony put their suspicions to rest. I'm officially nobility now. I've got a symbol and everything. So, now I just need to survive a few weeks."

"Okay." A wry smile flits over his lips. "Well, you'll be learning from me, the best possible teacher in the world. Pity I'm not in the competition. I'd eat them all alive."

"My most humble servant."

He laughs—a rare, warm laugh from Tristan that sends a pulse of heat through me. Firelight and shadows carve the masculine planes of his face, the inviting curve of his lips.

Owain and I only just broke up, but clearly, I'm on the rebound. It doesn't help that I've always dreamt of what it would feel like to kiss Tristan for the first time. He's taking care of me, and he always has. I'm fighting the urge to pull him into bed with me.

"What are you thinking about?" he asks quietly.

My heart races, and I can feel my chest flushing under my shirt. But I could never tell him what I'm really thinking. This is the one long-term friendship I have.

I lick my lips, and I see his gaze shift down to my mouth. "Just that I need to sleep."

But instead of turning to leave, he shifts closer, settling on the edge of my bed. I breathe in his delicious smell from here, and I lean closer.

His green eyes study my face. "Syn, I need you to tell

me every single thing you heard or saw tonight. Every person you met. Every detail you can remember about them. Nothing is too small, too insignificant."

"Now?"

"I'm here to keep you safe," he murmurs, and that ache returns. "And the best way for me to do that is to know everything. I need to know exactly what we're up against. And before dawn breaks tomorrow, we rise early and start training. We will train day and night until I think you can survive against them, because I will not let you die here."

Before dawn breaks.

The Undercroft never left Tristan. It never left either of us.

CHAPTER 14

As I finish my set of push-ups, my arms shake. My days of being the best fighter in the kingdom are long since over, that much is clear.

There's only one week left until the first round of combat trials, and I've spent every waking hour either training or searching for grail clues. So far, neither has amounted to much.

In this dark sepulcher, it smells of soil, moss, and bones. Bruises cover my body from the past week. Four hours of sleep per night.

Catching my breath, I curl back onto my hips in a kneeling position, arms stretched against the cool stone floor. My leather trousers have made me too hot, and I'm glowing with sweat. The cool, dank floor of the crypt feels good on my bare arms.

Niniane told us to enjoy life, lest we find ourselves

entombed by time—and here I am among the literal tombs beneath the castle.

I imagine the other contenders have been getting drunk on mead and zipping around on that castle roller coaster. Rion probably doesn't need to do push-ups in a crypt, inhaling skeleton dust. I imagine he was born muscular, a gods-blessed golden warrior baby who took his first steps just to slit a peasant's throat.

I suppose training down here is better than some of the jobs I've had. There's no one here saying things like, *Careful with that chair, it costs four thousand pounds,* while I calculate how many months it would take me to earn four thousand pounds. At least there's no blonde named Sharon saying things like, *Can you stay an extra two hours? I've got plans. You probably don't have anything on, do you? Cheers, darling, you're a star.*

I raise my eyes a little, wondering how long I've got until Tristan yells at me to get up again. Guttering candles cast dancing light over ancient stone effigies of knights and ladies.

"Syn." Tristan's deep voice echoes off the stone. "You need to get up. That's plenty of stretching."

Ah, there it is.

I swallow hard and push myself up on shaking legs, facing Tristan.

He raises his eyebrows, his moss-green eyes glinting, candlelight flickering over his dark hair. As he peers down at me, I know he's assessing me. He's got the clean orderliness of a soldier. His short-sleeved shirt is white as sun-bleached bones, and dark tattoos curl around his forearms. As he crosses his arms, I can see the fabric of his shirt strain over his muscles.

His expression tells me he's not pleased with me. Possibly because I haven't landed a single punch yet.

With the look he's giving me, I know what he's thinking, and I stare right back at him. "For the last time, I'm not quitting. I want the grail."

"You'll do a better job of looking after Vero alive than dead."

"While I'm hunted by the Cloaked Ones? No. I was raised a soldier, and I'll die one if I have to in pursuit of the grail."

He arches a dark eyebrow, and a muscle ticks in his sharp jawline. "Fine, then. Let's try this again. Remember what I said about balance and focus. But Syn? This time, I'm not going to hold back as much. Your opponents will be fighting to the death, and you need to get used to it. We don't know that you'll have a sword the entire time in the arena, or at all. So, you have to be prepared to fight unarmed."

I nod and slide my weight slightly onto my back leg.

Immediately, I swing for him. Tristan dodges easily. I'm off balance, and before I can right myself, Tristan's fist slams into my cheek. Pain vibrates through my skull. I hold my cheek and stagger back. I don't even get the chance to recover before his left fist smashes into my other cheek, and pain splinters through me. I wonder if he's using his magic. He did say he wouldn't hold back.

I fall flat on my back, lying on the dusty stones next to an effigy. Pain cracks through my head, and nausea wells in my gut.

When my vision clears again, I look up to see Tristan standing over me. He holds out his hand to me.

Fuck.

His expression is stony.

I take his hand, and he pulls me up.

"Were you using your magic?" I ask, holding my cheek.

He folds his arms, his brow furrowing. "No. I'm worried you won't survive this. I just hope this isn't some kind of penance," he mutters. "Because you don't need to repent for anything."

The unspoken memories freeze the air between us. "Ah. You want to talk about the past now?"

"Not really, no."

I clench my jaw. "I didn't ask for this, but I'm here now —and someone needs to heal Vero. Why should only the aristocrats have access to the grail?"

"I think I hit you too hard."

"I'm thinking *perfectly* clearly."

"No, I know that. You've always been unhinged. I mean, I literally hit you too hard." He's scrutinizing my face now, and he lifts my chin gently in his hand, carefully tracing the back of his fingers over my cheekbone. "You have a bruise forming there."

I swallow hard. "It's part of training. We used to hit each other all the time."

"Feels different now." He steps away again, his gaze shuttering.

I take a deep breath. "Are you going to tell me about your mission at some point? Why are you here in the first place?"

He shakes his head. "I can't tell you, Syn. You don't have clearance. But I'm heading to Avalon Tower for a few days. Maybe I can get you clearance while I'm there."

"How exactly are you getting in and out of here without anyone noticing?"

"I don't have a halo, and I have portals opening at very specific times, for short periods. But it's chaos at Avalon Tower right now. Some members of the Iron Legion have managed to find a way in through Camelot's magical protections. They're attacking Avalon Tower, and we're just trying to repel them from breaking into the fortress."

"When are you leaving?"

His green eyes pierce me. "Tonight. But I promise to come back before the first trial."

With Tristan gone, I'll be able to spend more time looking for grail clues and less time training.

I lean back against the wall, tilting my head against the cool stone. "Give it to me straight. What do you think my chances are of surviving the combat trials?"

A line forms between his dark eyebrows. "It depends who you're matched against. I don't know what magic anyone has, but I don't think Elizabeth and Lady Lunette will be formidable opponents. Duke Mabon, I think, is a skilled fighter, but he's been drunk the whole time. I think there are a number of people here you could beat, even if you haven't been training. We just have to hope you don't end up facing off against someone like Rion or Dagonet."

"Any other advice from the best teacher in the world?"

He folds his hands behind his head. "I guess you have a solid chance against many of them, even without the Song. And assuming you're evenly matched, your history gives you an advantage. Maybe your magic is gone, but you're used to combat. You can manage pain better than anyone, and you won't panic at the sight of blood."

"I do have that going for me."

"You remember what Auberon taught us. Simply keeping your mind clear and focused is the best advantage you can have. Rational thought is more powerful than anything. Make them panic if you can."

"How?"

"The sight of blood can instill fear immediately. Use that to your advantage. Go for the jugular, the arteries. Spill crimson all over the stones and let their primal terror take over. You can let them think you're weak before the start of the trial, but that will only work once. After that, you need to make them feel horror. End it all as quickly as you can. And if you're truly fucked in a fight, there's only ever one solution."

I swallow hard. "Surrender and hope they don't kill me."

He closes the distance between us, and I feel the heat washing off him. He brushes a finger over the bloom forming on my cheek again, sending hot shivers over my skin. "Surrender if you need to. I promised to get you out of here alive, and you will not make a liar out of me, Syn Malleore."

CHAPTER 15

Without Tristan to spar with, I set up a pell in the crypt. It's a wooden training dummy, and I can use it to practice my strikes with an oak sword. I still have no idea if weapons are involved in the trial by combat—Niniane won't tell us a thing. But I can hope. A sword has always been my preferred weapon.

For the past three days, I've been hunting around the castle for signs of the grail and coming up empty.

Then I take out my frustrations by battering the shit out of this pell. My palms have grown calloused and rough. I fashioned the pell and the sword from oak. For my sword, I carved the point with a knife, then tied cloth around the base to act as my makeshift hilt. It all came from the coffin oak of some poor dead knight named Bleoberis. And even if his skeleton now lies jumbled on top of the bones of one of his fellow knights, I hope their spirits will not haunt me.

Now, my biceps burn as I thrust at it, delivering cross-cuts, over-strokes, down-strokes, and cleaving blows. I practice the little windmill slices to build strength in my wrists again. Even without the Song, I find some of that fluidity I once honed with hours of daily practice.

It's cold in this crypt, but I've still managed to work up a sweat, and my skin glows with the heat. All the time I'm attacking this wooden man, I'm imagining Auberon's face—the crown gleaming over his platinum hair, my blade jabbing at his withered heart.

He used to wake us late at night with buckets of ice water dumped on us because for some mad reason, he was convinced that sleep deprivation made us *stronger*. After practicing all day, we'd practice at night in the forest, in storms. Some nights, he'd send us alone to the wintry woods and leave us to shiver against a tree, listening to the sound of wolves growing closer. It built strength, he said. Resilience.

Sometimes, he woke us just to beat us for no reason at all. He told us our parents no longer wanted us, that he was our protector now. He said he was the only one who cared for us. The only thing I'm thankful for when it comes to Auberon is that Vero wasn't born with a type of magic he could use.

I flick my wrist harder, faster, jabbing at the wood.

"There's the Syn Malleore I remember." Tristan's deep

voice echoes off the crypt ceiling, and Auberon's face disappears from my thoughts.

He's back. With a smile, I turn to see him.

"Any luck with the grail?" he asks.

My smile fades, and I notice a new scar across his cheekbone. "None, I'm afraid. What happened?"

"Just a scratch. We had a little skirmish with the Iron Legion." He steps closer, appraising me with his eyes. "But your speed is improving already. I saw it just now. The old Syn Malleore."

I turn back to the pell, showing off now with some rapid crosscuts to Auberon's heart.

Tristan stands behind me, and his familiar scent curls around me—cloves faintly tinged with tobacco. His hands settle on my hips, and heat slides through me. I want to lean back into him, but I resist.

"So much better. Just fix your form," he says quietly. "Because your power comes from here."

His hand slides around my stomach, and heat radiates from his palm. My lips open, my breath shallowing. I wonder if he can feel my pulse racing.

"And here," he murmurs. "Push from the ground up, let it rise through your core, and transfer the energy from your arm into the weapon. Like magic."

Heat from his body washes over me, and I lick my lips.

But before I can melt into the hard muscle of his chest, he pulls his hands from me. As I turn to face him, my heart is still racing, and heat rises to my cheeks.

"So, can you tell me about your mission now?"

He shakes his head. "Avalon Tower said they need to meet you before you can get clearance. But if we can make that happen, it would be great to have your help. I could bring you very briefly with me through a portal, quickly enough that the Cloaked Ones don't notice you're gone." He turns to stare at the pell. "Did you make this?"

"Sir Bleoberis donated his coffin. He was quite generous. Not that he was in a position to argue." I point at a pile of broken wood in the corner. "There's more sticks if you want to fight me."

"You think you can take me on with coffin sticks?"

"It's actually my weapon of choice."

He leans over and selects a straight piece of wood with a splintered edge, roughly the length of his arm. From his dagger sheath, he draws a blade and begins shaving away the jagged edges, smoothing the tip so he won't actually rip a hole in me. When he's finished, he pulls off his shirt and tears it into strips, wrapping them around the base to form a makeshift handle like mine.

As he works, my gaze drifts over the strong lines of his body. New tattoos mark him now, dark ink winding from his forearms to his biceps. Across the sculpted planes of his abs, the ink forms a hound, captured in motion.

He looks even more powerful than he did in the Undercroft, and I can only thank the *gods* he's not a telepath, because my thoughts are becoming indecent.

"Syn?"

"What?" I say in what comes out as an annoyed shout. Then, quieter, "When did you get that dog tattoo?"

"It's my Cornish hound, gods rest his soul. Petitcrieu."

"So, you gave yourself a sigil like a nobleman?"

"You're stalling." He slides into his fighting stance. Then, to my immense irritation, he starts twirling the wooden sword around in a display of his skill.

While he's showing off, I shift in for the attack, but he parries easily. We strike, back and forth, wood clashing.

I shift forward faster, aiming for his chest. As I swing, he ducks, then strikes me from below. His sword slams into my thighs, knocking me over, and I fall back hard. My head smacks against the floor, and pain flares through my skull.

Get up. Auberon's voice bellows in the hollow of my skull. At the sound, I feel like ice water drenches me.

I'm up again in moments, gripping the wooden sword tightly.

I used to be good at kicking. It all happened instinctively back then—but does that memory still live in my body?

Gripping our coffin swords, we circle each other like wild animals.

I strike for him, and he blocks it. "Almost."

Our swords clash again, then he jabs at me. I spin away like we're dancing, then whirl around to strike him in the back. He shifts just before my sword lands, but I barely manage to clip his bicep.

A wry smile from Tristan. "Getting better, Syn. You're no match for me yet, but—"

I strike again, bringing the sword down, and he ducks. I kick for his head—but he catches my foot, twisting it. I'm off my feet, suspended for a moment—until I slam down hard on the crypt stones. My sword skitters away from me. He lunges, and I barely roll away from the strike.

I kick backward at his knee with my free foot. *Whack.*

He stumbles.

Get up.

My heart pounds like this is real. I know we're only training, but it never feels like *just training*. Even with Tristan, it always feels like death is just a breath away. Which, strangely, makes me feel energized. It makes me feel more alive than I did making tea in an office for people who told me I was a star.

I scramble for my weapon, pulse racing.

Still on the floor, I spin back to him. He's bringing up his sword above me, and I only just manage to block it. From the ground, I lunge upwards, my shoulder slamming into his stomach, taking him down. But as I start to stand, he swings a *hard* kick at my legs.

I crash back onto the stone, my back aching. I grunt with frustration. He's starting to make me deeply irritated.

"Master your emotions," he says.

"Get fucked."

Anger starts to heat my blood, though I'm not sure if I'm mad at Tristan or myself. I want to remind him about the time he failed to master his emotions and ran through the woods naked.

I roll backward, snatching my sword off the ground.

I stand, then swing, and he blocks it, the force of it so hard this time that the wooden swords nearly splinter.

Tristan flashes me an infuriating half smile, practically glowing. He's enjoying himself. His magic coils around me, tingling over my skin, which means I don't stand a chance anymore. He launches off the floor toward the wall, then kicks off the stones. He's a blur above me for just a moment—gripping the wooden beams and swinging. Then, with a flip through the air, he lands behind me.

Still, my sword is at his throat. "Got you, you ridiculous show-off."

But only then do I notice the thrust of his wooden sword already at my abdomen, prodding at my stomach.

His eyebrow arches. "Do you *really?*"

The annoying thing about Tristan during sparring situations is that he can slow time—only for himself. To others, it looks like he's moving incredibly fast.

We spin away from each other, and the next time we meet, he slams the wooden sword into my hips once more, knocking me *hard* into a wall.

And before I can push away, Tristan is there, his weapon carving through the air. When his sword slashes into mine, it's with a force so powerful that the wood splinters.

I bring up a left hook that slams into his chin, because

I needed to get at least *one* good blow in. In the next moment, he's pressing me against the wall, one hand lightly around my throat and a faint smile ghosting over his lips. His other hand tightens around my waist.

His green eyes shine down at me, and a bead of sweat slides down his temple.

My gaze lingers on his mouth—that full lower lip that always invites me to stare.

"That was fun," he says quietly.

His gaze dips to my lips, and he leans in slightly closer once more. I lick my lips, and my hips shift forward, seemingly of their own volition. His fingers pulse on my waist. I want to wrap my arms around his shoulders and pull him in close—but then I'd be stepping over a boundary I'm afraid to cross. His thumb brushes the skin on my throat slowly, just above my clavicle, and I breathe in sharply at the touch. Heat radiates from the point of contact.

The air between us is charged as lightning, and warmth pounds through my blood. I glance at his neck, nearly overcome by the urge to run my tongue over the pulsing vein in his throat.

At last, his gaze shutters and he pulls away, releasing me. As he steps back, the cold air washes over me again, and I regret the loss of his warmth.

I'm catching my breath, scrambling to organize my thoughts. "See? I'm already getting better."

He's still close to me. "How's your head? And your body?"

Aches slide through my bones, and my skull is pounding. I smile anyway. "I know you were still holding back, by the way. But I'm absolutely fine, soldier. I don't feel a single sore point," I lie. I'm trying to sound normal but probably overdoing it. "What's your assessment of my chances of surviving?'

He arches an eyebrow. "Just make sure the Council of Nobles love you. Charm them. Ultimately, they decide who lives and dies after you surrender. They like a good fighter, of course, but you could also try to make them love you."

And what are the chances I can do that? I don't suppose any of them would be delighted by a long monologue about Tudor-era execution methods.

I slide down the wall, my body exhausted. "Any chance you checked up on Vero when you were away?"

He nods, his expression grave, and my stomach turns.

"She's okay," he says. "She's resting."

Every muscle in my body tenses. "Does she seem worse?"

"She's tired, yes. They found a healer, but he wasn't able to help her."

There's a quietness to his voice that sets my teeth on edge. Tristan always burnishes the truth. *Tired* probably means something far worse.

"A regular healer can't help. The toxin was specially

designed by Auberon's poisoners to be incurable by peasants. Only a royal relic like the grail can fix it."

I've been looking for *clues* to the grail's location, just like Cador said, but how can I recognize what they are?

My jaw clenches, and I stare up at him. "I'm running out of time, aren't I?"

CHAPTER 16

$\mathcal{I}$ stretch out in bed, unable to sleep. My body still aches from weeks of training day and night. Thirteen hours a day of strengthening, of hacking the shit out of the pell, and of scouring the castle for unnamed clues.

I need sleep. Auberon never understood that even the Fey need rest.

I roll over to stare out the window. The vast sky spreads out beyond the glass, and the two moons hang in the dark sky like crown jewels, shimmering over dark waves.

My pulse won't stop racing because I can't stop thinking about Vero. She's growing sicker by the day, and I'm not around to help her.

So, what am I doing wasting my time in bed? Sleep can wait.

Rising from my sheets, I cross to the window and stare out at the glittering sea. Then I pull open the glass door and step out onto the balcony. A bottle of mead still stands on the table from earlier, and I pour myself a glass. I take a sip, trying to figure out my next move. I need to search in a more focused way.

I breathe in the salty air and let the sweet mead linger over my tongue. It's balmy out here for April, and it's so peaceful and calm, I almost hate it.

I take another sip. The mead slides warmly down into my chest.

I'm going out to look for the grail one more time.

Cador said, *Here, secrets are hidden behind locked doors.*

But if that's literal, which locked door?

When I cross back into my room, I open the wardrobe and grab a soft blue cloak and one of the daggers. The misericorde *might* be thin enough for picking a lock, and I take a hairpin too. I slide the dagger into a thigh holster.

I stay barefoot. I want to walk as quietly as possible tonight and skulk around unnoticed.

Carefully, I open the door and slip into the stairwell. The hallway is empty, just guttering torches and shifting shadows. The only sound is the pounding of the waves floating through open arched windows.

Cador said that unlocking doors would be treason. And treason, as it happens, is my favorite hobby.

I begin the climb, spiraling to the tower's summit. At each landing, warm light dances over the sigils, painted with ladybirds, magpies, jackdaws, honeybees, pegasuses, and bats.

At last, I reach the crown of the tower.

A cool breeze slips over my skin as I step into the open space. Up here, there's no ceiling, just arched openings framing the sky itself. Silver-red moonlight bathes the floor, and wisps of clouds drift slowly overhead. From this height, the kingdom stretches out beneath me, an endless landscape of velvet-dark night and a star-dappled sea.

There's nothing in here, no adornment or decorations except the silent beauty of the night sky.

But from here, I have a perfect view of the entire fortress. My gaze lingers on a large stone building with a rounded red door with climbing ivy. Above the door is a carving of a chained book, painted bright colors. A library, I think. That will be worth exploring at some point.

There are new additions around Aether Tower now—our banner flags snap in the wind, one for each of us. Above the banners is a golden number: *180*. The number of contenders remaining after Blythe burned to death.

The wind toys with the fabric of my raven banner where it stands among the others from the Gloaming Tower. Elizabeth's owl flaps in the breeze near mine.

I survey the grounds again, and this time, it's Lyria that catches my eye. At the top, a still pool of water reflects the moons like a mirror. From the chambers below, waterfalls cascade into a misty basin at the bottom.

But something snags my attention at its summit.

Everything in the Veiled Court gleams with magical perfection except the top floor of Lyria. There, above the falling water, one of the mullioned windows hangs open, half shattered. A torn and tattered curtain flutters in the window, buffeted by the wind. It's dyed woad blue, an old style no one has used in centuries.

So, what's going on in there?

A locked room, perhaps? Completely off-limits—like some of the old derelict buildings in East London. I grip the side of the parapet, and the wind whips over me.

That's where I should start.

Halfway down the stairs, I hear the sound of footfalls, and voices echo off the stairwell stones. Guards, I think.

I don't want anyone catching me out of my room tonight, so I slip onto the balconies outside one of the open windows. There's only about a one-foot ledge out here. I press myself all the way to the side, staying out of view while trying not to fall off.

The guards round the stairwell and pass my hiding location. I catch my breath and wait until the guards' voices fade to silence, then step back into the quiet stairwell. The cool stones feel smooth against my bare soles, and I take a few steps down to the round door painted with the rolling cart. At last, I have a reason to use this, but I need to be somewhat discreet.

When I push through the door, I find myself standing on a stone balcony, where one of the wooden carts sits waiting on the tracks. The night air is cool, and I breathe in the scent of apples and honeysuckle. From this vantage point, I look out at the strange beauty of the towers and courtyards.

But my gaze is on Lyria, where the towering, blue-tinged standing stones glow behind streams of water.

The warm wind kisses my cheeks. I don't belong in this rarefied, elitist fortress. I'm not from one of Brocéliande's noble families, and my ancestors' nearest brush with royalty was digging the graves of those they executed. But deep down, I don't believe that people deserve things because of their ancestors. Bloodlines alone should not grant or withhold the healing powers of the grail. This place is mine as much as it is Rion's and Igraine's.

I climb into the cart, settling my arse on the hard oak seat. There are a few different track options, but one of them shoots over to Aether Tower, then curves around to Lyria.

I turn to inspect the mahogany lever to my left. There are six different settings marking the various destinations: a picture of Aether Tower, little animals for the menagerie, a sword for the arena, flowers for the garden, and so on.

Lyria Tower stands near an orchard, so I press the lever all the way down to a picture of an apple tree.

Then, I duck down into the cart. Immediately, I'm *off*, gripping the wooden bar and peering out the side. Even crouching like I am, I'm grinning ear to ear. A wild thrill rushes through me as I sweep around the courtyards, watching them barrel past me.

I zoom toward Aether, then curve sharply to whip past the spray of Lyria's waterfalls. Pure joy lights me as I pick up speed, hurtling through the night, until at last, the cart comes to a hard stop against a wooden barrier. The impact knocks me forward a little, and I bump my head inside the cart.

Rubbing my skull, I step out.

Quietly, I creep from the orchard and head for Lyria's door. I scan the courtyard for signs of movement and sneak across the grass and stone and shadows.

As I reach the base of the tower, the running water shoots mist into the air around me.

There's no reason for me to be in the Lyria Tower, no plausible deniability. My best hope is simply to move as fast as possible.

But this is all for Vero. All it will take is *one* sip from that grail, and she'll be healthy again forever.

Quietly, I push through the smooth ivory door and slink into the Lyria Tower.

CHAPTER 17

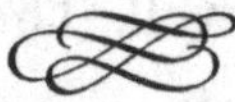

I spring barefoot up the stairs. There are no torches to light the way; rather, little floating will-o'-the-wisps drift around me as I run. The towering windows are open to the cascades of water, and droplets fleck my skin.

I sweep past images of otters, kelpies, eels, water goblins, and mermaids that glow under the shifting lights. The air here smells fresh, like water lilies, and a beautiful blue tone radiates beneath the ivory stone's surface.

Close to the top, I pass Rion's room, which is marked with the white stag. My breath catches as I think of that beautiful face from my nightmares. The last thing I need is for him to open that door and accuse me of treason.

But immediately after his room, the shadows grow thicker, and there are no more sigils. The will-o'-the-wisps disappear, like even they are afraid to climb this high. Now, the only light illuminating the stairwell is from the moons and stars.

From a narrow, open window, a thin blade of silver light streaks across a wooden door reinforced with metal nails. It's completely out of place here, a heavy door blocking a curving stairwell. There wasn't anything like this in the Gloaming Tower.

I listen for footfalls or voices and hear nothing. From the arrow-slit window, the breeze rushes into the stairs, kissing my skin.

I press my ear against the wood and am greeted by silence. Carefully, I try depressing the latch. It's locked, of course.

My pulse quickens, and I crouch to slide my hairpin into the keyhole. I use my dagger to keep tension on the lock. My pin scrapes against metal inside, and I hold my breath as I work. Again, I pause to listen for footfalls.

When I don't hear anything, I shift the pin again, feeling around inside the mechanism until I can slide it in deeper.

Softly, a click breaks the silence, and the door unlatches, opening just an inch.

I let out a long, slow breath and pull the door open on a shadowed stairwell.

After four more steps, I get to the top, where moonlight spills through a large, gothic window onto a second door. This one bears a sigil, but it's covered in a thick layer of dust. Beneath the dust is an image of a swan wearing a golden crown and chain around its throat. The bird carries a rose in its mouth, blood dripping from the red petals.

The image stirs an old, uneasy recognition in me. I can't quite put my finger on where I've seen it before.

Bending, I pick this new lock, trying not to cough as I inhale the dust. The door unlatches, revealing a circular room. Starlight streams through leaded windows onto utter chaos—bedclothes tossed on the floor, plates and glasses smashed and in disarray. A breeze howls through the shattered window.

Apart from cobwebs, the hearth lies empty.

Quietly, I creep around the room. On one of the walls, I find scratch marks etched in the stones, like a prisoner marking the passage of time. Faded tapestries line the other walls, one of them with the same heraldic emblem of the swan and the rose. I stare at it as recognition starts to bloom in my thoughts. It's the Lancastrian sigil from the War of the Roses—the symbol of Henry VI, the mad king in the fifteenth century.

This isn't his room, of course. He was mortal, murdered in the Tower of London by a rival king, his throne stolen from him. *My Crown is in my heart, not on my head...*

Carved on one of the walls is the text *KING EMRYS, FALSELY IMPRISONED.*

Could this really be Emrys's room? Only magic would

preserve this for so long. He was one of the early kings in the old days of Avalon, before the fall.

Vaguely, I remembered that Avalon lay in ruin during his reign, that he was a mad king, too. Emrys sent his army to terrorize his own people. When someone killed one of his soldiers, he dispatched his military to slaughter everyone in their village. The massacres only stopped when Queen Morgan took over.

No one ever knew what happened to him. By the old, dried blood on the pillowcase, I can guess.

It's just like Cador said—the mortal history of kings mirrors our own, centuries later.

I start to hunt through the room for any signs of the grail. I find a scrap of parchment and fragments of text.

> A wroth king, abandoned by reason…then
>   stood the realm in great jeopardy a long
>   while…kingdoms shall be in great
>   poverty, misery and wretchedness…the
>   white rose of Queen Morgan shall
>   restore…

It reads like a list of charges against Emrys, perhaps. Nothing to do with the grail, as far as I can tell.

I keep searching until I find a faint image carved in one of the windowpanes, as if etched with a diamond. There—a little chalice, like a grail. And words beneath it say:

A rose to grace the castle door, two princes'
heads shorn to the bone—
Two fallen crowns beneath the floor—dark
secrets brood in silent stone

I stare at the words.

Slowly, something Jasper said dawns on me. He was insulting how terrible I looked, and he said, *Might as well dig up the two princely corpses from Aether Tower...*

The echoes of the Tower's history ring even louder now. Just like Cadoc said, London's heart is a mimicry of this place.

Hundreds of years ago, in London's old castle, two princes' bodies were found stuffed under a stairwell, little victims of the Wars of the Roses.

Wind rushes through a broken window, and a dark chill ripples around the room, sliding over my skin. I feel as if I've woken the old king's vengeful ghost, and I don't want to spend another minute in here. Nor do I need to.

I know exactly where I need to go.

Of course, I *should* go to bed now. It's late, and I've found my clue.

And yet, I can see Vero's pale face in my thoughts. I can practically hear her wheezing. I won't sleep tonight until I know more.

I turn, heading out the door to the stairwell. I close both doors behind me, listening as the locks click shut again.

I hurry down the stairs and out the door into the fog around the tower's base.

Pulling my cloak tight, I rush across the courtyard to the bone-white tower in the center, my bare feet padding over cold cobbles.

At the base of the Aether Tower, ivy twines around the white stone. I climb a set of stairs to a large oak door. I half expect it to be locked, but I'm able to push through it into a spiral stairwell. Inside, torches light the pale walls.

A door nestles at the bottom of the stairs—and just like I expected, it's marked with the white rose of Queen Morgan.

A rose to grace the castle door...

I listen for the sound of footfalls, and when I hear nothing, I pull open the door, revealing a small, narrow set of stairs. At the bottom is a chamber no larger than the cart that brought me here, and within it lie two small skulls in the dirt.

Two princes' heads shorn to the bone...

My pulse picks up. I don't know who they are, exactly, but I can only guess they stood too close to a crown someone else claimed.

I know the path to the throne lies stained with blood.

I take down a torch and quietly creep toward the skulls. In the gloom, I find a carving marking the granite walls: *Truth grows among the violets and thorny roses. Once, we devoured our kings...*

Cryptic, confusing, and I have no idea what it means. The garden, perhaps?

I close the door to the stairwell and listen for footfalls. This time, I hear them.

And they're close.

I close my eyes and inhale. If I'm caught, I want to seem relaxed.

Just as I'm pulling open the door out of the tower, a deep voice says my name from behind.

I turn to see Lord Cador rounding the corner, his burgundy hair draped over a midnight cloak. My heart slams against my ribs, but I flash him a smile like I'm delighted to see him.

"Ah! Alis. What brings you to the Aether Tower tonight?"

Casually, I shrug. "Too excited to sleep. I'm just so in love with this place. It's like you said—it was built at a time of primal power. Maybe one of us can bring back the golden days of the Fey. I just hope I can help restore that glory."

He smiles at me. "I believe you can. I feel it."

I open my eyes wide. "You can really feel the ancient Fey magic here, the primal powers. I was going to pay a little visit to the Rhiannon Garden before sleep. I hope to see the grail someday."

He glances to the side, then leans down to whisper, "We have truly powerful relics here. They were lost for a thousand years, but we found them again in our time of need. But if you want to get your hands on that ancient power, Baroness, I suggest doing everything in your power to win the trials. Only someone with divine strength can grasp a relic."

I swallow hard. "And if I don't have magic?"

He shrugs. "Then surviving is the best you can hope for. Count it a blessing if you leave here alive."

CHAPTER 18

I turn and step out of the Aether Tower.

I *really* should go to bed now, but there's one last clue to search for among the violets and thorny roses.

I step over the cool stones on my way to the Rhiannon Garden.

An amber stone bridge arches overhead, joining the towers with a broad walkway. I pass beneath its looming gargoyles. On the other side lies the verdant flower garden. A cobbled path wends through gnarled trees, their trunks twined with ivy and hawthorn blossoms. Pale pink petals are scattered over the mossy earth.

I start searching for more carvings.

Roses bloom wildly here, even though April is a bit early for them. Violets, too. I keep looking, surveying the wild beauty of this place where apple branches sweep over me and moths flutter around my head. In the distance, Belenior burns, a flame against a dark sky.

I scan every rock and tree trunk for clues, stopping when I get to an altar tucked away in a corner. Honeysuckle clings to the pale stone. I move closer, studying its markings. Faintly, I can make out an engraving of what I think is a cauldron.

Beneath that, I read these words:

The grail is found—
Where bridges kill and swords collide—
Two houses torn by fratricide—
Cross the sword, face the fires
A test of might—a funeral pyre

My blood roars. *This* is what I've been looking for all along. Unfortunately, I'm no closer to getting the grail. That will only come at the end of a trial—one that involves murder and fire.

I don't *think* it will be the combat trial. That one is in the arena, with no bridges. It must come later in the trials, which means I must survive the first trial if I want to cure Vero.

No wonder Cador said only those with the most powerful magic will grasp the powerful relics.

Fuck. I need to get the Song back. If I possessed the power of my youth, I'd win every trial.

Is it possible to get it back? As I walk through the garden, I try to recall how it sounded.

For just a moment, when the baroness attacked me, I

felt my magic humming. Maybe it still lives somewhere deep inside me.

Before I cross under the bridge, I reach down to pick up a twig. If I have any magic left, a makeshift wand could help me channel it.

Gripping the end of the stick, I find my footing. As I extend my sword arm, I try to clear my thoughts of all the chatter, listening only to the breeze and the distant crash of waves. I call up the footwork I learned years ago—front foot, measured spacing. I change stance and strike in an X, my hips turning, blade tracing a clean line.

I move into slashes and thrusts, precise and memorized. I keep going this way, trying to hear the Morrigan's song the way I used to.

Dimly, I hear a few notes, but it's like the music is playing underwater. I can't really hear the melody at all. Maybe a rhythm? I try to match it with precise steps and strikes—one, two, thrust; one, two, step—an exact tempo. My stick whips through the air.

I hear Auberon's furious voice—*Guard yourself! Step in! Perfect your timing!*

But the melody is muddled, drowned under the sea. And inside, I just feel hollowed out.

I keep trying to hit the right rhythm, but it gets harder. Even the beats are slurred now, and I feel wrong and empty.

A strange note of panic starts to flow through my

mind, and all I can see is Auberon's furious face as he stands over me, asking me what I've done.

I stumble. Panic is death.

A soft, hazy rain mists the air.

I close my eyes, thinking of calming images. I'm not going to summon my magic if I'm in a complete state of fear.

I think of the little cottage where I grew up. The swing beneath the willow tree. The river that rushed by behind my house, the way the light streamed onto it. There was so much green outside, winding around the oak trunks, so much magic in the forest. And then, something I rarely remember anymore—my mother's face, smiling as I made a joke. It always thrilled me when I could make her laugh, because it seemed like such a hard thing, but what a golden reward. I hear her singing now as she gardens.

Faintly—very faintly—a distant melody returns, thin, rusty threads of something almost familiar. I begin to sway to it, willing it to swell louder, but the clarity of the tune is still out of reach.

And as I grasp for it, a thudding sound interrupts me. Heavy footfalls shake the nearby wall, and dust spills down from the stones. The loud, booming noise rumbles through my gut, making my heart race.

A low growl rolls out from the bridge. Slowly, I turn and find myself looking up into the red-scaled, reptilian face of Goch.

He's perching on the nearby bridge not ten feet away,

fiery eyes locked on me. Snorting, he leans closer, then cocks his head like he's studying a curious insect. Fire burns in his eyes, and his red scales catch the moonlight, gleaming like fresh blood.

My breath goes still. I freeze, staring at him, hardly daring to breathe.

He thrusts his head closer, and it feels like the world is tilting beneath my feet. He smells of iron and sulfur. When he exhales, his breath heats the air, and I breathe in death. His maw starts to part, and I'm now staring at his sharp, blood-stained jaws.

What is the blood from?

I stumble back, still clutching the stupid fucking twig, as if it could do anything.

My gaze darts around, searching for an exit, a better weapon.

My little misericord dagger is the best I've got, and I reach down to draw it from the holster on my thigh.

"Leave the baroness alone, Goch," a deep voice calls out from behind me.

I turn to see the Ruthless Knight himself in the shadows, resting against the trunk of an apple tree, arms folded. He's not wearing a shirt now, just the fur-lined cloak and trousers.

Goch growls again, breath rolling out in a searing burst of heat.

Rion prowls closer, looking utterly at ease with the

creature. "Goch. I believe you're frightening the lady," he drawls.

The dragon opens his mouth.

A pulse of dark magic bursts from Rion, slamming into the dragon like a shock wave. Goch whimpers, nostrils flaring. Yelping, he rears back, nearly falling off the bridge. In the next moment, he's airborne, retreating to the starry skies. He unleashes a gout of fire into the dark night sky and soars away from us.

I take a deep breath and slowly turn to Rion. Those unnerving pale gold tattoos glow across his face, and his silvery eyes burn bright from the shadows. His long, silver hair falls like liquid starlight over his black cloak.

As I look at him, a shiver of warning skims down my spine. *He's more dangerous than a dragon's fang.*

My gaze brushes down to his chest, where bright gold slashes across his muscles. The gilded tattoo there is almost like a primitive drawing of a tree that stretches over his chiseled abs. Strings of necklaces hang around his neck, one tipped with the sharp point of a stag's antler, and it draws my eyes in a slow pull to the V carved into his hips.

If he were anyone else, this sight alone might have me forgetting about the dragon.

"Thanks for that." I force the words out.

Amusement glints in his pale eyes. "I was hoping you'd return to that swaying dance you were doing before Goch arrived."

"Why, exactly, are you watching me?" I ask.

"I saw you whipping past my window earlier, crouched down in the cart. I scented you outside my door as well. Eventually, curiosity got the better of me." His gaze flicks to the stick on the ground. "Then I saw you playing with a twig, and I was not disappointed."

"I was practicing my swordsmanship."

He lifts an eyebrow. "Your swordsmanship, even with that stick, was precise. You've obviously been trained by someone who demanded complete perfection."

"Thanks, I guess," I say.

He takes a step closer, and his magic thrums over my skin. Power rolls off him, languid and intoxicating, making my nerves tingle with anticipation.

"It wasn't a compliment. I preferred the dancing. At least it looked like you enjoyed yourself, if only for a moment. When it comes to swordsmanship, your teacher left you with all the natural instinct of a mortal's pocket watch."

I frown up at him. "What does that even mean?"

"*Tick-tock.* Hitting all the right steps at all the right times. Predictable. Unfeeling." His mouth curves faintly. "Boring."

"*Boring.*" I narrow my eyes. "You seem pretty interested in me. I even got you out of bed."

"I didn't say *you* are boring. I said your swordsmanship is."

"And what am I supposed to feel with a weapon in my

hands?" I ask. "A deranged thrill at maiming people? We've all heard the stories about the high lord who tortures people to death as entertainment for his depraved party guests."

He leans in, his breath brushing my throat. His seductive scent wraps around me—musk and cedar and the irresistible allure of pure sin.

"Do you know what else is interesting? The sweet smell of your mortal blood." Slowly, his gaze drops to my mouth. "I'm not sure I've ever tasted one."

Fuck. My heart slams so hard I swear he can hear it, and I wonder if I'll be ashes in Goch's pit before the sun rises.

"I don't know what you mean," I whisper.

"I can always tell when someone lies. The racing pulse. The flushing cheeks. Maybe you're mostly Fey, but you *think* like a mortal. And you probably fight like one." His pale eyes narrow, icy as winter as they drag over me, assessing me. "Which means you'll die very quickly here."

My blood roars. "And here I am, plucked from the Waste Land to compete against you. The gods think I'm worthy, even if I don't have my own personal harem and torture dungeon."

"Mortal, your life will end at the tip of a blade." His eyes gleam, feline and cruel. "And no one will care enough to notice."

I'm willing to learn from people I hate. I certainly

spent ten years doing it. "And what do you suggest I should do to stay alive?"

"I suggest," he whispers, "that you remember what it is to be Fey."

Something tightens low in my stomach. "Meaning?"

He peers down at me. I'm only at his chest level. Between us, there's just a few inches of electrified air.

He circles me, slowly. "You're suffocating under your own restraints. Once, we ruled Britain with primal magic in our blood. We hunted and claimed what we desired. We took each other hard on the forest moss, and we fucked each other against rowan trunks. We thrived on instinct. But when mortals spread across the kingdom, they flooded us with their words, and then their iron weapons and machines. *You* think like a machine."

My pulse speeds faster, blood heating. "I'm very much not a machine."

Rion goes still. His silver eyes bore into me, rooting me in place. "Even mortals know what you've lost. Your own stories tried to warn you—the serpent and the garden and the fruit tree. The god who brought fire. A taste of knowledge that separated you from nature, words that warned of your own mortality. That was your fall from grace. Self-awareness breeds dread, and you're drowning in it."

"I see. So, that's your thing? You don't have any knowl-edge? Just hunting and murdering and fucking like beasts? I'm not sure I'd brag about that, Ruthless Knight."

His magic drips over my skin like warm honey. I hate this arrogant prick, but I feel a gravitational pull to him. Whether I like it or not, I crave his power, and I want to take it for myself.

"We were born to feel. To take what we wanted." His voice drops, sultry and low as a lover's caress. "To drag our fingers through the soil as we fuck and taste each other. To let desire silence our thoughts. We hunt for what we want—no fear, no dread, no shame on our tongues."

My blood pounds hard in my chest. "And your forest-fucking fantasies are supposed to help me get better at fighting?"

"You think so loudly it's a wonder you don't wake Merlin from his oak tomb. It's been a long time since pleasure made your thoughts go silent. That's what makes you mortal. You cannot commune with the eternal."

My chest is tight, breath shallow. "I have no idea what you're talking about."

"Deep down," he murmurs, "you know exactly what I mean."

CHAPTER 19

Elizabeth sits across from me on my balcony and plucks a strawberry from the plate.

Out here, the moons glitter off the dark sea, and brine floats on the wind. The peace before the storm.

"We should go to sleep, shouldn't we?" Elizabeth says.

"Sleep will be elusive tonight." I take a sip of mead, and the sweetness rolls over my tongue. "We don't want to be left alone with our fears the night before the combat trial."

"Unlike you, I haven't spent a moment preparing for it. I really should have. I was just so excited to be around people for once."

"But you have magic to help you, don't you? I think most of us here do."

She shrugs. "Mine is fairly useless. It's nothing like Rion's magic, anyway."

I draw in a sharp breath. "What sort of magic does he possess?"

"Dread magic. He can inspire a mind-bending terror in his victims. Drive them utterly out of their skulls by forcing them to experience their worst fears and memories."

My stomach tightens. Auberon taught me to shield my thoughts from dread magic, but that was long ago. If I were forced to experience my worst fears—well, it doesn't bear thinking about.

"We can always surrender," I say, "and hope the noble houses choose to keep us alive."

But it won't be enough if they send me home tomorrow. I still haven't found the grail. I *have* to both survive the trials and impress our judges enough to keep me around.

And right now, both of those things feel like a long shot.

She sighs. "I don't imagine the noble houses are very impressed with me so far. Mabon spilled wine on my dress the first night, and somehow, that made *me* a target, even though he's the clumsy idiot. When you were off training all that time, Igraine did it again. Worse, really. She dumped an entire drink on my head, and then just said, 'Oops!' Mabon laughed uproariously. I froze, then ran out of the hall and didn't return."

"They act like children. Children with lethal magic. It's a very bad combination."

"They do, yes, but it's calculated, too. They make other people look weak before our judges." She refills her glass. "And tomorrow morning, Igraine and her friends will be trying to kill us."

I drum my fingertips on the table. "I don't suppose we could make them find us intimidating."

"Yes. I want to be the sort of person who declares things like, 'I am not a woman to be trifled with.' Do you think that could work for me?"

"You're going to need to look angrier when you say it. Imagine someone you truly despise."

Her eyes flash with flames. "I am not a person to be trifled with," she hisses.

Goose bumps rise on my skin. "*That's* it, exactly. Bring that energy tomorrow morning."

With a smile, she slides her glass onto the table. "On that note, I should get to—"

A scream cuts through the air, interrupting her.

The hair rises on the back of my neck, and Elizabeth goes still. Her gaze meets mine.

Another cry. It's a bloodcurdling, almost animal sound, and it tears through the quiet night like a banshee's shriek. My blood turns to ice.

From here, we can't tell what's happening. We can only see the glittering waves crashing against the rocks.

The anguished shrieks float on the wind, carrying over the water.

"Is someone being tortured?" she whispers. "Should we go see?"

"Hard to ignore that kind of wailing. Maybe someone needs help?"

She nods. "Right. I'm also nosy as fuck."

We're both standing now, heading for the door. I slip into my shoes and wrap my blue velvet coat around myself.

We take a few steps down to the little round door with the cart and push through. Outside, the agonized cries echo off the castle walls, clearer now. A man is screaming that he's innocent, and he sounds out of his mind with terror.

From this vantage point, I can't really see what's happening, but I think it's coming from Goch's pit.

"Do you think we should just…stay inside?" Elizabeth whispers. "Are we being stupid?"

"I think so, yes."

"Right." The wind rakes through her dark hair. "Let's go anyway."

We climb into the cart together, and I pull my cloak tightly around me.

I push the levers down to the golden symbols of the unicorn and lion, and we shoot along the tracks, soaring over the courtyards. Most of the light is coming from the blaze of Belenior. Its flames warm my skin for a moment as we rush past, and then we swoop around a curve toward the menagerie.

We slam to a halt at the bottom, and my chest hits the bar, nearly knocking the wind out of me. As we step out of the cart, the man screams again in agony. Within the menagerie, the animals look spooked, fur raised, teeth bared. Some of them snarl and growl at the dragon pit.

I lead us on a path around their cage, heading for Goch's stone pit. A small crowd has gathered to watch, and the sight unfolding before us turns my stomach.

A man I've come to know as High Lord Hermance stands tied to a stake, bare-chested. Blood streaks down his skin, with the word *killer* etched into his chest.

Behind him, Goch's head is raised, his golden eyes alert. Watching. Steam puffs from his enormous nostrils.

Cador stalks closer, dressed in a black cloak. He pivots, facing the rest of the crowd. The moonlight gleams off his burgundy hair. "I hope you all realize now that if you are a liar, an imposter, or an enemy of the noble houses, we will discover your treachery."

"I didn't do it!" the man shouts, his words strangled.

Cador flicks his hand again, and new words slice into the man's skin. "My magic reveals the truth in your flesh. *That's* how I know you are lying. What happened to the real High Lord Hermance?"

The man's head hangs.

"You're not who you say you are," Cador bellows, his voice echoing off the stone. "Someone watching from the noble houses knows the real High Lord Hermance of Joyous Isle. You've done a reasonable job imitating him, but you're not actually him, are you? You killed him and took his spot."

Cador seemed so kind when I first met him. Now, he seems terrifying.

Elizabeth clutches my arm. When I look around, I see Tristan standing against the far wall with some of the other servants. He catches my eye, his jaw tight.

Niniane lurks in the shadows behind the stake, her face covered in a thin silver veil.

"So, why did you do it?" Cador turns, and his cloak swirls around him like smoke. He flicks his wrist again, and a faint shimmer of gold magic streams from his fingertips.

From his glittering magic, words begin to etch themselves into the arm of Hermance—or whoever he is. He shrieks again.

"Stop it," I mutter through clenched teeth.

Slowly, I watch the letters form one by one as he cries out, until I read the word *Fratricide*.

"Well, there you have it," Cador announces. "Your brother was the real High Lord Hermance, wasn't he?"

"Half brother! I found him with my wife," the man screams. "He promised her he'd make her queen if he won these trials. He's a half brother, that's it, but my father always loved him more."

Cador spins to face him. "You're a bastard, then? Do you even *have* a title?"

Tears stream down the man's face. "Some bastards get titles."

Niniane crosses into the center of the circle. "If you kill the person intended for these trials, you steal their halo. Even a commoner could murder their way in. But we will not tolerate liars and deceivers. Those who would cheat and steal their way onto the throne, those who would make a mockery of the noble houses, those who do not even have a title, cannot rule from the high throne. This is *treason!*"

A word I know all too well, one that always sends ice-cold needles dancing down my nape.

The word seems to have an effect on Goch, too, because his eyes blaze with flames.

When someone wields enough power, the definition of *treason* bends to their whims. Want someone's land? Treason. Worried they might threaten your power? Treason. Sick of your wife? She committed treason, too.

Cador turns to us, his eyes raking over our faces. "I suggest you all step back if you don't want to get singed."

At this, the prisoner starts screaming again, begging for mercy.

"Let's go," Elizabeth whispers. "I don't need to see another burning."

She loops her arm around mine, and we turn to walk toward the cart, trying not to look back. Behind us, the man's desperate cries are drowned out by Goch's roar.

The sound rumbles through my bones, setting my teeth on edge.

Heat singes the air behind us, a scorching blast that blows past, and the man's cries fall silent. The scent of charred flesh lingers in the air, and embers drift on the wind around us. Elizabeth is walking with her eyes closed, as if this will help her block out the sound, the smell.

Nausea twists in my stomach. If anyone learns the truth about me here, that same fate awaits me.

The sound of his shrieks still echoes in my skull, and smoke from his body coils into the night sky.

Traitor.

I taste the word like blood on my tongue.

As we pass the Aether Tower, I see the number on top has already changed. Now, the golden numbers read *179*.

* * *

IN MY ROOM, I sip a rose tea. After I rang the little bell for food, a young woman brought up a tray of tea and honey cakes for me, but I wasn't remotely hungry.

Even if I need to rest before tomorrow's trials, I feel as if I'll never fall asleep tonight. I can't forget the look of terror on that man's face. I imagine myself in his place. *Killer. Liar. Peasant.*

A quiet knock sounds on my door, making me jump. When I pull it open, Tristan is standing there, his green eyes flashing.

"Come on in," I say, my voice thin and weary. "Do you want some tea?"

He slips through the door, shutting it with a quiet click behind him.

"I think it's time to extract you," he says. "I won't let you die like that."

I drop into a chair and pour him some tea. Tea always makes the worst situations slightly better. "I will stay here until I get the grail or die trying. And as a bonus, maybe I'll kill some aristocrats while I'm at it. *Let us sit upon the ground, and tell sweet stories of the death of kings.*"

He scrubs a hand over his jaw. "You have a habit of bastardizing Shakespeare quotes. And what happens when they realize *you're* an imposter?"

I set my tea down, frowning. "Maybe I am supposed to be here. Why didn't the dragon burn me on the first night? Goch was supposed to kill the unworthy, but instead of killing me, he incinerated Lady Blythe."

Tristan shrugs. "He's a dragon, Syn. He doesn't follow rules or logic. Maybe he didn't like the color of Lady Blythe's dress. Maybe he thought she smelled like old onions. But if Niniane learns the truth, she'll have you killed."

I scowl, staring at the starry sky outside. "Niniane's priority is protecting the nobility. But the magic here is older than titles or lineages. Anyway, I have a benefit that man didn't. I was in the Undercroft from eleven, then

London. No one here could possibly recognize me or Alis."

"You could let down your guard. Your accent could slip."

"And what is the safe alternative? The halo returns the moment I leave. Of course I don't want to burn to death, but the Cloaked Ones will burn me, too. At least as long as I'm here, my death will serve a purpose. At least here, the danger also means I can save Vero."

"You have a point." He pulls out a chair across from me, sitting before the coiling steam of the tea. "Syn, you need to come with me to Avalon Tower. You need to meet our tarot reader and diviner in person."

"What's her name?"

"She's called Tana. If she approves of you, you'll get clearance, and then I can tell you what I'm actually doing here. You can work with us, which means you'll also have the help of Avalon Tower if we need to get you out."

Excitement flickers in my chest. I've always wanted to see Avalon Tower. "How do I get to Camelot?"

"In two nights, I'm scheduled to report back. If we move quickly enough, I can take you with me."

"After the first combat trial."

He nods. "And it won't be easy to get there."

"I don't suppose they can discreetly open a portal within the Veiled Court?"

"Not for this mission. Reporting to Avalon Tower is only half of my assignment. The other is transporting a dragon. And there's a battle raging nearby against the Iron Legion."

I blink. "Hang on. You know how to ride a dragon now?"

He raises an eyebrow. "I've learned to do a lot of things since I left Brocéliande."

And what have I learned in the past fifteen years? How to make tea for my colleagues so it's just the right shade of milky brown.

But maybe I gleaned important lessons from all those years of service among the English—how to be nice and polite and to smile sweetly, even when I want to scream. That mask of artifice is precisely what I'll need to survive here, because I need these people to think I'm one of them.

And when the time comes, I'm going to steal their most precious relic.

CHAPTER 20

I sit on my balcony, staring out as the sun rises and gold stains the pale blue clouds above us. Despite the beautiful morning, the air still smells of cinders and smoke. An inauspicious start to the day.

As if trying to cover up for the horror of last night, a servant slipped into my room a few minutes ago, leaving me with bouquets of flowers and a teapot—pretty diversions before we start hacking each other to death in a stone pit.

I'm already dressed for the trial, with a raven sigil embossed across my hardened leather doublet. I had the option of chain mail and a metal cuirass, but it felt too heavy and restrictive for fighting on foot. Being able to shift and dodge swiftly will offer me better protection than a heavy breastplate.

During the few hours I slept last night, I dreamt that I'd buried dragons' teeth in the soil, and an army of the dead rose from the ground to fight on my behalf. When I woke, it was just me again. And Rion's words keep rolling around in my head. *Tick-tock. Little machine.*

He sensed I've been trained by someone who demanded absolute perfection. Somehow, he knows I'm part human. It's as if he can pull me open like a book and read every secret inside. Is *he* a fucking telepath on top of the dread magic? Because if he heard me thinking about his hard, muscled chest and abs, I will make it my mission to slaughter him today.

A knock sounds on my door from across the room, and Tristan's muffled voice filters through the wood.

"Come in!" I shout.

Tristan crosses into the room, bearing a silver tray with my breakfast. As my head servant, some of these tasks fall to him. "Breakfast is served, Baroness Alis."

"I *do* hope it's hot. You know I flogged my last butler for serving me lukewarm tea."

"Careful what you promise, Baroness." He slides the tray onto the table and pulls off the silver dome.

Tristan and I joke about it, but he has actually been flogged with an iron-tipped whip. His back bears the scars. Once, he took a lashing for me. After weeks of brutal training, I'd vomited in the corner of the Undercroft. Weakness wasn't allowed, but Tristan told Auberon it was him. He took the whipping for me, and I will never forget it.

Before me are hot bread, scones, butter, strawberries, and a few pieces of cheese.

"Please eat with me, Tristan. How are the servants' quarters?" I ask.

He pours us both cups of hot tea. He's wearing a short-sleeved shirt today, and my gaze brushes over his tattoos, the beautifully rendered leaves that coil up his muscles.

"A maid named Arlene keeps climbing into my bed at night. She claims she's confused every time, then locks her legs around me."

I spread butter onto a piece of steaming bread. "I hope you don't get entangled in any romantic drama while we're here."

"Hard to avoid, sometimes. Perhaps it's my fate."

"Do you believe in fate, Tristan?"

He grabs a scone and leans back. The morning sun catches in his green eyes. "Fate is something people invent after they've already won. But the moment they lose, their destiny disappears."

"What do you mean?"

"Auberon ruled for fifteen hundred years. They called it destiny." His gaze flicks to mine, and a slow smile curls his lips. "Now that he's dead, they call him a usurper. It only takes one battle."

"One battle," I say. "Maybe my fate will change today."

He leans closer, his eyes locking on mine. "Don't die today."

"I will obviously be trying not to die."

"If you do, I won't let it go."

"You are fantasizing about saying *I told you so* to my corpse right now. But I'm not going to die. I'm still the same ruthless Syn I've always been."

He folds his arms, studying me with a cold appraisal. "Perhaps, yes. If you feel like your life is in danger, I think you'll eat your opponents alive. It's what happened with the real Alis, after all."

I swallow a sip of tea, and the steam coils around my face. "Took you long enough for that vote of confidence."

"I think you also have an advantage beyond your background in the Undercroft. You can charm the council. You're beautiful. A wildflower grown from the Waste Land—that's how they'll see you." He cocks his head, studying me. "Actually, I think we can play that up."

Tristan has never called me beautiful before, and that word brushes softly against me, slipping under my armor like a caress before I can stop it.

He rises from the chair and draws some of the lilies from the vase, then crosses behind me.

"What are you doing?"

"Fixing you."

I feel him twisting my dark curls behind me, then threading them with the flowers. "When did you learn to do women's hair, Tristan?"

"I've had reasons."

A lump rises in my throat. "Do you ever dream of your family?"

"Better not to think of those days."

The man never indulges my nosiness. It's infuriating. For example, I know he's broken the hearts of dozens of women, but I never get any of the details. And I think there's one woman who truly wrecked *him*, but he's never breathed a word about her—not even her name.

He steps around in front of me again, arms folded, appraising his work. "There. Better."

I slide my teacup onto the table. "Tristan, have you ever heard that perfection in swordsmanship can get in the way of real skill?"

"No, because that makes no sense."

I sigh, relieved that someone else thinks Rion was talking bollocks. "That's what I thought."

"Are you nervous?" he asks.

My heart flutters, but I don't want to admit to being nervous. "Not really. But I have a question for you. How do I make the noble houses love me so they'll spare my life if I surrender? You seem to think my beauty will charm them, but I imagine I need some social graces that I don't have."

He shrugs. "In my experience, many of the nobility are bored. Their lives are easy, but with little to entertain them. They don't work, obviously. They don't have real worries. They've run out of thrills. So, whatever you do today, Syn, make sure you don't bore them."

"Entertain them…" I roll the words over on my tongue.

Tristan casts an assessing gaze over me, his green eyes sweeping over my leather armor. "Are you ready, Baroness? It's time for you to kill some aristocrats."

CHAPTER 21

The route to the arena goes past the ashy dragon pit where a nameless man burned to death last night. Now, the only thing left of him is a charred skull half sunk in the cinders.

We walk onward toward the arena until we reach a stone tunnel. When we cross under its cool arches, we fall into silence. We're all unarmed for now. I have no idea if we'll get weapons today or just bash each other's heads in with our fists.

Elizabeth rubs her eyes. "How much sleep did we get? Three hours?"

"Not sure I even slept that much," I mutter.

A red-haired woman turns around to smile. She's dainty and pale, dressed in leather armor like mine. "Don't worry. Everything will be fine if we have faith in the gods.

I'm named after Rhiannon, the love goddess. She protects me."

I smile at her sympathetically. I'm afraid she won't last a minute in the ring.

As we walk, my gaze trails over the stone walls. Etchings are carved in the stone. In one of them, the crude figures seem to be tearing a crowned king to pieces.

Nice. If omens exist, that feels like a good one to me.

As we step into the arena, the sunlight dazzles me. There aren't many people here in person, only a few of the servants and squires sitting on curving stone benches. Tristan sits behind a row of veiled priestesses.

But the real crowd is observing through mirrors adorning the arena walls. Through those looking glasses, the nobles will watch our every move today and decide our fates.

The morning light burns brightly off their surfaces, then shimmers, showing me all the nobility watching us in their jewel-studded silks. I can hear them, too, murmuring faintly. Talking about us.

Lord Cador emerges from another entrance, riding a horse and dressed in armor. His burgundy hair hangs loose over silver chain mail.

Niniane sits on a raised stone dais, dressed in a blue gown and a crown of oak blossoms, as remote and resplendent as the moon. Behind her are three Cloaked Ones, their faces shadowed by dark cowls. I'm not even clear if they *have* faces because I've never seen them. Jeweled cinctures hang around their waists, each set with stones shaped like eggs. Such strange creatures. They're relics of the old days, guardians of rites most Fey have forgotten. I've never heard them speak, and I don't know if they can.

A carnyx sounds, the horn echoing across the stone and sending a chill down my spine.

Lord Cador pulls his horse to a halt. "Subjects of Brocéliande, sons and daughters of our noble families. Today, by the will of the gods, we bring you the first trial of the Veiled Court. Those who die today will die nobly as warriors of the great houses. Today, on the holiday of Tanos, we will feed the earth with blood sacrifice and renew life with an offering to the gods. When the trial ends, the survivors will celebrate with a festival. But we will also choose a handful of the weakest to send home."

My fingers start to shake a little, and I curl them into fists. I can't go home yet—not without the grail.

"In the great and ancient tradition of the Veiled Court," Cador continues, "the noble houses will choose two lead warriors for each round, and those fighters will in turn select three opponents to face."

Elizabeth leans in to whisper, "Choose their *opponents*? Why not their allies?"

I swallow hard. Auberon read from the *exact* same playbook.

"They'll say it's a testament to bravery, to see who chooses the strongest opponents," I whisper back, "but the real reason is to purge the weak fastest. Everyone always chooses the people they can kill the most easily."

"Fuck," she mutters under her breath.

Cador nudges his horse closer. "When another fighter defeats you, they can either kill you or give you a chance to surrender. When all fighters on a team have surrendered or died, the round is over. Now, if you surrender, the noble houses can demand your execution or choose mercy."

I breathe slowly, trying to maintain a sense of calm. I glance up at Elizabeth; her expression is tense.

Cador looks overhead. A dark wren circles above him, casting its shadows in a swooping arc over the stone. The bird carries something in his little talons. He dips down and drops the little piece of paper. It flutters into Cador's hand, and he unrolls it.

"The noble houses have chosen their first two fighters! The two lead fighters are Countess Igraine and Duke Mabon, both of Tintagol!"

Igraine smiles and stalks to the center of the arena. She's wearing chain mail with a breastplate emblazoned with her golden water serpent sigil.

Mabon actually looks uncharacteristically sober today. He stands tall as he faces her, his sigil—a fiery salamander —gleaming on his breastplate.

Still astride his horse, Cador calls Igraine forward. When she sidles up next to his stallion, he turns to face the mirrors.

"Lady Igraine. Tell our noble houses why you would make a good queen." Cador's voice booms across the arena.

She straightens, her hair shining like spun gold in the sunlight. "Once, I ruled as High Lady of the Court of Tintagol." Her accent drips with money. "My husband, High Lord Gorlois, was a strong ruler until a duke from another land took over our island. As they laid siege to our castle and rammed our gates, their leader tricked me into his bed. The filthy swine glamoured himself to look like Gorlois. Little did I know my husband was already dead, shot through the eye with an arrow outside the castle gates."

Through the mirrors, I can see the noble houses leaning closer, eating up the story.

"The invaders murdered my husband, the high lord," she continues. "They installed their own duke. And their army included filthy, bestial demi-Fey. But even that wasn't enough. Our new ruler tried to force me to marry him. When I objected, he threw me into a dungeon. I lost my husband, my title, and everything I cared about. I starved in a prison cell, but I grew strong, nursing my hatred for the demi-Fey into magic. No one will protect you like I will. I don't want to simply fend the enemy off at the gates. I want to destroy the so-called mortal *civiliza-tion* that threatens us."

She raises her fist into the air, and the noble houses clap on the other side of the looking glasses.

My eyebrows flick up. I didn't know this history.

Cador nods at her, and the smile on his face looks proud. "You are, as you said, from Tintagol, far from Brocéliande and our capital city. Since our noble houses have not yet made your acquaintance, what would you like them to know about you?"

She lifts her chin. "I'd like them to know that I have the utmost respect for their expertise. As queen, I would make the head of each noble house part of my council of advisors. I'd also confer vast new lands and titles onto those who pledge loyalty to me."

And here we go. That land will come straight from the peasants. The Melian Forest, the communal farmlands—all this will be split up among the nobility. The commoners will be back to renting from them and handing over half their crops.

I'm sure it's *exactly* what the nobility wants to hear. And what would happen to Vero? Turfed out of her cottage, forced to pay rent for the land she lived on for free.

I glance at Mabon to see how he's reacting. And what I read on his face is a look of utter and complete adoration. He's in *love* with Igraine.

This should be interesting.

Igraine saunters back to her place in the arena, her expression glowing. She's pleased with herself, and I'm sure the noble houses are lapping it up.

Mabon is up next, and he stalks toward the mirrors

with an uncharacteristic steadiness. Cador asks him about his past.

"Well, I've lived in Tintagol in recent years, but I'm from Brocéliande originally, of course. I know many of these faces on the other side of the mirrors. Studied with them, of course. Learned to ride with them. Hello, Lord Enion! Do you remember the parties we threw? Bit of gambling. Bit of fun. The commoners would fight each other, you see, to the death. And we'd place bets...well, much like we will fight today. And I do hope you all will be betting on me this morning..." He casts a quick glance back at Igraine. "Though I fear defeating such a beautiful woman would be like carving out my own heart."

It's one of the first things he's said that seems genuine.

"Thank you, Duke Mabon." Cador turns back to us. "Lady Igraine, choose your first opponent."

Igraine stalks over to the waiting contenders and walks slowly past us, her heels clacking on the stone. Casting her gaze up and down our bodies, she's examining us like we're livestock.

When she reaches me, she pauses. Her amber gaze sweeps down my body, and she cocks her head.

Truthfully, I'd rather take my chances with her than with Rion.

"Go on, then," I whisper. "I know you want to pick me."

Her eyes flick up to mine, the pale gold piercing me. "No, I don't think so. Not if you want me to."

Mabon passes me over, too, choosing Rhiannon, the

little red-haired woman with her faith in the gods. Even now, her faith seems to be holding strong, and her faint smile is serene. But I don't think she has any idea what's in store for her today, or how much blood will flow across these stones before the day is done.

And just as I suspected, each of them chooses the frailest-looking fighters to kill.

They're culling the weak.

I find a space in front of Tristan on a cold marble bench. Not too close, though. In public, I can't seem too familiar with him.

I catch his eye, and he holds my gaze longer than he should. When I turn around, he gives my shoulder a short, light squeeze for reassurance.

Cador's horse walks slowly across the arena before the contenders, the hooves echoing off the stones. Cador's eyes rake over the fighters. "Igraine's team, you will now move to the east side of the arena. Mabon's, to the west."

The fighters start to move, stalking to the arena's edges.

"To start, you won't have weapons," Cador calls out. "Our dragon, Goch, will soar overhead, and he will drop the weapons from the skies. You may not run for them until you hear the carnyx sound. Then, sprint to choose your sword. But you should be warned: there won't be enough for everyone."

I'm not even in this fight, and my heart is thudding like a war drum. The fighters settle in on each side, staring at each other across a pit that will run with blood by the end of the day.

Slowly, a dark, sweeping shadow swoops over the arena, making my blood go cold. When I glance up, I see Goch flying above us, gripping a wooden crate in his teeth. A cold breeze whips at us.

The dragon arcs in a circle a few times, casting the arena in darkness. He lets out a low, ominous roar that makes the stones quake around me, the sound rumbling through my gut. With one final arc, he releases the crate from his mouth, and the wood smashes into pieces on the stones. The contenders look tense, hunched over and ready to sprint, fingers twitching. Igraine leans over, her eyes gleaming as she looks at the weapons.

At last, the carnyx sounds—a deep howl that echoes off the stone, ringing in my skull like a bell.

They race, sprinting into the center. Igraine grabs a sword—Mabon, too. Only Rhiannon misses the chance to seize one.

With everyone else armed, she backs away, lifting her face to the skies like she's praying.

By the looks of it, Igraine plans to pick her off first.

Mabon is dueling with two of the men on Igraine's team. His swings are powerful and deadly. One of his opponents tries to dart forward and stab him, and Mabon easily parries it, then smashes the man's nose with the pommel of his sword. A snarling grin is etched on his face.

While the wind whips at her golden hair, Igraine stalks toward Rhiannon, her whiskey-gold eyes narrowing on her prey. For such a lithe, willowy woman, she looks terrifying, her body coiled tightly like a lioness about to strike.

The pious redhead still smiles up at the sky, waiting for her salvation. The morning sun washes her face in honey. She holds her hands out, palms up, like she's receiving a blessing.

As Igraine prowls closer, her fingers flex on the sword.

Rhiannon's eyes open, and her smile falters. She takes a step back, then another. Finally, her face pales, and her jaw drops.

My fingers gripping the marble seats, I fight the urge to leap in to help Rhiannon.

My heart races as Igraine lunges. With one clean, devastating strike, she cleaves the woman's head in two. Blood splashes against the stone.

Igraine pivots without a second look to stalk her next victim.

I close my eyes, fighting rising nausea. What is the *point* of all this?

I want to scream my outrage at the fucking mirrors.

But I suppose I know what it is, beyond the spectacle

and the primal celebration of brutality. Igraine helped me understand. Fewer aristocrats means fewer to share the plundered lands.

When I open my eyes again, I see Igraine's blade carve through a man's hardened leather armor like it's butter. She splits his chest and stomach open, and I'm starting to suspect her magic power might involve otherworldly strength.

Claret runs down the serpent embossed on her cuirass, bright as poppies. The scent of blood fills the air, turning my stomach. Smoothly, Igraine pivots to find her next kill.

On the other side of the arena, Mabon swings his sword in an arc, spraying blood. His opponent's head topples to the ground, his body collapsing just a second later.

Mabon turns around, surveying the killing ground.

Muttering spreads through the crowd, and I realize what attracted their attention.

Rhiannon is moving. It seems impossible—her skull is split, her face cleaved in two. And yet, as I gawk, she lurches to her knees, then to her feet. Perhaps I have misjudged her. Her prayers must have been answered, because this is a miracle.

She lunges forward in strange, jerky movements and leaps into the air, landing on one of Igraine's teammates. With a wild snarl, she bites his throat, tearing it. The man gurgles, collapsing. Igraine picks up his sword and whirls around.

Then, from the corner of my eye, I notice more movement.

The beheaded body. That, too, rises to its feet.

"Oh, my gods," someone moans from behind me.

The headless body takes a stumbling step forward, then another, blood streaking from the open wound on its neck. Next to the headless swordsman, his decapitated head jabbers. The head's mouth snaps open and shut, as if trying to bite an unseen foe.

Another dead body rises and lunges at one of the few living contestants, skewering him.

The dead are rising to fight again.

I can feel a magic thrum all over the arena. It's a dark, cold magic, and it's all wrong. I can feel the rot crawling through the air around us.

Necromancy.

Looking around the arena, I realize that Mabon isn't moving. His eyes have turned dark as coal, black holes that sweep over the carnage around him. Power radiates from him, warping the space around him.

Gods, he cannot be king.

Igraine is after another woman, this one clad in hardened leather like mine. As she stalks closer, the woman lifts her sword awkwardly. It's clear to me she's never trained a day in her life.

In the next moment, she falls to her knees.

"I surrender!" she shouts.

Igraine doesn't hear her. Or perhaps she pretends

not to.

One step forward—one swing—and half the woman's head is gone. Blood streams over the stones, pooling in rivulets in the cracks.

But already, the dead woman's body is jerking and moving as it rises again. She's no longer inexperienced. Now, she's a skilled fighter.

Mabon is in control.

Igraine jumps back and looks around her. All but her and Mabon are dead. But most of the contestants are still moving, circling her. Just to her left, an amputated arm is crawling toward her.

I shudder and look at the mirrors. Surely the nobles are horrified by what they are witnessing.

But all I see are fascinated smiles.

I should have known better. Nobles are drawn to power. And Mabon's is fucking immense.

"Surrender!" Mabon calls out. "My dearest friend, Countess Igraine."

She glowers at him. He could easily kill her now, but he's hesitating.

He stands safely beyond his army of the dead and spreads his arms wide. "Come now, Igraine, we can finish this. Surrender."

The dead just watch her, their eyes vacant.

And then Igraine lunges forward. She rolls on the ground and lops the feet off Rhiannon's corpse. The body collapses to the dirt, its arms grasping at Igraine, but she's long gone. By the time the dead manage to react, Igraine has leapt to her feet and crossed the distance to Mabon. She moves with an impossible speed.

She strikes, and he parries. Their swords clash with sharp rings, fast and powerful. Mabon's lip curls back from his teeth, and he snarls. But he's giving ground, forced into retreat by Igraine's relentless assault.

The dead are coming to his assistance, but their movements are slow, clumsy. Distracted, Mabon can't control his minions properly.

He thrusts at her, and she parries, then chops him from above. He blocks her swing, and his sword actually *dents* under her powerful strike.

One of the dead reaches her from behind, and she whirls, slicing off his sword-wielding arm. With another swing, she takes off one of his legs. She's truly breathtaking.

She darts sideways, keeping the rest of the dead as far from her as possible.

Mabon tries to use the distraction and strike at her, but as fast as he is, Igraine is faster. This time, she blocks his swing and cuts his arm. The point of her sword rises to his neck.

With a broken cry, he lets go of his sword and raises his hands into the air. Red-faced, he screams, "I surrender!"

All around Igraine, the dead topple to the ground. The victorious woman looks at Mabon, her face blank.

Slowly, after a minute, she turns to smile sweetly at the mirrors.

"Shall I let him live?" she asks the nobles. "I quite like him, you know. He *is* a jolly good friend."

Lord Cador guides his mount to the center of the bloodstained arena.

"We await now the verdict of the noble houses!"

After a few moments, a wren circles over his head. The bird swoops down, dropping two pieces of curled parchment into his hands.

Standing on the gore-spattered stones, he unrolls the first. "Mercy for Duke Mabon! The noble houses wish you to live."

Still on his knees, Mabon lets out a choked sound. I think he's trying to suppress a sob. He blinks furiously, gasping for breath. He takes a step back from Igraine's sword, lifts his eyes to the skies, and lets out a half-strangled moan.

Servants hurry to drag the bodies and the discarded weapons away, leaving crimson streaks in their wake. I try not to look at Rhiannon's abused body as it slides over the flagstones.

When I look at the others on the stone seats around me, I find a sea of ashen faces.

I imagine many of them are wondering if this is worth it, even for the crown.

Only Igraine appears delighted, radiating joy. As she crosses out of the arena, she smiles and waves to the nobles in the mirrors like a queen waving to her subjects. Blood spatters her hair and face.

Lord Cador turns his horse to the stands and unrolls the next piece of parchment. "The noble houses have chosen again. The two lead fighters are High Lord Rion du Lac and Sir Dagonet of the island of Ys."

Rion stalks to the center of the arena. He isn't even *wearing* armor. He's wearing a black tunic, his hair pulled back for the fight. I suppose he's arrogant enough to think he doesn't need armor.

The two enormous, muscular men—Dagonet and Rion—stand on either side of Lord Cador.

Dagonet wears leather, and his dragon banner is sewn into the front. He looks almost bored, with his arms crossed over his chest. His expression suggests he's just waiting for this all to be over so he can move on to something more interesting.

Cador levels his gaze on us. "We will not drop a crate this time. Rather, we will place weapons in the center, and you will run for them when you hear the carnyx. But this time, there will be fewer weapons."

I breathe in sharply. I wonder if they're going to keep making it harder with each round.

From his horse, Cador looks down at the two men. "Now, it's time for the lead fighters to choose their opponents. If Rion calls your name, you join Dagonet's side. If Dagonet chooses you, join Rion. Sir Dagonet, you may begin."

Dagonet's gaze slides over those of us on the stone benches. He stops scanning when he reaches a man who sits with a cane. "You," he barks.

With his dark curls and lace collar, the man doesn't look like a fighter. He's holding a stack of books under one arm, the other hand gripping his cane—though I think it's more for style than necessity. With his red cheeks and delicate curls, he looks like he could be a poetry student. He's quite clearly more suited to a library than an arena.

"Lord Aneirin of Brocéliande!" Cador calls out. "From Castle Catreath."

Aneirin looks startled, as if he thought he might somehow escape the carnage today. But under his blue cloak, he wears a breastplate of armor. A unicorn sigil adorns the front.

Reluctantly, he hands the books to a woman sitting next to him. "Right. Right. Please take good care of these. *Please*. They're rare."

Taking his cane with him, he crosses to stand by Rion's side.

The Ruthless Knight doesn't even bother to glance at his new ally. His ice-cold gaze scans the crowd of seated contestants, looking for anyone he thinks would make an easy kill.

And when that glacial gaze lands on me, I already know. Of course it would be me. He's already decided I'm a weak link here. He thinks I'm mortal and mechanical, and that I don't belong here at all.

Tick-tock.

"Baroness Alis of Listenoise." His voice echoes off the stones, and my blood roars in my ears.

Within the next fifteen minutes, Rion du Lac will be trying to kill me.

CHAPTER 23

As I leave the bench and move toward Dagonet, I breathe in, slow and deep. No matter what happens, I must keep my focus, and I can't panic.

Each team will choose fighters in turn—four to a side. When the horn sounds, we'll run for the weapons. Cador already announced that there will be fewer swords this time, so my first task is simply to focus on getting one in my hand.

My pulse hammers as I walk, trying to block out the scarlet streaks that gleam against the limestone. My gaze trails over the shattered pieces of the crate strewn over the rocks. At least they dragged the bodies away.

As I take my spot next to Sir Dagonet, I turn to look up at him. His black hair gleams like onyx in the morning light, and an iron scar runs down one side of his cheek.

"Countess Elizabeth!" He barks the name of his next opponent.

Fuck.

My throat goes dry as Elizabeth rises from her stone seat to take her spot next to Rion.

One of us will be on the losing side today, but I can't let myself get distracted by that.

Auberon's voice still echoes in my skull: *Sever your emotional ties. Compassion for an enemy is a weakness.* He taught us to freeze our own hearts, to trade empathy for calculation. *Cold logic is survival.*

The king taught us not to fear death. In his own way, he made us ready for it. Sometimes, we almost welcomed it. That's why he chose us from the most ragged enclaves of Brocéliande. He dragged us out of the slums because he knew a simple truth: those with nothing left to lose are the most terrifying of all. We'd kill and die for the chance to become knights, because what else was there?

I exhale and watch Rion pick his next victim: a tall, powerfully built viscount named Bedivere, his forearms thickly corded with muscle. No idea why Rion chose him, considering he looks like one of the stronger fighters. Maybe he's going for the *testament to bravery* angle.

As Bedivere crosses closer, he eyes me with open disdain. Even my own teammates don't seem to be impressed with me.

I close my eyes and picture myself rushing for the weapons; I imagine my hand closing on a sword hilt. My goals are simple: stay calm, move quickly, survive long enough to find the grail.

Dagonet calls out the last one for their side—this one a man named Mark. Immediately, I can see why Sir Dagonet chose him. Mark appears to be completely hammered, and he staggers toward Rion with a bottle of mead in his hand. He's literally still drinking it as he stumbles into the arena. Perhaps his nerves got the better of him this morning.

Rion's last choice is a seasoned, grizzled, red-haired knight named Sir Morholt, who looks like he could snap a smaller man in half.

Apparently, Rion isn't afraid of anything.

My thoughts churn wildly as I try to remember all my training. I close my eyes, breathing slowly, and Cador starts pulling over fighters to speak to the mirrors.

Rion is first, and he prowls to the mirrors with an easy half smile.

"High Lord Rion du Lac," Cador calls out. "Can you tell our noble houses why you would make a worthy king?"

Rion gives a slow, unbothered shrug. "My sword will speak for me today, and my blade will write my enemies' epitaphs."

He doesn't wait for another question—he simply stalks away with unhurried grace.

Cador pulls the contenders aside, one by one. Mark slurs his way through his answers, and I have no idea what he's saying.

I glance at the bookish man called Aneirin and find him gripping the top of his cane so tightly, his knuckles have gone white. He seems like he's going to be sick. When I look at Elizabeth, she's giving me an apologetic smile that seems more like a grimace.

Beside Rion, they all look easy to kill.

Dagonet turns to me, a faint smile curling his lips. "Don't worry, little one. No one here will touch us."

My eyebrows rise. "What makes you so certain of that?"

"I was imprisoned for years," he says gruffly. "And do you know why?"

"Did you kill someone?"

"I killed many. I was born on Ys with a forbidden magic—the Song of the Morrigan."

My breath catches. "You have the Song?" I whisper.

He nods. "I do."

With the Song, a man can break minds and bodies as easily as breathing. It's a godlike speed and strength, a whirlwind of violence. The other side doesn't stand a chance.

I breathe out a long sigh of relief. "Thank the gods."

Faintly, I can almost hear the Song emanating from him, a haunting melody that hums along his skin. I *crave* it, like I want to rip him open and steal the missing part of myself.

I scan the iron scars on his skin. I know the marks of

royal interrogations—I bear some of them on my waist and thighs, places that are hidden.

And on more than one occasion, I've inflicted them.

Not the worst thing I've ever done, but close. The absolute *worst* thing I've ever done? Well, I believe that's why I no longer have the Song.

Sadness pools in my mind, and I shove it away so I can ready myself. I need to stay in the moment.

Right now, Elizabeth is mid-interview.

"I can share a light with the world, I think." She smiles at the mirrors. "Some people want to put it out, but I think it's my time to shine. I crave adventure."

I point to her and lean closer to Dagonet. "Can you let her live? Let the crowd decide. Please. She's no threat."

He grunts noncommittally.

I regret even asking.

Empty your mind, Auberon says in my head.

I shouldn't be thinking about anything other than survival right now.

I realize Elizabeth has finished now, and Cador's gaze lands on me.

From his horse, he declares, "Baroness Alis. As a lady from the Waste Land, our ruling families have not yet had the honor of getting to know you." He beckons me toward the mirrors. "Will you tell them, Alis, what would make you a good monarch?"

Slowly, I walk closer. I don't like being the center of

attention, and everything feels wrong as I walk. I feel awkward, like I don't know what to do with my hands.

As I reach the mirrors, I stare into them. There I see the nobility, glittering and still like a king's tomb. To them, these are windows to a brutal game, one they can watch from the safety of a distant palace.

As I search their faces, I read hostility and disdain. No one is impressed by a baroness from the Waste Land. As far as the Brocéliande nobility are concerned, I might as well have crawled from a sewage pit.

Gods, I'd rather just get to the killing than this. My hands are shaking, and I fold them together to make them still. My mouth is dry, and I realize with a growing horror that I'm staying silent for an awkwardly long time, and that Cador asked me a question he's waiting for me to answer.

"Alis?" Cador prompts. "Are you all right?"

Tristan said to entertain them. What do people care about, besides wealth and power? They're not just bored, I think. They're lonely. They're in isolated palaces, probably married to people they hate because it got them the most land.

I close my eyes for a moment, and a haunting, horrifying phrase floats through my mind: *What would Vicky do?*

Her words drift through my brain.

If you hadn't noticed, everything around is fucking terrible these days. People want an escape. They want fantasy. They want—

I clear my throat. "Romance!" A single word, inelegantly blurted before I can stop it.

Cador looks startled, like I've just cursed him.

I clear my throat and try again, more softly. I force myself to smile, like I imagine Vicky would. "I'm hoping to find love here. After all, a kingdom is strongest when led by a sacred union between two people, isn't it? That's what I learned from the Rhiannon Garden as I spent time there. I found inspiration among the roses. In the Golden Age, the kings and queens found fated mates and formed a sovereignty bond that brought life to the land. Through a monarch's love, the land thrived. I believe Brocéliande will thrive when ruled by a queen *and* a king, together. And of course, Lord Cador, I am hoping to find love for myself."

With a smile, I lie through my fucking teeth. Silence follows for two, three breaths.

Then I hear cheers coming from the other side of the mirrors.

Thank the *gods*.

I smile, my mood already brightening. Maybe Vicky is a fucking genius. People really do just want to be entertained.

I glance at Tristan, and he nods, looking impressed. Whether it's from the speech I just gave or the allies on my side, he looks more relaxed now.

Exhaling slowly, I return to my place in the center of the arena and line up with the others on my side.

Dagonet gives me a curt nod, which I take as a sign that he was impressed.

Cador calls Aneirin forth to speak before the mirrors. He's telling them that his father and uncle were addicted to gambling, and they bankrupted his family. I can't imagine this is a winning strategy with the nobles.

As each person has their moment to speak, I feel as if time is moving too rapidly, like I'm hurtling toward something inexorable and disastrous.

But I remind myself again and again that Dagonet has the Song.

What is there to fear?

When the interviews have finished, Cador rides in again. A servant gives him two swords, and he ambles back into the center of the killing pit, a sword in each hand. He drops them among the pieces of shattered wood from the crate. "You will compete for these *two* weapons in this round," Cador declares. "May the gods grant you strength."

Only two? You've got to be kidding me.

As Cador's horse walks in a circle around the swords, Cador's voice booms over the arena: "Take your places now. Rion's team to the east, and Dagonet's to the west."

I look down at the stones as I move into position. The blood is pounding in my head, but I'm here for Vero. If I survive today, I have a chance of curing her at last.

I stand against the western side of the arena.

"Wait until the carnyx sounds!" Cador shouts.

My throat tightens as I look at Elizabeth opposite me, all the way across the gore-streaked swords and the broken crate. The silence yawns between us. I can tell she's even more nervous than I am. Aneirin, the book lover, clutches his cane to his chest like it's a treasured baby.

Then, my gaze slides to Rion, and I find his glacial eyes locked on me. Power coils around him, but his body is motionless as the arena's cold marble. He stands with an eerie, predatory stillness.

Each one of my muscles goes tense, and I can hear my own heartbeat, my blood roaring.

Steady, Syn. I remind myself to mark the angle of every opponent's attack. Each of them will telegraph a pattern. Time it right, and I can break the pattern.

My heart slams against my ribs, no matter how strongly I will it to be quiet. *Get a hold of yourself,* Auberon snarls.

At last, the carnyx sounds, and its knell reverberates through my bones.

$\mathscr{I}$ sprint for the two swords, pumping my arms hard. Adrenaline snaps through my nerve endings, spurring me on, and I feel as if I'm running as fast as the wind.

Ahead, Dagonet and Rion reach the swords just before me, swooping in to snatch them from the stone.

But that's what I expected, frankly. I was running for the sharpest piece of wood. I scan the ground and find a piece that's roughly my arm's length.

Once I've got my weapon, I turn to see Dagonet's sword clashing with Rion's, sparking in the light. Dagonet's Song floats on the wind, and I can hear the haunting melody. He's fighting ferociously, a blur of metal and fury. Around them, the weakest contenders wait, hoping for a weapon before we join the fray.

I move closer to Rion because I want to grab his sword

when he dies. I'm circling him like a vulture waiting to pick the carrion clean. A few paces away, Dagonet's blade sings as it sweeps through the air, his attacks furious. Thank the gods he's on my side today.

Really, I'm stunned that Rion has been holding his own against Dagonet this long.

But as I start to move closer, the skies darken overhead, and a chill ripples through the air. Wind sweeps over us, and the morning sky turns to dusk. In the gloom, the Ruthless Knight glows like a star, his silver hair gleaming.

My breath catches at the unearthly, sublime sight of him.

This is the full force of his dread magic, and it's much more powerful than the little demonstration I saw with Goch. He's not even targeting me, and terror runs over my skin like ice water.

Dagonet lowers his sword. He's not fighting anymore. Instead, he's retreating, his eyes wild and panicked.

Rion stalks toward him, closing the short distance between them, his footfalls reverberating over the stones like war drums.

Rion is a beautiful, living nightmare.

Instinctively, I take a step back. I should be hovering around them, waiting to snatch a dropped weapon, but I don't want Rion's attention on me for even a second.

Even now, his magic is sending a shiver of dread skittering down my spine. It's almost like a primal power from the old days, before the most powerful Fey magic withered from the world.

Rion possesses the graceful, careless cruelty of a god. It doesn't matter how beautiful he looks. He stalks the arena like death itself.

Drunken Mark, meanwhile, has no fear. Maybe his mead swilling really was part of a master plan to shield his thoughts from Rion's magic. Now, he's edging closer to the pair, coming in from the right.

He's also waiting for a fallen sword like a circling hawk.

As Dagonet staggers away from Rion, he begins to scream—holding his head, stumbling back. Shrieking like a child. Then he falls to his knees before Rion. He's still holding his sword, but loosely, awkwardly, like he's forgotten what it's for.

My breath goes still as I watch Rion close the distance between them. The Ruthless Knight towers over Dagonet, staring down at him, and the darkest recesses of my mind are screaming at me that I'm looking at a monster.

Finally, Dagonet seems to remember his sword, and he swings for Rion. But it's half-hearted, weak, and Rion blocks it easily.

Then, without waiting for Dagonet to yield, Rion carves his blade through Dagonet's neck, severing his head.

Sir Dagonet's headless body crumples to the ground,

and his blood streams across the flagstones. My stomach turns. I *must* shield my thoughts from Rion or it's all over.

From the other side of the mirror, the noble houses roar with excitement. Rion was right. He didn't need to give a speech—his skill in the arena is all the entertainment they need.

It hasn't even been ten seconds, and our strongest fighter lies headless on the ground.

Fucking focus, Syn.

I sprint straight toward Dagonet's fallen sword, but Mark is much nearer. He snatches it from the bloodied stones, then staggers closer to me. He wears a wild, ecstatic grin. When he swings for me with his sword, I use my wooden plank to block his attack, and his blade lodges in the oak. Before he gets the chance to yank his blade out, I twist the wood, trying to wrench the blade from his grasp. In response, he kicks me in the stomach. I fall hard, my head smacking the ground. Pain blooms through my skull like blood spilling through water.

Mark rips his blade free.

Thankfully, I'm still gripping my piece of wood, the splinters biting into my palm.

Pain is a gift. Auberon's voice rings in my thoughts. *A reminder of what's at stake.*

I lift my head to see Mark raising his sword above me, ready to bring it down on my head this time, but I roll out of the way. He lunges, but he's off-balance.

I kick out at his legs, toppling him. He falls backward

—hard. His head cracks on the stone. Still, he doesn't seem to feel it, because he bursts into laughter.

I jump back to my feet to face him. Apparently, the mead has dulled his sense of pain—he's already up again, lurching for me as blood drips down the back of his head.

I brace and grip the wood in my hand, holding it low. Timing is *everything*. And the moment Mark's a few feet away, I dart forward, *fast*.

With a lightning-quick strike, I jam the sharp piece of wood into his eye socket. He screams, and his sword clatters to the ground.

I reach down for it, but one of my own teammates snatches it from the stones first.

Fucker.

Mark slumps forward onto me, and I kick him in the chest, pulling my wooden stake from his brain, since it's all I've got.

As I catch my breath, I scan the rest of the arena.

Elizabeth is *fleeing* as fast as she can from my teammate with the sword.

My fingers tighten on my piece of wood.

As I watch her, she pivots, her eyes glowing bright with flames. Her lips curl back from her teeth, and she unleashes a shriek. A blinding white light bursts from her body, searing with intensity. I cover my eyes, my retinas burned.

When I open them again, I can hardly see a thing. Stars dance in my vision. Vaguely, I can make out shadows around me, amorphous forms. I blink, trying to clear my eyes, my heart slamming hard. I have no idea who has the sword now or where they might be. It's like I just stared directly into the sun.

I listen carefully, hoping to hear footfalls if someone is coming for me. The metallic scent of blood curls into the air around me, making my breath shallow.

When at last I can see again, the Ruthless Knight is stalking across the arena, sword in hand—a beast stalking his prey. But he's not coming for me. He's hunting Morholt, the man who snatched the sword from me.

Aneirin, the book lover, is rather unexpectedly unleashing tendrils of shadow magic from the end of his cane. They twist around my teammate, Bedivere. Threads of darkness suffocate him like a coiling serpent.

I focus on the two men with the swords. I still need to get my hands on one of them. Rion is after Morholt, who is tripping over his own feet to get away. He's not even trying to use the sword, the useless fucker.

Long ago, Auberon taught me to shield my mind, envisioning a cloud billowing in my skull. A veil in my thoughts. I practiced it, over and over, imagining a cloud in my head to block my thoughts from telepaths.

This time, I'll be ready. I start to gather the clouds.

Rion drives his blade through Morholt's ribs from behind, then draws it out again. Blood pours onto the stones.

I race for the fallen sword, sprinting across the arena

toward Morholt's body, my feet pounding hard. My fingers close around the metal hilt.

A pulse of magic skims over my skin, and I look up to face Rion. Frigid silver eyes pierce me, and a wicked smile curls his lips. He takes a slow, predatory step closer, gaze locked on me.

No one lies to me for long.

I feel his magic snaking into my thoughts, and I'm not sure my mental shield is strong enough.

Dread is making my heart race. He's a living nightmare, and I can no longer think clearly. I can't breathe.

Panic is death—and death has come for me today.

CHAPTER 25

My blood turns to ice as dark certainty takes hold of my mind. I'm going to die right here on the stones, and I'll never get the grail for Vero. There will never be a point to anything I've done.

The raw, primal terror makes it hard to think. Fear will be my doom, and I'm already dead—

I glance at the others he killed, their eyes gaping up at the clouds. Jaws open. If there is no point to my life, I should never have been born.

Overhead, the skies darken once more, and cold chills the air.

I can't think clearly through the roar of panic in my skull. Is that Rion's power, or am I predicting my own death because it's going to happen? Is this magic or understanding?

My thoughts flit with images from my past that make my stomach swoop.

Auberon is bringing prisoners into the Undercroft. He hands me a sword...

The image shifts. Now, Tristan's hands are tied to a post, and Auberon has forced another cadet to whip him...

Is it me?

And then the worst memory—

Two people kneel, arms tied, sacks over their heads...

I force the visions away. I'm shaking now, ready to vomit.

I *must* shield my thoughts from him. I try to summon it once more, a cloud in my mind, just like Auberon taught me. Gritting my teeth, I imagine the clouds in my skull like the ones from this morning: blue, with a golden tinge from the morning light.

Master your fear, Auberon's voice whispers. *Perfect your stance. Shoulders down. Weight forward. Let him come to you. No mercy. No hesitation.*

I manage to gather a fog in my skull, dulling his magic. I slow my breathing and tighten my grip on the hilt of my sword. He's left-handed, and I adjust my mental calculations to fight him.

Rion prowls closer, his icy gaze sharp as a blade. Another ripple of fear dances down my spine, but I block out the full force of his power.

He moves first, a little test. His blade glides slowly

through the air—slow enough for me to block. Our swords meet, but there's not much force to it.

I step and shift, blocking his next attack. He strikes again, faster, and I dodge his blade.

His eyes sharpen on me, head cocking with curiosity.

"You're used to fighting people who are mindless with fear, aren't you? Just staggering dullards."

I'm starting to think a little more clearly, and I track his patterns—the way his shoulder drops slightly before he lunges. The tick in his jawline before he feints. All those years of repetition with Auberon still live with me, marked on me like tattoos.

Our swords clash again, and a faint smile curls his lips. He's enjoying himself, obviously. And when he's actually trying, he's incredibly fucking skilled. I'm retreating a bit now, and he's pressing me with his attacks. Closing the space between us, pushing me back. Even without his magic, he can easily master a fight.

As he presses in harder, each clash rings through my bones like a funeral bell. Suddenly, I feel a kinship with that pell I've been battering, because now I'm the stupid piece of coffin wood taking a beating. And there it is again—the note of panic wending through my thoughts like a high-pitched scream.

Block it out, Syn.

Panic is a drug that poisons rational thought.

Now, my breath is shallow. My heart is pounding. I keep thinking of Dagonet, and the way Rion decapitated him within moments. Even if I had the Song, I don't know if it would protect me from Rion.

The only thing keeping me alive is the threadbare shield in my mind, barely holding itself together. And beneath that shield, it's Vero. She's the reason I have to get through this.

Maybe I can break his rhythm. He favors his left side, I think.

I swing for him in a fast arc, and he ducks. He strikes back, and his blade cuts through the air. Immediately, I dodge out of the way, but his blade nicks my ear.

I step in closer, trying to strike him. His range is nearly twice mine, and he's faster and stronger. He shifts inside my guard, moving in a blur of shadow. The hard line of his body slams into me, tossing me backward. I fall and hit the stones hard on my side, my cheek smashing against the ground, my head ringing like a bell.

My gaze flicks to my hand, and I see that I've lost my sword.

Shock cracks through my body like lightning. My cheek is split open, but I don't have time to think about that now. If I let the pain distract me, I'll die.

Rion stands over me, and I twist my body, reaching for the hilt of my sword. My old training takes over, and I kick up from the ground, my heel jamming hard into his knee. It shifts him back, just long enough for me to actually grip my hilt again.

"Surrender to me," he says. "You're only alive because I'm allowing it."

But I'm up again in moments. He circles me, his movements slow, graceful.

Auberon is yelling at me in my mind.

Grip tightly, use your thumb to guide. Cut upward. Break his guard, dodge left. Watch his eyes. Parry the thrust. Jab. Balance.

Too close, and I die, impaled on his blade. Too far, and I can't strike him. His enormous size is not fucking helpful.

A cold sweat glows over my skin.

When he strikes again, faster and harder this time, I parry—one, two, three times. Then I pivot and cut up sharply. My sword snaps toward his blade, but he blocks it so hard that I almost lose my grip.

The next time I strike, it's rushed and messy. Close to me now, he catches my arm mid-swing. He twists my forearm sharply in front of me, ready to break it. Grimacing, I drop my sword, and it clangs to the stones between us.

Fuck.

Hunched over, I catch my breath, and my heart slams against my ribs.

He stares at me, his silver eyes burning with a searing intensity. The breeze toys with his hair, and time stretches out. The shouts around me slow to a hush. Fear flares in my chest, stealing my breath.

There's a hungry look in his eyes. I wonder if he needs to replenish his magic, like I did. Even with the Song, it used to take me days to recover.

"You're skilled at blocking my magic," he says.

I jerk my hand free of his grasp and stagger back. Only I'm backing up against a wall, cornered. I'm trapped. There's nowhere else for me to retreat now, not with my shoulder blades jammed against the stone arena wall. My heart slams so hard, it's all I can hear. I try to slow my panicked breaths, to clear my head. He's towering over me, blade in his hand.

If I try to grab my sword off the stones, I'll be dead.

Improvise. Adapt. Do not give up.

I know the moment I bend down for my sword, his will carve into my throat.

Think, Syn. Think.

There's more than one way to dominate, isn't there?

Rion can kill everyone here, but that's not what determines who becomes king. He needs the nobility to *like* him. They're the kingmakers. And unfortunately for him, he's come here with the reputation of a monster. As far as anyone knows, he didn't even start off as a real noble—he got his title through violence. He's a warlord from nowhere who stole a throne on a distant island.

Killing me won't improve his reputation.

He strikes again, moving in closer. I duck, and his sword sings over my head.

When I rise again, I move *closer* to him, darting

forward. I'm out of range of his sword now, and I press myself against him. It was an instinctive move to close the distance, to make it hard for him to strike me. But a new idea starts to take root in my mind as the word *Vicky* rattles in my thoughts.

Catching my breath, I peer up at him. His oaky scent wraps around me, his hot body warming mine. He stares down at me, and his magic pulses over my skin. Now, his eyes have gone darker—a midnight blue. It's a primal, animalistic look that sends alarm bells ringing in my mind. There's a *hunger* in those shadowed eyes.

"You must submit to me to live."

His powerful magic licks at my body, making it hard for me to think straight.

He's towering over me, and I know he could simply tear my head off my body. He could end my life within seconds.

This is my time to play to the crowd.

"I don't trust you to let me live out of a sense of morality. Everyone here knows you don't have that. But I do hope you're smart enough to realize you can't kill me in front of the noble houses. After all, Rion..." On my tiptoes, I slide both arms up over his shoulders and press myself against his leather armor. "I'm just a girl looking for love. And you? Everyone knows you're a monster."

I leap up, wrapping my legs around his waist, arms around his shoulders. Distantly, I hear a roar of approval from the noble houses.

Something flickers in his eyes, but it's gone in an instant, replaced by a soft, dangerous smile that shows the edge of his elongated canines. "Do you really want to play with a monster?"

"Even the Ruthless Knight can find love, don't you think? It would make a great story."

I run my hand over his chest, feeling the hard muscles beneath his tunic.

He sighs faintly, and finally drops his sword at his feet like he's the one surrendering. "That's one way to disarm me," he says in a low purr.

This close, I can see everything. The sensuous curve of his lips. The angle of his jaw. The golden tattoos tracing his divine features, as if he's been kissed by the gods. The exquisite jewel dangling from one ear. I can't decide if this man was born to kill or seduce, or which side of him is more dangerous.

What I do know is that I can't look away from the Ruthless Knight, and I hate him for that.

"I hope you're willing to play for the crowd," I whisper. "They want romance."

His expression darkens. "And you're just a lonely girl looking for love, is that right?" His deep voice holds a sensual timbre.

"You keep saying I shouldn't be here," I whisper into his ear. "And what about you? You starved a demi-Fey high lord to death in an oubliette. Is that right?"

"I had my reasons." His hand slides into my hair,

fingers tangling in my curls. His other hand holds tightly to my bum, and he pulls me close.

He's so insanely large that I feel tiny in his arms and completely vulnerable.

"Mmm. But what's your noble lineage, darling?" I coo into his ear. "Isn't that what this is all about? For all we know, warlord, you could have crawled from the Corbinelle slums before you conquered Tintagol."

"I was born from the oaks."

"Like a jackdaw?" I whisper close to his lips, brushing a thumb over his cheek. "Or a beetle?"

Midnight blue bleeds into the silver in his eyes. "Like a god. Don't pretend you haven't noticed."

I wish I could say this was delusion, but he is the most powerful Fey I've ever met, and he *looks* like a god.

"Surrender," he whispers against my mouth. "You know you don't stand a chance against me. I let you live because I chose it."

"And why would you go easy on me? Out of the kindness of your warlord heart?"

"Maybe you amuse me." His magic strokes my skin. "Or, perhaps I know just as well as you do what the crowd wants."

"So, you're a filthy little liar, too."

"I must admit, you're stronger than I imagined," he says quietly. "And more brutal."

"See? We're not so different." Our lips are nearly touching. "So, what now?"

"Now? I'll let them think I've won you as my prize."

With his fingers curled into my hair, he tugs my head back a little, exposing my throat. He presses my back against the stone wall, pinning me in place.

I'm more vulnerable than ever as he lowers his mouth to my neck. He knows as well as I do that the crowd is watching, but I almost forget about them as I feel his teeth brushing over the pulsing vein in my throat. This is, perhaps, a threat, because he could rip through that vein in a second.

Something primal in the depths of my thoughts tells me to go still.

His teeth graze my throat again—just enough to remind me how easily this could end—before his lips replace them.

His scent is oaky and intoxicating, his magic tingling over my skin. I'm no longer sure who is in control of this act now, but I don't think it's me.

Unwelcome desire coils through me as he kisses my throat with a featherlight brush of his lips, followed by a gentle stroke of his tongue.

Is this his magic, too? Terror and pleasure, two sides of the same coin? Both make your heart race. Both make you lose control.

He raises his face to mine again, his eyes now dark as midnight. He's *very* good at this game of make-believe. Gently, he brushes his lips against mine, agonizingly lightly. And that brush of a kiss makes an ache build deep inside me.

My thighs tighten around him, and my hand slides into his long, silver hair. My breath is coming faster now, and I fight the urge to open my mouth to him. *He's the enemy, Syn.*

And yet, I can't stop thinking about what he said—about how we Fey seek pleasure and drag our fingers through the soil, how we fuck against rowan trees and primal magic roars through our veins like wildfire.

He pulls away from the kiss, but he's still holding my gaze.

Auberon taught me that panic was death—he never anticipated how much desire could unmoor someone, too. That doesn't usually tend to come up in battle.

The golden tattoos on Rion's cheekbones seem to glow brighter, radiantly. "You're a dangerous little liar, mortal, but you've done me a favor."

Slowly, he sets me down like he's lowering a child to the ground, and I slide against the stone.

He pulls me against him, leaning down to whisper, "But I demand a token of your defeat, and I will take my due."

He reaches out and rips the raven emblem off my chest with a cold smile. "Now, Baroness. Kneel before me and say my name when you submit."

Clenching my jaw, I drop to my knees—and already, his blade gleams with silver as it flicks toward my throat. I raise my hands. "I surrender to Rion du Lac!" I shout, and the sound echoes across the arena.

Rion faces the mirrors. "And what do the leaders of the noble houses say? Will you save this lady?"

From the stone dais, Niniane swans into the arena, her silver-blue gown trailing behind her. She smiles, lifting her face to the buttery sunlight. The three cloaked *cugol* glide behind her, their faces entirely shadowed.

"Only Baroness Alis survived on her side today, and she surrendered. And what do our noble houses say shall be the fate of our baroness today? Death or mercy?"

CHAPTER 26

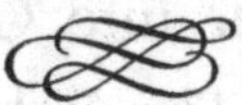

My pulse leaps as I await the verdict.

I think of what my life could be like if I get through these trials: a cottage with Vero, a warm hearth and fresh bread, books by a fireplace. And in this fantasy, Tristan would live with us, too.

I glance across the arena at him. He's gone pale, his shoulders tense. Igraine is sitting near him, glaring at me like she wants to end my life herself.

The mirrors shimmer, and the hooded *cugol* raise their arms, looking at the skies. The frigid stones bite into my knees. Overhead, clouds roil through the skies again. The Hooded Ones start to chant, a low and sonorous knell that sends a chill rippling down my spine. Now, all the heat of a few minutes ago has turned to a cold sweat, and my teeth chatter.

I glance up at Rion like he's going to help me. Apart

from the breeze toying with his hair, he is still as the stones beneath me. As we wait, his gaze slides down to me —cold, impassive. He's as remote and unreadable as a marble carving of a god.

At last, the wren circles overhead, and she drops a fluttering piece of paper into Cador's hands. When he unrolls it, he smiles. "The noble houses have chosen *mercy!*"

I close my eyes, whispering a silent thanks to the gods. Then I rise from my kneeling position. From the mirrors, the crowd roars their approval.

My head pounds like someone is hammering my skull from the inside.

Rion crosses into the center of the arena, accepting the cheers from the crowd. I follow behind him.

I'll keep the truth silent and swallow down my secrets. And before the crowd, I'll play the part.

I bow to the mirrors. "My deepest gratitude, noble houses, for your mercy," I coo, charming as I can be. "In the desolate Waste Land, I lived alone, broken and deprived of love. And you, most eminent houses of Brocéliande, have given me the chance to fill my life with warmth."

I let my eyes fill with tears. In reality, they're from exhaustion, but I hope they will look like gratitude.

"What a show," Rion murmurs.

I cross back to my seat and try to block out the smell of blood.

One hundred seventy people left. It's a miracle that I'm one of them.

My head throbs hard, and when I touch my cheek, a smear of blood streaks across my fingers.

I want to get away from the smell of death, but the day is only just beginning. I steal a quick glance at Mark's corpse and the gaping hole where his eye used to be.

His jaw hangs open, crooked, his good eye staring lifelessly at the sky. Already, his skin has taken on a grayish hue.

I stare at him. The nobility has forced us out here today to slaughter each other, all for their entertainment and profit.

I realize now that I don't simply want the grail. I want to destroy the entire thing. I want to *win* it—me, a peasant on the throne, someone who would give power to those who deserve it. I want to take the crown from the aristocrats and fucking smash it into pieces.

Because what if someone like Mabon wins? Or Rion?

And even if I can't win the trials, I will make it my mission to kill the next king.

I'm not letting another Auberon on the throne, or someone even worse.

I pull my gaze away from Mark and make my way back to the spectators.

When I resume my seat in front of Tristan, he touches the back of my neck. Warmth slides down my spine at the point of contact.

I hug myself and let my mind drift from the trials, back to the little cottage in the woods, where I once found Vero clinging to life after the River-Ague, asleep beneath the blankets of my childhood bed.

* * *

BY THE END of the trial, there are 114 of us left.

The combat trials didn't take very long. Twenty-two rounds today, most of them over within five or ten minutes. It's still only the late afternoon.

Sixty-five people died—bodies split open and dragged over the stones, then sent home to their families in pieces. The smell of blood still lingers in my thoughts, and no amount of mead will cleanse it from my mind.

In the center of the arena, Niniane opens her arms, palms up. "Now, blood has been spilled, a sacrifice to the gods. And we celebrate the end of the first trial with the festival of Tanos. Join us at the stone circle at sunset to celebrate."

Celebrate. Sure. Totally normal behavior after a bloodbath.

We walk in somber silence toward the stone tunnel that will take us out of here, and Tristan disappears with the other servants.

Elizabeth sidles up next to me and wraps her arm around my shoulder. "We made it, Alis. But that was fucking dreadful, wasn't it? Horrific. I've never seen so much death at once, have you?"

"Absolutely not," I lie. "Never."

"Do you know what the Fey used to do in the old days after a battle? It was a sort of ritualistic swim in the sea. Like, cleaning off the blood. We can swim from the Lyria Tower, you know. Something purifying before the festival of Tanos."

My head throbs. Rion is right—I'm hardly Fey at all these days.

I sigh. "Do you think the sea will get rid of my headache?"

"It was called the Rite of the Mor." From behind us, a male voice echoes off the stones. I turn to see Aneirin trying to catch up to us, clutching his books. "A ritual cleansing in the sea after a battle. Or a sacred well. Couldn't get enough of a sacred well in the old days. The ancients *loved* a well."

"Congratulations on surviving," I say.

He nods at me, and one of his dark curls falls on his forehead. "You as well. I think the noble houses adore you. Can't say they'll feel the same about me. I said all the wrong things. I ended up babbling about being in debt, which I don't imagine impressed anyone."

"You look completely unharmed from that trial," I say, with a touch of jealousy tinging my voice.

"Yes, well. The best fighter on *your* side was killed immediately." He pulls his books in tighter. "But fighting isn't really my thing, you know. I have shadow magic, yes. But I'd rather play music or shag a beautiful woman. Or read about the maligned heroes—Merlin, Mordred, Prince Talan, and the like. I also like to get high off snorting dried bisen-root and running around the forest with the wind in my hair, but I don't suppose that's an option here."

My eyebrows rise. "It would certainly be entertaining."

"Not sure that I want the crown at all," he says. "Not sure what I'm doing here, really. I like the parties, yes, but not all the fuss. I imagine being king is a lot of work. Lots of boring meetings. I'd rather stage a play or a masquerade."

I'm already starting to like him, even if we were supposed to kill each other moments ago.

"The three of us will go for a swim, then, shall we?" says Elizabeth. "Picnic, mead, a bit of sun. We can—"

But as we step out of the tunnel, I find Igraine waiting for me. Before I can react, she moves lightning fast. Gripping me by the throat, she slams me *hard* against the stone wall, choking me. Agony splinters through the back of my skull, and my lungs burn as she crushes my throat.

"Stay away from Rion du Lac," she snarls. "He and I are destined to end this together. We always have been."

From behind, Aneirin strikes her with shadow magic, and it coils around her neck. As he pulls his shadow magic away, she gasps for breath, doubling over.

Slowly, her golden gaze lifts to mine. "He's mine," she hisses.

* * *

DRIPPING WITH SEAWATER, I sit on a stone overlook with Aneirin and Elizabeth. The sparkling sea spreads out beneath the sun, and my belly is now full of bread, cheese, and fruit.

My head is already feeling better from the bracing swim. The saltwater stung my cheek when I first dipped into the sea, but I can feel it healing.

Elizabeth hands a strawberry tart to Aneirin, then one to me. "All right. Confess, Alis. What gave you the idea to kiss Rion du Lac? Were you simply hoping he'd spare your life if you turned him on, or did you have another play in mind?"

I want to tell them it's all bollocks and that I hate him. But do I trust them enough with the truth? If someone runs to the noble houses to tell them I lied, it won't go well for me here.

"It just came naturally," I say. "He's very handsome."

"Now we're done with the first trial." Elizabeth sighs. "But there will be more."

"Any idea what they might be?" I ask.

Aneirin shakes his head, his mouth full of strawberry tart. "No one knows."

"I want the trials to end," Elizabeth says. "But I don't miss my home at all. It's falling apart, and all the servants were loyal to my husband. What's your castle like, Aneirin?"

"It's an absolute ruin, but I like it that way. King Auberon took it from the Grand Clerics long ago, back when he was angry that they refused to worship him as a god. So, he started killing them and giving their castles and temples away. The king gave Castle Catreath to my uncle. When he arrived at his new home, he found the arms of the clerics nailed to the doors."

Sure sounds like Auberon. "Oh, that's… decorative," I say.

"My uncle used the clerics' skulls to make goblets, which I always thought seemed like bad luck. And apparently, it was. My uncle died, along with my father, during the invasion of France. My mother died from the River-Ague, thanks to Auberon, you know. We're not demi-Fey, *obviously*, but when you poison a river, it's hard to control who dies. But I don't miss any of them, if you're wondering. They left me with a castle and crushing debt. It's a quiet place, but the ghosts keep me company."

I lift my glass of mead, watching as the sun sparks brightly in the amber. "To the ghosts, then."

The scent of blood still clings to me, despite the sea and sun. I can still see the lifeless bodies in the arena and Mark's gaping eye socket.

I add, "And to the desperate hope that we don't join the ghosts soon on the other side."

CHAPTER 27

Elizabeth and I walk toward the door marked with the cart. She's dressed in a deep purple gown stitched with white owls on the sleeves, and primroses and pansies thread through her dark curls.

She smiles at me, and her shimmering violet eyeliner brings out the gold in her fiery eyes. "The sacrifice is done. We survived it. Now, let's drink toasts to the dead among the old stones. Summer is here."

It's the first of May—Tanos—one of two nights when the barrier thins between our world and the land of the dead. For the Fey, it's the start of summer.

Once, fires burned from hill to hill, lit by the king's torches. In the old days, the king would choose a priestess to mate with in the circle. People danced and shagged while the dead rose to bless the land, until dawn burned brighter than ever and the fields bloomed with barley and rye. Or so they say. It was all before my time.

We push through the round door to the rolling cart. The first thing I notice is that the banners have all changed position. They no longer stand on poles outside Aether Tower. Instead, they hang from its walls, festooned across the ivory stone.

At the top hangs Mabon's banner, a salamander with a crown of flames.

Beneath him hangs Igraine's water serpent, then Rion's sigil, a blue-eyed white stag wearing a golden crown.

The three contenders from Tintagol have taken the lead. Must be something in the water there.

My raven is about ten banners down from Rion's, and Elizabeth's another eight beyond.

Elizabeth points to it. "I imagine that's our ranking?"

"I think so. Shame that Mabon is in the lead."

Now, the golden number on Aether Tower reads *103*. Already, they've chosen eleven contenders to send home for generally being disappointing or uninteresting. Their sigils have been pulled from display, their halos removed.

I climb into the rolling cart.

Elizabeth slips in next to me. "Your banner is well placed. Nicely done, Alis."

When Elizabeth flicks the lever, we zoom off. The wind rushes over us, bringing with it the scent of apples and the brine of the sea. We zoom past the Belenior Tower and its blaze of fire. Sparks float on the wind, carrying the scent of burning cedar. We hurtle through the air, sweeping around to the grassy henge and ring stones.

The ride ends with a jolt near the stones.

The bells of Aether still ring, calling us all to Tanos. I step out of the cart, and Elizabeth loops her arm through mine. As we walk, a gentle breeze kisses my skin. The sound of the bells mingles with the rhythmic music floating from the circle of stones. Overhead, twilight streaks the sky with coral and indigo.

Aneirin waits for us just inside the ditch encircling the stones. I find it oddly endearing that he wanted us to go in with him, like he'd be too nervous on his own. He's dressed in a burgundy velvet suit with a white collar, and he leans on his cane, carved with his unicorn emblem. Really, he looks quite dashing with his dark waves gleaming under the light of the silver and red moons.

He smiles at us. "Happy Tanos, my fellow survivors. *Blessings of the fire*, as they used to say."

"Happy Tanos," I say.

"And we made the cut." He grins. "I was pleased to see both your banners flying on Aether."

"Shocking, isn't it?" says Elizabeth.

We cross the henge to join him, walking together between the large dolmen stones.

A great bonfire burns in the center of the standing stones, casting wavering light and shadow over the gathering Fey. Already, some of them are dancing around the roaring flames, bathed in the blazing light.

We're not far from one of the castle walls here, where large oak doors are inset in the stone, carved with spiral symbols.

As we move deeper into the circle, I feel an ancient magic thrumming over my skin, and the music pulses through my chest like a slow heartbeat.

Aneirin smiles. "I've always wanted to see these sorts of stone circles. No idea what they're for. I didn't know anyone still celebrated Tanos, but time seems to stand still here at the Veiled Court."

I survey the shape of the stones, counting the outer rings. "This one looks like Stonehenge when it was first built. Thirty stones, like the days of the month."

"Tell us more," Elizabeth says. "I don't know the first thing about Stonehenge."

I point to the oak doors. "On the summer solstice, I suspect those doors will open. You see that large stone over there? Lying flat? That's the heel stone, where the light will pour in when the doors open."

"Very romantic." Aneirin sighs.

"Sort of. This place is a bridge between worlds— between the human and the Fey, between the living and the dead. They might have sacrificed Fey here to the gods." I shrug. "Now I suppose we just murder each other in the arena and call it a day."

Elizabeth's eyebrows rise. "So, it's a calendar, a temple, and a burial site?"

"I still think it's romantic," says Aneirin. "I love a cemetery. Favorite place to shag. So, we're standing on warrior bones?"

"Not bones." I hug myself. "They cremated ancient warriors. Those doors—there's probably a path beyond them, leading to a river. It's life flowing toward death, just like at Stonehenge."

Elizabeth points to markings on the stones—axes and swords. "Why did they carve weapons? To honor the warriors?"

"I think they're meant to ward away mortal weapons," I guess. "It's protection."

"That makes sense," Aneirin says. "I can see why the ancient Fey had to create Brocéliande. The humans nearly hunted us to death when they discovered iron. We're not like the mortals, breeding like rabbits. I mean, it takes hundreds of years for a Fey to conceive—it wouldn't be hard to wipe us out at the rate we reproduce. Now, we need more than carvings in stone. We need a strong leader to keep us safe."

Elizabeth quirks a smile at me. "You really know a lot about Stonehenge."

Bollocks. I've said too much. "That's what I read, anyway. I had a book about it in the Waste Land. Not much else to do but read there."

"That's true anywhere, Alis." Aneirin sips his drink and

looks around. "Terrifying to think Duke Mabon could raise all the cremated warriors from the ground to murder us right now if he wanted."

A chill sweeps over me. Overhead, a crow caws. The torches affixed to the stones cast dancing shadows around us.

Elizabeth's eyes widen. "I had no idea his magic was so powerful. The entire time we've been here, I just thought he was a sniveling, drunk idiot."

Aneirin shrugs. "Powerful magic can take a toll on a person. It can drive you mad, and your mind never stops. Maybe the alcohol is the only thing that makes his thoughts go quiet."

"I've heard that necromancers hear the voices of the dead," I say.

My voice cracks on the word *dead* because I wish I could hear my parents' voices.

It must be the magic of Tanos, because I think of that overgrown garden in my dreams, and my eyes sting.

I wonder if Mabon could hear my parents if he stood above their graves. But I don't know where their bodies ended up. Nothing as grand and eternal as ring stones. A common grave, likely. A ditch for peasant traitors. Maybe their heads were stuck on the city gates—

I blink furiously, trying to master my emotions. These are some of the things no one wants to hear and no one should think.

I keep my eyes away from Elizabeth so she can't see

the sheen of tears. "I'll be back in a minute. I'm going to look for a drink."

I slip into the shadows outside the stone circle. I fold my arms, leaning back against one of the enormous, cold stones. Nearby, the wind rushes through the drooping branches of a willow tree, rustling the leaves. The May air is heavy and humid, tinged with salt.

My gaze flicks up to the sky, where the stars burn brightly, the constellations sweeping over me in a vault. Tonight, Brocéliande's red moon is a crescent, and the silver moon is a fat sphere hanging in the sky. My hands start to shake again, and I clench my fingers tightly together to stop the trembling.

I hear footfalls behind me on the grass. I'm not thrilled to see Duke Mabon step in front of me. His long, dark hair hangs over a white cloak. Again, he seems to be sober, though he's carrying two glasses of mead.

As he hands me a glass, he smiles. "Here you are, Baroness Alis. From such a meager provenance, and already a favorite among the noble houses. Well done. *Well done.*"

"Thank you. Though you're in the lead." I raise my glass, pausing as mental alarm bells go off.

Mabon isn't taking a sip. The chatter he must be hearing here from the dead must be maddening, and he *always* drinks.

Already, my hackles are rising, and I'm hearing Tristan's voice in my thoughts: *Don't trust a single fucking person here.*

Didn't Elizabeth say he poisoned his wife?

I look into my drink. He doesn't really have a reason to want me dead. Except, I think, he'd do anything to please Igraine.

"You don't want mead?" Mabon asks eagerly.

"I was hoping to find some food first. Just taking in the fresh air out here."

He nods. "Perhaps I could find you something to eat."

"The only thing you ever said to me before was that I stink of mortals. Why the change of heart?"

"Well, of course, I was drunk. I have to silence their voices...but you're not mortal. Of *course* not. Can't have *that sort* here." Mabon's gaze flicks past me, and his body tenses.

I turn to see Rion prowling closer. In the moonlight, he's all shadows and silver—the midnight darkness of his inky blue cloak clasped with a silver stag, the ice-cold gleam of his hair and eyes.

"I wouldn't drink that, Lady Alis." He arches an eyebrow. "Belladonna, if I'm not mistaken."

Mabon arches an eyebrow in turn. "Oh, dear. Are you suggesting someone is trying to poison us?"

Rion lifts his hand, and for a moment, it looks as if he's waving Mabon off. Then tendrils of magic coil from his fingertips, wrapping around Mabon in a dark embrace.

Mabon's eyes snap open, and he starts to moan and

shake. His legs give out, and he falls to the ground, smashing his mead glass.

"I am suggesting," Rion says softly, "that if you try to harm her again, you'll discover how imaginative I can be when I'm annoyed."

Mabon grunts, his eyes wide open like a terrified animal. Fear slackens his face. Panicked, he starts to smash his forehead backward on the rock.

"*Rion*," I snarl.

He shrugs slowly. "What? He was going to poison my lover."

"Those rocks are thousands of years old," I hiss. "Please don't destroy them."

"Fine." In a careless, lazy gesture, Rion flicks his hand, and his magic slips back around him.

Mabon looks up from the ground with an expression of fury. Blood spills down his face, staining his white cloak.

"I'm a direct descendant of the ancient king Vortigern," he snarls, climbing to his feet. "We're not in Tintagol anymore. You're not high lord here, and I could raise the dead to rip you to pieces. When I win the crown, *Rion*, I will marry Igraine. Then I'll have you cut into pieces— slowly—and eaten by crows. I'll leave your head to rot on my castle gates."

"So, it all comes out now, Mabon. You were so deferential to me on Tintagol, but all this time, you thought you should be in my place." Dark magic stains the air around

Rion like ink spilling into the night. "Your mead-addled brain is always feverish and incoherent. Your dreams of ruling as king are a fantasy and nothing more. Don't expect to stay on top for long."

"I will kill you," Mabon hisses. "In the next trial."

He shoots me one last furious look and skulks away.

Smoke from the bonfire floats on the wind and coils around Rion. His dangerous, seductive scent slips around me—musk warmed with fire-licked oak, tinged with a faint honeyed sweetness. It's a scent I want to taste on his skin, and I'm furious with myself for even having that thought.

Rion's gaze slides to mine, and he gives me a lazy smile. "I see you're making friends."

I pour out my poisoned mead onto the bluebells at my feet. "I guess I'll be needing a new drink. And to what do I owe this sudden chivalry, Rion du Lac? You nearly killed me earlier today."

The wind lifts a few strands of his long, silver hair, and a fleeting smile touches his beautiful mouth. "As I said, you're my new lover—as far as anyone knows."

"Let me guess." I sigh. "From a tactical perspective, you need me to help polish your brutal reputation. You're the monster who cut off people's heads on Tintagol. I imagine you don't get to overthrow a government without killing some aristocrats. A usurper took the throne from Igraine's husband. You took it from the usurper. But are you better than he was, really? The noble houses will want to know your lineage. And you're not like Mabon. He's *always* held the title of duke. He belongs."

"Now, now, Alis," he coos. "I don't believe *you*, of all people, object to killing aristocrats."

Ice slides through my veins. "What makes you say that?"

He leans down, and his breath feathers over my cheekbone. "I think that's how you got your halo."

The ground tilts beneath my feet. "What are you talking about?"

He straightens again, his pale eyes narrowing. "Just hints. Your accent slips occasionally, enough to make me curious. And that outfit you wore when you first arrived, those distinctly mortal clothes that smelled of mortal soap—"

"Bollocks," I hiss.

"Now I'm growing impatient with your lies."

My breath hitches. "I picked these clothes up on my way from the Waste Land."

"Such a shame what happened to Hermance for impersonating an aristocrat. Or whatever his real name was. Painful death, wasn't that? But we must have consequences for transgressions, don't you think? When a lowborn peasant snaps and kills, a price must be paid." A half smile plays on his lips as he leans in closer. "And I think it's what you do sometimes, isn't it? You lose your temper."

"I'm about to snap right now if you don't shut your mouth."

He straightens. Idly, he rolls his glass in slow circles, swirling the mead. "I think you relax around danger. Most people don't. You crave it. You *miss* violence when you're not around it. Chaos steadies your hands. So, you lean into the danger when you can find it. A dark part of you seeks it out. I think you're twisted, love."

My skin goes hot. "Nonsense. I'm just adjusting to being away from the Waste Land."

"Right." He sips his mead, then again swirls the glass slowly. "Except I don't think you're from the Waste Land at all. That first night we met, there were faint bloodstains on your clothes. I spotted a scarlet drop drying on your thumb. Everyone else is taking you at your word, but I don't believe a single thing that comes out of your pretty mouth."

Is he a telepath? To ask him would confirm that he was correct about everything, so I keep that question to myself. "I have *no* idea what you're talking about."

"You're not the sweet little romantic from a distant island. I think you're a ruthless soldier, forged in the crucible of battle. You thrive when death is all around you. You've been away from war too long, and you *miss* it. That's what I see. Am I close?"

Fury simmers in my chest. "I'm from the Waste Land," I say through clenched teeth.

It comes out too loud, laced with fury. Because unfortunately, yes, he is close to the truth.

A slow, easy smile. "There it is. A glimpse of the real you. That anger simmering beneath a placid surface. And who has made you so angry?"

"What do you want from me?" I breathe.

A wicked glint sparks in his eyes. "I'm just a man looking for love."

"And how many people did you kill on your way to power in Tintagol?"

"As many as I had to." His smile is as beautiful as it is deadly. "Perhaps a few more."

I stare up at him, trying to get control over myself. I breathe slowly. "And now you want me to help you win the trials by continuing the whole romance charade. Because if you don't win, Mabon will stick your head on the castle gates."

"And do you really want a drunken necromancer to win?"

"There are other options." I fold my arms. "You want me to soften your reputation."

"Would you really want to say no to a monster, love?" His sultry voice sharpens itself into an edge. "That sounds dangerous."

He turns, stalking away from me.

CHAPTER 28

$\mathcal{I}$t's midnight, and my arse is hanging out a window. I can't seem to get in or out.

I'm simply stuck, hips jammed in the frame.

I'm supposed to be sneaking out to Avalon Tower with Tristan, but my shimmering purple cloak snagged on something. Then I was thrown off balance, and now I'm dangling forty feet above the ground. But apparently, this is the only option for sneaking out tonight.

Tristan, of course, was out within seconds, but that's the advantage of being able to control time.

I wriggle out just a little more, and the window frame groans next to me.

Just a few feet below, Tristan has anchored himself to the thick vines on the wall. "Quite the view right here," he says.

"Enjoying yourself?" I mutter. "Because if you don't help me out soon, I may kick you off the wall."

He slides a hand onto one of my hips, and the warmth from his palms spreads through the thin fabric of my T-shirt. Gently, he shifts me against the stones, twisting my hips more vertically.

I wiggle out slowly, trusting him to catch me before I plummet to my death. And as I squeeze myself through, Tristan wraps an arm around my waist, pulling me tightly against him.

"I've got you," he whispers into my ear.

My arms encircle his neck. Pressed against his hard muscle, I breathe in his familiar scent, staring into his eyes, where the gold kisses the green.

My gaze flicks down to his lips.

"Shall we go?" he whispers.

"Right," I say. "Let's climb down."

"Are you okay to climb down on your own? I want to use my magic to rush over to the dragon keep."

Still wrapped in his arms, I peer down. It's only about four stories, which I think I can do. Especially with the vines growing over the stones.

"No problem." I shift off of him, grabbing a thick, woody piece of ivy that clings to the walls.

"When you get to the bottom," he says, "run east, close to the shore. Tarasque and I will find you fast."

And that's it.

Without another word, Tristan disappears in a blur of shadows.

I feel a million times colder without his nearness. I wish I'd dressed more warmly for the night.

I grip the ivy tightly, lowering myself down. As I do, a faint golden glow bounces off the rocks. My halo has already reappeared.

I start to move faster. According to Tristan, we have about four hours before the Cloaked Ones will realize I'm gone. Tristan won't tell me *how* he knows that, but if I had to guess, it's something to do with the fact that Mabon was found outside the castle walls last night, unconscious and with absolutely no memory of how he got there. And while I know Mabon is drunk most of the time, I suspect Tristan had a hand in that particular scenario, and that's how he knows how much time we have.

So, four hours until their hunt begins.

As fast as I can, I hurry down the ivy. When I'm only eight feet above the earth, I let go.

I land hard in the grass and spin, scanning for movement.

No sign of the Cloaked Ones, no soldiers. I glance up at the stars, orienting myself with the guiding star. Then I start running east.

The night wind howls over me as I race through the shadows, tasting the tang of sea salt. To my right, the ground sheers off in a steep cliff face, and a salty breeze whips off the water.

I sprint past flowering hawthorns and fields of wild thyme along the shoreline.

Tristan already prepared me for this—we'll be riding together on a dragon named Tarasque. I have no idea *why* we're doing this, only that he promises the dragon is *very* well trained. She belongs to Prince Talan, the one royal I actually like, since he had a chance to take the throne and abdicated instead.

I make it less than half a mile before a shadow sweeps over the moons, cloaking the world in darkness. It's an almost overpowering impulse, the urge to run and hide from the dragon circling overhead. It's an instinct I have to fight, especially when I see its red scales, so similar to Goch's. The creature unleashes a low, primal growl from her chest. I stand still as a statue in the grasses and try not to think of Blythe.

At last, Tarasque arcs lower, and her feet hit the ground first. Then she raises her head, letting out a roar that makes the soil tremble beneath my feet.

Fear steals my breath.

Her nostrils flare, and the scent of sulfur coils through the air. Her eyes slide to me, liquid silver that sends my heart racing.

Tristan sits on top of Tarasque's neck, smiling down at me like he's just brought me a friendly dog to play with. He's obviously very pleased with himself. He beckons me closer. "Come on, Syn. Before the Cloaked Ones find you. We don't have far to go."

Tarasque lowers her neck further, stretching it out in invitation.

My fingers curl into fists as I stalk closer to the dragon. I'm not about to admit how much dragons unnerve me, so I'm just going to shove my fears down deep and do what I need to do—climb on the creature.

I take Tristan's hand. I don't need his help balancing, but I appreciate the chivalrous gesture.

With a deep breath, I straddle her neck and nestle against Tristan. He slides a hand over my waist, pulling me against his warm, hard chest. When I brush a hand against Tarasque's scales, I find them softer than I expected.

Tristan's face is close to mine, his breath warming the shell of my ear. "See the ridge sticking out, by her spikes? Grab that to stay on."

I swallow hard. "That's it? Just grab the spikes?"

"You'll want to use your thighs as well." His grip around my waist tightens, pure iron around my stomach. "But mostly you'll be counting on me to keep you from falling into ruin, which really could be said for most of our time spent together. Don't you think?"

"I don't know, Tristan. Remember the time you tried to escape the Undercroft to live life to its fullest, and I found you three hours later, passed out drunk beneath a willow tree—"

"We don't need to rehash—"

"—and you had no trousers on? I believe I saved *you* from ruin that time."

"Syn, I made it clear I'm the one who will be keeping you alive on this mission, right?" I can hear the amusement in his deep voice.

He leans forward, grabbing onto another one of the dragon's ridges. His strong arm rests against mine, caging me in so I feel safe.

Tarasque raises her head and takes a few graceful steps. My muscles tense as I brace for the flight.

Tristan's thumb brushes up and down on my waist to reassure me. "Hold on tight, Syn. Rise, Tarasque!"

Tarasque lifts her neck higher and snorts, exhaling sulfurous steam into the air. As her neck lifts, I slide back against Tristan and grip the ridge of spikes, tightening my thighs to brace myself.

Her wings spread, then sweep up, beating the air as we take off. We rise from the ground, and the wind whips over me, rushing through my hair.

I peer down at the dark grasses and wildflowers as we pull away, leaving the comfort of solid earth far below. My breathing is fast and shallow, my knuckles white from gripping the dragon's ridges.

We soar over a cliffside, and dark waves churn below us, slamming against the rocks. The moons glimmer off the waves as we arc over the sea.

Tristan's hands clench more tightly around me. "You're

going to want to hang on. We're going to head through the portal."

We're picking up speed, racing above the star-flecked ocean. Tristan shifts his hand under one of Tarasque's scales, pressing on it. As he does, she arcs sharply through the air, tilting at almost forty-five degrees.

My stomach flips, but Tristan is keeping me firmly in place, using his arms to hold me rooted to the dragon. Unfortunately, he also seems to be guiding us *directly* into the sheer, chalky cliff face. My heart thunders, panic snapping through my nerve endings.

As we race closer to the cliff, I shout Tristan's name into the wind.

CHAPTER 29

Just before we crash into the white rock, a portal gapes open, and we soar through into a clear, starlit sky.

I exhale, my muscles relaxing, and Tarasque arcs lazily over an ivory castle with towering spires on a gently rising hill. *Camelot.*

Two sets of golden stone walls enclose an inner ward of halls and towers. In the grasses beneath us, crowds are gathering, staring up at us, even though it's past midnight.

It seems that even here at Avalon Tower, a dragon is still cause for excitement.

Slowly, we arc lower, until Tarasque touches down near an apple grove.

Distantly, the sounds of gunshots ring out from a battle, and Tarasque rears her head again, tensing. I slide off her, my heart still racing. And yet, I feel like we're old friends now, so I rub her neck a little.

As I step away from her, I scan the courtyard. From where I'm standing, the ivory castle looms over us, and the stone carving above the door marks it as Merlin's Tower. The walls connect gothic towers, sweeping around the flowering courtyards and a few Tudor-style cottages.

A man stalks toward us from the shadows, a silver-eyed Fey with sun-kissed skin and dark, wavy hair that falls to his chin. Demi-Fey, perhaps. Blood stains his white shirt, and the scent of it hits me from here.

"Léon!" The man calls out Tristan by his surname. "You actually fucking did it."

"Of course I did." Tristan sidles up next to me. "Syn, this is Raphael, our Seneschal, although frankly, he's far too young—"

"Pleased to meet you, Syn," Raphael says, cutting him off.

"And you."

I smile at Raphael. I trust demi-Fey more than anyone, I think, considering everyone else is always trying to murder us for being tainted by one side or the other.

"Is there a reason you're covered in blood, Sir Raphael?" Tristan asks.

"The paramilitaries are still here. The Iron Legion. But we've got it under control now."

"How did the Iron Legion get into Camelot?" I ask. "I thought this whole place was protected by magic."

Raphael's silver eyes slide to me. "Some of them are former members of Avalon Tower. Pendragons. They know how to get into Camelot, but they haven't breached our fortress walls yet, so there's no need to panic. Nice halo, by the way."

"Thanks."

Tristan crosses his arms. "Raph—are we at war with the British government?"

Raphael shakes his head. "They have the backing of some members of government. But it's not anything officially sanctioned, so let's not lose our heads and set everyone on fire."

"It would end the battle decisively if we used the dragon," says Tristan.

Raphael takes a step closer. "I'm ordering you not to. I don't want to have to lock you up for murder. *Again.* Or for starting an actual civil war, which would be a new one for you, but I wouldn't put it past you."

Tristan nods at Raphael's shirt. "You're literally covered in human blood."

"It was self-defense. This isn't technically a civil war, and they're just a splinter group of paramilitary extremists. In the current political reality, we have to treat them more like civilians."

Tristan's eyes gleam. "*In the current political reality,* what's the bloody point of bringing the dragon? The humans have guns. They have their own weapons. Our moral imperative is to protect the weak and to fight for the Round Table. It's not to get ensnared in mortal political squabbles or care about fucking paperwork and petty legal designations. You've become very human."

Raphael raises his eyebrows at me. "Well, I'm done with that conversation. Sir Tristan, you're going to debrief with me in an hour. I need to hear *every* detail about the Veiled Court. But stay with the dragon right now, will you? Make sure she doesn't eat or burn anyone while I take Syn to our soothsayer."

He turns and strides away at such a fast clip, I have to jog to keep up with him. I glance at the tattoos that coil over his forearms—thorny vines.

"Why *did* you want us to bring Tarasque?" I ask.

He shoots me a look that could freeze dragon fire. "You're not getting any more information until Tana clears you."

I don't feel like we hit it off very well, but I also gather that Tristan wasn't the right person to introduce me to Raphael.

I follow Raphael to an oak door in one of the inner walls, its surface carved with chalices and serpents. He pulls open the door, and I'm greeted by the scent of a cedarwood fire mixed with the smell of yarrow tea.

Raphael stands by the doorway, arms folded, and I take a step farther into the room.

A beautiful woman sits at a cluttered table, firelight casting a warm, shifting glow over her clear brown skin.

Long braids trail down over a red dress, and a tattoo of vines curls around her neck.

Hundreds of candles flicker around the room. It would be a real fire hazard, except I assume she can predict any disastrous conflagrations. In here, the shelves are crammed with strange objects—crystal balls, skulls, mortars and pestles. Moonlight streams in from a stained-glass window behind her, depicting a sword and a crown.

She hasn't even looked up at me yet. Instead, she's staring into a flickering candle flame, apparently oblivious to the fact that I've entered the room.

"You must be Tana," I say.

She looks startled for a moment, then smiles at me. "Ah, right. Today, yes? Come in, Syn. Please, have a seat."

I pull out a rough-hewn oak chair that creaks when I settle into it. "I've heard so much about you. In fact, no one will tell me a bloody thing until I meet you. From what I can gather, you're the most important person here."

"Well, that isn't a widely held belief," she says airily. "Yesterday I spoke to King Arthur, and he's certain he's the most important person here. But that's also because he doesn't know he's dead. And Merlin mistakenly believes he *is* dead, though he's not. He's just in an oak. Very mixed-up business." She pushes a plate of small golden pastries toward me. "Have some honey cake."

I'm starving, and I take one of the little cakes, biting into it. It has a delicious, faintly spiced center with hints of nutmeg and cloves.

Tana starts to pour some tea. The table in front of her is littered with crystals, mismatched teacups, and a chipped teapot with a rendering of a dragon on it.

She hands me a dandelion teacup full of tea that smells of yarrow. "There you are. We will do tea and tarot. I've already done some mirror scrying."

"And what did you see in it?"

"Absolute disaster," she says wistfully. "Brocéliande lies in ruins."

My pulse quickens. "It what?"

She cocks her head. "Something to do with a ruined world. I'm not sure if it's your fault or not, but it might be."

I stare at her. "I'm going to need more information."

"So am I," Raphael says quietly from behind me.

Then, Alis's words return to me.

You could destroy the world. Cursed is the hour you were born.

Because of you, the land will lie in ruin, the powerful will sicken, and sorrow will reign in our kingdom.

I clear my throat, suddenly at war with myself. Should I tell them what Alis said? I don't particularly want to, because it doesn't seem like the sort of information that would get someone clearance. It quite clearly makes me seem like a liability. *By the way, another psychic said I'm going to destroy the world. Can I get that secret intel now?*

On the other hand…what if I am, in fact, fated to accidentally cause a disaster? It seems like something people should know.

I narrow my eyes at Tana. For all I know, she can hear everything I'm thinking.

"Are you a telepath?" It comes out too loud, and it sounds like an accusation.

"No, darling, you can relax. I can see the future and the past, but I don't know what you're thinking." She frowns at my teacup. "I can, however, see that you are gripping the porcelain so tightly that it seems you might break it."

"And why would you be scared of someone overhearing your thoughts?" Raphael asks from behind me.

Alis's cursed words rattle inside my skull, refusing to be quiet. *You could destroy the world...*

I try to relax my muscles so I can strike a casual tone. "I take it you've both been briefed on the Lady Alis situation?"

"Of course," Tana says with a smile. "You killed her and took her spot in the Veiled Court. And now, Raphael wants to know if we can trust you."

"I killed her in self-defense," I say, echoing Raphael. "Anyway, as she attacked me, she said I'd destroy the world. Those were her words. She said the powerful would sicken, crops would fail. All because of me. Cursed be the day I was born, that sort of thing. I think it's because she overheard me thinking about killing Auberon." I clear my throat. "I just thought I should mention it."

Tana stares into the flickering flame of a candle on the table, and its light dances in her dark eyes. "*World* can mean many different things, you know. For some people, their lover is the whole world." She meets my eyes again. "For someone else, the world could be a book they've been working on for decades. The meaning isn't set in stone."

I nod. "The baroness was very aggressive about the point that one must never hurt a king. Maybe to her, the monarchy is 'the world.'"

"Exactly." Tana's eyebrows rise. "But maybe not."

"What do you think of Auberon?" Raphael asks.

I turn to look at him, standing with his arms folded, leaning against the wall.

I take a deep breath. "I won't trust that fucker is dead until I see his head on a pike, and if I see him again, I will kill him. I spent ten years with him. He's nearly indestructible. But everyone thinks he's a usurper now. If he's still alive, he'd be just another ruthless contender for the throne, one among many."

He nods curtly.

I turn back to Tana, who leans forward and hands me a deck of tarot cards. "Shuffle and think of the Veiled Court."

I take the cards from her and close my eyes. I shuffle the cards together, and my thoughts drift back to the Veiled Court, with the burning tower that flickers against a starry sky. I think of Goch, looming over me in the Rhiannon Garden. And then, against my will, I think of

Rion's silver eyes and the way they darkened to a midnight blue when I was close to him.

My eyes snap open, and I hand her the cards. "Finished."

She starts to lay them out. I consider taking another spiced honey cake, but I seem to have lost my appetite. I'm actually nervous about what Tana will discover in the cards.

I take a long sip of tea, draining the brew.

Tana lays out the strength card—a woman with a lion. Because it's reversed, I wonder if it's my lost magic.

"Is that me?" I ask.

She nods, laying out the emperor card, reversed. Then the devil, followed by a bunch of bloody swords, some of them jutting out of dead men's backs.

"Danger," she mutters, rather unnecessarily.

She looks up at me from the cards and holds out her hand. "I'll need your teacup."

I hand her the empty cup, and she stares into it.

"Interesting..." She looks up from the tea leaves. "Most people committing evil think they're doing something good, you know. Something to help their kingdom, their families, the world."

I'm not sure I like where this is going. "What does that mean in this context?"

Instead of responding, she returns to the tarot cards, flipping them over onto the table. She lays down pictures of people leaping from a burning tower, a skeleton decapitating people with a scythe, a heart pierced by blades, a reversed magician wearing a dark cloak…

It's not exactly getting more cheerful. Outside, thunder booms.

She mutters again, "Death chases you."

Nervousness skitters down my spine. "Anything good at all?"

More cards—a man hanging upside down by his foot, a priestess on a throne, and the Wheel of Fortune.

At last, she takes a deep breath and looks up at me with that startled expression that suggests she forgot I was here. "Ah, yes. Syn."

My chest is tight. "So. Is there any good news?" I ask again.

We lock eyes. "Ah, yes. It is your fault. You will destroy the world."

My stomach drops, and my mouth goes dry. "The actual world, or somebody's book?"

"Hard to say. But strangely, it's not a bad thing in the end. In fact, I think it *must* happen. Sometimes, creation is born from ruin. Sometimes, you must burn the forest to clear the brush, you know?"

I look down at my old T-shirt from Owain, suddenly feeling as if it's a portent from the gods. *Have you tried turning it off and on again?*

Raphael's footsteps sound behind me, and he stalks closer to the table. His silver eyes pierce the dim light. He's taken off his bloody shirt, and he's cleaning himself off with a wet cloth. Tattoos wind around his bicep and shoulder and spill onto his athletic chest—grapevines that twine around a sailboat and star. "Tana. Explain more about how she'll destroy the world."

Tana shakes her head, looking down at the cards again. She points to the burning tower. "I don't think it's permanent. Frankly, I see worse outcomes if we don't work with her. Without Syn, there's destruction with no rebirth. I think she's chaotic, with a dark past. She's done some terrible things. But I also think we need her. I think the Fey need her fire to burn it all down and start over."

Raphael still grips his bloodstained rag, and his icy eyes cut to me. "What terrible things has she done?"

I pointedly sweep my eyes back to the crimson-smeared rag in his hands, then slowly meet his gaze again. "Tristan and I were trained by King Auberon in the Undercroft, starting at age eleven. You already know that. We were assassins. Spies also, just like you. Except unlike you, we were teenagers in the thrall of a tyrant. And that's why I want to stop another person like Auberon from taking the throne. I don't know what, exactly, you are working on at the Veiled Court. But if it means stopping the next tyrant king, I want to be part of it."

Raphael nods and returns his gaze to Tana. "Are you absolutely sure this is the right thing to do?"

Tana nods. "I'm certain."

Raphael stares at her for a weirdly long time, then turns to me. "Will you help us protect the Republic of Brocéliande to the best of your ability?"

"Yes. And does that mean you want to prevent the return of the monarchy?"

He stares at me, still assessing me.

"Because I will help you destroy the next king who tries to take the throne," I add.

"Good," says Raphael. "This is a reciprocal relationship. We share information with you, and you share it with us."

Tana points to the reversed magician card and slides it forward on the table. "This is where you start. I need you to find him. We need his identity."

I frown. "An upside-down magician."

"Exactly." She smiles, as if this is sufficient information.

I wait for her to tell me more. When she doesn't, I ask, "How do I know when I've found the right person?"

But she's no longer looking at me. She drums her fingertips on the cluttered table, gazing at the cards again. I think she's lost in thought, possibly communing with a spirit.

Raphael pulls up a wooden chair and sits down next to me. The firelight wavers over the water on his skin, making his muscles glisten. "Talan dethroned his own father, but he decided not to take the crown himself. He wasn't interested. And yet, his claim remains. And now, someone has abducted him and his betrothed, Nia."

There's a flash of pain in his eyes at that last sentence, and I can only assume that he knows her very well. He doesn't seem like the kind of person who would show emotion unless he was completely overcome.

"Nia *also* has a claim to the throne," he continues. "But more importantly to us, she's the Lady of the Lake, and she's very important to Camelot. Nia and Talan disappeared one night from the island of Avalon. We suspect it was someone from the Veiled Court who wanted to get rid of any competition."

A cold shiver skims up my neck. "That's why we brought the prince's dragon back here. You want her to help find Talan. But who is the upside-down magician?"

Raphael's eyes gleam. "We intercepted correspondence from someone from Brocéliande, intended for the Veiled Court. The messenger managed to destroy most of the letter before we could read it all, but we have fragments. It included an image of the ouroboros—Prince Talan's sigil. Then just a fragment, and we think it says *the Order of the Green Knight.*"

"Do you think the captives are still alive?" I ask.

A thorny silence takes hold of the room, and I realize I've struck a nerve. Raphael's jaw ticks.

At last, Tana says, "I believe they are still alive, but we don't have proof."

"Anything else you can tell me about this magician?" I ask.

She picks up the card. "This comes up repeatedly when I ask about the Green Man from the Veiled Court. His magic is powerful and rooted in nature."

I was born from the oaks... "I have someone in mind."

Raphael's pale eyes narrow. "But you need to follow the evidence. Don't get hung up on your first hunch and ignore all the data that doesn't fit your theory. Watch *everyone*. Keep your eyes open at all times, and don't trust a single person there. If you do have a lead, get close to him. Find a way into his room. Find the proof, *carefully*. Then find out who he's working with. We need incontrovertible evidence before we act, because we will only get one chance. And we need you to be as careful as possible. If your cover is blown, we've got no one else in the Veiled Court."

And I'll be burned to death by dragon fire.

"Understood." I swallow hard. "But someone there has already figured out I'm not the real Baroness Alis."

Raphael's expression darkens. "Who is it?"

"Rion du Lac. You know, the Ruthless Knight who took over Tintagol? He already suspects that I'm an imposter, but he doesn't have any confirmation. He's not telling anyone. He wants to form a sort of alliance with me because the crowds like us together. He also might be the person you're looking for."

Raphael nods. "Okay. This is good. Find out if you can learn anything from him. Use this alliance to buy his silence and see if you can find anything that ties him to the Order of the Green Knight."

Just as I'm starting to worry about the time, the door bursts open, and Tristan stalks in.

"Did you make your decision yet? Syn needs to get back before anyone notices she's gone."

Raphael stands. "We've told her everything she needs to know for now. Tristan, we need to get her back to the portal, but then I want you to stay here for a few days. No one else can fly Tarasque."

"Where's the portal?" I ask.

"It's out in the lake—the altar in Nimuë's tower." Raphael looks at me. "I'll give you a key to open the portal."

Tristan glares at him. "I thought the Iron Legion was *also* outside the fortress walls."

"They're mostly taking cover within the orchards," Raphael says. "We'll take the bridge from Merlin's library to lead us directly to Nimuë's Tower. We can use the stone walls of the bridge to give us cover for the entire route."

A muscle twitches in Tristan's jaw. "Fine."

Raphael frowns at me. "There's one more thing I need to impart to you, Syn, before you leave Avalon Tower. At the Veiled Court, you'll be safest if you go unnoticed. You must do well enough that you stay in the trials, but not so well that you set yourself up as a target. The moment you're the center of attention, you're in danger, and people will want to kill you. Stay in the shadows as much as possible. Understood?"

I understand what he's saying, but I won't exactly be staying in the shadows if I get the grail. I'm going to try anyway. "Got it."

Tristan arches an eyebrow at me, his gaze lingering on my face. He knows that I'm lying, but he's not blowing my cover.

My fingers twitch as if searching for a hilt. "Listen, Raphael, I know you said we'll be taking cover using the bridge, but I'll take a sword anyway."

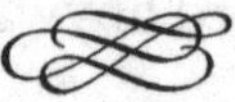

CHAPTER 31

We walk through a dark passage with an old, mossy stone ceiling. Raphael carries a torch, and its warm, guttering light dances over faded carvings in the walls. Beneath my feet, the stones are slick from centuries of foot traffic.

At Tristan's insistence, Raphael has thrown a cloak over his bare shoulders, and both of them have pulled up their dark cowls. The two men stalk before me in silence, shoulder to shoulder, neither one wanting the other to take the lead. Both of them have to hunch over to walk because the passage ceiling is barely high enough for me.

From behind, my halo casts a pale golden glow over their broad shoulders.

"Why is the portal outside of the fortress?" I ask.

Raphael glances back at me. "Nimuë was once the

Lady of the Lake, back in the days of primal magic. Her tower still has enough magical power to help us easily create a portal."

Tristan glances back at me with an amused smile. "So, Syn Malleore is going to destroy the world. Why am I not surprised?"

"Tana said it's necessary to restart things," I say. "A rebirth."

"Risky," Tristan murmurs.

"Tristan," I whisper. "It sounds like Avalon Tower can use me there. I want to stay at the Veiled Court as long as I can. I want to help protect the republic and stop the next tyrant."

Raphael scowls back at us. "Can we just focus on getting you to the portal alive first?"

"What kind of weapons do the Iron Legion have here?" I ask quietly. "In London, they're armed only with swords and blades."

"Some idiot politician has given them guns," Raphael says. "They have some supporters in high places. Government officials who claim they have absolute immunity."

As we get to a door, Raphael pulls a vial of glowing blue liquid from his pocket. "This will shield us in case we run into gunfire."

"And how would that happen? I thought the bridge walls would protect us." Tristan asks. "Because I know the magic of that potion doesn't last forever."

Raphael's eyebrows rise. "There's a *tiny* chance the paramilitaries will approach from the lake and get into Nimuë's Tower. We've been given the clear, but with a caveat that it's hard to have absolute certainty in the fog."

"Lunacy," Tristan mutters.

Raphael turns to me and dabs my forehead with the potion. As he does, I feel its magic like an icy, liquid metal dripping over me.

Tristan takes it from Raphael and dabs it on his forehead himself. Then he turns to look at me, his green eyes almost glowing under the cowl. "Once we get outside, keep low and cross the bridge to Nimuë's Tower. When you touch the altar, the portal will take you right into the Veiled Court."

When we're all shielded, Raphael pushes through the door. The bridge is longer than I expected, spanning hundreds of feet over the lake.

Raphael and Tristan start to move along the bridge, crouching down for cover, and I follow behind them. My scabbard drags along the stones. Beneath us, the lake laps at the base of the bridge.

Out here, the air smells of apple blossoms, reeds, and damp grass. Mist roils above us, coiling above the bridge. It *feels* peaceful, but looks can be deceiving.

In the thick fog, I can hardly see the tower ahead of us, only worn carvings in the ancient stone bridge around me. Moonlight tinges the fog with silver.

When we're three-quarters of the way to the end, I start to relax a little.

At least, until Tristan and Raphael freeze. My blood runs cold, and my gaze flicks over their shoulders. I have only a moment to see what's made them stop: a shadow moving through the mist that makes my heart skip a beat.

Fuck.

Two men stalk closer through the mist, their guns aimed at us.

My heart stutters. I reach for the hilt of my sword just as one of the figures ahead of us shouts, "Get on the ground!"

The man's not even from here. He's American, I think. I wonder if he's come all the way over here just for the chance to hunt Fey. In any case, they don't actually give us a chance to get on the ground before they open fire, and bullets slam into our magical armor.

I grit my teeth, thankful for the potion.

With swords drawn, we start to move closer to them.

The only other thing that can move fast as a bullet is Tristan, and he's already off in a lightning-quick blur of shadow. Within seconds, there's a shout and a spray of blood. As Tristan's first kill falls off the bridge, he's already stabbing the second man. He's slaughtered them both in moments.

But they're not alone. Already, more paramilitaries are running from Nimuë's Tower.

"Get on the fucking ground!" one of them roars, and even from here I can see his fury. A vein pulses on his forehead as he stares at me. "Fucking bitch!"

The three of us rush forward, and I swing for one of them. My blade bites into a man's shoulder, and I force it through his muscle and bone until his arm gives way. The gun falls to the ground along with his arm. He starts screaming, reaching for the gun with his good hand, but I kick it away.

They keep coming—gunfire pounding our shields, blades flashing from the fog—until all I know are my ragged gasps, the copper scent of blood, and bullets hammering against magic.

They're screaming at us as they shoot, calling us *Fey pigs*.

Most of the bullets ricochet off the stone around me, but one slams against the force field below my chest, hard enough to drive the air from my lungs. I know the potion is fading.

I strike one of the armed men, hefting my blade straight through his neck. His body crumples to the ground just as Tristan takes down another gunman. I turn and thrust my blade through a man's throat, slicing his jugular. His gun lets off a few more rounds into the air, but he collapses.

From the corner of my eye, I see one of the bullets pierce Raphael's shield, driving into his chest. He falls back, the force field around him cracking, sputtering out.

And just as I'm distracted, a bullet pierces my shield, driving into my bicep. Grimacing with agony, I can only watch as Tristan kills the last two gunmen, his sword slicing through their throats almost instantaneously. Their bodies collapse to the ground.

Blood stains the stones around us. It all happened so fast, and now corpses litter the bridge, and the air smells of death.

Raphael slumps against the side of the bridge, his hand pressed against his chest to staunch his blood.

A sharp ache lacerates my bicep. Iron is leaching from the bullet lodged in my shoulder, and it makes me want to vomit.

I wipe my mouth with shaking hands, tasting copper and salt. I don't know if it's someone else's blood or my own. My legs are trembling as my adrenaline crashes.

"Syn," Tristan says, turning to me with concern. "You were hit, let me see."

"I'm fine," I say. "I think Raphael needs help."

I turn to Raphael and find him clutching his collarbone, still trying to stop the bleeding. I kneel next to him. "Are you okay, Raphael?" I ask through labored breaths.

"Fine." Blood pours from his chest and leg.

I pull open his cloak—he's still not wearing a shirt under it. The bullet hit him near his collarbone, and blood flows from the wound. Another bullet hit him in the knee, probably shattering his bones.

If he gets to a healer soon, he'll survive.

"You need to go, Syn," Raphael says through clenched teeth. "You're almost at the portal."

"Wait," Tristan says, crouching next to me. "I need to get Syn's bullet out. If we send her back with that, her cover will already be blown. Plus, she could die from iron poisoning."

The excruciating pain is making me feel hot all over, and my limbs are shaking. I can only imagine how Raphael feels with two bullets in his body.

Blood seeps into my purple cloak. I pull it off and turn my injured arm toward Tristan, who stares at it with a deeply intent concentration. I look down to see my injured bicep, just beneath the cuff of my T-shirt.

His eyes lift to mine, and a line forms between his eyebrows. "This is going to hurt."

My teeth chatter. "It already does."

I close my eyes, trying to imagine myself anywhere but here. Tristan's hands reach for my arm, pressing, probing —and then he jolts the bullet with a hard, agonizing tug that makes my eyes water. A tear slips down my cheek, and I wipe it away with a bloodied hand before Tristan can see. Blood pours from the bullet wound, and I clamp my hand over it. I have no idea how I'm going to heal this in the Veiled Court, but I'll find something.

Distantly, I hear more shouts—probably more para-militaries heading for us, drawn by the sound of gunfire.

Tristan takes my face in his hands and stares into my

eyes with the intimacy of a lover. "Run to the portal and touch the altar. I'll take care of Raphael. Get your arm healed as soon as you get back. Tell them you were attacked by an unidentified assailant. I don't know."

"I'll think of something. Be careful," I whisper.

He kisses my forehead. "You've got the portal key?" he asks.

Hell of a time to ask that.

I reach into my pocket, pulling out a silver bracelet that glows in the mist. "Of course."

He slides his hand around the back of my neck, and warmth cascades through me. With his green eyes locked on me, he leans in closer. My halo gilds his features from below. My gaze lingers on his black eyelashes, the high cheekbones, the sharp jawline. Such pretty features on a hardened warrior of a man.

My heartbeat picks up, and I breathe in his scent.

For a moment, I think he's going to kiss me. Instead, he presses his forehead against mine and closes his eyes. He lets out a long, slow sigh. "I'll come back to the Veiled Court as soon as I can," he says in hardly a whisper. Then, he reaches into a small sheath at his waist and pulls out a dagger. "In case anyone sees you returning and wants to know how you were shot."

"Thanks. Will anyone notice that you're gone?"

He shakes his head. "Only Arlene, and she'll never tell on me."

I slip the dagger into my cloak and start to move for

the portal. As I reach the door, I turn back to see Tristan sliding his arms under Raphael's legs and back to carry him. Raphael looks unconscious at this point, and I have a feeling Tristan will never let him forget this moment.

The shouts of mortals draw closer, and I rush into the tower.

I breathe in the earthy, fruited air as I step into the tower carved with glowing triple spirals. I can feel the power of this place buzzing over my skin. As I enter, the air grows colder.

I take a few steps down into a room that looks like a temple, with sharply peaked gothic windows. There's no glass in them, and a cool wind sweeps inside, raising goose bumps on my skin. With the portal key around my wrist, I take a step closer to a dusty, circular altar in the center of the room. Carved into the stone are images of three women.

The moment I touch the altar, its magic surges into my fingertips, flowing up my arms and into my chest. Light blinds me, and I feel as if I'm falling through space for a moment. It's the strange sensation I get sometimes when

I'm drifting off to sleep, and it feels as if the world has been pulled out from under me.

I land on the cobbles outside the Aether Tower and struggle to regain my balance. My gaze flicks up to the stars and Brocéliande's two moons as I orient myself.

I take the portal key off my wrist and slip it into the pocket of my leather trousers, blocking out the screaming pain in my arm.

A footfall behind me makes the hair on the back of my neck stand up, and a chill slides through my veins.

Already, I'm gripping the dagger.

"I didn't expect it to be you," a voice says from behind me.

As I turn, I hide the dagger behind my back. Lord Cador is standing by the base of the Aether Tower, the torchlight gleaming off his burgundy hair.

My mind spins through a million calculations as Auberon's cold conditioning takes over. Once his poisonous seeds take root, the weeds he planted never stop growing.

"Didn't expect *what* to be me?" I ask quietly.

His eyes narrow. "The *cugol* just told me someone escaped the castle, but they didn't yet know who it was. I thought it might be Mabon, drunk again. What I didn't expect was to find you ripping open a portal into our fortress. And how, *exactly*, did you have the power to do that? You don't possess portal magic. So, my question is— who are you working with?"

I'm focusing on one thing—and that's the fact that no one else knows it was me yet. I take a step closer to Cador, making my eyes go wide, and inhale the scent of the linseed oil he uses in his hair.

I can feign ignorance, I suppose. At least to buy myself time. "I don't understand? I was asleep—"

He slashes his hand through the air, and a sharp gash opens up on my bicep, then rips through the bottom of my shirt. Pain tears across my skin, and for a few moments, I can hardly think clearly. When some of the initial shock subsides, I realize the gashes didn't go deep.

For a moment, I stand stunned and try to catch my breath, my arm throbbing painfully from the bullet wound.

Your sluggishness is giving him the upper hand, Auberon says in my thoughts. *Act now.*

I lunge forward and press my dagger against his jugular. "It will only take a moment to end your life, Lord Cador," I hiss. "So, you'd better listen very carefully to my instructions."

The first thing I need to do is get him inside. I'd like to interrogate him at least a little, and this isn't the place for it. If anyone looks out their window, I'm fucked.

He nods, nearly imperceptibly, his face pale.

"Open the door to your left," I whisper. "And we're going to go inside. Together. We're going to have a conversation at the base of the stairwell."

Trembling slightly, he does as instructed, and the oak

door creaks open. I keep my blade pressed against his throat, nicking his skin as we shift into the torchlight stairwell.

"Let's start with the grail," I say. "How do I get it? Is it a trial?"

"The next one." His throat bobs. "But you won't win it. You will die here, a traitor. And then we will find the rest of your family and kill them as a message to the others. Even if we have to break into the Waste Land to do it."

My jaw clenches. The thing about Cador's magic is that he could actually use it to learn my real identity. Then he really could hunt down Vero.

"You're not getting near my family," I snarl.

"I will peel off your skin, and then your family's—"

As an image of Vero flashes in my mind, I press the blade in deeper, drawing blood. He winces.

"Do not play with me." Darkness swirls inside my skull. "How do I win the trial?"

He whimpers, and I can see that he's already about to break. He may be a torturer himself, but the man doesn't have any pain tolerance when it comes to his own skin.

"It begins in about thirty hours," he blurts. "It's a race, and many of you will die. You must not go into the valley. The questing beast's howl is a thing you will never forget."

This isn't making any sense yet. "But how do I win?"

"Survive your competitors trying to kill you. Then, if you make it to the bridge of swords, you'll cross a long blade over a pit of flames."

"And is there a trick to it?"

Now, his cheeks are reddening, his temper rising. He's growing braver. "The trick is being brave, clever, and strong, so you don't have a chance."

"I've got this far."

His lip curls. "The gods will never accept you. The flames will claim you and burn you alive."

"You don't have the first fucking clue what the gods think." I'm running out of time. "Do you know anything about the Order of the Green Knight?"

His lips press into a thin line. He's not denying it, but he's not saying anything either. I press the blade in a little deeper, and he screams, a loud, panicked sound. And that, in turn, makes me nervous, because he's going to draw someone here.

He flicks his wrist again, ripping open the skin on my hand. A jagged, searing pain tears my palm, and I drop the dagger, clutching my bleeding hand.

"Now, traitor, I have questions for you." His eyes flash. "Who helped you make that portal?"

Shaking, cradling my injured hand, I take a slow step closer to him. My gaze flicks to the wavering torch by his head.

With my left hand, I smash his head into it, and the oil in his hair ignites, turning his head into a second torch.

He shouts, smacking at the flames in his hair to douse them, and I use the opportunity to grab my dagger again.

I bring it up into his chest and plunge the blade

between his ribs. His eyes snap open. I think I've hit his heart, but he's still breathing. A trickle of blood drips from his lip. His eyes are unfocused, staring at the wall behind me.

"What do you know about the Green Knight?" I ask.

The scent of blood and burnt hair fills the stairwell.

But what reason does he have to answer me now? We both knew the moment we came in here that only one of us would be leaving this tower alive.

His eyes focus again, and they slide to me. "Our next king will find the person who killed me. Then he will execute you, and everyone you love, in ways more brutal than you can imagine."

Not if I'm the next monarch.

I grit my teeth and twist the blade in his chest. Blood pours from him, and he lets out one final, rasping breath —a rattle in his throat. Then the light leaves his eyes, and I pull out my dagger, letting him slump down the wall.

Now, my hands are trembling, and my eyes sting. I can't stop thinking about how he threatened to peel Vero's skin off.

And once again, I've got a corpse on my hands.

There's blood everywhere, mine and Cador's. I don't imagine I'll be able to clean it all up, but maybe I can get some of it washed away.

I go still, listening for the sound of footfalls or any type of movement. When I don't hear anything, I turn to look at the door marked with the white rose.

I pull it open, and I'm hit by the scent of bones and soil. At the bottom of the short stairwell are the skulls of two princes murdered long ago. I drag Lord Cador's lifeless body over to the open doorway and shove him down the steps.

I cock my head, staring as his corpse rolls down. Cador lands with a thump at the bottom, stopping by the two skulls.

I close the door to the stairwell and lean against it. Blood covers my body.

As I catch my breath, the tower door opens.

Rion steps inside, his silver eyes burning into me.

In the next moment, my blade is pressed against his throat, and I'm starting to wonder how many bodies I'll collect by the end of the night.

With a dagger at someone's jugular, you'd expect them to show some sign of fear. A racing pulse. Wide eyes. A tightening jaw.

Instead, Rion looks almost bored. His pulse doesn't jump beneath my blade—not even a flicker as I reach up, pressing harder against his jugular. One quick movement, and the Ruthless Knight would be nothing but a story.

He actually leans into the knife, just a little, drawing a tiny bit of blood. A half smile plays over his full lips as he peers down at me, and amusement dances in his silver eyes. "Are you *trying* to turn me on, love?"

His sensual voice drips over my skin.

"Why are you calling me *love* when I could end your life at any moment?"

"Because I don't know your real name."

My first instinct, of course, is to kill him and add his

body to the stairwell collection. But that would ruin the entire mission, and piling up fresh corpses probably isn't the best way to stay out of trouble.

I *think* I can make a deal with him, buying his silence. Like Raphael said, I need this alliance. I've now pledged to help Avalon Tower destroy the next king, and I can't do that if I'm not in the Veiled Court.

Slowly, I pull the blade from his throat and back away. "You've caught me at an awkward time."

"I can see that." The torchlight washes over him, and shadows sculpt his cheekbones. He's dressed in dark clothes perfectly tailored to his broad frame, and his silver hair drapes over a cloak. A smile flits over his lips. "What was it you said to me? *Everyone knows you're a monster*, and yet, I was resting in my room when a horrified scream awoke me, and who do I find at the scene of the crime but you." He sniffs the air. "Did you set him on fire, too, or was the stabbing enough for you?"

My muscles have gone rigid. "It was self-defense."

I've been saying that a lot lately.

Rion's silver gaze flicks down to my arms and the tear in my shirt. Blood still spills from the bullet wound in my arm, too.

A muscle ticks in his jaw as he puts together what happened. "I think you killed him because he discovered the truth. You're not Alis at all."

"I don't owe you an explanation."

He steps closer, looming, and his magic prickles across

my skin like a warning. But he only brushes past me, then reaches for the door with the white rose. He pulls it open. "Well, *this* invites some questions."

I feel my chest flush. Rion has a real way of piercing me right down to the nerve. "It was a necessity."

I catch myself trying to justify my actions to him, and I wonder why I'm bothering.

"Is that the story you tell yourself?" He cuts me a sharp look.

I'm catching my breath. "What are you going to do?"

"As I said before, you're my new lover. I'm not sure I want to lose you to Goch's flames just yet, even if you are a murderous little vixen who probably deserves it."

I fold my bloodied arms, then immediately regret it as the torn skin pulls. "You expect me to believe you object to violence? You're the monster in children's tales, the legendary Ruthless Knight who hacks off limbs and leaves people screaming for sport. Stories can lie, of course. But as far as I can tell, you're proving them all accurate."

Amusement flickers in his eyes, and molten silver catches in the torchlight. His expression sends a shiver down my spine. "Then what does that make you?" he coos. "The Murderous *Peasant*? You should admit the truth to yourself. It's very liberating. We'd make a rather striking pair of monsters, don't you think?"

He takes a slow step closer.

Panic crackles through my veins. One word from him, and I die screaming. Vero will waste away from the ague.

And the kingdom could fall into the hands of someone like *him*.

"What do you want?" I grit out. "What do I need to do for you to keep my secret?"

"I could use you." A dark edge slides through his tone. "For now."

"Give me specifics."

The torchlight dances in his cold eyes. "You'll put on a show for the noble houses—one of desire and lust and a hint of obsession. If you fake being my lover, I can climb up to the top spot and unseat Mabon."

My cheeks flame. "You've got to be kidding me."

"And you will climb with me. When I win the crown, I will overlook your lies and deceit, and I will grant you a title and lands. Duchess, if you like. It's the best chance you have of rising." His expression darkens. "Or I could always tell everyone the truth I already suspected: you're an imposter. Now I know you've killed someone important to keep a secret. Cador was Niniane's lover. Oh, dear, I don't think she'll take this well."

It would be a sweet deal. But for one thing, I don't trust him. And for another, I'm going to try to kill anyone who gets close to the crown. Rion included.

My breathing is shallow, rapid. "Fine. I'll do what you want. The fake obsession. Whatever you need."

"Good."

At some point, I will need to kill him. For now, I'll play along.

His cold gaze sweeps down my body, assessing. "You're covered in your victim's blood. Take off your cloak. Use it to soak up as much blood as you can before you drip evidence all over the fortress."

"You really know your way around a murder scene cleanup, don't you?"

I pull off my cloak and brush the velvety material over my arms and T-shirt. I'm taking particular care with my hands so I don't leave bloody fingerprints everywhere.

"You'll need to properly heal those wounds quickly, though, or anyone here could immediately tie you to his disappearance."

I stare down at the ragged gash across my arm, then lift my shirt to look at the bloody red streak across my belly. Scarlet drips down my skin. "I have no idea how to do that without a healer."

"Lucky for you, I *am* a healer."

He pulls off his shirt, and I stare at him, my breath going still. My gaze lingers on the golden tattoos that glisten on his broad, sculpted chest, then dip down to the sharp V carved into his hips. My skin heats traitorously.

"Why are you taking off your clothes? Are you turned on by all the gore?"

"Love, if I were trying to seduce you, you'd know." He tosses his shirt to me. "You need to cover up the wounds on your way to my room. Head to the White Hart's Rill in Lyria on the top floor. I'll take care of everything in here."

I pull on his black shirt, and the soft, luxurious fabric

slips over my skin. It's ridiculously large on me, the hem and the sleeves hanging down to my knees. Still, I suppose if anyone saw me walking around in this, it would only help with the whole *lovers* charade.

His shirt smells of smoldering wood, faintly spiced. It brushes against my skin like cashmere. For a warlord, he has sophisticated style and obviously appreciates the finer things in life.

I step outside just as the first blush of dawn streaks across the sky.

Rion could destroy me with just a word, and now I'm putting my life in the hands of a man universally known for his cruelty.

* * *

I MAKE it to the White Hart's Rill without anyone seeing me, even though it's close to the top of Lyria. On Rion's door, I find a painted sign of a white stag standing by a river, wearing a golden crown marked with a triple spiral.

When I pull open the door, I find a breathtaking scene, like a great hall carved from misty forest. It's even better than my room. Rion's canopied bed stands nestled in one corner, and a winding stream burbles gently past it, flowing out a towering gothic window on the other side. Steam rises from the water, and the hall feels humid and misty. The floor is mossy stone, with bluebells growing alongside the stream. Azure flowers climb the stone walls

293

reaching for the vaulted ceiling. A bridge crosses over the stream, joining the two halves of the room.

I take off my boots and walk barefoot on the mossy stone.

The room is tidy—his bed neatly made. Everything is in its right place.

I move closer to the vast window, peering out above the light spray of water. Rion's view is of the courtyard—the bridge to the Aether Tower, the arena where we nearly killed each other, the cart track that I raced on one night.

I turn back into his room, looking for anything I can explore. There's a wardrobe across the little bridge, and I cross to that and pull it open. In there, I find his fine clothes and a vast array of daggers. I don't immediately find anything that stands out as evidence of Prince Talan's kidnapping.

A desk stands by his bed. I cross to it and listen for the sound of footfalls outside, then pull open the drawer.

I find a paper inside that stops me cold—a line drawing of an oak, its branches etched with royal symbols.

At its crown, there's a cauldron emblazoned with a skull, beaming with sun rays—the symbol of King Bran the Great.

On a lower branch is a swan wearing a golden crown, with a chain looped around its throat. I already discovered that one—King Emrys. I believe that was the king murdered in the room above.

Just beneath it, drawn on the bark itself, is a wild man with leaves spilling from his mouth and eyes. I think these leafy faces are called Green Men sometimes. It might be the symbol of Merlin—the great Fey—trapped in an oak.

The Order of the Green Knight?

And finally, I glance down at the last symbol—a raven, a moon, a white rose. The symbols adopted by Auberon when he claimed the throne.

I stare at it, my heartbeat picking up. Is this Auberon's family tree? I never knew he was descended from Bran the Great. Not that it really matters. He should have died an excruciating death, no matter who his ancestors were.

The important thing is that *Rion* seems interested in Auberon's claim to the throne. Does he suspect, like I do, that Auberon could be still alive? A rival to the throne he wants?

Just as I'm starting to slide the paper back into the drawer, I hear footfalls outside. My heart quickens, and I slide the drawer shut just before Rion steps into his room.

I fake a yawn and sit down on his bed like I'm bored. "How did the cleanup go?"

Buttery dawn light spills into the room, washing over his bare chest as he steps inside. When the sun hits his golden tattoos, they blaze like morning rays sparkling off the ocean.

His eyes spark, too. "Generally, I prefer killing to tidying up the aftermath, but luckily for you, I'm very good at both. Drink?"

"It's five a.m."

Ignoring my protest, he's already pouring mead into two glasses. "And you just murdered Niniane's lover, so I'm not sure why you suddenly care about propriety." He hands me a glass of mead. "Why don't you tell me who you are and what you were doing in the Aether Tower at such an ungodly hour?"

I take a sip of mead. "No, I don't think so. But I'll fake the romance with you, and that's all you need to move up."

He shrugs, and a dark smile curls his lips. "Fine. I know enough not to trust you either way."

"Likewise."

"You are, after all, the Murderous Peasant. Everyone knows you're a monster." His eyes drop. "Now. Take off your shirt."

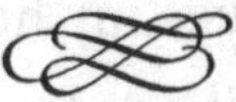

CHAPTER 34

I arch an eyebrow. "Is this the seduction you bragged about?"

His smile disarms me. For a moment, it's so heart-breakingly beautiful it catches me off guard, and I forget what he is. "It's really on your mind, isn't it, love? But no, I need to heal you so no one realizes you crossed Cador before he went missing."

I peel the soft black shirt over my head, revealing the ripped cartoon T-shirt underneath. Mist curls from the warm stream, twisting over the stone floor and thickening the air.

He frowns at the gaping wound in my shoulder left earlier by the bullet. "How did *that* happen?"

"Must have been Cador's magic."

"You wretched little liar." Venom drips from the words. "Let me see your arm first."

"Why do you have healing magic when your power is fear?" I ask.

"My power grows in the space between life and death."

I stare back into his gleaming silver eyes, shot through with metallic blue. There's something mesmerizing in the way he speaks, and it makes my heart race.

If I have to kill him, I'll need to forget this.

He holds out a hand. "Your arm."

I offer him my upturned wrist—and the moment I see the angry red gash, I remember its searing pain.

His fingertips hover over my skin, close enough for me to feel their warmth.

"Hold still," he says quietly.

His hand closes around my wrist, and even from that light contact, I can feel the power radiating from his body.

His fingertips brush over the wound in my arm, and I close my eyes at the sensation. It's almost ecstatic, like a cool pool of water I want to dive into.

I'm struggling to think of anything except the feel of his hand around my wrist and the lazy caress of his fingers over my arm. With each languid stroke, an ache ignites in my core. As his fingertips trace over my skin, the pain slips away, leaving behind only warmth.

I lick my lips. "What does that mean, *between life and death?*"

Silver eyes flick up to meet mine, and my heart skips a beat at his beauty.

"They call it amoromancy, as if it's about love." He

traces his fingers over my skin. "It isn't. But the world has forgotten the true sublime nature of Fey magic."

"So, what is the real nature of your magic?"

"Fear is born from a dread of death. People lie to themselves, and my magic strips those lies away." A wicked smile curls his lips. "They don't realize how deeply death terrifies them until its blade is at their throat."

I arch an eyebrow. "The healing magic comes from life, I take it?"

He leans in close, and my gaze dips to his full lips. "And desire. My magic reveals the truth about that as well. That's how I heal—myself and others."

A sensual need dances through my core, and I try to block out the way his magic makes my body flush. His mouth curves slightly, as if he notices.

I feel like the air itself has turned sultry.

I force my thoughts to cool down as I try to think clinically. "If the primal powers are gone from the world," I whisper, "then why do you have one of them?"

"Because I remember what it means to be Fey."

His voice is little more than a velvety murmur, brushing over my skin like a lover's caress.

That's his magic. It means nothing.

"And if you manage to become king, how will you wield such power?"

He cocks his head. "However I see fit, of course."

"No one keeps a crown without shedding blood." My breath is rapid. "The victor of the Veiled Court trials will likely slaughter the rest of their rivals before coronation day. Just like Mabon said."

He doesn't answer. He's focusing on my arm again, his dark eyelashes veiling his eyes.

I lean in closer, my face inches from his now. "Have you heard the rumors that Prince Talan is missing?"

Rion's fingers tighten nearly imperceptibly on my wrist. Slowly, his gaze lifts, unreadable. A sharp silence hangs in the air.

"What rumors?" His voice is low, controlled, but I can hear a note of tension cutting under the surface.

Our faces are nearly close enough to kiss now. "It's just something I heard. I have no idea where the rumor started."

His gaze sweeps down again to my arm, and he traces his fingertips over the bullet wound in my shoulder. Euphoria slides through me with each touch.

"Prince Talan didn't want the throne," he says quietly. "Gave it to the low-born, poorly educated peasants. Like you, love."

He moves over the last bit of cut skin on the inside of my elbow, and heat pulses along my arm. Pleasure ripples over my body from every point of contact. When he finally pulls away, my body hums with anticipation.

"Your stomach," he says simply.

With a deep breath, I tug up the hem of my T-shirt, and the humid air kisses my belly. He moves his right arm to my hip, while the left hand strokes my skin. *Oh, gods...*

As his seductive magic unfurls over me, I scramble to think about anything but kissing him. I think about the way he said, "I could use you. *For now.*"

Now my heart is pounding hard, and I try not to notice the way molten heat slides through my body at his touch, or the way he smells of spiced oak. Under my T-shirt, my nipples go hard. He's dangerous in every possible way.

I'm suddenly intensely aware of his right hand on my waist, his thumb resting in the hollow of my hipbone. A slow, languid stroke of his thumb makes warmth swoop low through my body. My breath is rapid, and my thighs clench.

He knows exactly what he's doing to me.

The heat in my belly smolders into need.

I look down at my stomach to find there's just a tiny dot left, and I stand up abruptly, catching my breath.

I gaze down at my perfectly healed skin, stunned by his magic.

"And we're finished," I say.

If his healing magic is this powerful, of course his dread magic is, too. And that's where this ends, of course. Either I kill him in the end or he'll take me apart with the same care he just used to put me together—mind first, then my body. Nothing of the real Syn would remain. Of *that* I'm certain.

"You'll need to wash the blood off before you go," he says. "I'll give you new clothes." He crosses to his wardrobe. "It won't hurt for people to see you leave here dressed in my things."

I glance at the burbling stream, where mist coils into the air. I can ask him to shut his eyes while I bathe, but that would give him the satisfaction of calling me an uptight mortal again. I'm petty enough to strip in front of a man I hate before I admit he was right.

While he's opening the door to his wardrobe, I pull off my leather trousers as fast as I can and peel out of my underwear and T-shirt. The humid air in his room kisses my skin, whispering over my bare breasts and nipples.

I slip into the water, and its warmth envelops me, flowing over my naked skin. The rising sunlight dapples the stream with flecks of gold. The ritual of the Mor.

I turn back to look at Rion.

Unexpectedly, I find that he's still looking in his wardrobe for something fitting.

If he were any other man, I'd interpret this as a gentlemanly act.

Quickly, I rinse myself off—my own blood from my stomach and arms, and Cador's from my face and hair and beneath my fingernails. By the time I look up again, I see that he's set out a soft towel and a long shirt for me on the mossy rocks by the stream.

He crosses the room, picking up a book. "Don't worry, love. I already know all about your mortal inhibitions."

He drops onto his bed with the book and flips a page.

Frankly, I'm surprised the man reads.

But perhaps we're both going to surprise each other this morning.

I rise from the spring, steam billowing around me. Water streams down my bare skin in little rivulets, tracing between my breasts and down my belly. Barefoot, I cross the mossy rocks to where he's sitting and pluck the book from his hands.

"What are you reading?" I ask.

As I said, I am petty and refuse to let him be right.

I turn it to read the spine: a small, leather-bound book of poems by Prince Talan.

My stomach tightens. This can't be a coincidence.

I don't see any other books in here. Did he take this from Talan when he abducted him?

I look up from the book to find Rion staring at me, his expression darkening as his gaze sweeps up from my breasts to my face. For a moment, hunger burns in his eyes.

He doesn't say a word.

Something about that feels like a victory. He's gone totally still—his control tightly coiled, and his eyes burning with a dark heat.

Then his expression shutters, and the intensity fades from his eyes so quickly, I start to wonder if I imagined it all. He pulls the book from my hands and turns the page.

"See you at the trial," he murmurs, sounding bored. "Duchess."

I turn to snatch up a towel and quickly dry off, then

pull on one of his expensive shirts. The soft wool caresses my skin. I slip on my shoes. At the door, I turn back to him to find his silver eyes are on me once again.

He doesn't know it yet, but tomorrow morning, we will be fighting to the death over the grail.

CHAPTER 35

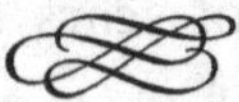

I'm walking through the Rhiannon Garden late at night. Flower petals dapple the mossy earth, and the humid air kisses my skin. I trace my fingertips over the altar. Then I feel someone moving closer to me, and his power radiates over me from behind.

I turn to see Rion walking barefoot over the moss. His golden tattoos illuminate the night. My heart races at the sight of him.

His eyes burn into me. When he reaches me, he lifts me by my waist onto the altar. He pulls out a blade, and it glints in the moonlight.

With a gasp, I wake from my dream and sit up straight in bed. I rub my eyes to wake up fully.

Enough sleeping for today. Already, it's the late afternoon. I have work to do.

* * *

Knights in silver armor roam the courtyard, searching for signs of Cador. Niniane has been tearing this place apart looking for him. She noticed his absence immediately this morning. After breakfast, her guardian knights questioned each of us. The man who interrogated me searched for any signs of scars on my body that would have betrayed a fight with Cador, but Rion's magic erased all traces.

Now, the sun is starting to set, and they still haven't found what's left of Cador.

I can only hope it stays that way.

And while they search for him, I'm going to see what else I can learn about the grail. Tomorrow might be my last chance to save Vero. At this point, I don't think she has much time left.

I follow a winding, cobbled path to the library I discovered earlier, a golden-stone building with soaring windows and a sharply peaked roof. Above an ivy-covered crimson door, there's a carving of a book.

I push through the door into a vast hall with an ornately carved rib-vaulted ceiling. Lanterns float beneath the arches, and a few wisps of glittering clouds drift between them. Warm light pours in through the windows onto stacks of books and mahogany desks, some of them set with tea kettles and cups.

There are thousands of books in here, stacked up two stories, with ladders on wheels to reach the highest shelves. Golden letters shift and spark on the spines of leather-bound tomes.

The question is, where can I learn anything about the path to the grail?

* * *

AFTER HOURS OF SEARCHING, I still haven't found anything about the grail trial.

But I did find something that I *think* refers to the questing beast.

So far, it's been utterly empty in here besides me, the books, and the many cups of tea. By now, the sun has set, and the lanterns cast golden light onto the book's pages.

The problem is that the texts are written in an archaic version of Fey, and I can only half understand them.

I think it's something about an *unhealed wound*. Something about dogs, maybe. On the right side, there's a poorly drawn picture of a large creature that looks half dragon and half leopard.

As I stare at the text, I hear the library door opening and slam the book shut. I slide it back into place, and I start to walk casually along the stacks of books until I see that it's Tristan, his dark hair ruffled rakishly. A smile warms his face.

I've been desperate to see him.

The lantern light bathes him in gold and shadow, and

warmth slides through my chest at the sight of him. It's lonely when he's not here.

"There you are." His gaze sweeps over me. "Do you have any idea how many knights I had to misdirect to find you?"

Already, I'm pulling the book off the shelf again. "I didn't know you were coming back so soon."

He closes the distance between us, and my back presses lightly against the stacks of books. He plants a hand on one side of me, caging me in. "I wasn't supposed to come back quite yet. Raphael wanted me to search for Talan in the air. I told him intel mattered more, but I mostly wanted to check on you."

I lean back against the bookshelves and tell him what I saw the day before—everything I found in Rion's room. The family tree, the symbol of King Bran, the cauldron—and the drawing that looked like the Green Man.

When I finish, Tristan folds his arms, frowning. "He has *Auberon's* family tree in his desk drawer? Considering Talan was the one who defeated Auberon, I'd say that paints him as a top suspect in the kidnapping. I'll get this back to Raphael. Anything else?"

"There was a bit of a hiccup as I came back last night," I whisper. "Cador caught me popping through the portal, and he didn't take it well. He threatened to peel my skin off—and Vero's, too, if he figured out who she was."

His jaw tightens. "He threatened to *what*?" His voice is low, lethal. "Where is he?"

"Dead and buried, of course. What do you think I am? An amateur?"

The corners of his lips lift in a half smile. "Well done."

I breathe in the safe, masculine scent of him. My breath catches whenever he's near. Imagine if Tristan and I had grown up with a normal life—without the Undercroft, without the memories that linger like aches in our bones. What if we had been two kids running through the woods, hunting conkers and butterflies, who grew into teenagers stealing kisses beneath willow branches, then adults who curled up in a safe bed, in a safe home?

It almost feels real for a moment, and an ache opens in my chest for this phantom world.

With a lump in my throat, I push the thought away.

I cross to the table and set down the book.

Tristan turns to one of the desks and starts to make tea with a metal kettle, its surface carved with magic runes.

"But I haven't told you the most important part. I will be competing for the grail tomorrow morning. I'm trying to learn more about the trial. Can you read ancient Fey?" I flip to the page with the beast. "I think this questing beast might be part of it. There's also a bridge of swords over a pit of flames."

He stares at me. "A pit of flames? Where, exactly, *is* this?"

"I remember Cador once saying that the grail wasn't here, exactly, but connected to the fortress. Maybe they'll bring it here for us to compete and create a pit of flames in the arena? I have no idea."

Tristan hands me a ceramic cup of steaming tea that smells of lavender, sweetened with mead. The steam coils in my face, warming me.

"Let me have a look." Tristan runs his finger over the text. "*And from his belly rose such a noise, like the din of thirty hounds questing.*"

"A hunting creature, then."

He's still tracing with his fingers. "*The noise it creates opens an unhealed wound…* I don't know what that means, exactly. It says a king named Pellinore woke the beast when he tried to extend his reign for longer than a year…"

"Who is King Pellinore?"

He looks up from the book. "No idea. He must have been a king before Bran, someone with a small kingdom. I don't understand the bit about only being king for a year. Anyway, he transgressed somehow, then a civil war broke out, and the bloodshed woke the questing beast, and it started to hunt him."

I frown. "What happened to him?"

Tristan takes a deep breath. "It tracked him, then chased him through the forest. Then King Pellinore lost his mind."

He flips the page to an illustration of a man running from the beast, his crown crooked on his head.

On the page after that, Pellinore is smashing his own head against a tree, and blood pours down his face.

"Cador said the questing beast's howl is a thing you never forget," I whisper.

Tristan looks up. "The questing beast caught the scent of his guilt. That's how he tracked him."

My stomach tightens.

Guilt follows me like a shadow wherever I go, my dark and constant companion. "I'll do everything I can to avoid that thing."

"Every instinct I have tells me to keep you somewhere safe where you can't burn to death or get carved by swords." He studies me closely, his gaze piercing mine like he's trying to read my secrets. The lantern light flickers between us, gilding the beautiful planes of his face. "But this is your choice to make, not mine."

My breath catches. "It isn't a choice. If I don't at least try to get the grail for Vero, I'll never forgive myself. She's all the family I have left. And you know I owe it to her after what I did."

CHAPTER 36

The sound of carnyx horns rouses me from a deep sleep, and for a moment, utter panic grips me. First, I'm terrified that I've lost my parents, then that Auberon is waking me to run in a wintry forest at night.

Then I remember where I am. I'm thirty-five, my parents are long dead, and I'm in the Veiled Court.

Outside, the first golden rays of dawn stain the sky with honey.

Yawning, I rub my eyes.

Tristan is already up, pouring tea at the table. I asked him to stay with me last night—just for comfort. He slept on the sofa.

I'm still blinking in bed while he sets out breakfast. "How did you wake so easily?"

"Easy. I didn't actually sleep at all." He's already dressed in dark clothes that hug his broad frame.

"What kept you up?" I ask.

His metallic green gaze flicks up to meet mine, and heat sweeps down to my belly. "Torments of all sorts. Get dressed."

I blink. "I take it the horns mean the next trial is starting soon."

"Yes. They slipped an invitation under the door. They're calling you to the Arthmail entrance, near the standing stones. They also left some supplies just outside your door—a sword, a scabbard, and dragon-scale armor."

I force myself out of bed and cross to the wardrobe. "A sword. Thank the gods. At least it's something I'm good at."

"But you need to move quickly, Syn. Dress. Eat something. You have half an hour to get there before they shut the Arthmail entrance. Anyone late will be dismissed from the trials."

I fling the wardrobe doors open and pull off my nightgown. I slip into leather trousers, a dark shirt. When I'm dressed, I cross to the table and grab a roll with butter and strawberry jam. I eat quickly, washing it down with the strong tea.

I glance out the window at the glittering, sun-dappled ocean, and magic tingles over my skin. Goose bumps rise on my arms. Outside, the sky shimmers and darkens, and my stomach swoops with a strange sensation, like I'm falling.

I brace myself, trying to find my footing. For a moment, I can't tell which way is up or down, if I'm in my body or floating outside it.

When the steadiness returns, the landscape outside has changed entirely. Instead of the sea, I'm staring out at a vast, rocky valley, where the jagged land sheers off to a ravine with a winding river hundreds of feet below.

This desolate, rugged landscape will be today's reaping grounds.

Now, the carnyx horns blare louder, making my stomach clench. And with the sound, a thick mist roils over the landscape outside, churning like a potion in a cauldron.

"Syn." Tristan's deep voice pulls me from my reverie, and his hand rests on the small of my back, warming my skin through my shirt. His thumb brushes up and down slowly, and I want to fold myself into him.

"Come back alive," he murmurs. "So I don't have to rip the rest of the court to pieces tonight and bury every last one of them."

* * *

FROM THE ARTHMAIL ENTRANCE, Aneirin, Elizabeth, and I climb down a worn set of stone stairs lit by flickering torches. There's a stream of contenders walking in silence, either terrified or still half asleep.

Fey aristocrats normally slumber through the morning.

Next to me, Elizabeth rubs her eyes. "Where the fuck are we going? I was only asleep for an hour. This is all very rude. I don't suppose they're going to serve us a lavish breakfast?"

"The weapons they gave us suggest otherwise," Aneirin says. I can hear the panic in his voice. "But no one knows what the trial is. Did you see the castle move this morning?"

"No." Elizabeth blinks. "I was in a blind panic trying to get ready in time. Feel like I'm in a nightmare. I haven't even eaten yet."

"Where were you yesterday evening, Alis?" Aneirin asks. "We knocked on your door around dinner. There was a party in the Aether Tower. It wasn't really sanctioned by Niniane, because she's upset about Cador, I think. But it just sort of happened. Everyone was shagging. Well, except Elizabeth and me, but not for lack of trying on my part."

I don't really want to lie to them, so I stay as close to the truth as I can. "I was being boring. Just hanging out in the library drinking tea, looking at books."

Elizabeth nods. "Oh, gods, you know what? I'm jealous. If I'd done that, I wouldn't have this brutal headache. I feel like I want to throw up."

"Do you think this will be an all-day thing?" Aneirin asks. "I'm starving."

I can't tell them what I know about the trial, but at least I can provide snacks.

"Here." I reach into the small bag I carry over my shoulder, and I pull out buttered rolls for each of them. "I already ate."

Elizabeth's eyes go wide. "You are a goddess, Alis. This should soak up some of the mead."

Aneirin takes the roll from me. "Brilliant. Thank you."

I glance at the aged stone walls on either side, where someone has chipped and hammered away to deface the carvings. I assume it's because one monarch was trying to erase a previous one—until I spot one image that the vandals missed. It looks like a king wearing a crown. He's on his knees, and a knight stands next to him, with a sword at his throat.

"You're in the way, Alis!" Igraine hisses from behind me. "Move."

I don't even bother to shoot her a dirty look. I just keep walking—but a little slower, since I know it annoys her. My sword's scabbard scrapes against the wall as I descend.

Up ahead, dim daylight illuminates the gloom of the stairwell, and it opens to the outside world. Mist drifts through the air around us, and I step onto a craggy, uneven path of rocks. Out here, the wind whips at us, carrying a biting chill and howling across a ravine.

I can't see much through the fog, but I try to reconstruct the view from memory as I glimpsed it from my room. If I remember correctly, it looked like a great valley carved through the rocks, with a river flowing beneath. The path I'm on now traces the side of the cliff, then veers down to the river, and one side sheers off hundreds of feet to the water.

On the other side of the valley, I think the slope is slightly less steep—forested and thick with greenery. I didn't see anything like a bridge of swords or a flaming pit. But in the far distance, on the other side of the river, I think there was a cave.

Moths flutter through the fog, strange bronze and silver creatures. I stare at one of them as it flies around me, trying to figure out what it might be, until I realize it's not a real insect at all.

I lean closer to Elizabeth and whisper, "I think that's how the nobles will be spying on us. The moths."

"Well spotted," she whispers.

I smooth out the raven emblem over my dragon-scale armor and flash a smile at the little metal spy.

"Alis? Elizabeth?" Aneirin says from behind us. "I can hardly see a fucking thing."

"There's a steep cliff to your right," I say. "Careful. We're hundreds of feet above a river, and the path just sort of falls away on one side."

"This is not the way to start a morning," he mutters.

The mist starts to thin a little, and I turn to see a few

people gathering around Niniane on a windswept hillside to my left. I loop arms with Elizabeth and Aneirin, and we walk on the uneven, grassy earth.

The royal contenders cluster around as we wait for the rest to come out the castle doors. Out here, the air smells rich and earthy, and the strong wind carries the scent of pines.

Wrapped in fog, Rion stalks slowly up to the group in his dragon-scale armor—iridescent, dark scales. His antler-tip necklace hangs down to his waist. The breeze toys with his silver hair, and his tattoos gleam with gold as if reflecting the sun.

Sometime today, I'll need to fake being *obsessed* with him.

"Noble contenders!" Niniane's voice calls out, echoing off stone. "The time is up. Anyone not already with us is out of the trials. A monarch must always be ready to fight for the Fey, even when exhaustion calls you back to your bed."

Her blue robes glitter with silver stars and moons. Today, she looks tired and tense.

"My knights are still searching for Lord Cador. He is not only my closest assistant, but, as some of you know, he has been my lover for decades. It was Cador's job to find traitors among you, and I can only assume that he did."

My stomach tightens. *Oh, fuck.*

Niniane takes a step forward, her gaze raking over us.

"And when I learn who hurt him, I will nail you to the door of the Veiled Court library, and I will slowly pull out your entrails. I will hunt and kill anyone you love. That's a promise."

CHAPTER 37

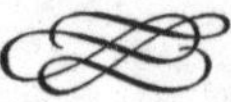

$\mathcal{I}$ let out a long, slow breath. Niniane's threat is how the monarchists try to keep control: through terror. My gaze sweeps around the rest of the group as I try to read people's faces, but all I see in their features is the usual low-level anxiety.

But when I look at Igraine, my heart skips a beat.

Standing next to Rion, she's glaring at me with unbridled hostility. Did she see something? Or is this just her usual unprovoked rage toward me?

By her side, Mabon stands straight, arms crossed. My gaze dips to his sword, and I can already tell by the hilt that it's finely crafted. It sits with a perfect balance at his hip, the kind of weapon that's been perfectly measured down to the slightest fraction of weight. The construction is seamless, and the guard and pommel flow together as if they grew naturally from the earth. Fine carvings and jewels spiral through the hilt.

Elizabeth sees where I'm looking, and she leans in, whispering to me, "It was a gift from the noble houses for his victory. An ancient sword of Avalon steel, forged during the Golden Age."

Jealousy flickers through me.

Mabon is glaring at Rion. He looks both angry and sober, which is unfortunate. He's less of a problem when he's drunk, but I suppose it would have been hard even for him to wake up wasted at the crack of dawn.

"The trial is a hunt and a battle," Niniane commands. "Search for King Bran's chalice. Survive attacks from other contenders. The grail is more than a cup. It's the first of three royal symbols and a token of the gods' favor. For centuries, these relics were lost. But in our time of chaos, without a king on the throne, the Veiled Court has found them again. Whoever touches the grail first wins the trial. Then you will keep it for a full week, basking in its power, until we return it to its place."

The crowd starts murmuring, and I'm already spinning through the mental calculations. *If* I manage to get the grail, I've got one week to get it to Vero and back again without anyone noticing.

I already know I'm outmatched here. But I'm not here for power. I'm here to save Vero. I'm not sure any of them are quite as desperate as I am.

Why should a healing relic be hidden away from those

like Vero who actually need it, just because they don't have royal lineage?

"But even without touching the grail," Niniane declares, "you can impress the noble houses with your bravery and skill. As ever, they will be watching. When the horns sound, you will begin."

"So, we're after the grail," Elizabeth mutters by my side, like she's still waking up. "We're supposed to search blindly for it?"

"Just try to put on a good show for the noble houses," I say. "And stay alive. Everyone's going to be trying to kill each other again today."

"Let's look after each other, then," says Aneirin. "We've got light magic, shadow magic, and…and Alis."

"Perfect." I bite my lip. "Rion might be joining us. He and I have spent a bit of time together at night."

I want to choke as the words come out of my mouth.

Elizabeth frowns at me. "Really? It's actually going somewhere?"

My stomach tightens. "Well, he's gorgeous, isn't he? And maybe he can help us stay alive."

"That's good," Aneirin says. "He's one of the most powerful people here. I wouldn't say no to having him in our group. Any idea where we should start?"

"I think we should take this path down toward the river. When the fog wasn't as thick, I saw a cave on the other side. The grail is hardly going to be out in the open, is it?"

"It's as good a guess as any," says Elizabeth. "And at least that way we'll be able to get some water. I feel like that might help my headache. That, or death. Perhaps your new friend Rion will oblige me with the second option."

As she says this, Rion is already stalking closer to me.

I glance at one of the moths fluttering around us. Time to put on a show so we can yank Mabon out of the top spot.

I smile coquettishly at Rion and sidle up to him, running my fingertips along his muscled forearm. I peer up at him and see a faint hint of amusement twinkling in his eyes. "Rion, darling," I say. "We're going to head down to the river first."

His silver hair catches in the wind, and the corner of his mouth curves in a faint smile. "I had the same idea. Head for the cave." He leans in close, whispering against my ear. "It's time to pull Mabon off his fucking perch."

I don't want to help Rion win, but I *do* like the sound of that.

The carnyx horns sound, a deep, sonorous battle cry that echoes off the rocks and makes my hair stand on end.

Immediately, people start to scatter in all directions— some of them running toward the path in front of us, others clambering up the steep hillside, all of them enveloped in fog. None of us knows where the grail is. We're simply guessing.

We're not the first to choose the route down to the

ravine. Two powerful men stalk ahead of us on the path, swords already drawn, their boots scattering loose gravel that tumbles off the side.

Rion strides after them, his towering body cutting swiftly through the mist. Aneirin follows behind him. Elizabeth stumbles along after me.

The two large men are a few steps ahead of Rion, and he closes the distance, drawing his sword. He rushes for them with the speed of a storm wind, his fur-lined cloak snapping behind him. Gracefully, he strikes right, carving through the first man's throat. Blood gleams on his blade. A gurgling choke interrupts the quiet.

Rion's sword is already arcing back in the other direction. The other man hardly has time to scream before the blade finds him. The man's head plummets into the ravine, followed by his body, tumbling off into the mist. Rion kicks the other corpse into the valley, and it bounces down the side.

He turns back to everyone still on the hillside, his blade dripping crimson. "If anyone else was considering joining us on this path, I suggest you find another route."

"Was that really necessary?" I whisper.

Rion's beautiful eyes gleam with a cold cruelty. "I don't know what your intentions are here, but mine are to get the grail in my hands, and I will not be deterred. This is life and death for me."

Life and death.

Would I kill a couple of aristocrats to save Vero? Yes, I

would. Vero's probably worth ten of them. So, I shut my mouth and follow after Rion and Aneirin, stepping over the blood-slicked stones.

I glance behind me. It seems like Rion's threat worked—no one is following us. For now, I leave my sword sheathed. Carrying it will only require more balance.

As I walk, the cold wind from the ravine bites my cheeks.

We follow the steep, slanting path as it zigs and zags along the cliffside. The path itself is slippery and too narrow to feel safe. A damp slick coats the rocks, and they're worn smooth, as though they've been trodden upon for centuries.

Thorny brambles grow from the jagged rock face. When I slip, I use one of them to steady myself. Loose rocks tumble off the side, bouncing off other rocks into the mist. The thorns on the brambles pierce my fingers, and blood drips onto the stones.

I glance up to make sure no one is about to murder us from above, but I can't see much. The fog is rolling in thickly around us.

Up ahead, Aneirin curses. The path is growing narrower—no longer a path at all, really, but a tiny, craggy outcrop that looms over the river.

We're getting nearer, though. Now, the sound of rushing water has grown louder.

Around us, gold and silver moths flutter by, watching our progress.

"Fuck this," Elizabeth mutters behind me. Her boots scrape on the smooth stones, and she's breathing hard. "Do you know what I think—"

A *thud* cuts off her words, and I whirl to see Igraine attacking Elizabeth. Igraine's sword has cut Elizabeth's shoulder down to the bone, and Elizabeth screams.

Igraine pulls her sword out again, and Elizabeth stumbles into me, nearly falling off the cliff face.

I grab her by the waist—one hand clinging to the brambles, the other clinging to Elizabeth.

I don't have space to fight back. The path is barely a foot wide, crumbling off into an abyss, and combat would be nearly impossible—which is probably the only reason Igraine hasn't slaughtered us all already.

I wrench Elizabeth away from Igraine, forcing her back. "Grab her, Aneirin!"

We shift around each other as I steady myself with one hand on the brambles.

The moment Elizabeth is secure in Aneirin's arms, I reach to draw my sword—

But Igraine stops me with a boot to my chest. The force of it is so hard, I'm sure she broke my ribs. My arms wheel in the air as I try to catch my balance.

A hard kick to my knees, and I tumble off the side of the cliff.

Now, there's nothing but the air and the fog and the rush of the wind whipping against me as I fall.

CHAPTER 38

I slam into a jagged ledge of rock, and pain rips through my back. Then I'm spinning through the air again until I bounce off another rocky ledge. If I didn't have the armor on, I'd probably be dead by now.

For a moment, I just want to give in to the fall and accept my fate.

But Vero's face burns in my thoughts—my little sister when she was eight, the way she'd sleep with both arms wrapped around a pillow.

A sharp hunger for the grail erupts in my chest.

I need to live.

Desperately, I reach out, grasping for the briars that grow from the rocks. They slip past my fingers, one after another. I brush against the side of a rock as I fall, scraping my limbs. Another craggy outcrop slams into my thigh, and a splintering pain rips through me.

And yet, the impact slows me enough that I finally manage to snag a briar sprouting from the cliffside. I clutch it with one hand, then the other, and the thorns pierce my fingers.

Pain racks my entire body, but I focus only on a single thing—clinging to this thicket, even as it draws blood from me.

I steal a glance down. Through the fog, I can see that the slope gets slightly gentler from here—but only slightly. It's gone from about a ninety-degree angle to seventy. I can't exactly walk down, and my body feels half shattered, anyway. My ribs are cracked. I think my leg is broken in several places. I don't think I can walk.

I grunt, clinging to the plants for dear life. Tears sting my eyes. Tristan is going to be so fucking furious with me if I die here.

Pain is shooting through one of my lungs. I can't breathe. I think the lung has collapsed, and every breath is agony.

Pebbles bounce and fall down the cliff, and time slows.

The plant I'm clutching starts to tear from the rocky surface, no longer supporting my weight.

Frantically, I search for a finger hold in the rock. There, one foot above me—

I miss it. My fingers slip, and I start sliding down again, too fast to grasp anything. My limbs drag painfully down the slope until I plunge into ice-cold water. The currents rush over me, pulling my broken body under the surface.

I scramble upward, but one of my legs isn't working properly, and agony is ripping my body apart. Even if I weren't shattered, the weight of the armor and my sword are pulling me under.

The cold pierces me down to my marrow, and I can't breathe. I can't move.

As I drift under the water, a buried memory surfaces.

I lie in a bed, and I trace my fingertips over little roses carved and painted above my bed by someone who loved me.

* * *

WHEN I WAKE, I'm coughing up icy water. As I gasp for breath, I feel like shards of glass are ripping through my lungs.

Every inch of my body—each nerve and bone—feels ripped to shreds. I can't stop shaking. I'm not quite sure if I'm alive or dead.

But surely, if I were dead, it would hurt less.

I think I'm lying on mossy ground.

Above me, sunlight tinges the mist with amber, turning the world hazy. I try to focus on that, to mentally detach from my broken body. Then I see his face above me—Rion's silver eyes, his golden tattoos that trace over perfect features, like sunlight kissing his skin, even in the mist.

Despite everything I know about him, I am certain that for this moment, I'm safe. He might be a monster, but he's my ally. For now.

"I've got you," he murmurs.

My body shakes as he unhooks the dragon-scale armor, moving down the front of my chest. The scales scrape softly, plate shifting against my body. My wet clothes cling to me, and the cold air bites at my skin.

My teeth chatter, and I close my eyes again, trying to let my mind drift. When I breathe in, pain screams through my chest until Rion slides his hand under my shirt and his warm magic starts to radiate over my body. Gently, he cradles my lower ribs. Heat pours from his palm, seeping into my bruised flesh and broken bones.

His hand moves slowly along my side. I gasp at the sensation of his touch on my skin, like molten honey sliding through my body. As I close my eyes, I inhale slowly. His magic is spring thawing the hard frost of pain.

Now, as I fill my lungs, each breath feels like a gift. Warmth licks along my skin, and his magic kisses my chest.

He's leaning closer to me, studying my face, and my eyes lock on his as he heals me. My pulse races faster. I realize his hair is soaking wet, just like mine, and the water makes his eyelashes cluster into dark peaks. His face moves nearer, and my eyes trace droplets of water dappling his golden skin. My gaze slides down to his sensual mouth, slightly parted.

My blood heats. When he uses his magic, he's mesmerizing.

This close, I see the way the silver in his eyes bleeds into a frosty blue. But the most surprising thing about them is a buried pain beneath that ice.

"Breathe slowly." His rich, velvet murmur makes my lips part.

Desire slides into my belly. The gold on his cheekbones seems to burn brighter, like it's responding to me. I try to keep reminding myself that this is just his magic.

He's my enemy, and I'm going to kill him someday.

I can breathe easily now, and his hand moves down to my broken thigh. Desire cascades through my body. Under my shirt, my nipples tighten into peaks.

His fingers move over my bare skin, where the leather has ripped away, and pleasure radiates out from the point of contact.

Hardly aware that I'm doing it, I grip his shirt and pull him closer to me. Our breath mingles, and his lips are only inches from mine. His beauty is overwhelming.

Staring at him, I inhale the scent of smoldering cedar embers.

I lick my lips, and my eyes flick down to his mouth. As his pupils dilate, the silver darkens into iron blue. Lazily, his thumb strokes up and down, gliding higher toward the apex of my thighs. What a wicked, dangerous sort of magic he possesses. Languidly, his fingers skim over the surface of my inner thigh.

Gods, it's like my dreams where he pins me against a tree.

It's wrong, I know. Even in my dreams, I know he's a monster, and I still want to taste the salt of his skin. I want to rake my fingernails down his back, leaving my mark.

But those are the dreams I try not to think about, because what if it means I'm as broken and brutal as he is?

Gods, I need to stop this. I clench my teeth.

"I think I'm healed," I finally manage.

I'm still clutching his shirt like it's the brambles I needed to keep myself alive. I think Rion's thorns would cut deeper.

Heat from his body washes over me, and I have the strongest impulse to lick the water droplets off his throat.

"Are you going to release me?" he whispers.

Now, I can see his faint, sly smile—

I loosen my grip on his shirt, and he sits next to me on the mossy earth. Slowly, I sit up again and take in my surroundings. My heart is still racing wildly.

Oaks loom tall above us. We're on a rocky slope beside the river, on the far side from where we started. But I don't recognize the landscape anymore.

Water drips down my skin. "What happened?"

"You plunged into the river. I got you out. But not before the current took you about a mile past the cave."

I turn to stare at him. "How did you find me?"

"The forest speaks to me."

"Right." I quirk a smile. "And I'm useful to you."

His eyes sparkle. "And if you were willing to admit it to yourself, you'd see that I'm useful to you, too. I've made you significant to the noble houses, and only I will grant you lands and a title. Without me, love, you've got nothing."

Only then do I catch the movement of the metallic moths sweeping around us and remember that the nobles are watching. Of course, this is all for their benefit— saving me, healing me. I'm sure he looks like a real hero now.

But while Rion wants to impress them, I want the grail in my hands.

"Well, I'm healed now. It's done."

His gaze sweeps down, pausing on my breasts. Through my sodden silk shirt, I know he can see my hard nipples, and my cheeks flush.

His gaze darkens, lingering for a beat too long.

"Did the forest tell you where the grail is?" I ask.

He arches a dark eyebrow. "In the cave. Let's make sure we get there before Mabon, shall we?"

As I stand, I realize I'm still armed with my sword. No wonder I couldn't swim out of that fucking current. Slowly, I pull on my dragon-scale armor. "Thank you for that."

He rises and peers down at me with a faint flicker of amusement in his eyes. "You're welcome, my *lover*."

I fasten my armor.

For the benefit of the moths, I smile sweetly up at him. I move closer, touching his cheek in a pantomime of affection. "What happened to Elizabeth? Did she make it?"

"She'll recover. Aneirin brought her to safety."

I stand on my tiptoes, my mouth close to his. "Your friend Igraine is a fucking arsehole."

His powerful, warm body presses against mine, and he studies my face. "She's a survivor."

"If she tries to kill my friend again, her surviving days will be over." I turn away from him. "Let's go."

We break into a sprint.

Minutes ago, I was half dead. Now? I feel amazing, and strength pounds through my body. I'm grateful to Rion's healing powers, even if he only did it for the benefit of the moths. My feet hasten over the mossy stones as I run along the riverside.

But we don't get far before I hear a howl—a sound that echoes like the screams of a hundred tormented souls.

My blood freezes, and a sharp tendril of dread coils through my chest.

I freeze, scanning the landscape, and Rion stops short by my side.

Catching my breath, I whisper, "Do you know what that is?"

"The questing beast," he murmurs. He brushes a wet strand of hair off my face. "If we see it, you need to bury your thoughts in silence."

"I have no idea what that means."

The beast's cries grow louder, and my stomach clenches. I clamp my hands over my ears, trying to block it out, but its howl is vibrating through my bones. And with the noise, a red-hot horror blooms in my chest.

I see it, then, flitting between the trees. It looks like an enormous, muscular leopard, only with a serpent's head. Its spotted body blends into iridescent scales at the throat, and a long, forked tongue lashes out, striking wildly at the air.

Fuck.

Its head whips in my direction, and amber eyes lock on me.

My heart skips a beat.

Raising its head, it unleashes a cry like a hundred agonized spirits trapped within its ribs.

My legs start to shake, my teeth to chatter. Its howl carries a magic that vibrates down to my marrow, making my body feel heavy. It's hard to breathe again—but not from a punctured lung. Now, I feel like rocks are crushing my chest.

Guilt presses down on me...

There was an old song the children used to chant, and it floats in my thoughts now, mingling with the cries of the questing beast.

Treason, treason, all around,
Drop the bones in hollow ground.
Ring the bells at Traitors' Gate,
On gallows beams the crows all prate.

Around me, the forest starts to change.

The trees thin, and the river changes shape.

Now, I stand in an unweeded garden. I'm back at home, where I grew up before Auberon took me. I stand outside the little cottage in the woods, where the swing creaks in the breeze, and hemlock and nettle have strangled the flowers...

Clouds cover the sun.

My parents have been gone so long that the wood is starting to rot.

I rasp for breath.

Where did the king bury the bodies? In an unmarked grave with the traitors.

Drop the bones in hollow ground.

Does it matter where their skeletons lie?

It matters more the way they died—

The vision around me shifts, and the sky fades. Stone sweeps over the soil beneath my feet, and the sky darkens above into shadowed stone arches. Now the world smells like damp rock and mold.

I'm in the Undercroft. Nausea turns my stomach, and my legs shake.

Auberon says that mortals are the enemy.

I pace the slick stones of the Undercroft. The famine has driven the king into a frenzy, I think.

Now, he's started burning demi-Fey. He incinerates them with dragon fire, and he sends his soldiers to slaughter their villages. When he's done, half his kingdom will molder under the soil. But maybe then they'll stop blaming him for the famine.

My father is half human. I don't think of my parents much. Auberon told us our parents abandoned us. Since we first arrived in the Undercroft as children, he told us that our parents never wanted us. We used to write them letters, but of course, we never heard back. They were glad to be rid of us. Auberon told us.

Now, demi-Fey are the enemy.

What does it mean that I'm one of them?

I don't know if Auberon remembers that I'm a quarter mortal, or that Tristan is half. You can't tell by looking at us.

I think he's pretending to forget. Right now, we're useful to him.

When we stop being useful, he'll call us traitors and drop our bones in the ground. If the king grows angry with us, our mortal blood will be all he can think about. We must do what he says so he doesn't think too long on it.

I pivot in the Undercroft, growing restless.

We all know demi-Fey started the famine. They tried to poison us all, and now the rest of us have to live with their actions.

It's midnight now.

Auberon brings two traitors into the Undercroft, arms bound behind their backs.

Another round of executions. We've done many like this, killing the demi-Fey traitors.

It's their fault, of course. They're conspiring to kill him. *They* poisoned the crops.

Torchlight wavers over the prisoners, and they're all shaking. I can't see their faces because hoods cover them. I know their eyes must burn with hatred behind the cloth. The mob loathes the king's instruments—people like me. Auberon says they'd mutilate us if they won. Devour us whole, eat our flesh. It's not my job to question him.

The king barks at them to kneel on the stone floor.

Tonight, I'm chosen as executioner, and I ready my blade. I don't enjoy killing, especially when my enemy is bound and helpless. But they've been tried and condemned, and who am I to argue with the king's courts? They had the evidence.

Without order, everything falls apart.

I'll do it quickly, I tell myself. They won't feel a thing. It will be over before they know it's their last moment.

They're bruised and injured—but they're traitors, so I turn my heart to stone.

They'd kill us if they had the chance.

He pulls off the first man's hood, and I don't see hatred in his eyes. I see sadness. Then, surprise. Then something almost like joy—

But my sword swings through his throat, and I snuff out the joy like a candle.

A woman is next, and it's the same with her—surprise, then a look of pure elation…

I think I recognize her lavender eyes before I strike— her cheekbones and her black hair. They're the same as mine. And I recognize her for an instant because I carry her face engraved on my heart. Even after I started to think she wanted me gone.

But Auberon taught me to strike first and think second.

Hesitation is death.

Auberon gave me a test, and I passed.

But why did they look happy as I held a sword above my head to kill them? Who could possibly feel joy moments before death?

It's only a few minutes after my sword carved through their heads that I put it together.

They thought I was dead. Auberon never sent our letters.

My parents were happy because they learned I was alive. But by then, it was too late.

The image shifts again, and I'm in the Undercroft once more. Two prisoners bound. No hoods this time. Maybe I saw their faces for more than just a moment—maybe I knew it was my mother before I dropped the blade—

I can't remember which memory is true.

For all those years in the Undercroft, I thought they'd sold me.

And hesitation is death, and acting quickly is also death, and the monster and the mob and the poison and the killer and the traitor is *me*—

I'm screaming now, and words are pouring out of me, and I need to stop it all—

Rion's earthy scent seeps into my thoughts.

Slowly, gently, the warmth of him wraps around me. I see him now. It's just him and me in the Undercroft. For some reason, he feels safe, even though he's not. His magic, I suppose.

In the Undercroft, Rion leans down, resting his forehead against mine. With his magic seeping into me, he's blanketing my thoughts with quiet.

The screaming in my skull falls to a hush.

I breathe in and out.

Smoldering oak. My feet stand on the forest floor. Sunlight pours into my thoughts, warming them again.

Breathe in. Breathe out—the scent of the forest, the humid air.

I open my eyes, and Rion's forehead is still pressed against mine, just like he was in my hallucination of the Undercroft. I'm shaking uncontrollably, and tears pour down my cheeks. Fuck. *Fuck.* Gods, I'm crying like a little child, and it's fucking mortifying.

I wipe at my cheeks as if I can hide it.

A soldier doesn't cry.

Rion takes my hands in his. He doesn't take his eyes off me, and that silver in his irises burns like the evening star.

My breath shakes as I look into his eyes. He's completely at ease. I suppose terror is his domain. He could sweep it out of my thoughts, blow the horrors away like dandelion seeds.

"You don't know what I've done," I whisper. My hands are shaking, legs trembling.

"You'll tell me someday."

I'm still breathing hard, in and out.

Rion pulled me out of madness, and if he weren't with me, it's entirely possible that I'd be bashing my head against an oak like King Pellinore in the old drawings. Without him here, I'd be floating dead in the river.

I take another breath, listening for the questing beast. Nothing, now. Just the sound of the river.

"Why did you wait for me instead of running off to find the grail without me?"

His long eyelashes cast a shadow on his cheeks. "Because if I didn't pull you out of the nightmarish memory, I'd have lost my best asset."

The moths flit around us, and I glance at them. I wonder what the noble houses think about me sobbing like a baby. "Right. You need me. And now you look like a hero again."

His brow furrows, but his expression is unreadable. "It doesn't hurt my chances."

I realize this is why he is holding my hands in his. I pull them back, trying to reclaim a sense of dignity. "Could you see my memory while you were calming my thoughts?"

His gold tattoos beam brighter. "I only saw you. But you've sparked my curiosity once again."

I feel his dread magic stroking against my thoughts like a dragon's claw, probing for things that terrify me.

As he does, I gather defenses in my mind, the way Auberon taught me—a veil to keep my secrets. "And why is that?"

His sharp thorn of power nudges against the cloud in my thoughts, trying to uncover my secrets. But I'm not letting him in. "Because I can't see your fears the way I can see other people's."

Good. Because if he slips into my mind, he might find me holding a knife to the throat of the next king.

He turns to run again. "Let's go. I want the grail in my hands."

CHAPTER 40

We sprint over gnarled roots and mossy rocks beneath the oak boughs. As we run, we crush acorns and leaves underfoot.

But it doesn't matter how hard I try—I cannot keep up with Rion. He sprints in a blur of silver, leaving me lumbering over the rocky ground.

Of course he'd leave me behind. I'd do the same. I want the grail as much as he does—and yet, I'm irrationally furious with him. I *need* that grail to save someone's life. He only wants it to win a crown.

Mostly, I'm furious with myself for being this out of shape. Ten years of puttering around London offices, making tea for people, eating buttered toast. I'm faster than a mortal, yes, but not fast enough to race past Rion.

I heave for breath, trying to fill my lungs. I wonder how many others got there first.

As my sword thuds against my thigh, I desperately try to run faster, pumping my arms to propel myself.

Heat thickens the air around me, sultry and suffocating. I'm sweating beneath my armor, and it runs down my temples.

As I run, I try to think of Vero, to keep her in the forefront of my mind so I don't let myself slow.

After I executed my parents, I started to fall apart. My magic stopped working.

It wasn't long before Tristan told me we needed to leave Brocéliande. I'd gone into a sort of daze for weeks, and I hardly spoke. I hardly ate.

Auberon had become fanatically obsessed with scapegoating the demi-Fey, and I was no longer useful to him. It was a distraction, I think. People blamed him for the famine and starvation, and he wanted them to look elsewhere. When I stopped being useful, Auberon would have killed me as an example. Tristan left to save my life. He found the information he needed. He learned of a portal into the mortal land of England, one used by the Fey army, and he pulled me from the Undercroft in the dead of night.

But I couldn't stop thinking about my parents. I remember screaming at Tristan that I had to check the cottage where my parents lived to see if maybe I was mistaken. Maybe it was just a woman who looked like Mother.

I remember the heartbroken look in his eyes. Tristan

knew they were dead. He saw me kill them. I could tell he thought I had lost my mind. He was talking to me like I was a child, but he indulged me anyway. So, the two of us went back to the cottage with the garden. By then, it was already growing wild, and the chickens were all gone— just feathers and blood left.

My parents weren't there. Instead, I found Vero inside, all skin and bones. She was so small, I thought she might be five or six instead of eight. She had a fever, and she kept falling asleep as we tried to talk to her. But when she was awake, she called me Mother because I looked just like her. I knew then I had to care for her. I'd killed her parents, after all.

Tristan carried her feverish body with us into England.

He didn't live with us long. I had a child to look after, and he craved adventure and revenge. He found Avalon Tower within a few months.

I never told Vero how our parents died or that it was my fault. But I owe it to her to make things right. So, even if I feel like I'm about to die, I force myself to sprint faster.

My breath rasps in my throat.

By the time I reach the cave, I'm tired enough that I'm stumbling and gasping, coughing to get enough oxygen.

Inside the cave, thick shadows pool around glistening rocks. I don't see a grail or a pit of fire, and I wonder if I've come to the wrong place.

I take a step inside, and it smells of wet, chalky limestone and soil. The cave floor is slippery and uneven, and I steady myself against a slick wall.

Around me, darkness starts to bleed into light as the landscape changes once more.

I'm seeing things. Fully hallucinating again. I don't think it's the questing beast because I'm not scared. It looks and feels like London around me now. A cold air bites at my skin, and freezing rain dampens my hair. I'm walking behind the train tracks, hungry. I had dry crackers for breakfast, and nothing since. My stomach rumbles.

I struggle to get back to where I was, to orient myself. I try to feel the cave walls. I touch the slick rock, but I'm still seeing Homicide Park. A newspaper blows across the dead grass. Men huddle over a burning bin, trying to warm their hands. Here, a rat drags a chicken bone across my path, and a dusky fog settles over the landscape. The air smells of old piss and diesel. Nearby, someone is shouting about the world ending, but there's no going home, because everyone is dead—

I'm in my Waste Land. I clamp my eyes shut and envision a fog in my brain, blocking out whatever magic this is. I bring up the veil in my thoughts, thicker this time.

When I open my eyes again, the vision is gone again.

I've returned to the dark cave, one hand on a dank wall.

Now, as I move farther in, I see the glow of warm light and breathe in the scent of burning meat.

My heart speeds up. Voices float through the air—and screams, too.

I move closer to the glow, and it illuminates the cave, allowing me to move faster.

The smell of burning flesh grows thicker, and it turns my stomach.

Ahead, a burning pit spreads out across a chasm. *This is the pit of fire I've been looking for.*

I break into a sprint now. When I reach the opening to the fiery rift, two bridges come into view.

Only one of them looks like something that could actually be crossed—made of wood and three feet across. The bottom of the wood is blackened by smoke, but the flames don't reach high enough to burn it.

It *would* be the perfect place to cross—except Rion is already using his sword to fight five different knights in a brutal melee that blocks the bridge. Even if he manages to defeat the knights, there's a bloody lion lurking at the far end of the bridge, waiting to kill anyone who makes it. What's the plan here, Rion—fight a lion?

As the creature watches the knights clash their swords, he opens his mouth and roars. A shudder runs down my spine.

Absolutely not.

And yet, the second bridge looks even more impossible. It's nothing but a long blade the width of a broadsword. It's long enough to span the crevasse, but deadly sharp. Maybe four inches across, pivoting in a shallow arc. Every second or so, it moves—tilting about forty-five degrees upward with a *click*—then horizontal again.

That tilt could throw off anyone who tries to cross it.

Taking a deep breath, I survey the far side of the bridge. Just twenty feet away stands a plinth with the grail. It's not at all what I expected, because it's made from what looks like a human skull. Around it, roses bloom, white and red.

My heart slams against its cage as I stare at the grail. One sip from that and I've cured Vero for good.

I glance at the blade again, and I'm actually starting to consider it.

Above me, the silver moths flutter. Watching me.

Aneirin, Elizabeth, and Igraine aren't here. Mabon hasn't made it, either.

Maybe they peeked inside, took one look at the setup, and had the good sense to turn around.

A scream echoes off the cave ceiling, and I turn to see one of the knights leaping from the bridge into the fire, just to get away from Rion's dread magic. Meanwhile, Rion's sword carves through the throat of another knight, and blood streaks across the air.

There's no fucking way I'm going to beat him on that bridge. And that means I have only one option.

I shift closer to the tilting blade, and the blazing pit heats my skin.

Gore coats the steel in a few places, the remnants of whoever tried and failed to cross it today.

Besides the blood, roses decorate the blade—the red bloom of King Emrys, the white of Queen Morgan. Symbols of royal houses, but also of anarchy, of civil war.

Is there a message here? I cock my head at it, letting my thoughts unfurl for a moment.

War is a dark magic. You cast a spell to get what you want. You know there will be unforeseen costs, but it's hard to predict how terrible the price might be until it comes back for you.

The red and white roses together suggest *ending* a civil war, I think.

And to cross, I would need perfect, impeccable balance. Timing too, leaping up for the clicks, landing perfectly at just the right time. The only way to cross this blade would be to take my armor off and abandon my weapons. I'd have to leave my sword behind. And I think that's what the grail wants.

Despite the carnage around me, I think the grail wants peace.

I unlatch my scabbard and let it fall to the floor. The sword clatters against the stone. Next, I unhook my dragon-scale armor. The weapons will only throw me off, and the armor will overheat me above the flames.

While Rion slaughters another knight on the bridge, I slide out of my boots. I'm going to need to do this barefoot if I have any hope of staying on the blade. I already know it's going to burn my feet, but the boots will be too stiff for landing perfectly. The socks will make me slip, so I pull them off too.

Auberon used to have us practice sword fighting across a thin rope, but this looks harder than even his most torturous constructions.

Two more knights rush into the cave, and they don't spend long deciding. They're going for the wooden bridge —probably because what I'm about to do is completely unhinged.

And yet, my gaze flicks up to the grail, and I feel its empty eyes inviting me closer.

I listen for the click, then the next one. I memorize the rhythm. *Tick-tock.*

I take my first step onto the blade, grimacing at its heat. I leap just as it clicks.

I land again on the balls of my feet.

Click.

When I land again, I hold my arms out to the side, keeping my balance. I wobble, dangerously close to falling. At the very last moment, I manage to stay upright.

Click.

The blade starts to tilt beneath me, and my heart plummets through my gut.

Sweat trickles down my temple, and the bottoms of my feet are excruciatingly hot. I land again on the balls of my feet, then lower my heel—but it's only there for a moment before I have to leap again.

Click.

I adjust. Step. Breathe. Jump. Balance.

Don't look down.

Cinders and ash drift through the air around me, and I inhale the charred air. The heat licks at my skin, drying my throat and searing my lungs.

From the other bridge, a man screams as he falls into the flames. They keep coming for him, more knights trying to challenge Rion.

I don't look. One step at a time. One breath at a time.

Click. I falter—arms wheeling, my weight shifting nearly out of control—

I catch myself just in time. My heart pounds hard as a drumbeat.

I glance down at the roaring flames beneath me, and my stomach leaps. They look *hungry* for me.

Another step.

Grimacing, I try not to think about the scorched skin on the balls of my feet. I'm nearly halfway there.

Now, the moths swirl around me, glittering with yellow and gold above the flames. I can't let them distract me, so I focus only on the blade. I keep my thoughts on the shallow arc of its tilt and bend my knees to stay in a strong position of balance.

Click.

Only now, the blade is moving faster. The rhythm is wrong—unpredictable, uneven.

Click. Click. Click.

Nearly there.

I almost want to leap into the fire because the balls of my feet are fucking burning and I need everything to *end*. I'm not sure if I can still match the rhythm, and my blood roars in my ears.

Now, I'm starting to lose balance. I leap again, trying to keep up with the pace. *Tick-tock.*

Fuck.

One last push.

I think of Vero instead when I first found her, snoring in my old bed.

I jump again, bringing my foot down hard onto the flat side of the blade. One last leap until the end.

I just barely land at the edge of the pit, and my feet are seared with agonizing pain. I glance at the other bridge, where Rion has killed every other knight. He's slowly approaching the lion with one hand out as if trying to tame it.

The grail is only ten feet away, and I sprint for it, faster than I've ever run in my life. I force all thoughts of pain out of my skull and simply hurtle through the air.

Time seems to slow, and out of the corner of my eye, I see Rion running for the grail, too.

J reach for it and close my hand around its stem.

Relief floods me, and my hands are shaking as I pull it closer to me. My eyes sting, and I clasp it to my chest.

I got it. I fucking got the grail that will heal Vero for good, and I don't need to worry anymore.

Tears stream down my cheeks.

When I open my eyes again, the first thing I see is the moths fluttering around me, watching it all.

On the other side of the bridges, Niniane appears. In the gloom, she radiates a pale, silver light, and her expression beams.

"Listen, all!" she calls out, her voice booming. "I declare Baroness Alis of Listenoise the ultimate victor of this trial! The rest of you will be judged by the noble houses on your displays of bravery, strength, and cunning. Let us return now to the Veiled Court, where we will celebrate the claiming of the grail!"

Still catching my breath, I turn to see the lion. The fierce creature is now slumbering on the bridge.

Then my gaze meets Rion's. Blood streaks down his body, and his knuckles are white where he grips the hilt of his sword. He stares intently at the grail.

He was *so* close to grabbing it, just two feet away from me.

The muscles flex in his jaw, and his gaze drags from the grail up to my face. His expression is coldly furious— and there's something else there I can't quite read.

Without another word, he turns and crosses back over the bridge, past the sleeping lion, stepping over the bodies of those he killed.

I start to limp toward the castle.

* * *

MY FRESHLY CLEANED and dried hair smells faintly of lavender, but I still haven't dressed yet for the ball.

Mostly because I have absolutely no desire to go. All I want to do right now is sneak out of the castle and get this grail to Vero. Only then can I truly relax. And after I've healed her, I want to sink into a soft bed and stay there for weeks.

Across the table from me, Tristan pours the mead, and

the pale liquid catches the dying light of the sun. The grail sits between us.

I cock my head. I can't stop staring at it. It seems to draw the sunlight toward it, and it glows like the dawn. The skull sits upside down on top of a stem carved from Avalon steel, its crown fitted into the base of the same metal.

Strangely, a symbol marks the stem. It looks nearly identical to the tattoo on Rion's chest—a vertical line with branches coming off it, like a primitive tree.

Tristan hands me the glass of mead. "And how many died during the trial?"

"Six were dismissed, halos removed, for failing to get to the trial on time. And twenty-six died, I heard." The number coils sharply between my ribs, but I force my voice to stay flat and keep my expression neutral. "Rion killed seven of them at least, and a few murdered each other. The rest burned in the fiery pit. I can still see the blade streaked with gore. It really was—"

"You made it across," Tristan cuts in, dropping into a chair just next to me. "That's what matters."

"I ran into the beast, by the way." My fingers tighten on the glass, but I'm keeping my voice even. "It was fine."

"Good," he says steadily. "I'm glad you didn't let it overwhelm you. No point in looking back to dwell on every horrible thing that happened to you."

I glance at the grail again, and it glows in the coral sunlight. "The legends say Bran's head was buried beneath the Tower of London. Have you heard that? His skull is supposed to protect Britain from invaders. Didn't always work, did it?"

A knock sounds on the door, and I stand to open it. A servant enters holding a tray with a golden gift box resting on top.

"A gift." She bows her head slightly. "From the noble houses."

"Thank you." Smiling, I take the box, carry it to the table, and open it.

A handwritten note rests on top, reading,

Let the raven guide your way.

Tucked beneath the note is a little bronze raven with clear quartz eyes. It's beautifully crafted, no larger than a sparrow. Its feathers are etched with a delicate precision, and little gold talons curl beneath it.

"They're lavishing you with gifts now," Tristan murmurs.

I set the golden raven on my bookshelf. "The greatest gift will be healing Vero."

Tristan picks up the grail. "Syn, everyone is going to be after you now. Time to slip into the obscurity of the shadows. It's dangerous too close to the throne. I don't want you as the top target."

"Unfortunately, tonight, I'm supposed to dress up in a gown and march into the Aether Tower ballroom carrying the grail in some kind of victory celebration. All eyes will be on me. Mabon's included. But when do we get this to Vero?"

Outside, the sun is dipping lower in the sky, bathing Tristan's tan skin in warm light and creating sparks in his eyes like flecks of gold. "In two nights. I'll find her in the Melian Forest and bring her to an abandoned cottage by the sea near the Veiled Court. You'll sneak out with the grail and join us there."

Joy blooms in my chest at the thought of handing this over to her. *That* will be the real victory celebration.

"Fucking incredible, Syn." Tristan raises the grail again, and a faint smile curls his lips. "If only I'd been born into a noble house, I could have joined you in the trials."

I lean in closer. "But then you and I would be competing for the throne, and only one of us could be crowned at the end. What would happen then?"

He glances at me, and his gaze brushes down to my lips, then sweeps up again. "I would hope you'd show me mercy, my queen, and make me your jester."

"And why would I show mercy? Everyone knows a monarch can't leave a rival breathing."

His eyes gleam. "Because you can't live without me, darling. You'd spare me, I think. You'd risk your crown just to keep me around."

He's right. I would.

"And would you spare me?" I ask with a smile.

"Of course I would. We grew up underground

together. You've been with me longer than I've had the sunlight on my skin."

My breath quickens as he leans in closer to brush a strand of hair off my face. The closeness heats my blood, and I desperately want to pull him closer, to feel his solid, warm body against my own.

Tristan's gaze moves to my mouth again, and I think he's going to kiss me, but the door opens.

We jump apart as Jasper the tailor strides into the room, a purple cocktail in one hand. Lifting the goblet to his lips, he takes a long sip and stumbles closer. A lock of his hair falls before his eyes. "There you are, darling. Someone told me that our little Waste Land gutter urchin found the grail. I want to see—ah! There it is. King Bran's drinking cup. Whose skull do you think this was?"

"Hello, Jasper."

He cocks his head. "Do you think I could sip my lavender libations from the grail?"

"Absolutely not," I say. "I am the grail's keeper for the week, and it's not a cocktail glass."

He shrugs and drags his heavy-lidded gaze to my face. "You know, isn't it just the most *interesting* thing to happen? Everyone expects the wealthier nobles to get the grail. The more powerful ones. You look at Igraine or Rion, and you think they're going to win it all, but that's boring. It's expected. Do you know what's a good twist?" He slurs his words. "The grail in the hands of a wretched waif who crawled from the slums."

I stare at him. "Can I help you with something?"

He snaps his fingers. "Ladies! Assistants! Come in, for fuck's sake."

Looking sullen, Tillie and Ranae slink into the room. Tillie carries a dark, feathered gown that gleams with faint shades of deep purple. Silver accents glint from the feathers. Tillie lays it out over a chair near my bed.

"The Raven Queen," says Jasper. "That's what they're calling you. Do you know what? Prince Talan would love you, I reckon. He collects strange creatures, like his wife from Cali...*fornia*. And Rion reminds me of that beautiful prince..."

Yes, well, Rion probably abducted and possibly murdered his favorite prince.

Tristan is still holding the grail, and Jasper suddenly notices. He lurches forward, snatching it from Tristan.

"Oh, no, no, no. That's not for a peasant to touch," Jasper sets it on the table. "Hands off. I've flogged servants for less."

Tristan stares at Jasper, and I know what he's thinking. If he didn't have the emotional restraint of a knight, Tristan would throw Jasper out the window and watch him fall to his death.

Jasper must sense it, because he edges out of Tristan's reach. Draining the rest of his cocktail, he shoves the empty glass onto a bookshelf near my new bronze raven.

He claps his hands. "All right, now, time to get you dressed, yeah? I've heard the gossip, you know. The noble houses are all aflutter about the passionate romance between the Raven Queen and the Ruthless Knight. They say you kissed him again today by the riverbank. Couldn't keep your hands off him. Is that right, you little minx?"

I glance at Tristan and find that his eyes are narrowed, his jaw tense. He cocks his head, and his green eyes blaze. Slowly, he raises an eyebrow.

I shrug and flutter my eyelashes. "How could I resist, Jasper? As you said, he reminds you of Prince Talan. What could be better?"

Jasper points at me, smiling. "You are truly skilled at entertaining the noble houses." His gaze drifts to Tristan. "You. Servant. What's *your name?*"

He enunciates each word as if Tristan were an idiot. Truly, Jasper is testing the bounds of Tristan's patience.

He stares back at Jasper without answering.

"I don't actually care what your name is, yeah?" Jasper drawls. "Just get me another cocktail. I'm *parched*, and I've got important things to do."

Tristan cuts me a sharp look, as if this is all my fault, then stalks from the room. I know he won't be coming back, but I doubt Jasper will remember the conversation in five minutes.

As Tristan leaves, Jasper leans back against the bookshelves, folding his arms. "Let's see the dress on you, Baroness. Igraine is competing for Rion, too. She wants a king and a crown, and you're in her way. So, you'd better look amazing tonight if you want to keep his attention.

She has that old money thing going on, you know. All gold."

"Oh, Baroness." Ranae's voice floats across the room, sugar-sweet and false. "We heard how he helped you today. That's how you got the grail. Rion helped you."

"We heard," Tillie adds, "that he would have the grail himself if he hadn't dragged you out of the river. We heard that he impressed them all with his chivalry. He's still most likely to win, you know."

Ranae steps close enough to twist one of my curls around her fingertip. "I think that when he grows bored of you, he'll discard you like an old rag. And everyone knows a king cannot allow his rivals to live. So, Baroness...you'd better find a way to make Rion happy."

"Shhh," Tillie cuts in. "If she wins, she'll have you executed for that."

These people are annoying, petty, and cruel, but they're also right about Rion.

Of all the Veiled Court's dangers, Rion might be the deadliest threat, and I need to find out exactly what he's planning behind the scenes.

CHAPTER 42

Carrying the grail, I stride across the high bridge. I'm dressed in my Raven Queen gown. A feathered collar brushes against my throat, and more dark feathers crown my head. The breeze kisses my bare arms and the skin exposed by my plunging neckline.

A slit in the skirt traces all the way up to my hip line.

Tillie did my makeup—black liner around my eyes, shimmering cheekbones, and berry-stained lips. If I'm honest, I feel very beautiful.

Twilight is falling, nearly night now, and silver stars streak a periwinkle sky. It doesn't matter how much time I spend here—this place still feels like a dream. A nightmare at times, too.

I remember as a kid looking up at the sky. Now, it makes me ache for a time when Tristan and I would lie in the grass, staring up at a dome of blue and white. We'd listen to the blackbirds sing and feel the sunlight washing over our skin. I want that quietness with him, when we could just *be*.

I glance at Aether Tower. The number has changed again—seventy-one remain after more deaths and dismissals.

And the banners have shifted places, too. Rion was right. Working together, we could take down Mabon. But even with the grail, I haven't made it to the top. I'm in second place, just above Mabon and Igraine.

Rion's white stag hangs in the prime spot, the sigil already crowned.

Clutching the grail, I cross into the Aether Tower and climb the worn steps. In the stairwell, haunting music floats through the air, raising goose bumps on my skin.

As I step into the hall, a hush falls over the room, and all eyes are on the grail. Those in the hall stare at it with raw hunger. A chill shudders over my skin. I feel like a rabbit who crossed into a den of starving wolves.

From the mirrors, the nobles watch me.

My skin prickles with discomfort at their notice, and I take a sip of the cocktail in my other hand. It tastes like strawberries and honey.

Mabon stares at me, his expression poisonous. Still, I think he's already downing drinks tonight. He won't be much of a threat after ten of them.

I scan the room. Between the soaring, open columns, the stars gleam brightly in a mulberry sky. A humid breeze sweeps inside, rustling the flowers and leaves. Floating lanterns sway, casting golden light over the guests.

I don't see Rion here yet, or my friends.

I could gloat and lift the grail above my head, brandishing it for the noble houses to see. But Raphael told me to retreat into the shadows, and that's what I'm going to do. Slipping to an arched window on one side of the hall with the grail, I hide among the vines climbing the amber stone walls.

The other Fey slowly pull their eyes from me, returning to their conversations.

I glance at the skull carvings in the fountain's stone basin. I saw them the first night here. Now, I realize that the skull carvings are the *grail*. And along with the grail, I see two more repeated symbols—a leafy branch and a sword.

I have no doubt we'll be looking for those in the next trials.

"Alis!" Elizabeth's voice pulls me from my thoughts, and I turn to see her coming toward me with Aneirin by her side. She looks like a goddess in a delicate bronze gown. Her arm is bandaged, but the Fey heal quickly.

Aneirin wears a red velvet doublet threaded with gold.

Elizabeth lifts her glass. "Water, tonight. I'm being boring, but I can't take any more alcohol."

"I can," says Aneirin, looking pale. "I need a break from my thoughts. I need to turn them off. Do you know? I think my happiest moments in life have been drunk."

Elizabeth frowns. "That's quite sad, Aneirin."

"What are your happiest moments, then?" Aneirin asks her.

"I don't know. I suppose when I married, but it turned out to be the worst moment in my life, looking back. So, I think it was when my husband died." She smiles.

"How did he die, exactly?" Aneirin asks.

Elizabeth shrugs. "Someone who'd had enough of being locked in a room put a pillow over his head while he slept."

Aneirin's eyebrows flick up. "Can't say I blame you."

I lift the grail, imagining how it will feel to hand it to Vero. "I think that our happiest moments haven't happened yet."

Aneirin cocks his head. "Yes, *your* happiest moments lie in your future, I'm sure, given your passionate romance with your warlord."

"Have you heard the rumors about him?" Elizabeth asks.

"The torture ones?" says Aneirin. "Everyone has."

Elizabeth shakes her head. "No, the *other* rumors."

I find myself leaning in closer to her, my pulse racing with anticipation. "Don't keep us in suspense."

Elizabeth's fiery eyes dart from side to side. "They say he's secretly King Auberon's son. Alis, you know him. Is that true?"

My heart skips a beat. "What? No, the king only had two sons. One is dead, and the other tried to kill him."

"Alis is right," says Aneirin. "Prince Talan is a hero or traitor, depending on who you ask, because he tried to kill Auberon. And Prince Lothyr died centuries ago. Apparently, Lothyr's death drove the king nearly out of his mind, and he started burning every peasant he could find. He blamed them all because Prince Lothyr died in the peasant revolt—"

"Hang on," I say. "You said Prince Talan *tried* to kill Auberon. You mean, he didn't succeed?"

It's what I suspected, but no one else has dared to speak the words out loud.

Aneirin's throat bobs. "Well, I don't know. We didn't see the body, did we? I certainly hope he's dead—otherwise, what's all this for?"

A hush falls over the room, and I turn to see Rion striding into the hall, his golden tattoos glowing over his high cheekbones. He wears a midnight-dark suit of a rich, velvety material, and a half smile curls his lips. He seems to radiate light, and he draws the eye like the sun. As he steps into the hall, his gaze sweeps around until it meets mine.

My mind is aflame with the whispers that he's a son of Auberon. It's only a rumor—but Rion *did* have Auberon's family tree hidden in his room.

I raise the grail as if in a toast.

Gracefully, he stalks closer to me.

He only makes it a few feet before Igraine sweeps over to peer adoringly up at him.

But his gaze darts to mine, and his eyebrows lift. Of course, he's seen that he's still winning, and he no longer looks as though he wants to murder me.

The slow curl of his lips tells me there's more in store for me. Apparently, he still thinks I'm useful to him. We are the top two contenders. It doesn't matter how fake the romance is because the noble houses are buying it.

Igraine follows his gaze and narrows her eyes at me. Her lips are pressed into a thin line.

Now, metallic moths dart and flutter around our heads, watching us.

But Rion stalks past her, gliding closer to me.

He ignores Elizabeth and Aneirin completely. They might as well be statues for all the attention he shows them.

His eyes sweep down my body slowly, then up again. "And here is my lover, cradling a king's head in her hands —not for the last time."

I lift the grail. "This is a king's skull?"

Instead of answering, he slides his hand onto the small of my back and guides me away from my friends. He leads me to an alcove, a stone bench with soft pillows and diaphanous curtains. He pulls aside the curtains, and we sit on the velvet.

When he glances at me, heat flares in the silver-blue eyes. "I've been waiting to see you all day."

A total lie, but he makes it seem convincing.

The moths flit around, their wings sparking with amber in the lantern lights. Rion reaches for the grail and lifts it to stare into its hollow eyes. "Beautiful, isn't it?"

He's *very* good at playing the part, letting others see him holding the grail as if it belonged to him. As if he were born to be king.

He hands it back to me, then leans in close, whispering, "Murderous Peasant." Despite his words, heat shivers over my skin. "You know I'll do whatever it takes to win."

Even slumming it with someone like me.

I lift my lips close to his ear. "So, are we still performing?"

He flashes me a disarming smile. If I didn't know any better, I'd think it was actually affectionate.

"Show them how much you want me," he whispers. "Fake it if you must. Because I need you to make them believe that you are so in love with me that you are willing to share the grail with me for the rest of the week."

I freeze. "No."

"Why not?"

I narrow my eyes at him. He thinks he can bully me, but he doesn't know that I have a greater purpose than simply winning power. "Because, *warlord*, I won it. And you lost."

He pulls me into his lap, and my breath catches as I am pressed against the hard angles of his muscled body. I lean into the solid heat of his chest, tilting my head up.

I can feel everyone's eyes on us—watching the golden couple. And yet, when I'm this close to his mesmerizing glow, the rest of the world fades to gray.

One of his hands wraps around the small of my back, and the other rests casually on my hip. Languidly, his thumb brushes up and down over the silk of my dress. The blue darkens in his eyes.

His mouth is close to mine. "You can't possibly hope to sit on the throne when you're lying to everyone about who you are. You'll be under far too much scrutiny. The best you can hope for is a title from me. I'll give you Mabon's ancestral palace near Corbinelle."

He smells of fire-kissed wood, a warm scent that coils around me.

"I'm not giving it to you," I whisper. "What do you even want it for? You're in the lead."

Still stroking my hip, he slides his gaze down my body, then up again. "Your heart is racing, love."

I nuzzle the side of his face, nearly kissing his ear. "That's because I'm worried about what you'll do."

His hand slips from my hip down to my thigh, caressing me. "Then do as I say."

He's not going to relent, is he?

My heart slams. No matter what, I need to give it to Vero first. "Fine. I'll give it to you for one day at the end."

"Your last chance will be Wednesday by noon. Four days. That's your deadline." He reaches for my face and strokes my lower lip. "Now, pretend to find me captivating so it's believable."

I kiss his thumb. "As long as you personally understand that I'd rather stab my eyes with hot pokers."

His lips hover inches from mine. "It would be a shame to ruin such pretty eyes."

I lean in closer, whispering into his ear, "Perhaps I should carve out yours instead."

For all the world, it looks like I'm whispering sweet nothings into his ear.

He brushes the hair off my face, leaving a trail of heat in the wake of his fingertips. "Is this how peasants seduce each other? With threats of maiming? I've always wondered how you did it. I must admit, it turns me on."

"Poor warlord." Our lips are nearly touching now. "Hurts to know a peasant holds your fate in her hands, doesn't it?"

He whispers, "I think you're an uncultured swine in a beautiful woman's body. But sometimes we use beasts to get a job done."

My lips brush against his jawline. "I should have killed you when I had the knife to your throat."

"Your hatred for me only makes this feel all the sweeter," he breathes in a ragged whisper.

One hand slides to the back of my neck, his fingers threading into my hair. His touch seems far too gentle for the brutal killer who spilled so much blood today.

His thumb brushes along my jaw, then over my lower

lip. Molten heat slides through me—low, dangerous, liquid fire. A man so vicious has no right to be this beautiful. And right now, I feel the full force of his power trained on me. It shouldn't, but it feels like I'm standing in the sun's rays.

His eyes darken, shadows sliding through the silver until they turn iron gray. Then they close.

His lips meet mine in a slow kiss. He's taking his time with me, like he's savoring a fine mead.

My body answers to his, and I want to drag my hands down his chest. This is a performance. A lie. A pantomime with a man I loathe. But my body is too stupid to know the difference.

When I part my lips, letting him deepen the kiss, I have to admit that *yes*, he's unbelievably hot, and *yes*, I've dreamt of exactly this. But even in my dreams, I don't feel desire lighting up my core the way it is now.

His tongue sweeps in, and a heated, unwelcome ache coils tightly inside me. Slowly, my tongue brushes against his. It must be his magic—nothing else explains this. For a moment, I imagine myself as one of the women in his harem, and in my imagination, his fingertips stroke between my thighs, lightly—

And just as the thought slides through my mind, his hand traces languidly up my thigh. Desire spills through me. When his hand moves higher, I have to bite back a moan—

Too late.

It slips out anyway, soft enough that only he can hear.

Get it together, Syn. Reality crashes into me. This is all fake. He wants the grail that I need to save Vero. And as Ranae said, he'll discard me like an old rag when he's done with me.

When I pull away from the kiss, his eyes are still dark, his chest rising and falling as if he's just come out of battle.

We *are* at war, the two of us, one fought with secrets and lies, and I'm pretty sure only one of us will be left standing.

"Four days," he whispers.

Before Rion snatches the grail from my hands, I *have* to get it to my sister. And if I fail, either Vero or I will end up dead.

CHAPTER 43

The hour has come, the moment I've been desperately waiting for. At last, it's time to save my sister.

Wrapped in a cloak, I stalk through a darkened tunnel with the grail safely tucked in a cloth inside a bag over my shoulder. I hold a candle to guide me through the underground tunnels. If anyone catches me, I'm armed with several daggers strapped to my thighs and around my waist.

I *refuse* to fuck this up.

This is my only chance to heal Vero.

All day, I mentally reviewed the plan for tonight. Tristan said I could no longer scale the wall outside. In the past few days, there have been extra patrols guarding that spot, but he found another way out for me. He mapped out the guards' movements and the exact timing of their patrols. I spent all day painstakingly memorizing every-thing I'll need to escape unnoticed.

Now I'm skulking through the ancient passages and wine vaults beneath the Veiled Court. A labyrinthine path leads from the servants' quarters through a crypt, more tunnels, a dungeon, and finally, out to the seashore.

Having spent ten years under a castle, I feel strangely at home down here in the mold and damp, breathing in the soil. This is my domain, among the scent of old bones.

Mentally, I go through the guards' rotations as I walk. In about ten minutes, a soldier will be stalking through the dungeons, searching for anything out of place. I'm counting every second and minute to make sure I have the timing right.

I reach an oak door fortified with metal nails and reach into my pocket for a skeleton key—another gift from Tristan.

I press my ear to the wood. Silence. Sliding the key into the lock, I open the door to the dungeons, the creak of the hinges echoing loudly in the quiet of the night. Wincing at the sound, I slip into a shadowed corridor.

The hallway smells of dirt, mold, and death. My candle gutters as I walk, flickering light over rusting metal cell bars. Skeletons lie on stone floors, their toothy grins agape. Starved to death, perhaps. Locked up and forgot-ten, a macabre menagerie of people who offended the last king in one way or another.

I swallow hard and walk faster, passing row after row

of cells as I head toward the crypt. It seems to go on forever, and my heart rate picks up until I'm nearly jogging. I count the minutes as I trot. Six and a half minutes now until a guard sweeps through this exact path. Ten minutes until someone crosses the crypt.

At last, I reach the other end of the dungeon. I slide the key into the lock again and unlock it with a click. I slip the key back into my pocket. Gently, I edge the door open.

The hinges creak again, and I wince, the sound as loud as a shriek in my ears. I hold my breath, then slip into another hall and carefully shut the door behind me. A long corridor takes me from here to the crypt, and I should be able to make it in time. I run through the corridor.

Eight minutes now until someone heads this way—

But as I reach the crypt, I already hear the footfalls. My breath catches.

Why are they early?

I can't turn back toward the dungeon—another guard will be heading past the cells any minute now.

Fuck. I'm trapped between two patrols heading through the crypt from opposite directions. They'll be closing in on me like pincers.

The sound of footfalls draws closer, and I blow out my candle as I scurry to the crypt wall. Carefully, I set down my candlestick and tuck the bag with the grail in the shadows by a coffin. I can't risk damaging it.

Quietly, I climb the stone catacomb niches, using them

as a ladder to reach the ceiling. At the top, I reach for the rafters, wooden beams that span the ceiling above the crypt. I grip one of them, then swing my legs up and climb on top of it, my heart pounding hard in my chest.

A moment later, the swaying light of a lantern comes into view, and a raven-haired soldier stalks into the crypt, shifting his light around.

From the dungeon side, the door groans open.

I'm hardly breathing up here, and fear flickers through my veins.

The second soldier marches into the crypt, and he nods. "Didn't expect you here."

The dark-haired soldier sighs. "They increased patrols, didn't they? Ever since someone murdered Lord Cador. Too much, if you ask me. No one's down here."

"Haven't slept in days." The second soldier starts to move on—then freezes. Slowly, he turns to look at the candle I left on the floor by the wall.

"Hang on." He kneels and picks up the candle, pressing a finger into the soft, warm wax.

"Is that new?" asks the other soldier.

"Still warm. Like someone just blew it out. Don't imagine it was these fellas, was it?"

The soldiers start to move their lanterns around the room, searching.

My blood hammers, and my gaze darts to the bag with the grail, still hidden in the shadows. I can't let them find that. And if they look up, I'm done for.

When the raven-haired soldier turns his back on the other one, I leap down onto the ground.

My blade carves through his throat before he has a chance to scream, and blood sprays from his neck. He drops his lantern with a bang, shattering the glass.

I whirl to face the other soldier just as he's turning to look.

He's starting to scream the word "Treason!" when my blade in his throat cuts the cry. His lantern smashes onto the stone, too, and the oil spills. Flames ignite, racing across the crypt floor, blazing over the spattered oil.

Heart galloping, I find the bag with the grail tucked in the shadows where I left it. The flames in the room leap and spread.

Seizing the bag, I run back to the crypt niches, climbing to the rafters once more. Heat scorches the room as I hoist myself over a wooden beam and crawl above the fire, sweating in the heat. The rafters are starting to smolder and blacken beneath me.

At last, I reach the door. I drop down again and move through the darkness.

An alarm bell sounds, the loud, clanging noise ringing off the stones. I'm *almost* there—nearly to the door, to the sea, and to freedom. Except I've lost track of my meticulous counting, and without my candle, I can hardly see a thing.

I no longer have any idea where the patrols are, but I can hear them shouting as they run to put out the fire.

I *think* I know where I'm going based on the map I memorized, but I can barely see the contours of the walls. Blindly, I feel along the damp stone. In the distance, the amber light of a lantern passes at the end of a passage, and I freeze, holding my breath.

He's not coming my way.

All it takes is one wrong turn for everything to be over. One noise, one false step, and Vero could die.

I stay still for a moment, slowing my breath, calming my thoughts. I call to mind once more the maps I memorized all day, their twists and turns that lead to the sea. I rebuild my mental image of the route and start moving again, ticking off each right and left as I walk.

At last, my fingers touch a new surface—damp, aged wood instead of stone.

Tears sting my eyes. I've made it to the door, and I still have the grail. Even if I never make it back here, I'll save Vero.

I turn to look back, where only darkness greets me, and the distant shouts about fire.

Gently, I pull open the door to the shoreline and the wide-open sea.

Tonight, clouds cover the sky. The only light out here comes from my own halo, but I keep my cowl raised, trying to cover its glow.

Reaching the shoreline, I break into a run, heading for the cottage where Tristan promised to bring my sister.

I pray to the gods that it's not too late for her.

I run down the beach, the wind whipping at my cloak.

When I think of Vero, I remember how I first found her—feverish, cheeks pink, rasping for breath. She slept with her arms wrapped around a pillow, and I always wondered if she slumbered with Mother like that when she was little, in her parents' bed instead of her own.

But when I found her, she didn't have anyone to look after her anymore. That was my fault.

I remember brushing her hair off her forehead. When she opened her eyes—big, lavender eyes—I immediately knew who her mother was. And when I picked her up, she clung to me like I was her new mum.

She would have died if we left her there. So, I scooped her up and clutched her to my chest. We rushed away from the forest, away from the Undercroft and Auberon's attacks on demi-Fey. Then Tristan led us to a portal into London.

The first few weeks in London, we slept under a bridge by a park. For the first time, my magic no longer worked. My life changed drastically. I wasn't a soldier or a spy anymore, and I didn't serve the king. I could no longer fight with the ferocity of the goddess. And as my life became slow and quiet, horrible memories haunted me. With nothing to fight or survive, I couldn't escape the memories of everything I'd seen and done.

And so, my world narrowed to one thing: taking care of Vero, making her feel safe and protected.

At night, a little shop would leave its unsold sandwiches on the windowsill. I'd snatch them up for my hungry sister to eat throughout the day.

After a month, Tristan found a place for us to live. I don't know how, but I always suspected it was his charm and beauty and the loneliness of a woman he'd just met. That's probably how he also found me a job, even when we barely spoke English. He found a school for Vero, too. He managed everything.

I never told Vero how our parents died. I couldn't take the look on her face if I did.

And now, at last, I'm going to fix what Auberon did to her.

I race into the forest, breathing in deeply as the oaks shield me. Rain slides from their leaves onto my cloak, dampening it. Lightning cracks the sky overhead, and thunder rumbles over the landscape.

I run along the rocky path, racing like the wind.

It's not long before I see a stone cottage in a clearing, where golden light beams through the windows. Smoke coils from its chimney.

I fling the cottage door open. Vero sits by the fireplace, wrapped in blankets. Her skin has taken on a yellow tinge, her lips the color of a bruise. Dark veins trace over her cheekbones toward her eyes. She isn't moving at all, and for one terrible second, I think she might be dead.

I freeze in place, staring at her with horror.

Tristan stands, relief on his face. "You made it."

"Is she okay?" I croak.

Balin crosses into the room with a cup of hot tea. "Oh, thank the gods. You're in time."

"Okay." My hands are shaking as I reach into my bag, and I pull out the grail. "Get some water."

Relief spirals through me as I hurry to her side. She's still breathing, rasping for breath, but her lungs are working all the same. The sharp, pained wheeze makes my own breath go shallow, like I'm the one dying.

I'm hardly aware of Tristan or Balin anymore—I'm just looking at Vero. She's shivering, her eyes half open. Even her cherry red hair looks faded, the ends bleached to bone-white, like the illness has drained every sign of vitality from her.

Tristan hastens over with a carafe of water and pours it into the grail.

It seems to hum with power between my hands. "I've got it. Let's do this now."

I sit next to Vero, halfway on the sofa with her. I bring the grail closer to her face. Her eyes flutter, and her pupils look white. I'm not sure she even knows I'm here.

From behind the sofa, Balin holds the back of her head.

I lift the skull to her lips and let the water trickle over her mouth. The first few drops spill down her chin, and Balin uses his other hand to try to open her mouth a little more.

I pour water directly into her mouth, and she sputters and coughs like she's choking. Then, her eyes snap open, and she grabs the grail from me.

Hungrily, she pulls it to her mouth. She tilts it back, drinking down every drop. When it's empty, she cradles the grail in her arms like a baby.

We stare at her, listening as the rough whistle in her breathing quiets. Slowly, the lavender returns to her eyes, and the dark veins beneath her skin begin to recede.

She looks shocked, and I gaze at her in awe.

She takes a deep breath, and a bit of color returns to her lips, then a pink blush to her cheeks.

For the first time, she seems to realize that she's holding a skull, and she stares down at it in shock. "Is this the grail? Oh, my gods, I can breathe again."

I wrap my arms around her, pulling her in tightly for a hug. I clamp my eyes shut, but tears start to stream down my cheeks anyway.

"You're crushing me, Syn," she says into my shoulder.

I pull away again, looking into her face. "Are you better? You can breathe fine now?"

She already said it, I know, but I want to hear it a million times.

A line forms between her eyebrows. "I feel amazing, actually. Is this how you feel all the time? Like you can run five miles?"

She pulls the blanket off and stands. Balin practically tackles her in a hug, and she breaks into laughter, hugging him back.

"Veroooooo." He's pulling her tightly against him.

She's still laughing when she pulls away from the hug, giddy with everything.

Tristan leans over to ruffle her hair like she's still a little girl.

I can't think of a time when I ever felt this elated. My happiness is a wild, uncontrolled thing, a roaring river of joy. I can't decide if I should laugh or sob with relief, and I end up sort of hiccupping between both.

The firelight wavers over Vero, and she looks down at her arms, grinning. "The weird veins are gone! Bloody amazing. Syn, I can't believe you got the fucking grail. How did you do it?"

I shrug. "Not a big deal. You *are* my sister, so of course I did."

Her smile is dazzling. "I knew you could do it." She lifts her shirt sleeve to her nose and makes a face. "Gods, I reek. I need a bath." Her smile spreads again. "But when can we have a party to celebrate? I need to bathe and find something clean to wear. And then we should get mead, and food, and music. And we will *not* invite Owain."

Tristan runs a hand through his hair. "You and Balin should have a party the moment you return. But Syn and I have to get back to our mission."

Vero's smile fades. "You're not coming to the cottage with me?"

I shake my head. "Not just yet. But I will, of course. I'm working with Avalon Tower still."

"Doing what?"

I actually have no idea what Tristan already told her, so I let him fill her in.

"We're monitoring a monarchist group," he says. "We need Syn's help. I promise to keep her safe."

Her frown deepens. "But how can you make that promise? That's not something you can actually promise."

"I'll be fine," I say.

She folds her arms. "You two always have secrets. From me, from each other, from yourselves…"

"All part of being a spy, darling," says Tristan.

I swallow hard, looking at Vero—completely healthy for the first time since I found her feverish in that little cottage. "What will you do now, Vero? What do you want to do with your life?"

She looks up at the ceiling, smiling as she thinks. "I could do anything now, right? I want to have a home library. And I could write books, maybe, in Fey about the mortal world. And maybe open a bookstore. And I want to learn how to swim and how to cook. Balin always cooks for me, but I'm sure I can learn. And a garden! I'm going to grow vegetables and flowers. I might learn to fight, also. And I want to play the drums."

I grin. "Beautiful."

"Are you sure you can't stay?" she asks.

She crosses to me and hugs me tightly against her.

I want to stay here with Vero, hiding out in the forest cottage with her forever. But I don't have much time before the *cugol* will notice I'm gone, and they'll come for me—and Vero, too.

Outside, I hear a twig snap, and I run to a window. But when I peer out, I see only shadows.

"What's wrong?" Vero asks.

I press my face to the glass, looking out. "Nothing. I thought I heard a twig. But I can't see a thing."

I turn back to Vero and wrap her in my arms again. I squeeze her, no longer worried that I'll break her. "I'll be with you soon. I promise."

* * *

TRISTAN LEADS me along the shoreline, and the waves crash against the rocks. Overhead, thunder rumbles across the horizon, and the dark clouds unleash a torrent of rain. Lightning spears the darkness.

And yet, I feel euphoric all the same. I've finally redeemed myself, just a little.

I pull my cowl up higher, hoping to hide the halo's glow from anyone who might look outside.

From here, we can't see the Veiled Court. It blends into the horizon—just the dark sea, the mist, and the night sky.

"What, exactly, happened?" Tristan asks, as he wipes the rain off his face. "You lit the crypt on fire?"

"No, not *me*. The soldiers' lanterns lit the crypt on fire when I startled them."

"Right. When you startled them by slitting their throats."

"I imagine that was a surprise to them, yes. In any case, I think we need a different route. There will be soldiers crawling all over the underkeep, trying to figure out who the murderer is."

He nods. "Okay. We'll need to scale a different wall and do it fast. I think our best option is the outside wall of the Gloaming Tower or Lyria, facing the sea. No one will be looking for the murderers in the middle of the ocean."

Rion lives in Lyria, and that fucker catches everything.

"Gloaming," I say. "We only need to make it up two stories, and we can climb through one of those big balcony windows into the stairwell." I turn to him, grabbing his arm. "Tristan? There's a little situation I have to tell you about."

His eyes flash in the darkness, and I can see a line of concern between his eyebrows. "What happened?"

"Rion is blackmailing me into giving him the grail. If I don't give it to him by Wednesday, he'll tell everyone that I'm an imposter, and I'll be tortured and burned."

"Fuck. I want to rip that man's heart from his chest."

"Right?"

"But we can't kill him yet. What does he want the grail for? He's already winning."

I shake my head. "I have no idea."

"Order of the Green Knight, perhaps?"

"I can't say I'm much closer to figuring that part out. So, what do you want me to do?"

"I need to report this to Avalon Tower. But I might not be able to get back here in time. I'm not even sure how I'll get a portal open. I think I can get to one tomorrow morning." He turns, grabbing me lightly by my biceps. "Syn, if you don't hear from me by the time the deadline is up—I want you to give it to him. Don't risk your life for the grail. Whatever he plans to do with it is a problem for later. Your immediate problem is staying alive."

"Okay." I turn away from him, looking for the Veiled Court. I know it's near here, but I still can't see it. "And our immediate problem is also getting back inside."

Tristan guides me with his hand on the small of my back. "We're almost there. I can feel it."

He leads me into the shallow waves, and seawater sprays through the air around us as the waves crash. Magic crackles over my skin, raising the hair on my nape.

Then, it comes into view—the fortress, and the Gloaming Tower looming above us. It's dizzying, this sudden appearance of a grand fortress before us, and I stare up at the hulking tower.

"The exterior walls are slick, with hardly any finger holds," he says. "Do you think you can do it?"

"What other choice do we have?" I ask.

"None."

"Then we'll make it happen."

As we reach the base of the tower, I look up at the climb. Rain lashes against the smooth, honey-colored rocks and slides down the sides. This looks nearly impossible.

From the lapping waves, Tristan nods up at the rain-slicked tower walls. "You go first."

I know he wants to catch me if I fall, but I don't argue. He's a better climber than I am.

Arching my neck, I look up for any uneven stones. Lightning flashes again, and I spot a slight grip in the momentary glare. I reach for the little outcrop of stone, then feel around for a foothold. My toe finds a tiny ledge, and I hoist myself up.

Even with the cowl over my head, the halo's light catches on the slick stones, glowing back at me.

I climb slowly, scanning the wet surface, just barely

holding on. I breathe in the scent of wet wool, my sodden cloak weighing me down. The rain picks up, slamming down on us from behind, completely soaking my clothes.

After one story, I reach for a grip, but my fingers slip off again, and then I'm falling—

Tristan's left arm shoots out, and he catches me like I don't weigh a thing. He pulls me in close to him.

For a moment, I stare at the way the rain slides down his golden skin. "Thanks," I whisper.

"Climb onto my back. I'll get you up."

It's not glorious, but his limbs are much longer than mine. He has a lot more options when it comes to finding grips. Plus, he's incredibly strong.

I shift around his body, wrapping my arms over his shoulders and my legs around his waist. His white shirt clings to his skin.

As he climbs, I feel his muscles shift and flex until at last, we reach the balcony. I raise my arms and reach for the balcony that juts from the window. I pull myself up, then shift out of the way and slip into the stairwell. Tristan hauls himself up next and slides inside with me.

Catching his breath, he turns to me with a half smile. "Victory."

Rain trails down his cheekbones.

I smile and let out a little laugh. "We did it."

From below, I hear rapid footfalls, and I freeze. Someone is about to round the corner.

I nod at the window, then slip outside. Tristan follows,

and we press in close, just out of view. There isn't much room here, and he wraps his arms around me. As the rain hammers down on us, I press my head against his chest, listening to his heartbeat.

I'm no longer paying attention to what's happening in the stairwell or if we can go inside now. All I want to think about is the warmth and solidity of his body, the steady drum of his heart.

I steal a look at his gorgeous face and shining green eyes. When he looks down at me, I see it for the first time —the hunger. My gaze flicks down to his sensual lips, then slowly drags itself up again. Gold shoots through his irises, then it smolders to a fiery copper.

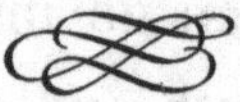

CHAPTER 45

My pulse speeds up. He smells like sunlight on freshly cleaned cotton—like summer. The curve of his full lips entrances me.

I've thought about kissing him a million times, wondering where my mouth would draw the loudest sound from him, what touch would make him come undone…

He's gorgeous, of course, but it's not just that. It's also all the nights he lay behind me in the Undercroft. In those ten years, he was the only person who made me feel safe. The way he took lashings for me, the way he pulled me into his arms when I fell apart. I think of him as the only spark of light in a decade of darkness.

And with all this in my head, all I say is a whispered "Do you think they're gone?"

"What if I like it out here?" The low, rough sound of his voice sends heat pulsing through my veins.

The copper in his eyes burns brighter, and the intensity of his look takes my breath away. His breath mingles with mine, warm despite the rain. He looks enraptured with me in a way he never has before.

Standing on my tiptoes, I press against his rain-soaked shirt. I close my eyes and brush my lips against his tentatively, like I might shatter something fragile between us.

His fingers tighten in response, and his body coils with tension.

Even that first light brush of our lips sends a hot shiver through me. Then a dark, dangerous heat curls in my belly as his mouth slides against mine. The storm, the guards, it all fades around me. As I kiss him, everything narrows to just *Tristan:* his delicious mouth, his warm body, his powerful arms wrapped around me.

His hand slides behind my neck, his fingers curling into my hair. His mouth opens first, his tongue sweeping in, and my back arches into him before I can stop it. Desire pours through me as we taste each other for the first time, slowly at first, then with a growing, sensual hunger.

I press against him, my breasts brushing against his chest. I remember how he looked without his shirt on, the way his dark tattoos slash over his hard abs, the ink and shadow tracing his muscles.

He slides a hand over my bum, pulling me in tightly

against him as he kisses me deeply like he's been starving for me. Oh, gods, no wonder this man broke hearts all over Brocéliande.

There's nothing tentative now. The way his mouth moves against mine—desperately, hungrily—answers every question I've had about how he feels about me. I can tell he's thought about this as much as I have.

I crave him, body and soul, because ever since the Undercroft, he's been the missing piece of me that I need to live.

As he pulls me into him, the rest of the world dims around me. He is the sunlight through the oak leaves; he is the gold of a slow summer afternoon—warmth and light and sky.

I'm where I always wanted to be.

My hand slides into his shirt, feeling the hard planes of his abs. My thumb brushes low, and he lets out a quiet growl.

Then a voice cuts through the moment—sharp and jarring. "Lady Lunette is in her room!"

I pull away from the kiss, but I'm still clinging to him. We stare at each other, neither willing to let go. What I want to do is drag him into my bedroom, rip his clothes off, and explore every inch of his body.

From above, someone else shouts, "Lord Oran is in his room. Clear!"

My lips still hover inches from Tristan's, and I feel his fingers flex behind me.

His eyes widen a little, and he mouths, "They're checking every room."

Bollocks. They're patrolling the stairs, too.

I swallow hard and look up. The stones glisten dimly in the rain, and lightning spears the sky again, flashing off the wet rock. Thunder booms, echoing in my ears.

Tristan leans closer, and he whispers in my ear. "I'll carry you up. Climb onto my back again."

He turns to face the tower, and I wrap my arms over his broad shoulders. I jump up a little, clamping my thighs around his waist from behind. As he climbs, I feel his muscles tighten and release between my thighs.

I rest my head against his shoulders and breathe in his scent.

With me on his back, he climbs the wall. I lick my lips, tasting salt—but I can still taste him, too, faintly.

At last, we reach the balcony outside my room, a stone overhang that juts out over the sea. Tristan climbs up close enough that I can shift off his back, sliding my legs over the stone rail and onto the balcony.

Tristan follows me onto the balcony, and I open the door to my room.

I turn back to look at him.

His green eyes search mine. "If they're looking for the killer, they're going to wonder why you're wet."

"I'll get in the bath."

"I should go. I don't think I can be here without raising suspicion."

But I'm not quite ready to let him go yet. I want more from him.

I grab him by his soaked shirt collar and pull him closer. "Give me one more thing before you go."

His gaze brushes down to my lips. "Another kiss?"

"No. The truth. What happened to you that night you lost your mind in the forest?"

I almost want to take it back, but I don't.

Pain flashes in his eyes, then confusion. "This is what you need to know right now?"

"Yes. Because you never tell me anything, and you never want to talk about the past. I know you better than I know anyone else on earth, but you still keep secrets from me."

A line forms between his dark eyebrows, and a muscle ticks in his jaw. "Her name was Isolde. She was a countess and noble, and I was sent to bring her from the Joyous Isle to Brocéliande. We fell in love on the way, but she was engaged to the king's cousin. And the king also planned to make her his mistress. When Auberon learned that she had a peasant lover, he tortured her, demanding to know my name. She refused to give it to him. Eventually, when every one of her bones was broken, and he'd cut out her tongue, he threw her off a balcony. I found her there." His voice roughens. "That's how I ended up running through the forest, half mad."

"I'm sorry," I whisper.

His eyes gleam, and he cups the side of my face. "It's a sad fact that I'm ruinous for people I get close to."

A sharp sadness carves through my chest, and I pull him closer in a crushing embrace. His arms slide around the small of my back. Then I stand on my toes, pressing his warm lips against mine again for one last kiss.

At last, I let him go and watch as he climbs down the wall again.

When I hear the shouts of the guards drawing closer, I pull the grail from my bag, and I set it to rest on the table just beside my bed.

Then I run into the bathroom, stripping off my clothes.

By the time they fling open the door to my room, I'm wrapped in a towel.

The soldier glowers at me as I feign a surprised expression.

Staring at me, the soldier shouts, "All clear in Baroness Alis's room!"

He turns, slamming the door behind him.

I slip into silk underwear and pajamas and climb into my bed. More than anything, I wish Tristan were here with me.

My mind races, and I can't stop thinking about the feel of him, the way he held me, and the delicious taste of him still lingering on my lips.

But why now? I was always there, waiting for him to

want to kiss me, and his mind was always on other women. Beautiful, rich, aristocratic women.

Married women.

And they all have one thing in common. They were never truly his to have.

I slide down under my covers, watching the rain hit the diamond-pane glass.

And now, here I am, playing at being an aristocrat. In public, I'm in Rion's arms. Now, I have Tristan's attention as a baroness vying for the throne. I'm another version of the woman he always wanted—rich, polished, and untouchable.

But it's not really me.

That's the legacy of the Undercroft, isn't it?

Tristan always ends up in a cage, one way or another. And he will only let himself love the people out of his reach. It's like he said—he believes he's ruinous for the people he gets close to. And I'm no better.

I think if we ever got what we wanted, we wouldn't know how to keep it.

* * *

I WAKE AT DAWN, as the rising sun paints the sky with nectarine and gold. I raise my arms over my head, and a knock sounds on my door.

Slowly, I drag myself out of bed, rubbing my eyes. I tug my silk nightgown down my thighs as I walk.

When I pull open the door, I find Tristan waiting for me, his arms folded. "Good morning, Baroness."

With a smile at him, I open the door wider. "Come in."

He steps inside. "I can't stay long. I came to tell you that I need to go back to Avalon Tower for a night or two to help lead a search team for the prince."

He closes the distance between us and cups the side of my face, searching my eyes.

"Any chance you can check on Vero when you leave here?"

"I'll see what I can do."

I peer up at him and wrap my arms around his shoulders. "Tristan. When did you first think you wanted to kiss me?"

A line forms between his eyebrows as he looks down at me. "I don't know. I suppose when I saw you fight in the arena."

My stomach sinks. "You mean, when you saw me kiss Rion?"

"Well, I didn't love seeing you in his arms. It was the first time I realized I was jealous of you with another man. I wanted to slit his throat, so I suppose that's how I realized. And you?"

"I was probably thirteen. You always reminded me of the times before everything fell apart. When we were kids, we ran around the woods without any worries. You remind me of the last time I felt safe."

"Thirteen?" His jaw drops, and a devilish smile curls his lips. "All that time?"

"But that's the thing, Tristan. I think…I think you want women you could never truly have."

A look of confusion crosses his features. "What are you talking about?"

"Married women. Aristocratic women. The thing is, I can't risk losing you. I *need* you in my life more than anyone else. You are the missing piece of me, and I'm not whole without you. But what if that means I need you as my best friend? Because if we were lovers, and one of us moved on…then I'd be missing a piece of myself."

His throat bobs, and a look of pain flashes in his eyes—but only for a moment before he regains control of himself. "I understand."

He pulls away from me and reaches for the doorknob. At the last moment, he turns back to me. "You remember our childhoods differently, Syn. I remember my mother growing thin and sick with worry. We were always hungry. My father hanged himself. One night, nobles beat your father nearly to death for no reason at all. Don't you remember that?"

My throat tightens. "No."

"We ran through the woods because we were foraging for acorns. All I knew as a kid was that you could never be happy when you're poor. I think, Syn, you remember a childhood that never existed, but you've invented it for yourself…I think you and I *both* only want things we can't have." He flashes me a sad smile. "Perhaps that does make us perfect friends."

When he turns and slips out the door, I drop into a chair. A tear streaks down my cheek. I wipe it away.

I don't know if it's because I just told Tristan we should stay friends or because of what he said about my childhood that never existed, but I feel like my heart is breaking.

Tonight, I'm going to drink all the mead.

If there is one thing the English and the Fey have in common, it's that you drown your pain in drink.

CHAPTER 46

*E*lizabeth, Aneirin, and I lie on top of the Gloaming Tower, staring up at the night's starry vault. The two moons hang in the sky, both full. Red and silver light pours over us.

I can't stop thinking about what Tristan said. Ever since he mentioned that we grew up starving, I keep remembering more glimpses of the real past. And yes, now I *do* remember when my father came home battered and bruised, with a punctured lung. He said he fell off a horse, but now that I think about it as an adult, a fall from a horse wouldn't do that kind of damage to his entire body...

Back then, I believed everything was fine because my parents made it seem that way. They made collecting acorns and foraging for fallen apples into a game.

Tristan's parents didn't spare him the truth.

"I don't want to leave this place," Aneirin says. "I was scared at first, but now I want to stay. I'd rather deal with the terror than go home to an empty, provincial ruin in the middle of nowhere. There's absolutely no one around Castle Catreath except a few forest-dwelling peasants."

Elizabeth sits up. "Maybe you won't have to leave. Alis is probably going to win the entire thing. Then she can make us knights of the Veiled Court, or we can join her at court in the capital."

I sit and reach for the bottle of mead. What I want to say is, *This is all fake. I am, in fact, a forest-dwelling peasant. I don't love Rion, and the moment he no longer needs me, I'm sure he'll feed me to Goch, and he's forcing me to give him the grail tomorrow for what I can only imagine is a truly horrific reason.*

But if I want to stay here as a spy, I have to play along.

Everyone needs to think I love Rion so much that I'd just hand him the grail for a few days.

I try to look starry-eyed and heave a wistful sigh. "Rion would make the most perfect king, truly. You know? He's just very…regal."

The words taste bitter on my tongue, and it feels ridiculous. I wonder how long I can keep this going.

"Do you think so?" Aneirin asks skeptically. "What does it even mean to be regal?"

"He's very powerful and clever. And he's *winning*." I realize this is a more realistic tactic than trying to convince them I've fallen head over heels in love. "I think I might let him have the grail for a few days to stay on his good side."

Aneirin sits bolt upright. "You don't need to help him. Even if you love the man, you should be fighting for yourself first. If you win, you'd be queen. Then he'd be consort. You'd have all the power."

Elizabeth nods. "Or you could just, you know, not get married because it's bloody terrible."

I shrug casually. "I just thought it would be a romantic gesture."

Aneirin narrows his eyes. "You're *framing* it as romance, but this is a calculated move, isn't it? Igraine is still after him. Giving him the grail keeps you as his favorite, and therefore a favorite of the noble houses, too. It's not the stupidest idea I've heard."

Making this a calculated move at least preserves some of my dignity. "Well, yes."

Aneirin holds a glass out toward me. "I'll be out of here soon, I'm sure. Hopefully with my life. The best-case scenario is that I'll end up back in my lonely palace with the dead clerics and the howling wind, and the peasants trying to behead the nobility. But that's only the very best case."

"Why not come to court?" Elizabeth says. "Maybe the new monarch will invite us both to Castle Perillos. We'll have a new Golden Age. Poetry. Theater. Balls. We'll have vast, sumptuous banquets. I'd rather stay a countess than a queen, you know. I'd rather just show up for the parties than throw them. I'm hoping for a dismissal also."

Aneirin drains his glass. "Yes, if Alis wins, that would be perfect. But anyone else? We've all been trying to kill each other. Do you really think they'll let us live? Someone like Mabon or Igraine? They fucking hate everyone else here. And you know what kings are like."

Darkness slips through my thoughts. "Maybe it would be better if we didn't have a king."

Aneirin scoffs. "Well, it's a very pretty notion, but the rest of the kingdom is in chaos right now."

"You're awfully gloomy tonight, Aneirin," Elizabeth says.

His expression brightens. "Sorry. It's the hangover. No, you're right, Elizabeth. Let's think of the new Golden Age. We will all be there for it. Let's try to help Alis win, shall we? She's our best chance of surviving."

And yet, I only have until tomorrow to give the grail to Rion.

I'm only making him more powerful until he rids the court of the rest of us.

* * *

BY THE TIME I get back to my room, it's nearly two in the morning, and my brain is addled with mead. I'm half drunk. Not *completely* drunk, or I would have risked spilling all my secrets to my friends.

By the way, I'm actually a peasant working with a spy agency to ruin the nascent monarchy, and I murdered my way in here.

A few more glasses of mead, and it would have all come out.

I cross into the bathroom and fill the tub with warm water. Steam coils into the air, and I strip off my clothes. As the tub fills, I slip into the bath.

I am *just* buzzed enough to take the edge off my heartbreak, and I know that giddiness will turn into sadness soon. But for the moment, it's working. It's dulled the pain.

In the bath, the hot water heats my skin.

As I lie back and close my eyes, Tristan's handsome face floats into my thoughts. Then, his muscled chest with the tattoo of his hound, the dark ink that slashes over his abs. And now I'm thinking of running my tongue over his stomach, and moving lower, feeling his hardness—

After everything I said to him, I should *not* be thinking of him this way.

Rion asked me why I hate pleasure, and the answer is that it's dangerous.

And now, I'm thinking of Rion, which is worse. The idea that he has an entire harem of women begging him to fuck them is unfortunately not that far-fetched. But why am I thinking about it?

Elizabeth said he tortures them by not letting them come.

I imagine him behind me, stroking me—

I bite my lip, because now that's all I can think about. I slide my hand between my thighs.

I can still see Rion in my thoughts—the way he looked in the garden that night with his shirt off and the tattoo glowing on his chest. Around me, the warm bath water laps at my skin. In my mind, Rion is spreading my thighs—

Then I bite down on my lip. This is the man currently ruining my life by blackmailing me.

I refuse to find him attractive.

I rise from the bath and yank a towel off the rack. I dry myself off roughly, dragging the towel over my skin. When I cross back into my room, I quickly dress in a pair of black underwear and a matching little nightgown that comes down to the tops of my thighs.

A knock sounds on my door, and for a moment, I hope it's Tristan. Instead, I see a letter slide under my door, addressed to *Alis*.

I frown and pick it up, turning it over.

Opening the door, I peer out into the hallway. Whoever left the letter is already gone, and I can only hear the faint sound of footfalls echoing down the stairs.

Still frowning, I turn back to the letter. I close the door and lean against it.

And when I unseal it, my heart stops. A lock of hair falls out, ripped off at the roots. It's cherry red, and the roots are bone-white.

Vero's hair.

My hands shake as I read the note.

I have captured Vero.

Leave your room now. Bring the grail to the dungeons within the hour. Leave it in the third open cell. Take the south entrance route to the dungeons.

Do not linger around the cells. Do not try to fight back. Do not bring help.

If you fail to follow any of these instructions, your little sister will die an excruciating death. I will carve out her organs, one by one.

And then I'll reveal to the court who you really are...

White-hot rage slides through my blood, and I crumple the paper in my fist.

I run to the wardrobe and arm myself with a holster and an iron dagger strapped to my thigh.

I will not be letting Vero's attacker leave the dungeons alive.

I whirl and grab the grail from the table by my bed. Shaking, I shove it into the bag.

I race out the door, thundering barefoot down the stairs. I waited too long reading the note, staring at the lock of hair, and I've lost my chance to catch up with the kidnapper.

I run, clutching Vero's hair in my fist—the lock of white blending to red.

Fury snaps through my body as I think of Vero. I was *so close* to keeping her safe. Someone from the Veiled Court must have followed me out last night, stalking me all the way to the cottage. *That's* how he learned about Vero.

My first thought is that this is Rion's work, since I know he wants the grail. But what's the point? I already agreed to give it to him by noon tomorrow.

As I run into the courtyard, the cold breeze buffets my skin, chilling away the last vestiges of my tipsiness.

I sprint for the door that leads down to the crypt, and my heart slams against my ribs.

Cold stones chill my soles. It's empty out here.

I reach the stairwell door to the catacombs and pull a torch off the wall. It's completely dark down in the underkeep.

I fling open the door, and my torchlight wavers over the rough stone stairs. I descend as fast as I can, my bare feet on dirty stone. I move swiftly through dark tunnels, taking the paths I already memorized.

In the distance, I hear soldiers' voices, and I snuff out the torch. I can't risk getting caught by patrols while I'm trying to save Vero.

I can find my way to the crypt by the smell of burnt coffins and bones. As I walk, I listen intently for more soldiers, or for Vero calling for me. Anything.

I cross into a hall lit with a few torches, their fiery light dancing over dark stone walls. I'm almost to the crypt when a sound makes my stomach lurch.

A footfall, directly behind me.

I whirl to see Rion stalking closer, his silver eyes burning like a wolf's in the dark.

He moves quickly as a storm wind, and he grabs me—one hand clamped around my waist, the other around my throat. In the next moment, he's pinning me against the stone wall.

His fingers curl around my throat. It's a light touch—just enough to trap me in place.

My pulse hammers, breath hitching.

"What do you think you're doing with the grail?" His low, lethal voice vibrates over my body. "I gave you until tomorrow to give it to me. And then I see you running across the courtyard like your nightgown was on fire, stealing away the relic."

"And how did you know I'm carrying it?"

"Because you have a very grail-shaped thing in a bag."

My pulse races. "I take it the note wasn't from you."

"What note?"

All I can think about is Vero and the brutal threats in the note.

I will carve out her organs, one by one—

She's only just become healthy, and now someone wants to kill her.

Distantly, from the depths of my skull, I hear the faintest hum of the Song. It's blurred, barely audible—a melody that whispers in the hollows of my mind.

I take a deep breath. "Okay. I'll give it to you."

I feel his hands relax, just slightly, on my hip.

He leans down to say something to me. The moment his grip loosens by a fraction, I slam my forehead into his chin and drive my elbow into his face.

It's just enough for me to slip away from him. But as I try to turn toward the crypt, he grabs me from behind, yanking me back and crushing me against his body. A blade flashes at my side, and my heart skips a beat—but he's not stabbing me. He slashes the bag from my shoulder, and it drops to the ground.

Panic ignites in my chest as he continues to pin my arms against my body in his vise-like grip.

"Take the dagger from your thigh holster," he murmurs, "and throw it across the room. I don't need you trying to murder me on my way out."

I look down at the bag on the floor. Rion is going to fuck this whole thing up for me.

"What do you even want with it?" I ask.

He brings his blade up to my throat in a warning, just barely grazing my skin.

But that movement frees up one of my arms.

Auberon trained me for this.

The Song is humming louder in the back of my mind, a distant, distorted melody, enough to spur me on.

I grab his knife-wielding wrist and yank it down hard, twisting. I duck under his arm and wrench it behind his back, but he tears himself free in the next moment.

I turn to run from him into the dungeons, but a powerful arm clamps around my shoulders from behind, pinning me again. I kick off the wall, using the stones for leverage, and thrust hard, slamming us both back onto the ground.

I land on top, but he rolls us over. Now my nightgown is up to my waist, and he's pinning me to the crypt floor, crushing me with his weight.

"You really need to stop trying to kill me," he mutters.

I jerk my hips upward and drive my elbow into his ribs. The impact knocks him off me.

I roll, reaching for the dagger at my thigh—

I'm too slow.

His blade is at my throat again.

But this time, I see it in his eyes—a flicker of hesitation.

Hesitation is death. He has the chance to kill me, and he's not taking it.

I draw my iron blade and drive it into his chest, between his ribs.

The moment I do, guilt twines through me. I don't know if he'll live. I avoided his heart, but I stabbed him with iron. Without a healer, he'll die down here.

My thoughts go dark, my blood roaring.

Vero.

I need to fix the mistakes I made long ago and keep my family safe. Then I'll come back for Rion.

So, I scramble for the grail.

"Sorry," I whisper to Rion. "I'm sorry."

He slumps back, clutching his chest, and blood pours between his fingertips.

For a moment, I look into his silver eyes, and I read the pain there. My twisting thread of guilt grows sharper, angrier, coiling in my chest like a poisonous serpent.

He could have killed me the moment he found me in here. He didn't. Am I the monster here?

My eyes sting, and I blink it away.

I rush toward the dungeons, through the next tunnel.

CHAPTER 48

Alone and clutching the grail, I creep into the dungeon. I can hardly see anything. Only a few slivers of moonlight pierce the darkness through cracks in the stone walls.

I count the cells, and when I get to three, I feel for an open door.

The note didn't say how I'd get Vero back, only that she'd die an excruciating death if I didn't bring the grail here.

My heart sinks when I realize the cell is empty. I'd hoped to find her here in some sort of trade-off.

But what leverage do I have?

I pull it wider. The metal creaks, and I step inside. With shaking hands, I set the grail on the dungeon floor.

I look around, sniffing the air for any trace of Fey. I breathe in only the smell of damp and mold, of old bones.

My breath is shallow and fast, and I try to scan the shadows for signs of movement.

As I close the cell door behind me, it groans loudly on its hinges.

I'll pretend to leave. But I'm not *actually* leaving here without trying to figure out who took Vero.

I creep back to the corridor just outside the dungeon and close the dungeon door. The kidnapper told me to come in through the south entrance, which means he'll be arriving from the north to avoid me.

But that cell door was fucking loud, thank the gods. I'll be able to hear him as soon as he comes in for it.

I wait, my heart racing, and press my ear against the wooden door. I try not to think of Rion, because why am I worrying about the Ruthless Knight when my sister is in danger?

I've seen him kill dozens of people without a second thought. The man has a pile of bodies behind him. So what if he hesitated when it came to me? I couldn't prioritize someone I barely know above my own family.

Still, a thread of remorse twists between my ribs.

I try to focus.

I close my eyes, listening closely. I count the seconds, hearing only my own breath.

At last, the rusty sound of metal scraping against metal pierces the door.

I fling the door open and rush into the dungeons. The man is holding a torch, and its warm light glows over a mask—one shaped like a fox's face. It's grotesque and absurd that the person who kidnapped and threatened to *eviscerate* my sister is wearing a fucking vixen mask.

As I run for him, he grips the grail in one hand and his torch in the other. He seems to freeze.

I've got my blade to his throat within seconds, my arm wrapped around his neck from behind. Around us, the shadows thicken and coil.

"I don't care about the grail," I say. "But where is my sister?"

"I don't have her. Don't kill me. All I had was her hair."

His voice is…familiar. The words slightly slurred. "Where *is* she? What happened to her?"

"I needed the grail, Alis. Whatever your name is. I followed you out the night you brought her the grail. I saw you give it to this peasant to drink from. I *heard* you call her your sister. I chased after her, trying to find out who she was, who you are. But I couldn't capture her. Her male companion was bloody powerful. His magic incinerated mine. I couldn't trap her."

"And her hair?"

Around us, the shadows twist unnaturally at our feet.

"I ripped out a chunk as she was fleeing from me. They were running into the forest."

"And *why*—"

My words are cut short by a burst of shadows—ice-cold, dark tendrils that snake around me, binding my arms, trapping me. I drop the knife, and it clatters loudly to the dungeon floor. As I struggle, my attacker darts away.

I rake at the magic, trying to free myself from the frigid, slick bindings.

Rage pounds through my blood, and I scramble to free myself, but the restraints only seem to be getting tighter.

Shadow magic wraps around my mouth and nose, suffocating me. My lungs burn as I claw at the strands that twine around me like strangler ivy. I'm going to die down here.

At last, I free my mouth, and I take a deep, gasping breath, filling my lungs.

From there, I start to loosen more of the ensnaring strands of shadow magic.

That's how I recognize the voice, and why his words were slightly slurred. We'd both been drinking on top of the Gloaming Tower tonight. That's probably *also* why his plan was so ill thought out.

For whatever reason, Aneirin decided to blackmail me for the grail.

But what, *exactly*, is everyone planning to do with it? The Veiled Court wants it back. What the fuck is the play here?

At last, the last of his magic dissipates from my body, drifting away from me like smoke. I'm left here by myself now.

Wherever Aneirin is, he's too far gone for me to catch.

I close my eyes. Rion's image blooms in my mind, the blood pouring between his fingers.

I lean over, hands on my knees, and take a moment to catch my breath.

I stagger away from the dungeon as the last threads of shadow magic drift from my arms. My mind races. Was he telling the truth when he said Vero got away from him?

Somehow, I think he was. And if she's free, then I only have one more immediate problem.

I start to head back to Rion. I sprint through the dark tunnel, navigating now by the smell of blood. The air grows colder. When I reach the crypt, a shadow moves.

I pause at the doorway, searching the room. Then, I see his golden tattoos, glowing from the shadows. And before I can even say his name, he lunges for me, his hands around my ribcage. He pushes me back, crushing me against the wall. Fear detonates in my skull.

I look up into his eyes, and they burn with a dark heat. But I can't quite see Rion in there—just an uncontrolled, animal lust for either sex or death, I can't tell which. Blood stains his shirt, but he doesn't seem to be paying attention to it.

"You're still alive," I whisper.

His only answer is a low growl. By the primal look in his eyes, I think he's in a place beyond words. He's not quite Rion anymore.

His hands are gripping me so hard around my ribs that

I'm sure he'll leave bruises. My heart hammers, but a memory stirs as I call to mind how to fix him.

His words echo in my thoughts.

Desire. That's how I heal—myself and others.

Am I going to have to kiss him to get out of this alive? I've done worse to survive.

Slowly, tentatively, I wrap my arms over his shoulders. My breasts shift against him.

Another low growl rises from his chest and trembles through my ribs. But this time, I think I see the faintest flicker of recognition in his eyes.

Looking up at him, I lick my lips. He's lethal, otherworldly—and heartbreakingly beautiful.

His large hands slide down lower, moving possessively from my ribs to my waist. Then lower, down around my arse. He lifts me into the air, pinning me against the wall, and my thighs wrap around him. One of his hands wraps under my bum, holding me up.

My nightgown slides up to the top of my thighs as I tighten my thighs around him. We grip each other like we did in the arena—except this time, I'm wearing thin silk instead of armor.

His free hand threads into my hair, and he tugs my head back, exposing my neck. My breath shallows.

He could easily kill me like this. Snap my neck. Tear out my throat. I've put myself in a wildly dangerous position. I can't tell yet if this is a mistake or the only way out.

Between my thighs, his body feels hard as steel. I'm

completely vulnerable here, pinned at his mercy. My pulse races as I hope for the best.

Slowly, he lowers his mouth to my neck, his hot breath feathering over my skin. Then his teeth drag over the pulse in my throat. It feels like a warning—that I'm his. Down here, I'm a prize he's claimed, and he'll do with me what he wants. His teeth feel sharp as he drags his canines over my neck, testing me.

For a moment, I wonder if he's going to rip out my jugular and end my life.

After all, I did just stab him.

I'm hardly daring to move. I simply breathe in, breathe out. My heart thunders against his chest.

Then, slowly, his warm lips press against my throat, and I let out a quiet moan. I'm shocked by how gentle his mouth feels on me. His grip is rough as a warrior's, but his kiss on my throat is exquisite.

Warmth radiates from his body as he crushes me in place.

I take no pleasure in this, of course. I'm only—

I'm only lying to myself.

His mouth moves lower down my throat, brushing over my collarbone. *Oh, gods.*

My hips shift against him.

He moves lower, his tongue grazing over the curve of my breast. My thighs clench, and I gasp for breath.

He lifts his face to mine now, searching my expression. If he's hoping to find desire in my flushed cheeks, I'm sure he has.

I reach up to touch his face, and my thumb brushes over his lower lip. The torchlight wavers on him. Gods, he's beautiful.

"I don't even know your name," he whispers. "Nor you mine. But I can hear how your heart races, and I can feel that you want me, and I want to claim you."

He leans in, pressing his lips against mine. As I kiss him back, my tongue slides against his. It's a heated, sensual kiss. The exquisite ache building between my thighs has my hips rocking against him. Another moan escapes me.

Now I hardly remember who he is, or who I am, or what I'm doing here. Molten heat slides through my core.

Slowly, he pulls away from the kiss with a nip to my lower lip and stares into my eyes.

"What do you mean?" I ask, remembering myself. "That I don't know *your* name?"

He shakes his head slowly. In his eyes, I can see him returning to himself.

His lips still heat the air, just an inch from mine. "I don't know what I was saying."

"But you're healed now, yes?" I almost hate myself for saying it. "We can stop now."

Slowly, he lowers me, and I slide down his body. As I start to take a step away from him, he pulls me back. The strap of my nightgown has fallen off my shoulder, exposing my nipple. The cool air kisses my skin, and my breast aches for his touch. Rion's hand slides up, caressing me, palming my breast.

"You need release." His voice skims over my skin. "Let me give it to you."

His other hand moves down between my thighs, touching me through the silk. My head rolls back against his chest.

I gasp at the contact, moving against his hand. Desire coils tightly in me, and I shift my hips back into him, feeling his hardness. I know he's as turned on as I am.

Part of me is *desperate* to say yes.

I want him to hike up my dress, rip off my underwear, and fuck me hard on the crypt floor. In just this moment, I want him to take total control of me, to make me forget the rest of the world. My body aches with need at the thought.

But I'll never admit how much I want him—even if he can see it, feel it, scent it.

I won't say yes. I've pledged to destroy anyone who tries to take the crown. I will kill anyone who threatens the republic. And right now, Rion is the top contender.

If I'm going to kill the next king, I can't let myself fall under his spell or lose myself in his dark allure.

At least I'm leaving him as unsatisfied as I am.

Still, it feels like another's voice is speaking for me when I say, "I don't need anything."

The lie feels ice cold on my tongue.

Even I can hear the falsehood as I step away, tugging

my nightgown back into place. Cold regret sets in for a moment—not because I stopped him, but because I almost let my enemy seduce me.

Then, I turn back to him and catch his gaze. "I suppose I should tell you now that Aneirin stole the grail. He blackmailed me."

"With *what*?"

I smile at him. "Do you think I would tell *you* that? You have enough leverage on me."

"Aneirin," he murmurs. "You gave the grail to that worm?"

"I'm going to try to get it back. Give me another day, please, before you tell anyone. Just one more day.

He slides his hands into his pockets and cocks his head contemplatively. "You ask a lot of favors for someone who keeps declaring how much you hate me." An arched eyebrow. "Do you think my patience is endless?"

"Just one more day." I swallow hard. "But what is it, exactly, that you both want to do with it?"

"Do you think I would tell *you* that?" He steps into the torchlight, and it gilds his perfect features. "I think, little mortal, you should worry more about what Niniane will do to you. Losing the grail is a mistake even I can't fix for you."

CHAPTER 49

$\mathcal{I}$ sink into my bath, exhausted. My body flickers with memories of Rion's kiss and the way his lips brushed over my collarbone. I can't stop thinking about the feel of his hand moving down my body, over the silk.

At the same time, I feel drained of all life, like a piece of paper bleached by the sun. My muscles burn with exhaustion, and my eyelids are heavy.

I slept a few hours today, but I still feel exhausted. About five hours after Aneirin stole the grail from me, alarm bells began to ring across the castle. They're still ringing now, reverberating in my skull. They can't possibly serve a purpose. Everyone knows by now that Aneirin escaped.

After four hours, the Cloaked Ones alerted Niniane,

and she set the whole fortress on alert with the bloody bell.

But apart from Rion, no one knows *why* Aneirin ran away, or that he took the grail with him. I pray to the gods that he'll keep my secret while I try to get it back.

I'm going to do everything I can to hold the grail in my hands once more.

But right now, the bell ringing is setting my teeth on edge. I feel like Niniane is furious with the world and wants us all to wallow in misery with her. She's doing a good job of making me feel unhinged. No wonder Mabon drinks so much to quiet his thoughts.

I run the soap over my skin.

Steam rises from the bath around me, and it gleams rose-gold as the setting sunlight slants in through the windows.

My jaw clenches. It now seems more likely than ever that these will be my last few days here—one way or another. Unless I get the grail back by Sunday, I'll probably be executed, either hunted by the Cloaked Ones or burned to death right here.

Losing the grail means everything is over for me.

More than anything, I need Tristan back. I need guidance and answers. I need a portal to Aneirin.

And most importantly, I need an update about Vero.

If all else fails, I need Tristan to help me escape this place so I can spend the rest of my life on the run.

I rinse the rest of the soap off my body and rise from

the bath. Warm water drips down my skin, catching in the sunlight. I towel off.

It's tempting to slip on my pajamas and crawl into bed, but I'll never be able to sleep with everything hanging over me.

Naked, I cross into my room. I dress in soft leggings and a plain black shirt.

As I'm pulling on my clothes, something catches my attention out of the corner of my eye. It's the little golden raven sitting on my bookshelf.

I cross to the table, where the note sits on the oak.

Let the raven guide your way, it says.

My gaze flicks back up to the object. The finely crafted wings seem to have delicate hinges, like joints.

I pick it up and inspect it. When I tilt the raven, the feathers shift a little. The head is connected separately, like it's designed to swivel.

When I look closely, it seems too intricately crafted to be just ornamental.

What if it's a magical tool of some kind? Like the moths.

I turn the little bird in my palm. "Guide me," I say. "Tell me what to do."

Nothing happens. For a second, I feel stupid, but no one else is here to witness my shame.

I look closer. The wings are definitely designed to move, I think.

Carefully, I pry my fingernail under one of the wings, shifting it up a little.

The raven hums to life, its head turning back and forth, wings outspread. From my palm, it lifts into the air, then settles on a bookshelf and cocks its head at me.

I'm so startled, I'm not even sure what to ask first. My pulse races, and I stare at it in wonder. At last, I ask it the most burning question in my mind: "Where is Vero?"

And with that, the raven takes off.

Quickly, I slip into my shoes and chase the bronze raven down the stairwell. Through the windows, coral light streams inside, catching on the raven's wings. I'm so sleep deprived, I feel like a child chasing a toy.

I rush after him into the courtyard.

I wonder where it's going, because clearly, Vero isn't in the fortress. I have a terrible feeling he's simply going to fly to Vero, and I'll be stuck here.

As I pass the Aether Tower, I see that Aneirin's unicorn banner has been ripped down.

The raven arcs over to the library, where he flutters in front of the painted image of the chained book.

I pull open the bright red door, and the raven zooms inside. I race to keep up with him as he sweeps into the library, soaring beneath the rib-vaulted ceiling.

As I run, swaying lanterns light my way with warm light. I chase the bird beneath the twinkling wisps of clouds that float through the library.

At last, he hovers before a cabinet of rolled maps. I

open the cabinet, and he swoops in, pecking at a roll of parchment. I pull it out and lay the map on a table.

The raven hops south until he finally lands in the Melian Forest, exactly in the spot where Vero lives, an hour from the capital.

Brilliant.

I close my eyes, exhaling a shaky breath. I was almost positive Aneirin was telling the truth about her, but now it's confirmed.

I clear my throat. "Where do I find Aneirin of Castle Catreath?"

The raven hops north, closer to the Veiled Court, not far from the Barenton River.

It's about thirty miles from here. Judging by the route, I *think* Aneirin might be heading back home to his castle.

What's he planning to do with the grail in his empty palace?

I imagine he could sell it to get out of his debt. Sell it to whom, though? And what's he planning to do about the Cloaked Ones who will hound him to the ends of the earth?

"And Tristan?" I ask, hoping to learn he's already back in Brocéliande.

But the little raven flits back to the maps again, selecting a new one. When I unroll this map, I'm frustrated to find it's of England. The raven pecks at the West Country, where Camelot lies hidden behind a veil.

Bollocks.

I slide the maps into place, then pick up the bird again and hold him in my palm. "Can you help me understand? What are they doing with the grail?"

The bird flies into the air again. He loops around a few times, appearing confused. This question is probably more complex than he can handle. Still, I get the impression he's trying.

He sweeps across the library to a dark alcove flanked by stone pillars. Inside the alcove, a tapestry hangs at the back, depicting a cauldron.

I have no idea what to do at this point. I'm not sure the raven and I can communicate very well. But he seems to be growing more insistent, slapping against the tapestry. He cocks his head and makes a clucking sound, like he's angry with me.

And the space almost sounds hollow behind him—

I peel back the tapestry and find a shelf with a wooden cabinet—just about two feet high.

It's locked, and this time, I don't have any lock-picking tools with me.

What I do have is a wild combination of desperation, sleep deprivation, and utter impatience.

I turn back to look at the library. Not a single person here. I breathe in the scent of old oak and books, and all I hear are the bells ringing outside. It's only me and the floating lanterns.

Pulling back the tapestry again, I slam my boot through the wood of the little wooden cabinet, then reach through the splintered mahogany and open it from the inside.

A single book lies inside, barely thirty pages long. Golden lines trace images of the grail, a leafy bough, and a sword. The metallic lines shift and glimmer over a velvety green cover. In my hands, the little book hums with magic.

I pull the book out and start reading, slowly translating the language of ancient Fey. I flip past the names of kings and a few queens—so many of them. Each of them ruled for a single year, each reign beginning on Tanos and ending the day before the festival.

Who *are* these rulers? Apart from the name Vortigern, I haven't heard of any of them.

Once I get past all their names, I find a few handwritten paragraphs about the ancient Fey monarchy.

My jaw drops open as I read.

For one year, we grant a monarch the three sacred relics—the sword, the grail, and the golden bough. With these relics, our gardens and crops grow verdant with life. Through a ritual bond between the monarch and the land, Fey power blossoms. Life, crops, and magic grow stronger when a king's power is bound to the earth.

So the relics are part of some kind of ritual to amplify a monarch's power. If Aneirin is going to sell the grail, who could possibly buy it?

Then, I read on.

Tanos starts our year, and Tanos Eve ends it. A Fey monarch rules during this time.

When the year ends, we return the monarch's life to the earth. We open the body, and his blood feeds the soil, renewing the bond.

Thus, we complete the ritual.

My breath quickens. I close the book, and I stare at the empty library before me.

There's the missing piece. And I doubt all these people after the grail have this information.

In the Golden Age of the Fey, we killed our kings.

CHAPTER 50

I pace my bedroom floor with a glass of mead in my hands. It's close to midnight now, and the fucking bells are still going. They're vibrating in my bones, my brain.

A knock sounds on my door, and I rush over to it, hoping to find Tristan.

I open it and find Elizabeth instead.

"There you are!" Her eyes are wide. "I came by earlier a few times, but you didn't answer."

I run my hand through my hair. "Yeah. Sorry. I've just been—"

"Worried about Aneirin?" Her brow furrows.

"Exactly." I'm too much of a mess to carry on this conversation in a normal way.

Fire burns in her eyes. "But I don't understand what happened. He seemed fine last night, didn't he? We all know what happens when you run away from here without permission. Why would he do such a reckless thing? He was doing all right in the trials. There was no immediate danger. He could have left with a dismissal."

My head throbs, and I don't want her to see what I've got laid out on the table behind me. "I don't know, Elizabeth. I wish they'd stop with the bells. I can't think clearly."

"Right." She nods at me. "I'll let you get some rest. Come find me if you hear anything."

"Of course."

I close the door and return to my new obsession, the maps. When I left the library, I took the maps of England and Brocéliande back to my room with me.

With a sip of mead, I turn back to my table. Once more, I spread the maps out, using books to pin down the curled ends.

I pick up my little bronze raven friend. "Where is Aneirin now?"

The raven hops out of my hand, landing in the forest. He's about an hour from Castle Catreath now, still fleeing with my grail.

"Raven, where are the *cugol*?"

He hops north, and I can see that they're on the right track. Still, they're a few hours behind Aneirin.

"And Tristan?" I ask, my voice breaking.

The last time I asked this—about half an hour ago—he was in the Melian Forest, where Vero lives. I know, at least, that he's on his way back to me. Just as I asked him to, he stopped to check on my sister.

But this time, the raven hops farther north—in Brocéliande. He lands on the spot where the Veiled Court stands now, by the sea.

With a deep breath, I close my eyes. "Thank the gods."

In just a few more minutes, a knock sounds on the door.

I fling it open and find Tristan standing there. I throw my arms around him and press my head against his chest. He wraps his arms around my back, his warmth enveloping me as I breathe in his familiar scent.

"What's wrong?" he asks quietly.

I peer up at him. "Did you see Vero?"

A line forms between his eyebrows, and he nods. "Yeah. She and Balin are fine. I think I interrupted them shagging—"

"I don't need to know that part." I pull away from the hug and tug him into my room, shutting the door behind him. "So, she's totally fine?"

"Someone with shadow magic attacked her immediately after she was healed. I take it you already know that?"

"Yes. Tristan?" My breath catches. "I think we're going to need to steal another dragon. We need to get the grail back from Aneirin."

* * *

I WAIT by a cliffside a few miles from the Veiled Court, armed to the teeth with a sword and as many daggers as I could slip into my holsters.

It's a cloudy night, and I stand in almost total darkness. The cool marine wind whips over me. My halo beams in the air around me, but I'm not as worried this time about the *cugol* hunting me. They're a bit preoccupied at the moment.

As I stare out at the sea, the ground shakes with heavy, thundering footfalls. My stomach swoops.

I turn to see a midnight blue dragon stalking closer over the seagrasses, and my breath leaves my lungs. He's almost impossible to see in the dark except for the silver flecks that shine from his scales. He looks like the night sky in living form. Slowly, his silver eyes cut to me, and he narrows them. Tristan clings to his neck as the dragon rears back his head and roars. The sound trembles through my body, and the dragon unleashes a great stream of fire into the night sky.

My heart races as the air heats above me. Is Tristan in control of this thing?

I step back toward the edge of the cliff as the dragon thunders into the air, and pebbles trip down the cliffside behind me.

At last, the dragon lowers his neck to the ground. Tristan sits on the creature's neck, and rubs his scales, trying to soothe him.

When the dragon seems to have calmed, Tristan looks

up at me. "It's okay, Syn. I've got him under control. He's ready for you."

I swallow my fear and cross over to the dragon. Tristan helps me up, and I mount the creature, sliding into place in front of him. As he taught me before, I squeeze my thighs around the dragon's neck, and Tristan wraps an arm around my waist, locking me in place with an iron-clad grip. I lean back into his strong chest and grab one of the dragon's spikes.

"Seronos is a little wild," Tristan whispers, "but he blends in with the sky. The *cugol* are less likely to notice us."

"Okay." I take a deep breath. "I trust you know what you're doing."

"Seronos," Tristan calls out. "Rise!"

Slowly, the dragon takes a few lumbering steps, pounding the soil with his feet. The ground shudders beneath us with every footfall.

The dragon raises his neck, and I slide back into Tristan. His strong grip tightens around me as we tilt and the ground seems to fall away beneath us. I cling to the spike harder and clench my teeth. Slowly, his wings start to beat, great strokes that pound against the sea air.

And with a lurch of my stomach, we lift off, soaring into the night sky. The wind rakes at us as we sweep above the forest. I hang on, gripping hard with my thighs. Wisps of clouds float in front of the moon, darkening the world around us.

Seronos flies higher, shooting through the line of clouds. Silver and red moonlight bathes us as we soar.

The dragon spreads his wings, and we race south.

* * *

THE CLOUDS HAVE THINNED, and as Tristan said, Seronos's scales blend with the night sky. As we sweep closer to Castle Catreath, the dragon glides over a gleaming lake, where the still waters reflect the moons. His dark shadow sweeps over the swells.

Tristan keeps his arm locked around me as the dragon glides lower toward a beautiful ruin.

Moonlight glints off the gothic spires and arches. Three walls ring a courtyard, with the fourth lying in ruin, just a few crumbled stones and columns left.

With a boom, we land on the grass in the square courtyard, and I shift forward a little.

Slowly, Tristan relaxes his grip, and the dragon lowers his head. Tristan slides off, then helps me down.

I breathe a sigh of relief to be on solid ground once more and step away from the dragon, surveying the castle.

Through some of the sharply peaked windows, warm light glows. But even as I look at the ruins, the lights start snuffing out, one by one.

Seronos wasn't exactly quiet with his landing. Whoever is inside is trying to hide from us.

"Should we search together?" I ask.

Tristan turns back to me, his eyes flashing green in the dark. "No, I can go much faster than you. Let me use my speed to race around. I'll find him within minutes."

"His magic is powerful," I say. "Especially if he has his cane with him to magnify it. The moment you spot him, call me, and I'll come help you. I'll wait near the castle and listen."

"Shelter somewhere out of view. I'll call for help if I need it." A cocky half smile. "Of course, I don't think I will."

Then he's off in a blur of speed.

As I walk closer, I draw my sword. The hair rises on the back of my neck, and my fingers tighten on my hilt. With every step toward the ivy-clad walls, I feel like someone could be watching me.

I cross under an arch, where no one can see me from the windows. As I wait here, I listen for Tristan.

My eyes dart, left and right, searching for signs of movement. Around me, the shadows seem to darken. My muscles tense, and alarm bells ring in the recesses of my mind.

Sword in hand, I whirl. I barely have time to glimpse Aneirin before his shadows slide from his cane, wrapping around my mouth and throat. Immediately, I lose my grip on the sword.

He's not choking me—but he's silenced me. Another tendril slips around my ribs and binds my arms together. Then, he tugs me down to the ground—*hard.*

His halo beams from his skull, staining the air around him with gold. A few wisps of his shadows curl before his halo, like smoke is rising from his body.

"I don't have it anymore." His voice is ice-cold, and he has a strange lisp. "And if you've come here for revenge, you needn't bother. I came home to die, anyway. That is all that's left for me."

I writhe, frantically trying to free myself from his magic.

"I know, I betrayed you," he adds. "But you're not who you said you were, are you? I followed you to the cottage. I heard you call that peasant girl sister."

He takes another step closer on the gravel, peering down at me. Still, shadows cloak his face.

"I was betrayed, too," he lisps. "It's justice, isn't it? I didn't have a chance, Alis. Whoever you are. The noble houses would never choose someone like me to rise up. I'd never win more titles, more land. I was either going to die in the trials or be dismissed. And then what? Back here, to my crushing debts and the fucking isolation. What do I have to offer anyone? Even the servants don't like my company. And really, I can't even pay them."

I try to scream, but the bindings around my mouth are choking me.

"I might as well be dead," Aneirin says. "But then someone powerful approached me. The Order of the Green Knight, it's called. He wanted three relics, and he offered to pay me *very* handsomely for any of them. Just one was all it took. He wants the throne, you see. Not only did he promise to settle my debts, but he promised me protection from the *cugol* and vast tracts of land. And if anyone is in a position to make those promises, it's him."

From the ground, I inch closer to him, trying to kick out his legs, but it's useless.

The shadows clear from his face. Now, as I look up at him, I see someone has already beaten the shit out of him. They must have used iron to smash his face, because he's not healing as rapidly as a Fey should. Blood spatters his white collar, and he's missing all his front teeth. One of his eyes has been gouged out.

Nausea turns my stomach as he keeps talking.

"But my benefactor never intended to keep his promises. He simply took the grail from me, then battered me half to death with an iron rod. He was angry that I let myself be identified. He said that was messy. He doesn't tolerate mistakes. You know, I don't know why he left me alive. I think he liked the cruelty of it, leaving me to suffer, mutilated like this. No money, no friends. He didn't really need me in the end. He has a more powerful ally in the trials. His own son. And why bother with me when Rion is winning the whole thing? You helped him get to the top, Alis. Was that really a good idea?"

I shriek into the bindings around my mouth.

At that moment, Tristan whips into the archway and presses his blade to Aneirin's throat. "Pull your magic away from her," Tristan hisses, "or you'll be dead in moments."

A smile curls Aneirin's lips. "If you think you can threaten me with death, you're sorely mistaken. I *long* for it. Cut away."

"Where is the grail?" Tristan snarls.

"Not here." Aneirin says through clenched teeth. "Isn't that clear by the state I'm in? Don't you think I would have sipped from it to cure myself, you contemptible moron?"

His magic still binds me, which means I still can't speak. I want to ask him who the fuck Rion's father is.

"And who took it from you?" Tristan's voice echoes off the archway.

"Ah." Aneirin's single eye holds a dull sheen. "Well, King Auberon isn't dead. He plans to reclaim the throne. And you know who else isn't dead? Prince Lothyr. Alis's new lover. For the past few centuries, Lothyr has been living as a high lord on Tintagol. He's changed, but it's him all the same. You think *I'm* evil? He's a fucking monster. They want to bring the whole world to its knees, and Alis seems to be along for the ride."

Shadows burst from Aneirin's body, knocking Tristan back. Tristan's head slams hard against the stone.

Aneirin runs just outside the archway, where another stream of shadows shoots from his body, racing up toward the sky. It loops around his throat, forming a noose—and jerks him sharply upward.

The loud snap of his neck makes me gasp, and then silence unfurls over the courtyard.

Aneirin swings above the ground for a few moments, his head limp, feet swaying.

As the shadows slide from my body, evaporating into the air, I step out of the archway. His magic loops over a gargoyle on the façade above him until the shadow magic drifts away like smoke into the sky, and then his broken body falls to the ground in a heap.

My body shakes as I stare at him.

Auberon. Of course he's still here, still pulling strings. Still demanding perfection.

And Rion is there to help him.

"Auberon wants the throne back," I say, my voice choked. "I knew he was still alive."

Tristan steps out of the shadows. "Why would he need the relics?"

Tears blur my eyes, and I stare down at Aneirin's broken body. "Auberon was defeated in combat. In the old days, that's how a reign ended. No one will accept him as king now. He looks weak, dethroned by his son. A monarch has to defend his crown. But with the relics, he can claim the gods blessed him."

"Then our mission has changed," Tristan says. "Now, we're after Auberon."

I meet his gaze. "Kill the king."

CHAPTER 51

 stare down at Aneirin's body, and a wave of pity crashes over me. Blood from his bashed face stains the gravel, and the scent of death curls into the air.

He did all this because he was terrified of being lonely. Here in this forsaken ruin, he'd spent too much time by himself, too deep in debt for a place in society. He believed that Auberon would bring him into his court. I don't think it was just about money. He wanted to belong.

I'm still reeling from everything he said.

Auberon lives. That's not a shock to me, but I didn't imagine he'd be trying to steal the ancient relics.

And I had no idea that *Rion* is the heir. Why did he fake his death and disappear for centuries? For a moment, I wonder if it's true.

But then again, he told me I didn't know his real name.

Now I know why. I cast my mind back to the family tree —Lothyr's family tree. Grandson of Merlin the Great. No wonder his magic is powerful and the oaks speak to him.

They want to bring the whole world to its knees.

There must be something beyond the relics' symbolism, a ritual that will give them terrifying power.

Tristan sidles up next to me, looking at what's left of Aneirin.

"Should we bury him?" I ask quietly.

But when I look at Tristan, I see his attention is already elsewhere, and a muscle ticks in his jaw. "They're here already," Tristan says.

My heart lurches, and I look up. At first, they're only shadows moving strangely against the night. Then, the cloaks catch in the wind. The *cugol*'s strange jeweled belts sway silently as they move toward us.

The *cugol* have already caught up to us, and they are gliding across the darkened courtyard, faster than I've ever seen them move before.

"Tristan!" I scream. "We need to get out of here right now!"

We run for the dragon, sprinting across the courtyard.

Already, my body is starting to heat. I never understood before how they would light you on fire. I imagined they'd drag you to a stake, just like in the Veiled Court. But it seems that their magic is at work from a distance because my body burns with a fever, oppressively hot.

It starts in my chest, like I've swallowed fire. Then it spreads out, burning my throat, my limbs, and my skin.

Tristan, of course, reaches the dragon within seconds. His magical speed has him already on the dragon's neck while I'm still trying to run across the courtyard, my cloak smoldering in the scorched air.

But Seronos seems to be panicked, and he's already lumbering away from me. *Please, no!*

His footfalls boom across the landscape, shaking the ground with his weight, and his wings spread out.

My heart is ready to leap out of my chest as I try to chase after Seronos. The dragon takes off into the air, stretching out his wings to fly away. Then, as heat sears my skin and singes my clothes, the dragon swoops back down again. Tristan angles low, grabs me, and wrenches me upward. We lift off into the air, and I'm dangling from the dragon, kicking my legs in reflex as the ground drops away from me.

The winds rush over my body, cooling me from the heat of the *cugol* magic.

Tristan's grip on me is as powerful as stone.

I force my legs to be still, trying not to make the dragon's flight any more difficult. But just dangling here, I can tell that my weight alone is affecting Seronos's flight. He keeps tilting to the right, frantically flapping his wings.

I twist my head to look behind me, and my gaze lands on one of the dragon's spikes.

I reach for the spike with my left arm. When my

fingers wrap around it, I start to turn my body a little bit, still supported by Tristan. Grunting with the effort, I manage to grab it with my right hand also. With a tremendous strain, I start to pull myself up, my muscles shaking as I shift, inch by inch. As I try to maneuver into position, the wind whips at me, making my cloak flap like a banner around me. I pull myself up with Tristan's help, and he hoists me higher until I can hook my left leg over the dragon's neck.

I lean back into him and breathe in the night air. The cool wind chills my body after the heat. My clothes are singed, but the redness of my skin is already returning to normal.

"That was close," he whispers.

We climb higher into the sky, and I close my eyes for a moment, thanking the gods that I didn't burn to death.

But what do I do now?

"They saw you," Tristan says.

"I know. I'm fucked. I'll be on the run forever now." I am envisioning a future where I live permanently on this dragon, fleeing eternally from the Cloaked Ones and their fire magic.

"Maybe we can bargain for a dismissal," Tristan says. "Maybe we can persuade Niniane that none of this was your fault. We can tell them about Auberon—"

He stops himself.

"She doesn't care who's at fault," I say. "She only demands utter loyalty. And what leverage do I have? I don't have the grail anymore. We shouldn't let them know a thing about Auberon. She could help him. She wants a monarchy. For all we know, she might give him the relics. Better to let everyone think he's dead for now."

"You risked your life to save a relic of the Veiled Court. That's the story."

I shake my head. "You know it's not enough, Tristan. There's no room for failure in a monarchist's court."

Slowly, an idea sparks in my mind.

What if I do have leverage?

* * *

THE BELLS ARE STILL RINGING by the time we return—funeral bells, now. Aneirin lies on dirty gravel with his neck snapped and his eye gouged out. The bells ring for his death, even if no one here knows it.

Carried by Seronos, we circle over the fortress. Beneath us, nobles of the Veiled Court begin to creep out of their rooms, staring at the strange new dragon.

Goch perches on one of the outer walls of the castle, glaring at us. As we swoop closer, he roars, unleashing a blast of fire in our direction. I crouch down, taking cover behind Seronos's neck. Our dragon answers with flame, his roar rumbling through me. Around me, the air burns hot.

We circle again, and when it seems as if Goch won't attack, Tristan guides Seronos down into the dragon pit, right near the menagerie. We land on ashes and charred bones, and they crunch beneath the dragon's weight. The scent of old smoke clings to the stones around us.

I'm not getting off this dragon yet.

From the shadows by the menagerie, Niniane prowls slowly, draped in blue. Wrath blazes in her eyes, and her lips press into a thin line. But she's not in a rush. She still thinks she's in control here.

As she walks, she draws a dagger from a holster. A *cugol* glides behind her, his face covered by his cowl.

"What do you think you're doing here, Baroness?" she hisses. "You left the Veiled Court and returned with a stolen *dragon?*"

Still clinging to Seronos's neck, I lift my chin. "Aneirin escaped because he stole the grail from me. I tried to reclaim it."

Niniane makes a subtle gesture with her hand, and two soldiers move closer, aiming arrows at me.

Tristan's hand tightens around my waist, and I can tell he's ready to lift off with Seronos any moment.

"Treason," she snarls. "You're in league with him, aren't you?"

I scan the little crowd that clusters around the pit. From the shadows, Rion is staring at me, his arms folded.

"He's dead," I say. "And before he killed himself, someone robbed him of the grail. I don't know who, but I will make it my mission to get it back."

"There's no place for you here, Alis," Niniane says.

"You failed. You lost the grail. You broke the rules. You should burn."

"Then you'll never know who killed Cador," I say.

All the color drains from her face, and she takes a step closer. "Was it you?"

My jaw clenches. "Remove the halo, and I will tell you."

She arches an eyebrow. "Do you really think removing the halo would end all this? Do you think I'd just let it go?"

My gaze darts to the mirrors, where the noble houses watch us. "There's no room for failure in a monarchist's court," I say. "You were the keeper of the grail, ultimately. And it was stolen under your watch. Do you really think this will impress the noble houses? One of your—"

She raises a hand. "Silence! Stop speaking. Branos! Dismiss this wretch."

The *cugol* steps forward, reaching for my hand. He grabs it in his, and for the first time, I catch a glimpse of his eyes—pale, beautiful blue eyes. His magic sweeps over me, wrapping around my skull like a warm embrace, then heating to a sharp blaze for a second. It sizzles in the air around me until it goes silent.

"It's done." Niniane's lip curled. "Who killed Cador?"

I sit tall on Seronos. What's one more lie when I'm drowning in them? "Aneirin did. He confessed before he died. He was trying to interrogate Cador for information about the grail."

She stares at me. "And I have no idea if you're telling the truth. Cador is the one who could have carved it out of you. But what a shame you let us all down, Alis. You could have had a chance, you know. Especially for what the noble houses are demanding that we do next. You, of all people, had the best chance."

She's trying to keep me here by dropping tantalizing hints, but I can't be lured into her games.

"Time to go," Tristan whispers. He tugs on one of Seronos's spikes, and the dragon takes a few booming steps across the pit, angling his wings.

And now, everything lies in ruin. I saved Vero, but Avalon Tower has lost its only two spies in the court. Auberon lives, plotting from the sidelines to amass a greater power than ever.

Exiled from the Veiled Court, I can't do a single fucking thing to stop him.

It's over.

CHAPTER 52

My legs ache as I walk through the forest, and light pierces the oak leaves. Dusk is falling, staining the light with copper. Tristan had to race back to Avalon Tower, and he dropped me off miles from my home, with a pocket of silver coins to get by. I didn't mind. Whenever I feel like I'm barely hanging on, walking long distances is the one thing that makes me feel normal again.

And yet, I deeply regret the route I've taken. I should have planned this a bit better. Because on the other side of the river, a marble mansion rises from the banks like a grand, ancient temple.

It's Owain's aunt's home.

There, in that palace, is the life I was *supposed* to have.

Somewhere in there, Vicky lives my stolen life. She's probably drinking a mead cocktail with fresh berries floating in the amber. I imagine her draped in the finest silks while a servant hangs around, waiting on her every wish.

From the muddy riverbank, I stare across the water.

The setting sun washes the palace's marble in gold and honey. Serpentine ivy twines around marble columns and balconies overlooking the river. Behind the mansion, vast fields stretch out into the distance, alive with the blooms of hawthorn and forget-me-nots. A curving stairwell sweeps up to grand doors, twenty feet high.

Around me, the shadows grow thicker, colder. I stare with a growing horror as a blonde woman in an emerald-green gown walks out onto the balcony, a drink in her hand. *Vicky.*

Then Owain steps out, and he slides up behind her, resting his chin on her shoulder. And all at once, I feel like I'm staring up at that Tudor window again, soaked in the April rain.

Swallowing hard, I turn away from them and march on toward Vero's house. But it all worked out in the end, didn't it? Without Owain's betrayal, I might not have saved Vero at all. She's alive now—and even if I failed in my mission, at least I'm alive, too.

Still, I can't stop reviewing every mistake I made. It was going well until I got that letter. Maybe I should have seen that Aneirin wasn't what he seemed. If I'd only pulled the door open the moment he left the letter—

That memory plays in my mind on a loop, and I shiver

with the cold. A few minutes, a split second of a mistake that changed the course of everything.

I was supposed to help Avalon Tower, and I can't do that from outside the Veiled Court at all. So, what am I going to do with my life now?

I wonder when I'll see Tristan again, but I have a terrible feeling it could be years. We're not even in the same realm anymore.

As I walk, I think of Aneirin, broken by loneliness. He was already suffering, but Auberon twisted the knife. Auberon preys on the weak, and he'll keep doing so until someone stops him.

I dread to think what he has planned with the relics.

I shove my hands into my pockets, feeling the silver coins that Tristan gave me.

I could pop into town to grab some food and mead, but really, I just want to see my sister as soon as possible. I haven't laid eyes on her since the night she drank from the grail.

I keep walking as the sun sets lower and a periwinkle gray spreads over the sky. When the trees grow thicker and ivy climbs the oak, I see it at last. My sister's new cottage is not far from where we grew up.

A stone house, wrapped in ivy, stands by the river. Its windows glow with warm light. The wooden shutters still need paint, and the glass is cracked in a few places, but they've tidied the gardens outside. Already, they bloom with violets, cowslips, and lilies. Most importantly, they've repaired the thatched roof. After years of abandonment, that must have been falling apart.

Someone painted the front door a deep, mossy green, Vero's favorite color. A metal doorknocker shaped like a hand hangs on the door.

I knock twice and hear the soft sound of voices inside through the wood. After a minute, Balin opens the door, and a grin spreads over his face. His eyes light up at the sight of me, and he pulls me in for a big hug. "Vero!" he calls out.

But she's already running closer. She joins in, wrapping her arms around me, and the three of us stand clustered together.

At last, I pull away from them and take a minute to look Vero over. Her cheeks are full, with a healthy glow to her skin. Her lips still hold a coral hue instead of purple. She looks so *young* now.

"You look incredible, Vero. How do you feel?"

"I feel great." She smiles at me. "But what are you doing here? I thought you were working with Avalon Tower on the secret mission."

I sigh. "Yeah, that's over. I'm free now." I try to smile, but I suspect I simply look exhausted.

"So, what happened?" Vero asks.

I swallow hard. At some point, I'm going to need to tell her about Auberon, but maybe not just yet. "Everything will be okay."

It doesn't even sound confident.

"Right," says Vero.

I step into their cottage and cast an appreciative glance around the room. From an abandoned cottage, they've really fixed this place up. The stone walls are painted white, and they've set up bookshelves, with three books so far.

There are plants all over the place. Vases around the cottage hold wildflowers, and something delicious in the oven smells of apples and honey.

On one side, cut flowers are set out on a rough-hewn table. A washbasin stands by a warmly lit hearth. On the other side, chairs and a sofa cluster around a wood-burning stove. And through a door I can see the bedroom. Just one bedroom, with one bed.

"I'm going to make tea," Balin declares. "Have a seat. You'll stay with us now, right?"

As Balin makes tea, Vero drops onto the sofa and curls her legs underneath her. She's dressed comfortably in soft leggings and a bright red shirt that matches her hair. The roots are starting to grow back in cherry red.

"What do you mean, everything will be okay?" she asks. "You were monitoring the monarchists, right? What are they up to?"

I swallow hard, trying to figure out how much to tell her. But she's not exactly a little girl anymore, even if I think of her that way.

I look between Vero and Balin. "What I'm about to say cannot leave this cottage. The fewer people who know, the better. Auberon is still alive, and some people are working to put him back on the throne. Someone stole the grail from me and gave it to him, and I have no idea where he is or what he plans to do with it. But Avalon Tower will be trying to find him, I'm sure. They'll try to stop him, as they did before. And if they ever need my help again, I'll jump at the chance."

Silence hangs in the air, and I know what they're thinking. *What good could you do? Your magic is broken.*

"How could he possibly rule again?" asks Balin. "His reputation is ruined, even with the nobility."

I shrug. "He thinks possessing the ancient relics like the grail will prove he's meant to rule. Or maybe they'll give him more power through some sort of ritual. I don't know. I think I need weeks of rest before I can even think clearly again."

Vero brightens. "Perfect! Stay here, then. We're making apple cake, but it's always best the way you make it."

My mouth already starts to water.

"You can stay in the bed with Vero," Balin says, handing me a cup of tea. "I'll take the sofa."

As I take a sip of my tea, Balin slides onto the sofa next to Vero. He wraps an arm around her shoulder, and she leans into him.

Tristan said he found them shagging, and I wasn't entirely sure if he was joking. They never were lovers before. Now, I see that Tristan was serious.

Maybe Balin was waiting all this time for her to

recover. Before, she was dependent on him. She would have been trapped. Now, she can leave him if she wants. It was the only way for them to be together.

And clearly, she doesn't want to leave him.

As if suddenly remembering that I'm here, they both straighten, and Balin pulls his arm away again.

"What's Tristan doing?" Vero asks.

I shrug. "Back to Avalon Tower. I'm sure he'll come see us sometime."

My heart squeezes as I remember what happened the last time we escaped the Fey realm. Tristan practically dragged Vero and me into London, and we were so close for a few months. But he needed more than just looking after a little girl, more than the day-to-day tasks of making lunches, cleaning clothes, and working in shops. The boredom was driving him mad. So, after a few months, Tristan joined Avalon Tower. He found a new life, and I'd go months without seeing him. Sometimes over a year.

I *say* that Tristan will come visit us, but I'm not even sure I believe it.

I wonder, for a moment, if I made a mistake when I told him we should only be friends. I know that *no one* is more important to Vero than Balin at this point, and she's taking the risk of love with him.

The steam coils before my face, and I wonder what would have happened if I hadn't pushed Tristan away. Would we have stayed lovers after I was banished from court and I was no longer playing the role of a baroness? Or perhaps I'd bore him now, too.

I suppose I'll never know.

When I look up from my tea, I see Vero and Balin staring into each other's eyes, smiling at one another like idiots. They start to lean in closer, and I'm certain they've already forgotten that I'm here.

I clear my throat. "You know, Vero, I was thinking I might actually find our old cottage and try to fix it up. I might move in there for a bit. It's not far from here, and there will be more room."

Vero's attention snaps back to me as if I startled her awake. "You don't want to stay with us?"

"Of course I do. At some point. But wouldn't it be nice to have our old home again? I have so many beautiful memories there. Might as well claim it before someone else does."

She nods wanly, and I wonder if she's thinking the same thing that Tristan did—that my memories are a rose-tinted version of the truth.

* * *

I FIND my old house by the river, and a crack opens in my chest at the sight of it.

It is smaller than I remember and crooked, practically tumbling into the river. Brambles, thistles, and nettles grow over the garden.

A rope hangs from the tree where Father made me a swing, but the hemp rotted through, and the wooden seat fell into the dirt. I cross to the little rotten plank and pick it up where it's sitting among the thorns. The red paint is mostly chipped off.

I trace my finger over the hole my father drilled in the wood to slide the rope through. I imagine him using a metal gimlet to pierce the wood. He made this before I left. This is what's left of him.

I blink the tears from my eyes and carry the wooden plank into the house with me like I'm a little girl holding a treasured doll.

Inside the cottage, weeds are growing from the dirt floor, and cobwebs hang from every dusty corner. The thatched roof is barely hanging on, thinned in places to expose the wooden ribs. Wind whistles through holes in the roof.

There's only one bedroom. I used to sleep in a little oak bed next to my parents. When I found Vero here, she was sleeping on a canvas sack stuffed with straw and rushes. Now, it's ripped and threadbare and smells of mold. Above the bed frame, I see the little flowers my father carved for me, worn with time. Mother painted them red and white to add color to the drab room, but most of the paint has chipped off now.

On one of the walls, I see small ink marks. Father was keeping track of our heights as we grew. Mine stops abruptly at eleven, Vero's at eight.

I pull the wooden swing tighter to me and blink to clear the haze from my eyes.

By the hearth, I find sticks with paper animals and figures of people glued to them—a raven, a king, a stag, a queen…once, they were painted bright colors, though they've now faded to the color of pale tea stains. A memory sparks in my mind of my mother telling me stories and using lantern lights to cast shadows with these little figures. In all her stories, the kings and queens were kind people who wanted to keep everyone safe, and they'd protect the kingdom from ravening wolves and monsters.

Why burden children with the truth?

I pick up a figure of a knight with black armor and faded golden tattoos across his cheekbones.

The Ruthless Knight. I'd all but forgotten her story about him. Maybe this is why I dreamt of him and he slipped into the depths of my thoughts, setting up a home there. In Mother's stories, he rampaged through the kingdom, threatening to do terrible things. Every time, a queen would stop him with her powerful magic.

Then she'd bury him.

I twirl the stick between my fingers.

My stomach rumbles, and my first thought is of collecting acorns. That's what we used to do, forage for acorns and fruits that the forest gave us. Tristan is right, of course. It was never enough. We were starving half the time. And yet, I was actually happy here because my parents turned our meager life into magic.

It wasn't the house or the forest that made me happy—it was *them*.

But you can't really go back, can you? There's no idyll, no sylvan paradise, because I'm not the same person I was before. I was happy then in my ignorance.

What did Rion say? *Your own stories tried to warn you—the serpent and the garden and the fruit tree. The god who brought fire...*

Before my fall, I didn't yet understand the violence and brutality that lurked beneath the glittering surface of the world. I didn't understand the evil that flowed under the blooms like a poisoned river.

Now I carry the poisons with me in my bones.

My chest feels hollow as I set to work dusting away the cobwebs from the bedroom.

CHAPTER 53

Instead of spending my silver coins on food that would quickly disappear, I decided to invest in a bow and arrows. That way, I can hunt for my food. I can keep some of the meat for myself and sell the rest at the Corbinelle market.

Maybe actually make something of my life here.

The bow is finely carved of yew wood, the tree of the death god, and strung with waxed hemp. By the forest's edge, I carry a quiver of arrows trimmed with goose feathers and tipped with steel. These cost me almost all my silver, but I'll make more.

This patch of forest can be tricky. There's sometimes heavy foot traffic on the path to the city, but it's also full of game.

So far, I've struck out everywhere else. I've been hunting for days without a single kill. I'm starving, and my empty belly has put me in a terrible mood. And for some reason, since I've returned to my parents' old house, all I want to do is sleep. I don't have an alarm clock like I did in London. Every morning, I find myself waking late with the sun halfway up the sky. When I open my eyes, I'm still lethargic and tempted to sink back into my bed.

When I left Vero's house, she sent me off with bread and fruit and told me to come back for more. But she's my younger sister, and I'm not going to keep taking food from her. She needs it. So, I've been rationing: a few dates per day, one apple, two slices of bread. I supplement with acorns and chestnuts that I forage.

It's not enough, though.

I'm so hungry I can hardly think straight. Once, I was very good at hunting, but years of office work and ready-made lunches have dulled my skills.

Gods, London did make me soft. I ache for a ham and cheese sandwich so sharply that I can almost taste it.

It makes me furious to admit that Rion was right. Sorry, *Prince Lothyr*.

I think like a mortal now. I've forgotten how to live as a Fey.

A flicker of movement catches my eye, and I see a doe walking through the brush, eyes bright. She seems unaware of me.

I freeze, crouching low. Her ears twitch, and she sniffs the air. I move quietly closer, taking care not to snap a twig or rustle leaves. Carefully, I draw an arrow.

The deer keeps walking slowly, munching on leaves. When I have a clear shot, I nock the arrow and draw the string.

My breath slows. I watch her chest rise and fall. Holding my breath, I aim for the heart and release. The steel-tipped arrow flies straight and drives right into her chest.

She staggers, then collapses onto the moss.

I run for her and set down my bow by her side. As she bleeds out, the light fades from her eyes, and her body stops twitching. In the quiet forest, the only sound now is the wind through the oaks.

I kneel by the deer and draw my knife. As I carve into her belly, blood splashes onto my hands and sleeves, and the metallic scent fills the air. Steam rises from the gash where I slice along her belly and start to pull out the entrails. *This* will make me some good money.

"Oh, dear. Oh, Owain?"

I freeze at the voice, and the hair rises on the back of my neck.

Slowly, I lift my gaze to see Owain and Vicky walking on a nearby path. "Is that your friend?"

I close my eyes for a moment, horribly aware of the fact that I'm covered in blood and crouching over a dead animal.

I open my eyes again and see Vicky and Owain peering at me from the path.

Vicky wears a sapphire-blue gown, and Owain is

dressed in a sleek black suit. And yet, I'm deeply gratified to see he looks haggard with exhaustion, and that Vicky's roots have grown in mousy brown.

"Syn!" Owain says, his expression brightening as he sees me. "I've been worried about you."

He walks closer.

I crouch over the dead deer, blood dripping from my blade. "I'm fine. Better than fine, really. I'll be having venison tonight."

"Incredible job," Owain says. "I didn't realize you could hunt."

"It never came up in London."

Owain's eyebrows rise hopefully. "Would you like to come to my aunt's house for dinner this week?"

Only if I were on the verge of starvation, I think. "This week is a bit busy," I lie aloud.

Vicky tramples over the brambles to get to us. "Oh, wow. That is…how rustic! Did you kill that? With a knife? You stabbed a deer?"

She's slurring her words, which delights me because it's early afternoon.

As she sidles up next to Owain, she stumbles, and he catches her elbow, looking irritated. His cheeks turn pink, and I'm struck by how shockingly *young* he seems. "Perhaps we should keep walking, Vicky. Let's get to town for lunch."

"I miss London," Vicky blurts. "And apparently, no one knows how to get back to civilization. There was a portal here, but there's no portal *back*. And there's nothing *here*. I miss being in a real city."

"We're not far from Corbinelle."

She scowls at me. "No, I mean a *real* city, with entertainment, and, like…fun things?"

Owain practically drags her away.

I turn back to my kill with a small, satisfied smile.

When I'm done selling the extra meat, I'll still have plenty for Vero, Balin, and myself tonight. I'll serve it with hazelnuts and blackberries and a nice mead that I'll buy with my profits.

All things considered, my morning is turning out *far* better than I could have hoped.

And maybe I'm not in the Veiled Court anymore, but at least I'm slowly starting to remember how to be Fey again.

Perhaps when the time comes, I will hunt and slaughter Auberon like I did this doe.

I just need to figure out *how*.

* * *

A KNOCK SOUNDS on my door, and I snort as I wake. I still haven't fully patched the roof, and rainwater drips into my bedroom, turning the dirt floor into mud. I have no idea what time it is. At least, for once, I'm not waking up starving.

Disoriented, I look around the room. Dull gray light seeps through the holes in the ramshackle wooden walls.

Thunder booms outside, and I wonder for a moment if that was the knock.

Then I hear it again.

No, it's clearly a knock.

Slowly, I climb out of bed and go to the door.

There, standing in the rain, is Prince Lothyr, a cowl pulled up over his silver hair. His golden halo beams underneath it.

My muscles go tense, and for a moment, I consider running. I did, after all, stab him and nearly kill him. Why else would he be here?

"I appreciate that you're not stabbing me this time." He arches an eyebrow. "But aren't you going to invite me in?"

Only now do I realize that I'm clutching the seat swing, which I was sleeping with. I look down at it, slowly waking.

"Oh." Somehow, it's all I can muster.

I open the door wider in an unspoken invitation and turn back into my hovel. I slide the piece of wood onto a table, and Rion steps inside.

I've never felt quite this shabby before. I'm not sure when I last washed my clothes, and my feet are muddy from the dirt floor.

"Is this where you grew up?" he asks quietly.

"Yes. Part of the time, anyway."

I expect him to make fun of the appalling conditions, but he doesn't.

I drop into a rough wooden chair and stare at him. "I can't decide what to ask first, so what are you doing here, and how did you find me?"

He pulls down his cowl, and the golden light beams over the room. He looks like a god standing there—coldly judgmental, dripping in wealth, radiating light like the sun.

"I asked the first mortal I saw. A little blonde from a mortal empire. And wouldn't you know it, she knew exactly where I could find you, *Syn*."

My jaw tightens. "Are you here to gloat, or is there actually a purpose to this visit?"

"No, I'm here to tell you to come back to the Veiled Court."

I stare at him. "Why?"

"I've convinced the noble houses that you belong with me there. I planted one of Aneirin's gloves on Cador's body and pretended to find it. So, now they believe your lies."

My pulse races. "What's your plan, Rion?"

"To win the crown."

In the old days, Rion, we killed our kings. I let the words die on my tongue because he's offering to give me what I want. Only by getting close to him can I find out more about what he and his father have planned.

The problem is that now, he'll have even more rope to

hang me with. He knows where I live, knows my real name. He'd be able to find Vero in a heartbeat.

I stand, folding my arms. "And why do you need me for this task?"

He shrugs slowly. "The noble houses like us together, and I also want to keep an eye on you."

"For what reason?"

"I believe you're dangerous."

My jaw drops. "*I'm* dangerous?"

"In my dreams, you destroy the world. When you're done with it, Brocéliande lies in ruin. The rivers dry up, and crops wither. I don't yet know what it means."

Cursed is the hour you were born.

The baroness's words ring in my skull.

"Then why not kill me?" I ask. "You could have, over and over again. And you chose me in that first combat round—"

"I wanted to know why I've dreamt of you. I chose you in the combat round so no one else would."

My pulse races. "And why do you still need me in the trials?"

He takes a step closer, and his silver eyes burn brighter. When he's only inches from me, I feel his magic skim over my skin in a dark caress that makes my heart race. The scent of smoldering cedar drifts from him like sparks.

"Because, Syn, the noble houses liked us so much together that they are now saying a monarch must find a consort. Only someone with a fated mate can win the trials. In the old days, they called it the sovereignty bond. Only those blessed by Rhiannon can bring back the Golden Age. That's what they say."

"Do they?"

He leans closer until I can see the rings of blue in his eyes. The light from his halo drips over me, and the warmth of his magic skims over my body, making my breath catch. "To win the next trials, I need you to play the role of my consort."

* * *

THANK you so much for reading The Veiled Court.

While you are waiting for book two, you should check out the related series, Fey Academy for Spies.

In the next chapter, you can read a sample from **Avalon Tower,** where we spend more time with Raphael and the spy academy.

EXCERPT FROM AVALON TOWER

Prologue

Alix glances at the top floor of an apartment building, staring at the couple shagging against the window. Even from here, she can see the pleasure on the man's face, his breath misting the glass.

That would be an infinitely better way to spend the day than the mission she has planned. She can imagine Agent Rein holding her like that, gripping her as he kisses her throat.

But it will never happen. Love is strictly forbidden for the spies of Avalon Tower. The problem is, banning desire doesn't douse the heat. If anything, it fuels it. Sometimes, Alix thinks all the Avalon spies are unsatisfied, obsessed, lost in fantasies. Today, especially, her head isn't in the game—even though Fey soldiers probably lurk all around this place, waiting to run their swords through agents like her.

Distraction is death, she reminds herself.

She turns away, scanning the street for signs of her Fey enemies. She doesn't see anything amiss. In fact, it all looks perfectly calm, picturesque and quaint. Wrought iron balconies overhang the cobbled alley. Here, in the south of France, the scent of lavender mingles with the brine of the sea. The streets of this coastal town are ancient, stony, labyrinthine. At the bottom of the sloping road, wisps of fog curl over the Mediterranean. A cafe overlooks the sea—Café de la Forêt Enchantée. The meeting point is by the back door.

She peers out across the outdoor tables, where a pretty woman with raven hair is eating cake and flirting with a waiter. Alix feels a pang of jealousy. For normal women—those who aren't spies trying to save the world—love is always a possibility.

Focus, Alix.

Still a picture of serenity around her. No sign of the Fey soldiers. But no sign of Rein, either.

A church bell tolls, making her heart skip a beat. Rein should be here. He's usually early.

She takes a slow, calming breath. She's always thinking of him, which is exactly why love is forbidden in the first place. It takes your mind off the mission and leads to stupid decisions. She's never told him how she feels, how she seems to always be looking for him. Every time she sees a reflection, she checks the glass to see if *he's* behind her, hoping to see his boyish smile instead of looking out for the enemy. Whenever she walks into the dining hall at Avalon Tower, she scans the room for his slender form. She's always coming up with excuses to get close to him, but she can never quite tell if he feels the same about her.

The clouds slide over the sun, and she feels a chill. She should stay at the beach, alert for any sign of the Fey, those terrifying soldiers in royal blue. But she's not going to leave here without Rein. He's late for the rendezvous, and her mind spins in a million horrible directions.

Pulse racing, she climbs back up the hill. Her skin tingles with the hum of the veil emanating from the streets nearby, the misty barrier that separates this world from that of the Fey. In theory, it's a boundary that keeps them on one side and humans on the other, but it's not that simple. For one thing, you can never be sure exactly where the veil is. Sure, the Fey control it, but sometimes, it seems to have a mind of its own. The magical boundary roams a bit, shifting its location ever so slightly. It's a hungry thing, and if it consumes you, you die. Every few weeks, it leaves a curious tourist dead on the winding streets of southern France. Alix is one of the few people alive who can actually control it, who can stop it from killing those passing through.

Casually, she checks her watch, and dread skitters up her spine. Rein was supposed to be here six minutes ago. He's *never* late, especially not for an exfiltration operation.

The fugitives should be just beyond the veil by now. She feels like she can hardly breathe.

Spies are taught to suppress emotion, to maintain complete control of themselves, even when danger lurks in the shadows of every alley. But now, Alix feels her training fail as the terrifying possibilities race through her mind. What if he was slaughtered already? What if the veil shifted location and killed him? She'd lose her mind if anything happened to Rein, if she never got to see his brown eyes again or had the chance to wrap her arms around him.

She grits her teeth so hard that she nearly bites her tongue. *Get it together.*

She masks her feelings with a wistful smile as she crosses the road to the gold- and salmon-colored shops on the opposite side. She pretends to look in the windows at the madeleines and croissants, the slices of cake. Anyone watching her would think she's just a hungry tourist on vacation, a cute blonde in a sundress.

Fog drifts across the street.

Eleven minutes late now. Alix's blood roars. Something is *definitely* wrong. She starts to march back to Café de la Forêt Enchantée.

At last, she hears the whistle that is their signal, and she heaves a sigh of relief. It's coming from behind her. Did she miss him somehow?

The signal is coming from a narrow lane, and Alix hurries over to it.

She turns the corner, and the world tilts beneath her feet. Now, she's face-to-face with a towering Fey. Silver hair flows down his back, and he wears the dark blue velvet of a Fey soldier. There's something about his eerie stillness, about the sharpness of his gaze that sends fear ringing through Alix's bones. It's the metallic sheen in his green eyes that's so disorienting, otherworldly. His lip curls, exposing one of his sharpened canines.

Alix reads nothing in his eyes except loathing.

We've been compromised. Alix's heart slams, and she turns to run.

But her path is blocked by a second Fey soldier, and Alix is caught between them. She reaches for her dagger, but it's too late.

A blade plunges into Alix's stomach, and pain rushes through her. Her training takes over, and she tries to pull her dagger, to dodge, to parry, to run, but her limbs don't obey her for some reason. She falls to her knees.

Strange. Her wound doesn't hurt that much. She hardly feels it at all.

Thoughts of Rein flicker through her mind as she bleeds onto the stones.

CHAPTER ONE
Seven minutes earlier.
I breathe in the scent of the ocean, a fragrance tinged

with cypress, and sip my coffee. It's hot for early spring, and it almost looks like steam is rising from the sea. From my spot at Café de la Forêt Enchantée, I see the cloud of shimmering mist shearing across the landscape.

My vacation has been heaven so far. The breeze rushes off the water and leaves a faint taste of salt on my lips. This place is good for my asthma, I think.

The atmosphere in the south of France feels different than California. Here, the light is soft, honeyed, not the glaring, overwhelming harshness of the LA sun.

Nearby, the magical veil rises to the sky like a wall of fog. It's eerie and undeniably beautiful. It moves sometimes, but I'm at a safe distance here. Just beyond the tables of the outdoor café, waves crash over the white rocks. This might just be my favorite place in the world.

I manifested this trip with positive thoughts and vision boards. Also, many hours of minimum-wage labor and eating cereal for dinner instead of going out to bars. This two-week vacation is my destiny.

Sure, I feel a twinge of guilt at leaving Mom behind, but there's no way I could pay for us both. And it *would* be better to have my friend Leila with me, but she's scared of going anywhere near the Fey border. She thinks they might still leap out of the veil and murder you at any moment, even if the guidebooks from our bookshop and the U.S. State Department *clearly* say it's safe.

I pick up a sprig of lavender from the vase on the table and inhale.

I'm still enjoying the lovely scent when a dark-haired waiter slides a slice of a blackberry cake onto the lace tablecloth before me. "Bon appétit."

I definitely ordered the *lavender* cake, but cake is cake. "Thank you."

As I take a bite, the fruity flavor bursts on my tongue. This slice costs the equivalent of three hours of work at the bookshop, but I try not to think about it. Fifteen years ago, the war made prices soar, and they never went down again. Luxuries like cake are stupidly expensive. *Vacation*, I remind myself.

Another bite. The sugary, tart flavors coat my tongue. Mom would be horrified. *So many carbs, darling.* She lives on vodka and boiled eggs.

The waiter watches me take a bite and smiles. With his bright blue eyes and square jaw, he reminds me of someone, but I can't quite put my finger on it.

"Is delicious, yes?" he asks. He must have pegged me as a tourist because he's speaking in heavily accented English.

I nod. "C'est délicieux."

His shoulders relax as he shifts to French himself. "I'm glad. Are you here on holiday?" He wears a flat cap over wavy brown hair.

"I arrived a week ago. Only one week left." My chest clenches at the realization that my trip is already half over. For five years, I've looked forward to this, but I can't spend the other half of my vacation mourning the end of it, can I? "I wish I could stay."

Sure, it's a teensy bit lonely having my birthday cake at a table for one, but it's probably better than what I'd be doing at home.

"Where are you from?" he asks.

"The U.S. west coast. LA."

"LA, as in Hollywood? Are you an actress? A model?" He lowers his eyelashes, then looks up again. "Your hair is very striking. So unusually dark."

Is he flirting with me? "Thank you. No, I'm not an actress."

I glance at the veil again. I can't seem to keep my gaze off it. What's happening on the other side?

"Have you seen any?" I turn to him and whisper, "Fey."

He blanches. It's almost like saying the word out loud sends a ripple of terror across the café, and for a moment, I regret it.

I catch the brief tightening of the muscles around his mouth until he softens them into a smile. He shrugs. "Sometimes, they patrol the border on our side. But most of the south of France remains independent. We're safe here, and there's nothing to worry about. King Auberon has no interest in claiming more of France than he already has."

That's what I told Leila. Except I'd sounded convincing, and when he says it, it sounds distinctly rehearsed. What is he *not* saying?

What I do know is this: fifteen years ago, the Fey invaded France. When it first happened, the world was stunned. Until that point, no one even knew they existed. And then, suddenly, they were marching through Paris, commanding the boulevards. Their dragons circled above the Eiffel Tower. The Fey were beautiful, otherworldly, seductive…

Lethally violent and hell-bent on conquest.

The French military fought back and managed to keep some of the south free and under human control. Unoccupied. It's supposed to be safe.

But as the clouds slide over the sun, I feel the atmosphere suddenly grow tense around me. It's hard to put my finger on it, but there's something sharp and grim in the air now, replacing the soft ambience.

I glance at the waiter, who still lingers by my table.

Maybe there *is* more danger here than the tourist boards are willing to admit. Maybe Leila had a point.

The night before, as I ate bouillabaisse in a restaurant by the sea, I overheard a man arguing with his wife, telling her that an anti-Fey resistance was fighting King Auberon. A magical cold war that played out behind the scenes, one with spies and secret missions. He made it sound like these spies had legendary skills, that they could kill a Fey in two seconds flat with their bare hands. That a highly skilled, elite force was our only hope if we wanted to stop the evil king from taking the rest of France.

His wife called him an idiot and told him to stop talking.

But there's a tension here that makes me want to know more…

I flutter my eyelashes. "Have you heard anything about the secret resistance?" I whisper.

The waiter smiles, a dimple in one cheek. "Ah, that." His smile is patronizing, and he rolls his eyes theatrically. "Rumors only. How would they fight the Fey in their lands? You cannot cross the veil into the Fey realm, and even if you did, the Fey would spot you as a human instantly. And anyway, they have magic. We don't. I really doubt such a resistance exists."

I glance at the veil again. Misty shades of faint violet and green twist and spiral, plunging into the ocean and rising up to dissipate in the clouds.

If cell phones still worked, I'd be snapping photos like crazy. But electronics fizzled out with the arrival of the Fey. For whatever reason, Fey magic destroyed our most modern technology.

The waiter sighs wistfully. "The veil is beautiful, isn't it? Is that what you came here to see?"

Something about this waiter makes me uneasy, but I'm not sure what it is. He reminds me of someone I hate, but that's a completely irrational reason to dislike someone. "I did want to see the veil," I admit, "but also, I used to come to France, years after the Fey invasion. Starting when I was fifteen, my mom would take me here. We stayed at a château in Bordeaux during the summers."

He flashes me a smile. "I've been. Amazing vineyards, of course. Shame that we lost half of them to the occupation."

My stomach tightens as I remember those summer vacations. Our days were spent with my mom drinking all the wine in the vineyard. Then, when she was properly wasted, she'd urge me to flirt with rich French guys who "could do a lot for me." I remember she was so loud and drunk one night—

Oh. That's why he looks familiar. He resembles the dark-haired, aristocratic demi-Fey who broke my heart when I was a teenager. What a great example of a memory that should have stayed repressed.

The waiter is nearly as handsome as that demi-Fey, but not quite. Humans rarely have the shocking, heart-breaking beauty of the Fey.

I stare at him over the rim of my coffee cup. "What's your name?"

"Jules." He seems to think this is an invitation, and he pulls out the chair across from me. He stares at me dreamily across the table. "And yours?"

"Nia."

"I'm finishing my shift soon." This is clearly suggestive. But what does Jules have in mind, exactly? Maybe he wants to whisk me off to a beautiful hidden bookstore full of rare volumes. Or maybe he wants a quick fumble in a hotel room, in which case the answer is no.

I take another bite of the cake, tasting the confiture, and dab at my lips with the napkin. I still haven't satisfied my curiosity, so I lean forward and whisper, "What do you think it's like now? In the occupied regions? In Fey France?"

His eyes dart furtively to the left, then the right. He leans forward on his elbows and quietly says, "I try not to think about it. I hear things I wish I could forget." He keeps his blue eyes locked on me, as if suggesting I should do the same.

I wait for him to go on. When he doesn't, I ask, "What sort of things?"

"I see them coming through here, sometimes," he says. "Fugitives."

I stare at him. This *definitely* wasn't in the tourist guidebooks. "What fugitives?"

"The Fey king, Auberon, hunts anyone who doesn't support him. He accuses scores of people of treason and slaughters them. I think he particularly hates the demi-Fey. He suspects them of disloyalty, and he demands complete fealty. The police here are supposed to report any demi-Fey they see escaping. Otherwise, Auberon might invade the rest of France." He straightens. "I mean, he won't. He knows he can't win. Even if electronics don't work, we have guns and iron bullets. And we help to keep things under control. We protect what we have."

A shiver runs over my skin. "I see. And how do you do that?"

"We report any fugitives we see. No one is allowed to help them. It keeps the status quo intact." He opens his hands and shrugs again. "What can we do? We have to keep the peace. We can only enjoy life and keep things the way they are."

A tendril of guilt twines through me, and I try to push it away.

-Avalon Tower, Fey Academy for Spies.

ACKNOWLEDGEMENTS

I owe so much to Alex Rivers for helping me develop the world of the Veiled Court through our Fey Academy for Spies series, during which we worked together to create this lush landscape of Brocéliande. In this series, he gave me feedback on the plot as I wrote, reading and critiquing the whole book. He also helped to write one of the action scenes (when Mabon reanimates the dead).

Thanks to my husband (and sometimes co-author) Nick, who read the book and gave me in-depth feedback. Literature with Linsey was another amazing beta reader who gave me incredibly helpful feedback.

Thank you to my new PA, Kirstie, for helping me to market this book with gorgeous graphics.

Thanks to these amazing authors, who all read the opening of my book and provided reassurance while gently suggesting I could cut a few things: Sable Sorensen, Vasilisa Drake, Caty Rogan, Jenna Wolfhart. On a writer retreat, Sable Sorenson also helped me figure out some name changes so I didn't have a bunch of confusing R names.

I loved working with my first editor, Margot Harrison,

who meticulously edited the book and offered suggestions on word choice. Thanks to Lauren and Lexi from Wicked Pen Editorial for the final edits and for fully polishing the book into its final form.

Nerd Fam always creates gorgeous graphics, and Rachel worked with me to design symbols for each of my towers and the tagline, as well as to organize a book club to read The Veiled Court.

Thank you to Heather Becht from Crowns and Chaos PR for helping me put together a Discord server for readers and for generally guiding me through marketing!

Last but not least, I really feel like I have the best book designer in the business: MerryBookRound. But don't steal her. I need her.